GABBY
GREENE
KNOWS
WHODUNIT

I0590460

ALSO BY SAM TSCHIDA

Errands & Espionage

GABBY GREENE KNOWS WHODUNIT

SAM TSCHIDA

FOREVER

New York   Boston

This book is a work of fiction. Names, characters, places, and incidents are the product of the author's imagination or are used fictitiously. Any resemblance to actual events, locales, or persons, living or dead, is coincidental.

Copyright © 2026 by Inked Entertainment Ltd

Cover design by Caitlin Sacks
Cover copyright © 2026 by Hachette Book Group, Inc.

Hachette Book Group supports the right to free expression and the value of copyright. The purpose of copyright is to encourage writers and artists to produce the creative works that enrich our culture.

The scanning, uploading, and distribution of this book without permission is a theft of the author's intellectual property. If you would like permission to use material from the book (other than for review purposes), please contact permissions@hbgusa.com. Thank you for your support of the author's rights.

Forever
Hachette Book Group
1290 Avenue of the Americas, New York, NY 10104
read-forever.com
@readforeverpub

First Edition: January 2026

Forever is an imprint of Grand Central Publishing. The Forever name and logo are registered trademarks of Hachette Book Group, Inc.

The publisher is not responsible for websites (or their content) that are not owned by the publisher.

The Hachette Speakers Bureau provides a wide range of authors for speaking events. To find out more, go to hachettespeakersbureau.com or email HachetteSpeakers@hbgusa.com.

Forever books may be purchased in bulk for business, educational, or promotional use. For information, please contact your local bookseller or the Hachette Book Group Special Markets Department at special.markets@hbgusa.com.

Library of Congress Cataloging-in-Publication Data
Names: Tschida, Sam, author
Title: Gabby Greene knows whodunit / Sam Tschida.
Description: First edition. | New York : Forever, 2026.
Identifiers: LCCN 2025032099 | ISBN 9781538757239 trade paperback | ISBN 9781538757246 ebook
Subjects: LCGFT: Fiction | Romance fiction | Spy fiction | Novels
Classification: LCC PS3620.S44 G33 2026
LC record available at https://lccn.loc.gov/2025032099

ISBN: 9781538757239 (trade paperback), 9781538757246 (ebook)

Printed in the United States of America

LSC-C

Printing 1, 2025

To my husband, Terrell, for providing detailed instructions on how to strangle a man with my thighs without asking why I needed to know. All my absurd action scenes make more sense because of you. (Don't ask how Terrell knows these things. I didn't.)

PROLOGUE

Private Jetway, Jackson Hole, Wyoming

On the way out the door to the airport, Sheridan opened her purse to check for the essentials: driver's license, Air-Pods, red lipstick. Sheridan frowned. For a moment, the way the November sun cut through the windows made the new tooled leather look plain pink instead of its actual rich merlot. Either the light in the Village Booterie was off or she was.

While sliding her sunglasses into the purse, she shuddered like she'd just been hit with an icy blast, and all the hair on her arms stood straight up. She knew this feeling. It wasn't a bad or good feeling, just a premonition—and a vague one, at that. It didn't come with an associated word or image. But still, a feeling like this meant something was about to happen. Not the kind of feeling you want on your way out the door to the airport.

No matter. Sheridan Lane was a psychic. *The* psychic in certain circles. One vague feeling wasn't going to interfere with her schedule. Sheridan slipped the purse over her body and gripped her wheelie bag like she was in charge. But as she locked the front door, the feeling lingered. The heavy unease slowed her pace until she came to a full stop on the sidewalk in front of her Jackson Hole condo, hanging on for dear life to a rolling bag.

A glance at her phone didn't confirm or deny her premonition. There were no urgent texts regarding illness, death, or divorce, no weather alerts, no shocking national news—except for the burning secrets she was keeping to herself. Was she conflating fear and foresight? No, she understood her fear and had accepted it. This premonition was different.

Then her phone dinged, making her jump out of her skin. She had a text.

"Can't remember. Do I need to feed Leonard today or is it tomorrow?"

Jesus. She had forgotten to check in with the neighbor. Sheridan responded: "Both. I'll be gone through Sunday. I left his food bin on the counter. He's gonna beg but only give him ½ cup a day. Thanks!"

Sheridan sighed. The only emergency was her cat's waistline.

She didn't have time for vague feelings today. She was on her way to DC. The president of the United States was waiting for her.

It's not like she had clear plane-crash vibes. She simply felt unsettled, like she'd left the stove on, and the house might burn down . . . but probably wouldn't. While she waited for the driver to arrive, she shut her eyes and listened. Being a psychic was eighty percent paying attention.

That's what she was always telling her clients. *Listen to yourself— your thoughts and intuitions, to the world around you.*

There were fewer actual psychics in 2025 than there ever had been. The human attention span had reduced to the point that people couldn't watch to the end of a TikTok reel without scrolling to the next, let alone be in the moment enough to listen to the universe or read even the most obvious signs. For about the tenth year in a row, humanity was in the Year of the . . . "Squirrel!" If you can't focus for longer than five seconds, you can't be a psychic. End of story. Bottom line.

Her clients loved it when she used phrases like "Bottom line" or "Here's the deal." It's part of how Sheridan kept her client list. She'd been described before as "If George Bush were a psychic." Now there's a man she could have helped. You didn't need to be a psychic to know a guerrilla war in the Middle East was not going to be quick or winnable. That was a man for you—start a war instead of listening.

That's part of the reason she'd gone into politics, not as a politician of course, but as a guide to some of the biggest fools on the planet—politicians. Someone needed to do something. Men understood the way she talked to them. How many times had she been like, "Gary, shut up and listen."

Not that psychics don't lie. She was a damn dyed-in-the-wool liar.

A driver pulled up in a black SUV and helped her load her luggage into the back.

While she buckled up, he asked, "What kind of music would you like for the drive, ma'am?"

"Ma'am? Do I look like your mother?" Sheridan snapped. She might be fifty-five, but she looked forty-seven, tops. Before the big man could apologize, she said, "Country." People always expected her to listen exclusively to yoga background music, but she couldn't help it if she was from Wyoming.

The ride to the airport was peaceful. They drove past the

Jackson Hole Square with its elk antler arches and cute shops. She was probably just headed into a difficult session with President Simon. The reelection campaign was really getting to him and starting to wear on her, with all the emotional labor she'd have to do on his behalf.

When she finally looked up from her thoughts, they were pulling up to the private jetway.

"Sir," she called into the front, "I'm sorry. I'm going to the regular airport. I'm flying Delta." She had a layover in Denver before landing in DC, much later than she would have wanted.

"I got instructions from the higher-ups to take you to the private jetway. A plane is waiting."

She leaned back in her seat. "Really?"

It kind of made sense. She was flying out at the president's request. "No one told me about this." Sheridan kept still. "Do I have this plane all to myself?" Had she suddenly become Taylor Swift?

"I believe there is one other passenger."

"Who?"

"Genesis Love."

She'd choked on a hot dog at the Laramie County Fair when she was a child. She hadn't been that starved for oxygen again until this moment.

When Sheridan caught her breath, she said, "Genesis Love, the movie star?" His last movie, *Power Couple*, was like a three-hour-long acid trip. If he hadn't been wearing a Speedo throughout, she probably wouldn't have been able to sit through it. Maybe if you were high on something, it would make more sense. He used to be an A-list action star, but she'd mostly heard about his wellness empire lately. He'd gone Gwyneth Paltrow.

"I can get someone from the White House on the phone. They really should have talked to you about the changed flight plans." The man looked concerned that she was concerned, but Sheridan shook off his worry like she shook off her bad feeling from earlier.

"No need to make a fuss. Who am I to complain about an upgrade?" Maybe this had been what the premonition was about, an upgrade to a private plane with Genesis. Not all anxiety was bad.

Unlike the regular airport, she didn't have to go through TSA. The driver took her right out to the tarmac where the private plane was waiting.

Moments later, dazed and a little starstruck, Sheridan was walking up a staircase to the main cabin door, each footfall punctuated by her bootheel on hollow metal. Just like on a regular plane, a flight attendant welcomed her when she stepped into the main cabin. "So glad to have you aboard, Miss Lane."

The flight attendant watched as Sheridan took in the jet's interior.

"I guess Delta can go suck an egg."

The flight attendant laughed.

"You're going to love it, Miss Lane. I can promise the food is much better."

"How long is the trip to DC?" Sheridan asked as she settled into what must be a Nappa leather airplane chair, pretending she wasn't desperate to know what the in-flight meal would be.

The flight attendant's eyes went wide. "I'm so sorry. This flight isn't going to DC."

"What?" Sheridan sputtered. "Camp David?" She hazarded another guess.

The flight attendant shook her head. Behind her, the staircase began to pull away from the side of the plane.

"Where are we going?" Maybe the president's home in Massachusetts?

"The Azores," the flight attendant said with a smile. "The Hawaii of Europe."

"Is the president there?" Sheridan asked, confused. What would the president be doing in the Azores? Where even were the Azores?

When the flight attendant didn't answer, Sheridan sat up straighter. "There's been a mistake. I'm supposed to be on a flight to DC to meet President Simon. Can someone grab my bag for me? I'd like to get off this plane right now." If she pulled her boots off and ran like hell, she might still have time to make her Delta flight.

"I'm so sorry. Let me see what I can do."

Behind her, they were shutting the cabin door. A man in an orange vest was driving the movable stairway down the tarmac.

Sheridan's voice pitched up as she said, "I need to get off this plane immediately. I do not want to go to the Azores."

"Let me talk to the Big G," the attendant offered.

"Who the hell is the Big G?" Sheridan asked.

"We'll get this figured out." The attendant smiled again.

"I don't need to figure it out."

The airplane's engine shifted into gear.

The attendant smiled and walked toward the rear of the plane as it prepared for takeoff.

"What is so hard about opening the door and letting me off? I don't understand." But Sheridan did understand. She was being abducted. Instead of getting into a stranger's panel van after being offered candy, she'd gotten into a Hollywood star's private jet after seeing his abs.

"Unfortunately, we are unable to let anyone off the plane at this time," the flight attendant said in a too-cute intercom voice as the plane started taxiing down the runway. "It should be a clear flight to the Azores. We are serving a delicious lunch, and Genesis would love for you to enjoy the in-flight movie."

"Let me guess. *Power Couple*?" Sheridan rolled her eyes and settled tensely into her seat.

The flight attendant laughed, but really, the joke was on Sheridan. "How'd you know?"

"I'm a psychic." But apparently not as good a one as she thought.

CHAPTER 1

I got this." Gabby Greene slipped on her bike shoes and strode into the Elite Operatives Division gym like she owned it, but with the awkward gait of someone who had put on their clip-on shoes too far away from the bike. Those things were not made for walking. In a stiff-legged, might-as-well-be-wearing-ski-boots gait, she made it to the exercise bike for some cardio. It was Gabby's second month of being a field agent for the EOD, making her a Top Gun of the spy world. "Highway to the Danger Zone" might as well be her theme song, which also betrayed her age. Did the younger operatives know that movie?

The Thirty-Eight-Year-Old Female with Two Kids and a Muffin Top division of the espionage world was almost nonexistent, even in 2026. No female president and not too many chubby middle-aged ladies in the field. It was a dog-eat-dog, grab-em-by-the-pussy world out there. If your mascara wasn't waterproof, don't bother. Although tubing mascara did seem to be a good alternative. Women were changing the world for the better every day.

Agent Greene had to be able to handle any muscled-up Navy

SEAL who came at her. She had kids waiting for her at home, so failure was not an option. It's not like Lucas was going to brush his teeth if she didn't remind him, and if Gabby died, Kyle would never put her phone down. She had to be as badass of a mom as she was a spy.

She glanced in the mirror and squared her shoulders. Also, she adjusted her yoga pants.

Gabby, with or without camel toe, was going to have it all, damn it. If she could take down a money laundering ring of the Russian Mafia, she could handle anything. Well, most anything. Things got a little cloudy when it came to Markus, but more like cloudy with a chance of sausage. Dear god, she'd read too many children's books.

Gabby went dreamy for a moment—the man looked like Regé-Jean Page, the spy version. He'd gone from being her handler to her trainer. Unlike Regé-Jean, Markus showed up for work and for her. Not that Gabby had a chip on her shoulder about Regé-Jean Page quitting *Bridgerton* or anything.

Gabby set her Stanley on the bike seat and put as much of her hair into a ponytail as would fit. While she was trying to get a few more hairs into the rubber band, the cup crashed to the ground, and the clatter echoed against the concrete walls of the training basement.

"Damn." She grabbed a newspaper someone had left on the bike's console and ineffectively dabbed at the spill. "Who Killed Amanda Duvall?"—a headline with a picture of a beautiful young woman caught her attention. Gabby stopped mopping and climbed onto the bike holding the damp newspaper. With her "rolling hills" program selected, she read:

Amanda Duvall, thirty-four, was found dead in her Columbia Heights townhome last Saturday. Ms. Duvall was a political journalist who recently quit the *Washington Post* to focus on her Substack magazine, *ThinkPiece*. The cause of death was a gunshot wound to the head. Suicide has not been ruled out.

No one who knows Amanda believes she would have taken her own life. Hours before her death, she registered for a candle-making class the next day. If it was murder, the motive just might be a cover-up. This reporter can't help but wonder: What was Amanda Duvall investigating?

The program on Gabby's exercise bike shifted to uphill mode. She stopped reading as she struggled to make it up the pretend hill. The ink was too smeared from her drink to read the rest anyway.

As she "climbed," Gabby's thoughts shifted back to Markus, her sexy spy trainer. Her pedaling slowed to almost zero at the thought of introducing him to her kids. She could pedal up a twenty percent incline but not when she was dragging all her worries. With her momentum gone, she couldn't get the pedals moving again. Kyle was usually a petulant teenage girl, but, for the first time in a long time, there had been a tenuous peace, and one she didn't want to lose by telling her kids about Markus.

The bike's screen flashed a notice, "Keep moving. You can do it."

Of course she could. Prior planning, compartmentalization, communication, contingency plans. She had the skills to balance romance, bad guys, and her kids. No big deal.

Just as she gave another push, a noise near the stairwell drew her attention.

"Carl?" She called the EOD janitor's name.

But the footsteps sounded more deliberate than Carl's, and they were coming toward her. "Carl? Is that you?"

A form stepped into the hallway under the glow of the red exit sign, and Gabby's senses went on high alert.

This was not Carl.

The man took another step forward, and then another, still without any greeting. Markus had told her to be on alert for a double agent in the building while he was training her a couple of weeks ago. He'd explained the danger while she was eating lunch, an Athenian pizza with extra olives and feta. She remembered the pizza being a little dry. The exact danger—she couldn't recall.

But this looked like trouble. No one with good intentions wore a ski mask, and he was still heading in her direction. With no one else in the gym, there was no calling for help. And her gun was across the mats. There was no shooting her way out of this, unless she played it cool.

As casually as she could, she got off the bike. She tripped a little and laughed at her perceived ineptitude (one of her biggest strengths as an agent). After walking like she was wearing a storm trooper uniform for a few steps, she pulled off her shoes. "It's impossible to walk in these things," she said.

Halfway to her gun, the man caught her eye. She gave him a friendly wave.

He grunted a noncommittal reply.

Her heart was hammering in her ears.

Ten feet from her gun, he said, "Stop where you are, Agent Greene."

"Really? Are we doing this? I have to get home to the kids. I was already pushing it, trying to get in a workout. I'll just pretend like

I didn't see you, and we can all go about our business." She was running at the mouth.

The man reasserted himself. "Don't take one more step."

"Are you going to shoot me?" she asked, subtly getting into a fight stance.

After a pause for reflection, he said, "I'd rather a fair fight. No weapons, just you and me on the mat."

"And I really thought I wouldn't have to fight anyone for gym space at this time of day."

He didn't laugh.

There was no such thing as a fair fight. He was a lot bigger than her, but she had a few advantages. 1) Markus was always telling her she had better leverage. Use your body weight to take down your opponent. If nothing else, she could just hang on to this opponent's leg toddler-style. From experience, she knew that was very annoying.

2) A lower center of gravity made her harder to knock down. Just like why skid steer loaders carry their buckets low to the ground. Gabby's life had been nothing but diggers for a while: Luca's picture books, YouTube videos of digging, and visiting a nearby construction project in her neighborhood until it got weird when one of the workmen thought she was there for him.

At any rate, she had some junk in the trunk, and for once, it was to her advantage. Well, that workman had seemed to like it too.

The masked man barreled toward her, head down. Instead of sidestepping, she braced herself and prepared a defense. He had so much momentum already. All she had to do was change his trajectory and throw him over her shoulder.

Surprise flashed in his eyes when he realized what she was going to attempt. "Nice try, Agent Greene," he said, respect in his voice.

But that's all it had been, a try. Before she could come up with her next move, he swept a leg out, taking her feet right out from under her and sending Gabby flying ass over teakettle.

She hit the ground with a thud, and the breath left her lungs in a rush. Before she could roll away, the man was on top of her, using his weight to pin her to the ground. She bucked her hips and tried to sit up to take a swing, but he didn't budge.

"I thought you were going to make this harder?" he said.

How dare he? She was a force to be reckoned with. There had to be something she could do. She wasn't strong enough to punch him from the angle she was at, but... if she stretched, she could almost reach her shoe.

It was just out of reach, and he knew it. He laughed. She never should have signed up for this job. People were counting on her. She couldn't die on a Wednesday at the office.

A bead of sweat dripped down her face as she stretched as far as she could. If only she were an inch taller—or more serious about yoga.

When he laughed at her pathetic effort, he relaxed just enough to let her stretch out a little farther. She snatched her bike shoe with the metal clips and swung it toward him with all the force she could muster. He blocked the attack. Running out of options, she wrapped her thighs around his upper body and squeezed. If he would just hold still for a few seconds.

At this point, the masked man was smashed into her crotch. "Why do you look so surprised?" Gabby said through gritted teeth.

She squeezed harder, smashing his face even closer into her crotch. It was a good move, but the voices started getting louder in her head. Who did she think she was? Could she really kill a man with her thighs? It was the end of the day, and she was already tired from a twenty-minute hill workout on a bike.

"What's the holdup? Are you going to strangle me or what?"

She wanted to say something quippy before killing him, but all she could think was: She probably smelled like a barn.

Before she could answer, he said, "Squeeze! C'mon, kill me! Any man should be so lucky to die between a woman's thighs."

She was done playing along.

"Markus, I can't. Get your face out of my crotch, please."

"Gabby, come on."

"Markus, I'm serious. This role-playing isn't working. I have to get home."

She couldn't pretend it wasn't Markus anymore.

"Gabby," he said sharply, "for this to work, you need to participate. You need some real experience before you are out in the field. I want you prepared."

"I'm trying, but . . . It's just—" It was hard to have a serious conversation with a guy whose cheeks were smooshed between her legs.

"Get out of your head, Gabby. Strangle me with your thighs."

She stared back. Had she just heard that come out of his mouth? Was this a training thing or a sexual tension thing? In the interest of being direct-ish, she said, "This isn't the way I imagined things going, you know, you between my legs like that."

"Hmmm." He looked up at her in a way that made her think she might not smell like an old barn, or, if she did, maybe he was into it. Before he got more playful, she twisted the arm she was still holding in the wrong direction, forcing him to roll onto his back and bringing her with him. She scooted back, settled directly on his stomach.

Her phone buzzed with a text. Markus handed it to her. "Just in case it's your kids," he said.

At that little gesture, she melted. He was so thoughtful and unselfish. The barn was his if he wanted it.

"It's just Justin," she reported. He had texted: Your boudoir is ready. Get ready for reveal.

Justin had been giving her bedroom a makeover for the past week. She hadn't been allowed to see it. Was it a sign? Markus between her thighs, her bedroom finally ready to inhabit after a reno...

"Markus—" she started to say. "I don't know if I can do that thigh move."

"It's a classic for a reason, not that I want your thighs wrapped around another guy's head, but you have strong legs. When it comes down to it, they're more dangerous than your fists."

"I just feel like I should shower before we practice that one. There's this yoni oil that is supposed to make your crotch smell like candy."

"Gabby!" he said. "This is combat. Do you think dudes are worried if their balls smell?"

Probably not.

"You have to imagine that I'm the bad guy in these exercises, take it one hundred percent seriously." In a softer voice, he said, "And skip the oil."

"Is this foreplay or training?" she blurted out. It was unclear.

He wrapped his arms around her and brought her closer, answering her question.

"Oh." She relaxed in his arms. As their breath mingled, he ran his hands down her back in a way that was turning her into a pile of mindless goo. With her senses fully obliterated by his magnetism, she brought her lips to his and let her eyelids flutter shut.

It had been a month of absolute torture, holding Markus at arm's length, but she'd been firm with her boundaries, and he'd respected that she needed some time. He was waiting.

Was waiting. Past tense.

He let out a sigh and kissed her back softly. Not needy or demanding, just perfect. He broke the kiss, his eyes heavy-lidded with desire. "Are you ready to upgrade our coffee date to an actual date?"

Could she do it all? Fully kissed with swollen lips and a need that she couldn't ignore, it seemed possible. She said, "Yes, let's have dinner." But she still needed that boundary. It's not like she had time for a real relationship. "Maybe we can call it a working dinner?"

Markus rubbed the back of his neck. "I want to respect your boundaries, but I would actually like to date."

Gabby tensed up. This was so delicate. She wanted Markus, but she couldn't. Could she? "We could date, if we keep it casual."

Markus looked disappointed. "Are we really that casual after what we've been through together?"

Gabby thought on it. She looked at him. He was right. They weren't totally casual, but there's no way they could be totally serious. "What if..." she said thoughtfully, summoning all the power of the cool badass spy she almost was. "What if you were my work wife?"

"Did you just ask me to be your work wife?" Markus smiled, but there was an edge of sadness in it.

"We won't be regular work wives. More like work wives with benefits."

"Okay." He didn't look totally convinced, but she'd make him see. This could work.

Gabby smiled brightly and pulled up the calendar on her phone. "All right, work wife, I gotta get home, but I'm putting you," she said with a flirtatious lilt, "on my calendar. How about the Friday after next?"

"Really?" He looked skeptical, probably because he didn't think she'd follow through.

She gave him a sexy nod. "Oh yeah, we're going to do it." In the calendar event, she tapped out the words, Dinner with Work Wife.

Change her call sign to Maverick, because there was a new Top Gun in town.

Gabby glanced at her watch. "Shit. I was supposed to be home already." Wednesday was spaghetti night and the only night without any activities. She and the kids ate spaghetti, watched a show, and bonded. She slipped on some tennis shoes and collected her things.

"What are you doing tonight?" she asked Markus.

"Meal prep," he said. "Seven days of chicken and rice. I'm trying a Szechuan chicken recipe." Markus was the type to meal prep his meal prep.

High heels on the wooden gym floor interrupted their conversation. Their boss, Special Supervisory Agent Valentina Monroe, hurried into the training gym. In addition to being the boss, Valentina also happened to be Markus's ex-wife. Not intimidating at all, especially since Valentina could make picking up dog poop look sexy. Her boss-lady wardrobe upgrade was all sexy pantsuits, elegant chignons, and classic heels that Gabby had seen her run in. Her whole look said, "Yes, mistress."

Gabby's look generally said, "Ma'am, do you need help?" But that was her magic as a spy. No one, and she meant no one, saw her coming.

"You two, my office. Now."

Gabby glanced at the time again. "Umm, Valentina, I was supposed to be home a while ago—"

Valentina stopped and looked over her shoulder, Miranda Priestley style. "Agent Greene, national security trumps spaghetti night."

"How did you know that?" Gabby asked, her jaw on the floor.

"I'm a spy. I know everything, and so should you."

"So this one can't wait until morning?"

"No," she said sharply. "It absolutely cannot. I have an assignment. You need to start prepping tonight."

Damn it. She texted Granny, who was at home with the kids. "Running late."

Granny responded.

> **Granny:** Get 'em, tiger!
> **Granny:** But can you pick up a plunger on your way home?

Geez. Valentina stopped and adjusted a Louboutin. "I think I have a rock in my shoe."

> **Granny:** Lucas flushed something.

"Don't you just hate it when that happens?" Valentina said, frowning at her designer shoe.

"It's the worst," Gabby lied. A rock in her Louboutin sounded like a dream.

Valentina was everything Gabby wasn't. It's not like Gabby was jealous, mostly confused. How could Markus go from Valentina to her? Was she Markus's not-quite-midlife crisis? Instead of a Ferrari, he decided to get a middle-aged mom. It was almost unbelievable.

Once they were in her office, Valentina sat behind her desk and waited for Markus and Gabby to settle into the chairs across the desk. "Have you been following the Sheridan Lane story?"

Markus leaned forward in his chair eagerly. "Of course."

"Where's that?" Gabby asked.

"Not where. Who," Valentina said with a click of her pen cap. "Sheridan Lane. You two need to find her."

CHAPTER 2

1700 hours, should have left work an hour ago, Valentina's Office

Valentina turned her desktop monitor screen toward Markus and Gabby and pulled up a website. *Uncommon Sense* was written across the top in large, bold font. Below the title was a candid photo of a middle-aged white woman with startling green eyes and brown, gray-streaked hair. While the woman hadn't bothered with glamour or even makeup, something about her face drew a person in. It wasn't her features or style— it was her intelligence.

Valentina gestured to the brunette. "This is Sheridan Lane."

The website didn't offer any description of Sheridan or her job, other than *Uncommon Sense*, which Gabby believed simply from her expression. Her gray-streaked hair and button-down shirt said no-nonsense. She looked like the kind of person who wouldn't even consider visiting a psychic. The website tabs indicated that Sheridan had a podcast and a Substack, but good luck if you wanted to email her because there was no contact section.

Valentina pulled up an MPG file and clicked play. "This is security camera footage taken from Ms. Lane's street cam yesterday morning."

Valentina clicked play. In the video, the door opened, and a woman exited the building and turned to lock the door. It was clearly Sheridan in a turtleneck and a fleece vest. After adjusting her purse, she gripped the handle on the rolling luggage and wheeled it toward the street. A man helped her into a waiting car. The license plate was not visible.

"Ms. Lane was expected in Washington three hours after this footage was taken, but she never boarded the plane in Jackson Hole and missed her appointment with the president. There's been no word from her since."

Had the woman been wearing a fleece vest to the White House? Gabby was impressed.

"We're trying to track down the car that picked her up, but as you can see, the license plate is not visible. Neither Uber nor Lyft has been able to identify the person at the wheel as one of their drivers."

"Why was she meeting the president?" Gabby was on the edge of her seat. Maybe Sheridan Lane was a fundraiser, and all the funds had gone missing, or she was advising the president on environmental practices, and an oil company had intercepted her on the way to deliver the news.

"She's his psychic, Agent Greene."

"What?" Gabby tried to wrap her mind around that. "The president has a psychic?" Some of the moms at parent pickup had a psychic. Justin regularly saw a psychic because of course he did, but the president... Shouldn't he be dealing with facts and figures? Not to mention, shouldn't a psychic look more like a grown-up Luna Lovegood? Sheridan Lane looked like a federal judge.

Valentina forged on without even looking up. "The president's *psychic*—don't ask questions right now. Save them for the field."

"What kind of things does he talk about with the psychic?" Gabby had nothing but questions.

"Why do you think we're worried, Agent Greene?" Valentina asked. "Ms. Lane, or someone with access to her accounts, posted earlier today that she would be taking a social media break for a couple of weeks with a promise to return refreshed and more insightful soon."

It was a lot to take in all at once. She decided to grab a coffee. "Does anyone else want one?" Gabby asked as she poured a cup from a carafe at a side table.

The way Valentina said no made it sound like Gabby shouldn't have wanted one either.

All business, Markus asked, "Do we have any ideas where to start looking?"

Gabby mopped up some creamer and looked for a trash can. When she didn't see one, she left her stir stick and creamer in a shameful pile by the coffee things.

Valentina clicked on another screen, bringing up a globe. Google Maps–style, she zoomed in on a location, a string of islands in the Atlantic Ocean. Gabby's adrenaline spiked. She'd never been to Europe. She'd never even been to an island other than Catalina, where she'd gone on a school field trip with Kyle, and she'd spent most of her time there taking kids to the bathroom.

"Ms. Lane's cell phone pinged off a tower near Ponta Delgada on São Miguel Island." Valentina indicated one of the islands.

Markus exhaled as if that meant something to him.

"Ponta Delgada?" Gabby leaned forward, peering at the map while gripping her coffee like a lover's hand.

"Ponta Delgada is the capital of the Azores, a chain of islands located a thousand kilometers off Portugal's coast. It's not a country, but an autonomous region of Portugal known for its dramatic landscapes and fishing villages," Valentina explained like she was giving a fifth-grade report on the region. Gabby was familiar with fifth-grade reports. She'd helped Kyle do a last-minute one on Venezuela, capital Caracas, population: twenty-eight million, largest export: crude petroleum.

"The Azores are known as the Hawaii of Europe."

Well, that sounded nice.

"I assume she's at Inner-G," Markus said, looking like he already knew a lot more about this assignment than Gabby did.

Valentina confirmed with a nod. Looking directly at Markus, she said, "Before we do anything, I want you to chat up Genesis and see what you can get out of him. Maybe they're not hiding anything."

"Genesis?" Gabby was officially on the last-to-know list. "What am I missing? Can someone catch me up?"

"Inner-G is a yoga and wellness brand run by Genesis and Jasmine Love." Markus waited for her to recognize the names. "It's basically goop but run by The Rock and his swimsuit model wife."

Gabby was all ears.

Markus continued his report. "Inner-G is a known security risk and has been for some time. On the surface, it appears to be nothing but a yoga and wellness retreat, but there are a few red flags, which is why I've gotten involved. Number one: the money. Genesis and Jasmine are living well beyond their means. The luxury resort, the yacht, the private jet. Mr. Love claims that all Inner-G's wealth comes from member tithing, but the numbers don't add up. Number two: The retreat has been tied to several major leaked news stories. We're concerned they're selling member secrets."

Pop Princess Sunbathes Nude!
Congressman Marries Nanny on Beach!
Oscar Winner Snorts Coke Off Sex Worker!

On her last mission, the bad guys had been Russian Mafia. This time it was Hollywood. Talk about leveling up!

Valentina cut in. "Sheridan Lane has spent countless hours in private audience with the president. Whatever secrets she has heard, it's a matter of national security that they stay in the vault. She's not the person we want on gossip island."

Markus rolled his chair back. "Not that I don't want to go to the Azores, but can we just send the local operatives in to grab her? That'd be quick and easy. Less cost for the taxpayers too."

Valentina shook her head. "She has too much sensitive information, apparently. The president doesn't want Sheridan in the hands of foreign intelligence until we get there. He wants our best American field agents on it as soon as possible."

Gabby sat up a little straighter at the compliment. Was *she* the best field agent?

Valentina clarified, "Make that our best *positioned* field agents."

"How so?" Gabby asked. She didn't know anyone in Hollywood, and yoga hadn't worked out for her. Balance was not her thing.

"I've gotten to know Genesis," Markus said. When Gabby looked skeptical, he added, "We're once-a-day, text-level friendly."

"So that's why you've been doing all the yoga." Gabby was putting it all together.

"Wasn't it believable?" he asked.

"I thought you were more of a karate, rugby, sports-that-require-a-helmet kind of guy."

Ignoring them, Valentina said, "Congratulations, Markus. After embedding yourself in with Genesis and his inner circle, you and your fiancée are about to take your commitment to Inner-G to the next level."

Fiancée. Gabby let the word wash over her.

All business, Valentina continued, "Genesis is expecting you at Inner-G's resort on Friday." It was almost like she was introducing the Showcase Showdown prize on *The Price Is Right. You are about to win a trip for two at a lovely tropical resort!*

Gabby blinked at Valentina. "This weekend?"

"As I said, Friday. Bright and early."

"The day after tomorrow Friday?" How was she going to leave Friday? Her color-coded calendar was a rainbow of obligation from now until the end of time. It would be one thing to shift things a week out, but the day after tomorrow . . . There were appointments, conferences, and vegetables that no one would eat without her.

"Don't worry. Markus has done the paperwork and reconnaissance. You only need to familiarize yourself with your cover identity and the organization itself."

That was hardly enough time to prepare for an afternoon at the beach with her kids.

"Markus, you should be familiar with your identity. But make sure you know everything about George Alexander." Turning her attention to Gabby, she said, "Gabby, you're going to be Gia Glanville on this mission. You have an extensive backstory and a digital footprint."

It was a lot to take in. She had to become a whole other person by Friday. It was hard enough being herself.

Markus gave her an encouraging nod. "We got this."

That was easy for the meal prep king to say. The man had been infiltrating the group for long enough to get pretty good at yoga. His bags were probably already packed.

"It's a multiphase mission. Your first task is to find Sheridan."

Gabby nodded distractedly.

"If she has been abducted, you need to get her to safety as soon as possible. If she's *actually* on a social media break, then just keep an eye on things. Assess potential security risks. If these people are trading in gossip, that psychic needs to get out. And I need a full report on the structure of the organization. I want to know more about Inner-G than they know about themselves."

Gabby pushed her chair back. If she was leaving for a work trip, she needed to get ready now. The least she could do would be to fill up the freezer with enough frozen pizzas to last a week.

"Hold up, Agent Greene." With a wicked smile, Valentina said, "I haven't told you the good part yet."

Gabby braced herself.

"You two are down there to get married. *That's* why Genesis was so excited to have you."

Bombs exploded in Gabby's head.

Markus grumbled. "Really, Val?"

Gabby fell back in her chair, speechless. Her coffee sloshed over the rim onto her pants.

Valentina handed her a towel. "Get it together, Greene. It's just pretend. No need to sign a prenup."

Role-playing a fight had already been hard enough this morning.

"Why?" Markus asked, looking no more excited than she was.

While Gabby mopped up coffee, Valentina continued. "Inner-G is hosting its Power Couples Retreat this weekend."

Markus snickered, and Valentina said, "I know."

"What's so funny?" Gabby asked, glancing between them.

"It's based on his movie *Power Couple*."

"It's genius," Markus said, "turning his classic movie into a cult."

"Wasn't that an action movie?"

Valentina sighed. "I don't know if it's genius, but it starts on Saturday morning. Markus, you make the arrangements. Genesis is going to be thrilled you're finally signing up."

Gabby's head was spinning. She and Markus were in the middle of trying to figure out workable boundaries in their relationship. They were work wives, which might or might not involve sex but definitely didn't involve trips to the Azores and marriage.

Valentina explained, "By getting married, you're jumping straight to the inner circle. It guarantees more time with Genesis and Jasmine. They love when their cult members get married, especially to potential new cult members."

Markus, with his pecs and his gray sweatpants and a pheromone cocktail that made her woozy and pliable . . . she wasn't ready to bring him home yet. What if he didn't do the dishes? She had kids, and a mortgage, and a Granny who was going to need more help than she offered before long. The stakes for making a bad decision were too high. Gabby was dating without a net.

Valentina cocked her head. Channeling a drill sergeant, she said, "Is this too hard of an assignment for you, Agent Greene?" Gabby half expected to tell her to drop and give her twenty or clean the latrine with a toothbrush.

"I got this," Gabby said with more volume than confidence.

"You better." Valentina nodded. "I've emailed you our encrypted files on Genesis, Jasmine, and Inner-G. I expect you to have it all memorized by tomorrow. This is not a drill."

Markus held the door for Gabby, and they walked down the hall away from the office. Before this meeting, the amount of open-ended business between them had felt like a lot. On the way out of the office, with a fake marriage on the calendar for next week, she and Markus barely fit in the hall with all the unspoken business and big feelings between them.

"So, uh, we're getting married, huh?" she said, if for no other reason than to fill the awkward silence. Work wife wedding bells were ringing. Gabby could almost pretend that didn't make her actually, really worried she couldn't do it all. Almost. For a job that required compartmentalizing, the lines were getting very blurry.

CHAPTER 3

1800 hours, late for dinner, Greene household

Gabby drove home in a daze. She had two nights to get everything in order before she left for the Azores. A quick Google search had shown shots of beautiful volcanic islands, velvety green conical mountains, waterfalls, and ocean views— basically, it was the bad guy's island lair from *The Incredibles* and a twenty-four-hour trip from LA. Her last mission had turned into an unmitigated disaster, but at least it had been a short commute. This job—international travel, away from her kids twenty-four seven for . . . had Valentina said a week? She started to sweat more than she had during her twenty-minute workout that Markus had interrupted. In retrospect, had that really been necessary? Markus needed to get a dog. It was just him and his protein shakes and his hot ex-wife.

And Gabby needed to calm down. Spiraling anxiety would do nothing but suck up time.

She hit her blinker and made a slow, controlled turn onto Avocado Avenue. She might be about to go on the work trip from hell. The kids didn't need to know that. When she walked through the door, she was Mom.

Avocado Avenue was just as she'd left it this morning. The biggest excitement on the block was Shelly's new privacy fence, erected shortly after their recent conflict. But really, it wasn't Gabby's fault that Shelly had gotten arrested. Sure, it wouldn't have happened if the Russian Mafia hadn't been staking out Gabby's house, but still, if she'd stayed out of it, she would have been fine.

The only other change was Justin's new lawn furniture. Now every time she went over there, he name-dropped the designer of his new chairs and table. "Dinner on the patio. Did you know this table is by Alphonse?" She didn't have the heart to tell him that the Alphonse de Picnic Table was kind of wobbly. Gabby had the Costco set he'd replaced in her backyard now.

As her Spanish-style home with an orange tile roof and a lemon tree in the front came into view, she couldn't help but smile. It was warm, welcoming, and filled with everyone she loved. Well, except for Burt, but even he was growing on her.

Tonight, Granny and Burt had picked up the kids and taken care of dinner. Justin was waiting eagerly to do the big reveal on her redecorated bedroom. Maybe she'd only be home for two nights, but at least she could sleep in a bed. A week on the couch had been enough. Hopefully, Justin hadn't spent a fortune on brand-name nightstands or something ridiculous. When he'd asked for keywords to describe her vision, she had said: "tasteful," "soft blankets," "Joanna Gaines." She had just been saying words. Gabby didn't have a design aesthetic.

He'd responded with a huffy, "You know I can't do Joanna Gaines. If I ever bring out shiplap, just make a casket out of it and bury me, because I've already died inside."

"What's shiplap?" she'd asked.

At least she would have a room that she could maybe,

foreseeably, if the stars aligned, bring Markus to. Someday. Really, bringing someone back to her house at her age was trickier than when she'd been fooling around as a teenager.

Before she even had a chance to put her bags down, her fourteen-year-old greeted her. "Mom, I need new shoes. I can't find mine." Kyle was a classic teen in oversized sweats, EarPods, and knockoff Uggs. Her hair, which she'd dyed red to match Gabby's, was shoved under a beanie, along with her love for her mother.

Wrinkling her nose, Kyle said, "Eww. Why are you so sweaty?"

"Hello to you too."

"But really, I need shoes. I had to wear Uggs in gym today." At which point, she noticed Gabby's feet. "Mom! Why are you wearing my shoes?"

"Sorry, sweetie. I was in a rush. I guess we all need some new shoes."

Gabby took her phone out of her pocket and shoved it at Kyle. "Just go online and pick something out."

Already scrolling, Kyle headed toward her bedroom, and Gabby called after her, "Don't order anything until you show me!" She was making decent money, but she was still a government employee paying California prices for everything.

In the kitchen, Granny was putting away leftovers. Justin was sitting at the counter, sipping a glass of rosé like he was just there for the show. He probably was.

"Where's Burt?" Gabby glanced at the empty La-Z-Boy. Her grandmother's boyfriend, Burt, was in a committed relationship with the television, Steve Harvey in particular.

Looking over her shoulder from the fridge, Granny said, "I made him take Bubbles for a walk. I'm not sure if the man can bend over to pick up the dog poo so I sent Lucas too."

At least Burt and Lucas had both gotten out from behind their screens for a few minutes.

From upstairs, Kyle yelled, "MOM!" and then something Gabby couldn't understand because Kyle was in another room.

Gabby walked to the bottom of the stairs. "Kyle, if you're speaking to me, please come into the same room as me." Not to mention, "The shoes aren't that important." Kyle needed to develop some patience.

Kyle appeared at the top of the stairs. Instead of mentioning shoes, she announced, "The toilet is being weird."

Weird... "Weird like Uncle Jim or weird like it's clogged?"

"Not funny, Mom!"

Which is when she remembered: Granny had asked her to get a plunger.

"Kyle, go to the utility closet and get the plunger. It's wrapped in a garbage bag. Plunge the toilet, and I'll check on it after." These kids needed to figure out how to solve a few basic problems.

"Gross." Kyle made a noise of horror. "I don't think I need to get that involved."

Did she have to do everything? "Just put the plunger over the hole and push down. It might take a couple of times. It's simple, Kyle."

"Can't you do it?" Kyle whined.

"See if you can figure it out first." She had been trying to set her expectations for the kids higher with mixed results. Some days, Kyle would make scrambled eggs and pack her own lunch and Lucas's. Then there would be two weeks where Gabby would need a crowbar just to get her off the couch to carry her own dirty dishes to the sink. And the EarPods. She was connected to the outside world and unavailable to her own mother.

With an *oof*, Gabby plopped down on a kitchen stool next to Justin, and Granny slid a glass of wine across the counter toward her.

"Thanks, Granny. I don't know what I'd do without you."

Granny patted Gabby's hand. "It'd be ugly."

Justin huffed. "What am I, chopped liver?"

Gabby gave him a side hug. "I love you too, Justin."

She would like to tell them she was going to the Azores. She needed to tell them she was leaving for a work trip, but she and Markus hadn't gotten around to making up a cover story yet. Everyone at home thought she was an executive assistant. They'd met Markus, so she'd simply said he was a coworker. They were boring employees of a boring company no one would ever want to ask a second question about.

Granny spoke up. "Shouldn't you go home, Justin? I don't want you neglecting Hugh and getting divorced like Gabby here."

Justin laughed off the idea like it was preposterous. "I'm the hot, fun one with personality. There's no way Hugh can leave."

Had her ex, Phil, thought he was the hot, fun one? Not that she needed to make everything about herself.

Granny turned her attention back to Gabby. "Not to suggest that you neglected Phil, dear. I never liked him."

"Thanks, Granny." The loyalty warmed her soul.

"And what is he doing with his hair lately?" Granny grimaced. "Is he dyeing it?"

Granny had a solid point about Phil's hair. "I'm not sure if he dyed it or if just looks funny against the spray tan."

Justin's eyes went wide, and he mouthed something to Gabby.

Gabby ignored him and went on. "You know what I mean. His hair and skin are kind of all the same color now, like a cheap plastic doll." A thought just struck her. "Do you think he's getting Botox?" If he was getting Botox and she wasn't, talk about a cruel world.

Justin started gesturing wildly and choking on his rosé.

"Slow down on the alcohol, young man!" Granny admonished. With a glance at her granddaughter, she said, "Botox won't solve Phil's problems. He needs a—"

Before she could finish her sentence, Justin caught his breath and blurted out, "Hi, Phil."

"I'm pretty sure there's more to life than being really, really ridiculously good-looking," Phil said. He made a *Zoolander* face.

Gabby's jaw dropped, and she turned to see her ex-husband standing in the entrance to the kitchen, toffee-colored from head to toe and holding a bouquet of flowers and a heart-shaped box of chocolates.

Gabby suppressed a moan. He must have broken up with whoever he'd been dating this week. That was his pattern. Find a woman, break up, run back to Gabby. He was nothing if not predictable.

"Hey, Gabs," he said with a smile, "I thought I'd surprise you."

"Did you just walk in?" Granny asked. "I didn't hear the bell."

"I bought—" From Phil's indignant tone, she knew he was going to say something like, *I bought this house. Of course I can walk in,* but he stopped himself, took a breath, and held out the bouquet. "I bought these flowers for you, Gabby. I know they're your favorite kind." It was a bouquet of carnations from the grocery store with a small helium balloon on a stick in the center.

Her favorite kind? It's like he'd never been married to her. "Thank you, Phil." Not to mention the man was a high-powered investment banker for a huge firm. Carnations?

"And here are some chocolates."

They were cheap gas station chocolates in a plastic container. She didn't want them any more than she wanted Phil. Worse yet, she could see from the tag that they were from a facility that also processed tree nuts, which meant that Lucas would be allergic.

Gabby set them on the counter without a word, winding up to give Phil a piece of her mind. It would be better than stabbing him with the helium balloon's stick. That would be a murder scene—stabbed through the heart, a tiny "Get well!" balloon protruding from the wound.

Justin stood, undoubtedly feeling the gathering storm in the air. "Well, I better be going. Gabby, we can do the reveal tomorrow."

"No!" she said forcefully. She would not give up sleeping in her new room because Phil decided to show up uninvited. "Phil's not staying."

Phil perked up at the mention of a bedroom reveal. "Don't mind me. I'd like to see what you did with my old office."

Gabby cringed. How could Phil make this any more uncomfortable?

Justin shook his head *no* a little too emphatically. "Later would be better. A bedroom is supposed to be a private retreat." The way he said "private" rang alarm bells in Gabby's mind.

Granny wasn't having it. "Gabby has been sleeping on a couch for a week." She started marching toward Gabby's bedroom. "Why are you acting like it's a secret? A bedroom has a bed, a dresser, and a laundry basket. That's it."

Justin scoffed. "Granny, what do you think I am, a Communist?"

Granny, who had defected from the USSR during the Moscow Olympics, raised an eyebrow.

Kyle appeared again and said, "The toilet is still like not right."

"Is it an emergency?"

"I guess not."

"Okay. I'll plunge it after I see the room."

Dismissing the "weird" toilet, Gabby turned toward her bedroom door. It was locked, and there was a Do NOT DISTURB sign hanging on the doorknob. Justin had already suggested she put the sign to use for real.

Before opening the door, Justin took a deep breath and made the sign of the cross.

Phil, uninvited guest of the century, stood at the front with a handful of pretzels. He popped one in his mouth and peered into *her* brand-new room.

Gabby was seething, but she held her tongue. She did not want to kick him out of the house in front of the kids, who had also joined the tour. If she could go back in time and divorce him before he had a chance to leave her, she would.

Like it was still his house, Phil said, "I'm curious to see what you did. There's that one awkward corner that I never knew what to do with. What'd we use to keep there, Gabs?"

Gabby glared at him. How dare he act like they'd lived together for fifteen years. Sure, they had, but he didn't have to relive it so fondly.

Justin smiled. "Oh, I made good use of the corner."

Gabby followed Phil, who had already pushed through the streamers stretched across the door to find…She'd watched that Netflix series, *How to Build a Sex Room*, a year or so ago. This wasn't that, but it wasn't not that either.

The walls were painted a deep pink, and all the furniture was glossy black, including a dresser and two nightstands. The comforter was black and splashed with oversized peonies. Justin had managed to create a small seating area with a TV. The loveseat was hot pink tufted velvet with a cream-colored throw.

There was nothing funny about it, but Phil laughed too loudly anyway. "What is this, a Victoria's Secret?"

"It's beautiful, Justin!" It was decadent, a retreat for wearing eye masks and fluffy slippers. The bedding was cozy and inviting. She was ready to crawl in and...Oh no, that wouldn't do. She quickly tucked a vibrator charging upright on the nightstand into the drawer, shooting dagger eyes at Justin.

He shrugged. "I was supposed to give *you* a tour, not you and everyone you know."

This was Gabby after dark.

Instead of kid art and family photos on the wall, he'd hung Georgia O'Keeffe flowers and an oil painting of a fox and hounds scene. When she looked closer, it was hard not to notice that the hunter was in very tight pants.

Justin whispered, "Vintage bulge because I'm keeping it classy."

Phil put a pretzel in his mouth and chewed violently.

Lucas, who had returned from his walk and joined the group without a hello, hopped on the bed and started rolling around. If she wasn't so overwhelmed, she would remind him to say *hi* to his father. When he flopped over and started sticking his tongue out, she looked up. They all did.

"A mirror?"

"Of course," Justin said, like he'd never considered not putting a mirror above a bed. Gabby couldn't help but think of Justin's husband, Hugh. No one had ever looked more like a history professor.

Phil scowled. "This doesn't feel like a bedroom for a mom."

The mirror was suggestive and playful, and no one needed toys on display, but besides that, the room was feminine and luxurious. After she cleared Phil out and compartmentalized everyone in her family, Markus could come over.

She gave Justin a huge hug. "Thank you."

"You're welcome. Hugh and I have been meaning to get you a divorce present."

Phil blanched at "divorce present," but oh well. That's what you get when you leave your wife, and then after it's all said and done, insist on going on a tour of her renovated single-woman bedroom. He shouldn't be here at all.

Justin kissed her on the cheek and said, "I'll see you tomorrow. Your grandma is right. I should go home to Hugh. Can't be neglecting my man."

As everyone filtered out, Gabby turned to Lucas. "Did you clog the toilet, Lucas?"

"No, but..."

From the look on his face, she knew he did. They would have the courtesy flush talk again tomorrow. But for now, "Just use the downstairs bathroom. I'll get to it before bed."

Phil touched her upper arm. "Do you need help with something?"

"No, I got it." She hoped.

Accepting that, he said, "Gabby, can we talk?"

"I guess." All she wanted to do was watch a show and crawl into her brand-new bed.

"Did you like the flowers and chocolate?" he asked.

"No, Phil. That's not something I want from you. If you want to help, how about some money for the kids? Kyle needs shoes."

"Of course I'll help with the kids, but..."

Phil had been nothing but missteps, and she could feel him about to make another.

"I want to get back together. Leaving was a mistake."

She started to respond, but he held up his hand in protest. "I was having a midlife crisis."

"Phil—"

He pressed a finger to her lips. "Your mom said you've been missing me. She thinks it's a good idea for us to get back together."

"What?" Her mom? Why was she talking to Phil?

"Just think about it. We have kids together."

She couldn't even with this. He had left her nearly a year ago now. She had moved on. Their chapter was closed. She opened the door and gestured for him to leave. "Thank you for the flowers, but no."

"And that bedroom, Gabby. I mean . . . that isn't you."

"Good night, Phil."

After she shut the door, she sagged against it to collect herself. Kyle walked around the corner. "Mom—"

The look on Kyle's face was one of mild distress, and it brought Gabby right back to her to-do list—the toilet. "Ohmygod. I almost forgot."

In the upstairs bathroom, she stared into the toilet bowl, plunger in hand. Thankfully, it wasn't filled with a giant poop. It was important to be grateful for the small things. She lined up the plunger over the hole and went for it. *Squelch*, followed by a giant sucking sound, and then nothing. She did it again. And then again.

After about five times with no success, she sagged in front of the bowl.

Kyle, softer than earlier, a tender hope in her voice said, "Are you and Dad getting back together?"

Plunger still in hand, her glasses splattered with drops of toilet water, Gabby stared at her daughter, who needed so much. It was the end of a long day, and Gabby had nothing left to give. Damn Phil with his flowers and apologies.

"Sweetie, it's so late. I love you so much, and I'll always love your dad for giving me you, but right now I'm only interested in getting together with a plumber." She smiled and gave the toilet another plunge.

Kyle's eyes narrowed to a fierce glare, and she stormed out, leaving Gabby with nothing but an incurably clogged toilet.

Gabby called out the door, "Lucas, what did you flush down this toilet?" Was he pooping like a grown man at seven?

Lucas peeked in the door and said, "A tennis ball. But it's okay. It went down."

Gabby dropped back onto the edge of the tub while Lucas prattled on. Something about playing fetch with Mr. Bubbles, Kyle flushing the toilet, and the ball bouncing off the shower wall and into the toilet mid-flush.

She started laughing because some monsters you just couldn't fight. The old Gabby might have primal-screamed into the toilet bowl or just put caution tape over the door, but she was Agent Greene. She could handle this. All she needed was a plumber and three more hours in the day.

Not picking up on the source of her maniacal laughter, Lucas said proudly, "It was awesome."

CHAPTER 4

0730 hours, morning rush, Avocado Avenue

Gabby normally listened to her favorite self-help guru, Sloane Ellis, on the way to work. Today, she pulled up Sheridan Lane's podcast. She hit play on an episode titled "Balance." After some acoustic intro music, Sheridan said, "Welcome to *Uncommon Sense*. I am your host, Sheridan Lane. Today we are talking about the greatest myth of all: balance."

Gabby scoffed. All you had to do was try harder.

"Balance is difficult if you have too little or too much. Too little and you become the focus, time becomes a swamp. If you have too much, you want more. Oof. Women, I see you."

If you wanted to balance more, you had to be faster, harder, stronger, smarter. Gabby knew that, if she could be more, she could do more.

Sheridan took a call. The caller, a woman named Tanya, said, "I have it all, a job and kids and everything, but I feel like I'm falling apart all the time."

Gabby fought the impulse to press STOP. She didn't need to hear this depressing garbage. Be More. Do More—that's all there was to it.

"Do you really have it all?" Sheridan asked. "If you have a big job and a lot of family responsibility, are you having any fun?"

The caller actually sobbed into the phone. "No."

"Well, then you don't have it all. You just have all the work."

Oh shit.

Frustrated, the woman asked, "How can I add some fun if I can barely do my job and take care of the kids?"

"If you can't carry what you have, sounds like you need to set something down, and that is okay."

What good was this psychic? "Help her!"

"Tell me what to do. Can you see a different future for me?"

"You determine your future. It's time to dig deep and use your uncommon sense. I only call it uncommon because most people don't have it, and if they do, they don't use it."

If Gabby wanted to add anything, or anyone, she needed to set something down. But what?

In a calm, but firm tone, Sheridan said, "Don't forget. It's your life, and you make the rules."

Now she was talking! Gabby turned her up like she was listening to a girl-power anthem.

Everyone had an opinion on Gabby's purely hypothetical love life lately. Sheridan was right—she needed to make the rules. There was one other person who needed this reminder.

In a loud, clear voice, Gabby said, "Hey Siri, call Mom."

Elena Greene picked up the phone on the first ring.

"Gabby, how are you? How're the kids?"

She could not small talk, not when her mom had been colluding with Phil. "Mom." She said the word with all the force of a stop sign.

"How is Kyle doing in school? I've been worried about her being bullied. It's all they talk about on the news."

Thanks, Katie Couric.

The irony of her mom talking about bullying. "Mom, Phil came over last night—"

"Oh good!" she said in a high-pitched, drawn-out tone, as if she hadn't instigated the visit. "How'd it go?"

Gabby took a deep breath. "Mom, he said you've been talking to him about us getting together."

"You say that like it's a bad thing?" Gabby could hear Elena shaking her head over the phone. "It would be so much better for the kids if you could put your differences aside."

"You can think that, but you need to stay out of it."

After a pregnant pause, Elena said, "Phil has a great job, and he provided a really nice life for you and the kids. Are you doing better now? You're hardly ever home anymore, and for what—an executive assistant job? It's not like you're saving lives or something."

"Mom," she said, a heavy note of caution in her voice.

"It seems like you're only thinking about yourself with all of these decisions."

And what was her mom even talking about? Of course she was thinking about herself. Why was that a bad thing? It was her marriage, and it was her divorce. Not to mention, the whole point of her job was saving lives. Not that she could say it.

"It's not the 1950s anymore. I don't want Kyle to see that having kids means she can't have a job, not to mention joy." Did her pleasure count? Even if it did, did she have time for it?

That made her mom laugh. "Joy—what are you talking about? You're a mother."

Yikes. Sheridan was right.

"Gabby," her mom sighed like Gabby was a recalcitrant child, "you are being selfish. It isn't about you. It's about your kids."

Gabby took a deep breath. "Stay out of it, Mom. This isn't your business."

"Fine, Gabriella."

Her mom had sucked all the air out of the car.

Violently, she pressed PLAY on Sheridan. Gabby was going to make her own rules, damn it. And the first rule she was making? *She* would be the one to rescue this psychic. Gabby might need her advice.

Today was the only workday before Operation Heartache to Heartache, so called because someone was listening to Pat Benatar, but for no other reason. Hopefully, Gabby wasn't missing something, but she had the vague sense that someone was making fun of her.

She slipped into her cubical for a quick email check before a meeting with Valentina at oh-nine-hundred. The cubes were right where International Rug, Inc., had kept the pasta and specialty sauces; the EOD had moved into the big box store's warehouse property after it had gone bankrupt. Gabby was still hoping to find a stash of candles or throw pillows somewhere.

Markus wasn't at his desk so, for the moment, her brain was free to answer emails. Spy email wasn't that much more exciting than regular email. There were endless calendar invites for various meetings, notices regarding which parts of the building were being cleaned or updated, and office refrigerator etiquette. She wasn't going to name names but there were a lot of national security experts who didn't make a new pot of coffee after taking the last cup. In good news, she received an email regarding her sidearm.

> Agent Greene, you have been cleared
> to carry a sidearm. Please report to the
> armory before the end of the day.

She wasn't just a baby agent anymore. The EOD trusted her enough to give her a gun.

Another agent, Ed, popped his head into her space. "Heard you're headed to the Azores, hot shot."

"Seems like it," she said.

"When you get back, we'll have to celebrate, go out for drinks."

Gabby smiled tightly. There was no way she was going out with work people when she got back from a work trip.

"We haven't been able to get Markus out for a while."

"Really?" That didn't sound like the man who'd been inviting her out for dinner on the reg.

A second later, the man himself sidled up to the desk.

"Hey, Markus," Ed said, "I was just saying we haven't seen you at happy hour for a while. That darts championship could be yours if you wanted."

"I've been focused."

"You know what they say about 'all work and no play...'"

"Is the path to success?" Markus answered.

"No, makes a dull boy. You're going to be boring, alone, and successful."

Maybe Gabby wasn't the only one out of balance.

Markus dismissed Ed's prophecy and turned his attention to

Gabby. "Let's meet on the mats. I want to talk without everyone listening in." He gestured to the other cubicles filled with spies.

Her stomach dropped. "Um, okay."

With a feeling of dread, she hit the locker room and changed into a matching set from Target, leggings and a shirt with a built-in bra. Why were people on the internet trying so hard to convince the world that a bra was a shirt? In Gabby's world, a shirt was still a shirt, and it was going to stay that way, damn it.

Markus was waiting for her in a muscle shirt and pants that left her struggling to keep her eyes up.

"How was your night?" he asked.

"Um…" She strained to focus on his face and keep from drooling. "Just the usual chaos at home." She shut her eyes as she reached for her toes. Focus on stretching.

"That bad, huh?"

"Yes, although Justin let me into my bedroom again, finally."

When Markus gave her a funny look, she explained. "I guess that sounds weird. He redecorated it for me and wanted to surprise me like it was a reality show reveal."

"Your bedroom…"

"Yep, my bedroom." She said the word slowly and glanced up from under her eyelashes to gauge his reaction.

He was very alert, she might even say eager, to hear about her bedroom. "Is it nice?" he asked.

She smiled softly and leaned into the flirting, angling toward him. "Very."

"What color is it?" He might as well have asked what color her panties were.

"Pink." She let the "p" pop on her tongue.

In a less flirty tone, she said, "Honestly, it's sort of a disaster.

Justin kind of forgot I have two kids and live with my grand-mother." She shook her head. "It's gorgeous, but—" She shook her head. It was a little too Samantha from *Sex in the City*. She'd have to tone it down.

"What did he do?"

She shook her head. "I can't even say it out loud. Lucas is going to be scarred for life."

Nodding in an "aww yeah baby" way, he said, "It sounds like Justin did an A+ job."

Gabby had never been so relieved to flirt. They were back to normal. Flirting at the office.

Markus stopped doing what he was doing. "Can we talk?"

"We are talking." Gabby smiled.

He ignored her flip response. "You're not going to back out of this mission, are you?"

She shook her head. "Absolutely not."

Markus's features relaxed. "Good." His eyes were downcast. "I trust you. I haven't been in the field for real since Darcy died."

Gabby released her thigh stretch and stumbled. "That's not entirely true. You were in the club the night we took Orlov down."

He huffed out a laugh. "Gabby, let me walk you through that night from my perspective."

"Oh-kay." That had been a great night.

"That was the night you tranquilized me. It was my first night in the field after getting pulled because Agent Strong didn't think I was psychologically ready after losing a good friend."

She could see his point. "It wasn't your fault. You trusted me, and I—"

"You tied me up and tossed me in a closet with a bunch of Russian Mafia." He paused to let it sink in. "Gabby, you didn't even have training, and you took me out of the game before it even started."

"It wasn't just you. I tied up Alice, and I tranquilized Valentina. I had to. I didn't know who to trust."

"I remember," he said. "I was there. How many agents would have been able to pull that off?"

"Everyone underestimates me. That's the only reason it worked."

"That mission was a huge success," he said.

With a smile, she acknowledged, "Yeah, I got a lot of congrats for that one."

He held up a hand. "You did get a lot of congratulations. Do you know how much ribbing I've gotten in the office since then?"

Her jaw dropped. "Are you sure it's not in your head? Ed just said he wished you'd hang out more." How had she missed this? "I'm sorry. It probably didn't help that I was brand-new."

"Yep, and a foot shorter," he reminded her. "With about a week of training."

It was the first time she'd thought about that mission from his perspective.

She nodded solemnly. "I understand. I'm sorry. Sometimes I forget that you are even human. You are so confident and handsome." She had been so wrapped up in her own world, what she needed, what her family needed, that she'd forgotten that Markus was a person with needs and wants and insecurities.

"I've got your back, partner," she said.

"Same."

This was a real mission with real people who depended on her. She had a job to do.

Valentina's voice cut through the gym. "Agent Greene, my office. Now."

Gabby startled at the sound of her boss's voice.

Standing over them and tapping her toe impatiently, Valentina gave Markus an up-and-down look, stopping on his pants and then drifting to his muscle shirt. She shook her head with exasperation. "Markus, what are you wearing?"

"What?" He held up his hands defensively.

"We're all onto the gray sweatpants trick by now. Quit playing."

He feigned innocence. "I don't know what you're talking about."

"Do I need to start picking out your clothes again?"

With a hint of "na-na, na-na, boo-boo" in his voice, he said, "I get to dress myself these days."

She gestured for them to follow her. Without even looking back, she volleyed, "I can institute a dress code."

Gabby followed Valentina out of the training gym. With a glance over her shoulder, Gabby said, "I got you."

The tension went out of his shoulders. Markus needed her.

CHAPTER 5

Thursday, one day before the mission, EOD headquarters

Gabby sat down across from Valentina, the clean expanse of Valentina's desk between them. The only decoration an award. There were no personal photos. Gabby's desk was the opposite. She had a recent picture of her family in its most current form, taken at Granny's favorite bingo hall. At first, Gabby had been upset about the kids gambling, but it was mostly just time with their grandma. In the picture, Lucas had a plastic water cup sucked to his face. Kyle was looking at the ceiling, waiting for the aliens to rescue her, maybe. Granny wasn't smiling because her partial was at the shop. Burt was beaming. Justin had also given her a framed headshot of his drag persona, Betty Danger. Beside the photo was a tray of succulents that were hanging on for dear life and some reminders about upcoming school events.

Was Gabby doing this wrong?

"I have a separate assignment for you to complete while you're at the resort." Valentina didn't smile.

"Who, me?" Before Gabby could think about it, she blurted out, "Shouldn't you be giving Markus the extra assignments?" He was the senior field agent. Gabby had one mission under her belt.

"Markus can't do this one."

"Oh no, you don't want me to seduce someone, do you? I'm not sure if that's in my skill set." It wasn't.

"Noted," Valentina said with zero expression, "But that's not what I'm asking for."

"Oh." Gabby's cheeks flushed with embarrassment.

"The assignment is to keep tabs on Markus."

Uh-oh.

"Why? Markus is the most competent agent I know."

"That's true, but everyone has a breaking point. It's my job to make sure you are all healthy and fit to do your jobs. Darcy's death brought Markus to his lowest. I haven't seen him bounce back yet."

What the hell did that mean? Gabby chewed the inside of her cheek. She did not like the sound of this.

"I've been married to the man, Gabby. I know his weaknesses."

Valentina was imagining things.

"I need you to keep me briefed on Markus. Specifically, on his relationship with Genesis."

"Why?" Gabby felt like the rug had been ripped out from under her. "Why would you do that? He's such a good agent."

Valentina sighed. "To be frank, I need to know if we can fully trust Markus. He's become very friendly with Genesis at one of his lowest points. This mission is two birds, one stone: Recover the psychic and make sure Markus didn't drink the Kool-Aid."

"Fine, I'll keep an eye on him."

"I'll need a full daily report."

Gabby had no intention of filing a bad report on Markus. Unless the man murdered someone, she was going to tell Valentina that he was the best agent she'd ever seen.

"Agent Greene, do you copy?" Valentina's voice was sharp.

Gabby's nod must not have inspired trust because Valentina reiterated, "Agent Greene, are you prepared to do this assignment, even if you don't like what you find?"

Gabby wasn't going to find anything she didn't like. Markus was perfect. She smiled and said, "Of course. I'm a professional."

This entire job was about establishing and betraying trust. It was like her relationship with Phil all over again, except Valentina was asking her to play the part of Phil. Gabby's stomach soured at the thought.

A knock at the door interrupted her shame spiral. Markus poked his head into the room, unaware that the woman who had just agreed to have his back was now a double agent.

"Hey, Markus," Valentina said, shifting from "spy on Markus" to "this morning's agenda" as smoothly as a German sports car. "Glad you're here. Gabby and I were just getting caught up."

He took a seat next to Gabby and smiled. "Hey, partner."

She died a little inside.

"You two need to get to Disguises, but let's go over a few last-minute details." Valentina tapped on her desk with a pen. "The travel arrangements are set. Agent Greene arranged plane tickets under her alias. You leave LAX at 8:40 a.m. tomorrow morning with a layover in Boston and should be in the Azores by tomorrow morning."

"I'll pick you up at oh-six-hundred," Markus said.

He looked unfazed by any of it. Then again, he just had to pack. Gabby had a lot of planning to do: schedules, groceries, and she had better make sure Granny and Burt had all their beta-blockers and cholesterol pills and an unexpired epi for Lucas. While she was at it, she should flush Burt's Viagra down the drain. She needed him to focus while she was gone, or at least not be a major distraction for everyone else. Burt was growing on her, but not really.

When Gabby had suggested that Granny could do better, Granny had fired back: "I'm eighty-three, sweetheart. There's not a lot to pick from. It's a pretty limited pool to begin with, and it's getting smaller by the minute. Men don't live as long as women."

Burt had some of his hair, most of his teeth, and could still drive.

"Inner-G doesn't allow phones."

This horrifying statement brought Gabby back to the present.

"You're supposed to leave yours at the front desk when you arrive." Valentina checked her reflection in the mirror and swiped on some lipstick. Casually beautiful.

Gabby gasped, not casually anything. "How will I keep in touch with my family?"

"I'll set up a dummy front desk number for them to call that can serve as an answering service while you're gone."

"Okay. Can we have that every day?" she joked. The EOD could screen tummy aches for her. That would be cool. But behind the joke, she couldn't imagine not talking to her kids. That wasn't something she wanted to outsource to a front desk.

Valentina swept her hair up into a ponytail. Clearly, the meeting was almost over because she was getting ready for the next thing. "It sounds like Inner-G assumes everyone will follow its no-phone rule and is not using jammers. We're going to take advantage of this arrogance and supply you with sat phones to keep in contact. Several key locations have already been bugged, and our liaison in the Azores will dead drop everything you need for the mission."

"Isn't it illegal to spy on American citizens? Is Genesis American?"

"Jasmine is conveniently Australian, and the resort is in Portuguese territory. We have a US citizen with potential knowledge of sensitive information who was possibly abducted and brought to a foreign nation. The jurisdiction is clear." Valentina glanced at them. "You will be doing the primary data collection and liaising with an operative from the Portuguese Intelligence Service."

Gabby normally had trouble following a television plot this complicated.

"Right now, I want you both to head down to the Disguises department." Valentina raised an eyebrow. "Gabby, I'm guessing you don't have any resort wear."

"Resort wear?"

"Exactly." Valentina turned back to her computer. "I have to get back to work. You two get your wardrobe straightened out."

Gabby hadn't been to the Disguises department since she had transformed into Darcy. Darcy hadn't been a bombshell, but she'd had better hair than Gabby and didn't wear sweatpants and Crocs every day. Her original Darcy makeover had been life-changing. Sometimes it takes the CIA to get you out of your sad clothes.

Tina welcomed her into the department. "Gabby! You're back." Before she had a chance to respond, Tina said, "So I was thinking we'd give you a little hair refresher, and obviously, you're going to need a mani/pedi."

That normally would have sent a wave of pleasure through her, but today she couldn't. "I don't know if I have time for all of that. I have a lot of errands, and I haven't even told the kids I'm leaving."

"Sit down, Gabby. You need a manicure. It's a matter of national security."

Gabby relented. Who knew the CIA had a manicure department?

After a trim, a color refresh, and a gloss, Tina said, "Seriously, did you think you could go on mission with an inch of roots? Keeping you looking good is my job."

Gabby relaxed and let Tina take control.

"You're done with bangs."

She swallowed a laugh. "Whatever you say."

"They're pretty much grown out."

After an hour of getting her hair washed, dyed, and blown out into the perfect style, Gabby was starting to feel like nothing mattered. It would all be fine. Snacks? Who cared. Pharmacy? Why did she need to go again? Fake marrying Markus? Whatever.

Dante, on wardrobe, entered the room with a flourish. "Now for resort wear."

Gabby gave Dante a wave and smiled blissfully. She couldn't care less what he packed for her.

"I'm sending you with several evening looks, about ten swimsuits, some cover-ups, and espadrilles."

"Swimsuits?" The icy hand of fear clenched her chest and constricted her breathing. She sat up in her chair. Not a swimsuit. No. There was no way. A dress with shapewear underneath was as far as she was willing to go. She would rather take on the Russian Mafia again.

Dante put a hand on his hip and looked down his nose. "Of course you need swimsuits."

"That seems really unnecessary." Yoga was bad enough.

"I'm sending you and Markus fully prepared for a beach vacation. Rich people don't show up to a resort with one swimsuit they bought fifteen years ago." He looked at Gabby skeptically. "Unless you have a nice suit?"

Gabby hadn't put on a swimsuit since Lucas's last mommy and me swimming lesson. Getting herself and a toddler in and out of swimwear in a damp YMCA locker room had been her version of hell. When he'd graduated to big boy swim lessons, she'd retired her swimsuit. It was in the bottom of a drawer somewhere.

"I don't have a beach body, Dante."

"Gabby, that's enough. There is no such thing as a beach body. If your body is on the beach, it's a beach body."

"You know what I mean. No one wants to see me in a swimsuit."

Gabby shook her head in abject terror as Dante brought out a few swimsuits. She actually shouted, "A TWO-PIECE? You've got to be kidding me."

"Tina, get the CBD oil, and maybe some restraints." With a stern look, Dante said, "I need to know if these fit. I can't have you showing up to the Azores and finding out that your suit is too small." He angled a gaze at her. "You looking good is my responsibility." He handed her a couple of suits. "I'm a stylist. I know what looks good and what doesn't."

She could do this. She'd birthed two children. She'd survived ten years of parent pickup. She could wear a swimsuit.

Calmly, her mind somewhere else, she stepped out of her clothes and put her feet in the swimsuit, one at a time.

When she stepped out of the room, Dante looked up. "See? You look great."

"Really?"

"Beautiful."

He sucked air through his teeth. "After I finish with you, I'm making one more appointment."

"For what?"

"You need to get waxed."

Gabby groaned. Markus was already done and had been for about an hour. "Does Markus have to get waxed?"

"You know the answer to that," he said. "This is the world we live in."

"Also, where am I going to hide my gun?"

"No body hair. No pockets. Them's the rules."

Gabby hung her head. To prevent international terrorism and protect the nation, she needed a wax. National security was riding on her bikini line.

At the end of the day, Gabby was a mix of relaxed, pampered, hairless, and completely freaked out. She had a suitcase professionally packed by the CIA, a huge file of backstory to memorize, and a beach bag filled with spy gadgets handed over with the comment, "Everything in there is self-explanatory."

Inside the house, it was remarkably calm. Kyle was doing her homework at the kitchen table. Lucas was doing Legos. The TV was on. There was no yelling.

When she stepped into the kitchen, Kyle looked up with surprise. "Whoa, Mom, what happened to you today?"

The day had been so chaotic that she'd almost forgotten about her makeover. She brushed her hand through her freshly styled hair. "Oh, I had a hair appointment."

Kyle narrowed her eyes with suspicion. "And a manicure. And someone did your makeup?"

"Do you like it?"

Kyle gave a single nod. "Is this a dating thing? River's mom got a makeover when she started dating."

"No! Of course not, sweetie."

Kyle released a breath.

"It's for work. My boss is sending me to a conference, and she said I needed to get it together if I was going to be representing the company."

Kyle let out a giggle. "What, she didn't like your Crocs?"

"I know, right?"

"Maybe she doesn't know about sport mode," Kyle scoffed. Whenever Lucas ran, he put his Crocs in "sport mode," which just meant putting the heel strap down so they didn't fall off. Apparently, it was a thing on TikTok.

Gabby sat down next to her girl. "My boss definitely doesn't know about sport mode. I've seen her run in four-inch heels."

"Is she Barbie or something?"

Pretty much.

When Lucas wandered in, Gabby decided to break the news to them. Gabby steeled herself for complaints and announced, "I'm going to be gone for a whole week." The way she said "week" made it sound like a year. "My boss says I have to go." Neither kid said anything. In fact, they looked completely unfazed. Phil went on work trips all the time. They were used to the concept. She was the only one who was freaked out.

"Dad will be around. And Granny and Burt. And I'll be a phone call away the whole time."

"Where are you going?" Kyle asked, seeming very reasonable about the whole thing.

"Cleveland." Cleveland was the fastest way to shut down any conversation.

"What's that?" Lucas asked. "Is it a waterpark?"

CHAPTER 6

0400 hours, pancakes in the kitchen, Greene house, Avocado Avenue

It was the morning of her departure. No one was worried, except Gabby. She woke up fifteen minutes before her alarm went off to a dark, silent house, her nerves jumping and her mind at least twenty-four hours ahead of her body. Bubbles groaned when she disturbed him on her way out of bed. By five o'clock, she was packed, showered, dressed, and flipping her second batch of pancakes.

Kyle wandered into the kitchen hours before any teen should make a voluntary appearance, looking sleepy and rumpled. Gabby barely moved a muscle. Her teenager had gotten up early to see her off.

Kyle was still blinking the sleep away when Gabby handed her a perfect stack of pancakes. The pancakes were stacked as high as her love for the kids. Butter + syrup = love. Fact.

Lucas was next. It wasn't as big a surprise to see him up early. Gabby handed him a plate and said, "I'll miss you."

"Miss you too, Mom. How many days is a week? Is that a long time?" Lucas still didn't have a great grasp of time.

"It's seven sleeps."

He proceeded to count to seven and nodded. Her heart squeezed hard. She'd never been away from the kids for a whole week, and not just in time, but in space. For one week, she was going to be a whole ocean away from her babies.

From the kitchen table, Kyle eyed her mom suspiciously. "What are you wearing?"

Gabby was dressed in her rich lady travel wear. Her loose cream-colored sweater draped expensively off one shoulder over some $500 leggings. In her hair, an Hermès scarf. Her travel bag, a Birkin. With the Gucci shades and expensive lipstick to finish the look, she was channeling Princess Grace.

"My boss told me I needed to dress up."

Kyle squinted, clearly not buying it. "What are you supposed to be?"

Gabby had spent all night studying the answer to that question—Gia Glanville, thirty-five, executive assistant, engaged to rich inventor, yoga enthusiast. Before she thought of an answer other than her cover identity, the doorbell rang.

She smoothed her cream top and collected herself. She could handle this. One week on mission, and it was probably a blessing in disguise that the "conference" was all the way in the Azores. At least it was separate from her family. There was zero chance of them mixing up with the bad guys like her last mission. Just thinking of Smirnov breaking into her house in the middle of the night and stationing men with guns out front made her blood run cold.

And for a blessed week, she'd only have to wear one hat. It might be easier being a sexy undercover spy than a spy, a mom, a daughter, a granddaughter, an ex-wife, and a neighbor.

At the front door, her Crocs were sitting on top of her travel bag. She hadn't put them there. Kyle? Gabby glanced up, and Kyle shrugged like it was no big deal, but it might be the sweetest thing that had ever happened to her.

"They're not going to go with your outfit."

Gabby picked them up and clutched them to her heart. "Thank you, sweetie."

Still clutching the Crocs, she opened the door to find Markus standing in the early morning light, looking like a Hollywood star going on vacation.

When Kyle caught sight of Markus, she narrowed her eyes, and all the walls went up. She looked between Gabby and Markus and then back again. Her voice accusatory, she said, "I thought you were going on a *work* trip?"

"I am. I work with Markus."

Markus, not fully picking up on the dynamics, waved. "Morning, Kyle! You're up and at 'em."

While he grabbed Gabby's bag and took it out to the car, Gabby tried to reason with Kyle. "It's a work trip. Markus just happens to look like that." She gestured to him like he was offending her. "He can't help it." That was true. The man couldn't be casual.

Like she was the parent, Kyle said, "Mom, don't even. You've been working out." She punctuated that with a glare. "You got a makeover." She said "makeover" like a dirty word. "You packed a bikini." She said bikini the way that Gabby felt about it. "I'm not stupid, Mom." All the softness Kyle showed a minute ago was gone.

"Kyle, I don't like your tone of voice."

"What are you going to do, send me to my room? You're going to Cleveland." With that, she walked off. "Or are you lying about that too?"

Gabby took a deep breath. She didn't have time to chase Kyle down. "Kyle, I don't like your attitude. I'm going to cut off your screen time if you keep talking to me like that." It was the only power she had.

Lucas gave her a hug, and she felt him not-very-sneakily put a Post-it note on her back. Knowing Lucas, it probably said, "Kick me," or simply "Butt." It was just the touch her outfit had been missing.

While she instructed Granny on a few last-minute things, Markus collected more items to put in the car.

Burt held up his hand. "Hold on, sport."

"Did I forget something?" Markus scanned the ground where the bags had been.

"Nope, I'm driving you two to the airport. That's a grandpa's job. And I'll pick you up when you land. No need to pay for an Uber or parking."

Markus smiled. "That's a great offer, but the car's already loaded, and I drove."

"I can drive your car. Looks like the regular kind."

Gabby shook her head vehemently over Burt's shoulder. Please, God, no. It didn't even make sense. Were they going to leave Markus's car at her house all week? Could Burt get to the airport?

Burt was having none of it, though. In saggy boxers and a T-shirt that read, "Shady Acres Cheer Squad," he settled himself into the front seat.

Granny saw the problem and shouted, "Burt, get out of the car. I need you."

After grumbling for a second, Burt swung one pasty white leg out, and then the other, showcasing his compression sock–loafer combo. He crossed his arms over his chest. "Well, you're forcing me to have an awkward conversation here in the driveway, then."

"Burt, we gotta go," Gabby said. "Whatever it is, we can talk about it later."

Looking very serious, he shook his head and took a step closer to Markus. "I need to talk to this young man, Gabby."

Gabby almost died. She loud-whispered, "Burt, this is a work trip. Markus is a co-worker. I don't think you need to say anything."

Burt held up his hand.

Markus gave her a look that said, "I can handle it."

Gabby couldn't.

"I just want to say that you need to take care of our Gabby. Watch out for her. Please help her with her bags because it looks like she overpacked."

Gabby breathed a sigh of relief. He wasn't being too weird.

"And remember to use protection. Vera and I can't be watching any babies. Our knees aren't good enough."

Gabby started choking on nothing but air. Markus smiled and said, "Yessir. Thanks for all the advice."

Burt gave him a salute and tapped the car on its ass.

A minute down the road, Gabby was still shell-shocked. "Sorry about Burt," she said. "I'm not actually related to him." Every time she started to give him a pass, he opened his big mouth and said something absolutely appalling. "At least everyone is suffering through Burt together. Maybe it'll be a bonding thing." She took another deep breath and focused on the hula girl dancing atop Markus's dashboard.

"Let's get you a Starbucks," Markus said. "I could use a coffee too."

Gabby started to chill. She might as well enjoy it. And they were on a mission. This was a serious job with high stakes. All she had to do was shove her feelings into a box. They'd probably pop out, jack-in-the-box style, when she was watching a commercial for life insurance later, but for now, she needed them out of the way.

"Gia Glanville, born in 1990, birthday of June 5, sign is Gemini, and my favorite hobbies are yoga, meditation, and healing." She shook her head. "What does that mean?"

"Just be vague and you'll stay out of trouble."

"Glanville..." Gabby said. "It sounds like a glandular problem. Or like a Midwestern casserole mom."

"Speaking of that, are you going to take my name?" He side-eyed her with a smile. "We should probably figure that out before we get there."

"I just went back to my maiden name," Gabby said. She could take another man's name, but maybe it was too soon. Even if she got married, she needed to be Gabby this time.

"What? Is Gia divorced?" Markus asked, sounding confused, which made Gabby realize they were no longer talking about the same scenario. He wasn't asking if she wanted to stay Gabby Greene.

In a soft voice, she said, "Markus, you know what a mess my life is, right?"

"Gabby—" He took a steadying breath. "Sure, you have chaos, but I don't see a mess. You're always stretched a little thin, I get that, but I see a competent, caring, beautiful woman."

Before she could haul her jaw off the floor, Markus pulled into the drive-thru. "What kind of coffee do you want?"

"The usual," she choked out.

Markus shouted their orders to the speaker: "One tall pumpkin spice latte and one grande iced oatmilk latte." He pulled forward toward the window. "I see how you are showing up for everyone else all the time. I respect that. You show up for me. I think you would be better off if you gave someone the chance to show up for you."

Gabby was legitimately tongue-tied. Sure, she liked a compliment, but once someone said something nice, could she respond like a normal person? No.

She'd promised to have his back and, minutes later, agreed to spy on him. Gabby was a dirty, dirty double agent.

"Let me get the coffee," she said. It was the least she could do given her double-crossing.

"No, I got it," he said.

"That'll be fourteen dollars," the woman at the window said.

While they were waiting for the coffees, Markus reached into his pocket and pulled out a small package. "I almost forgot the ring."

Gabby's brain screeched to a halt, and her soul was almost ejected from her body.

"You okay?"

She collected herself. "Just surprised."

"Let's see if it fits."

She held out her left hand, and he slipped a diamond ring on. It was simple, beautiful, sparkling in the bright California sun.

"This isn't your grandma's, is it?" she said. It looked like an heirloom.

With a laugh, he said, "No. I picked it out yesterday. Don't worry, on the EOD's dime."

She stared at her hand like any newly engaged woman.

"You couldn't show up without a ring," he said. "It looks nice on you."

He handed her a pumpkin spice latte, and they drove off, officially fake engaged. Why did it feel real?

She took a sip. "I'm sorry about the work-wife thing."

"I get your hesitation." He merged onto the 405, accelerating and sliding into traffic without once applying the brakes. As he moved into one of the middle lanes, he said, "I'm more than you're ready for."

At that, she laughed. "Markus, you just picked me up. Did you see all those people?" She gave him a moment to recall Burt. "I think *I'm* more than you're ready for."

"Oh, I've met your people. I get it." He accelerated and passed a semi. "I'm ready to show up for you and the people you love. You're the one looking for a work-wife-with-benefits situation."

"Markus, you make it sound like I'm just out here looking for..."

"Dick? You can say it, Gabby."

She gasped, "Markus! Don't say that." But...was that what she wanted? He wasn't wrong.

He took a sip of his coffee calmly while she clutched her pumpkin spice latte and stared straight ahead, feeling naked in her desires. Was she the frat boy? She couldn't be. "I...uh..."

"I get it if that's where you're at. I have a dick. It's available."

"Thanks." She swallowed too loudly. "I've never had a guy show up for me in the million little ways that count. When Phil left, it was almost simpler." If he was being honest, so could she. "Sure, he paid the bills, but he never helped with the kids, the cooking, the cleaning, the shopping, the chauffeuring, so I just did my regular, but without also worrying what he wanted for dinner, or his opinions on all the choices I made throughout the day." She twisted the sleeve on her coffee cup. "I don't trust that you'll be there for me.

It's not because of who you are, it's because that's how it always is with men and women. I hear about guys who went to liberal arts colleges and do equal work, but I haven't met one yet."

Markus nodded. "I guess I'll have to show you I mean business then."

They drove in silence for a few miles, while Gabby added caffeine to her conflicting emotions. It seemed like she'd found the right guy at the wrong time. Not to mention that she was spying on him.

"Let's go over our plan."

"Make contact with the liaison," Gabby said. "Pick up the dead drop. Look for Sheridan."

Markus changed lanes. "I've been doing yoga with the Big G—" He glanced at Gabby and said, "That's what the insiders call him. Anyway, I've been practicing with G for a year and getting the basics, but I haven't done the couples stuff. This will be new to both of us."

That was kind of nice.

Markus side-eyed her. "From the way I understand it, we'll be marrying each other *and* Inner-G."

"What?" She tried to wrap her mind around that. "Literally or metaphorically?"

He flashed a mischievous grin. "We'll find out, I guess."

Now, that was something Gabby never saw coming. She'd fallen asleep to several of Genesis's multi-million-dollar blockbusters. For years, she'd seen pictures of him on red carpets wearing a tux with the sleeves ripped off to show off his bulging muscles and tribal art tattoos. A recipe for baked nachos she'd ripped out of *People* had a picture of him at the Golden Globes. There was a grease stain on his face. Now she was going to be his cult bride.

"Wedding planning...that could be a lot, given that we're on a mission."

If this was anything like her last wedding, he was going to be deep sea fishing and getting buddy-buddy with Genesis while she made centerpieces with Jasmine or something.

"I don't anticipate the wedding interfering with our mission," Markus said. "The resort staff will help out. I don't think many people at this place do anything for themselves."

Maybe that's what money could do for a relationship. If you hire out all the labor and paper over all the underlying inequalities, everyone lives happily ever after, except for the hired help. She was going to be living the *Downton Abbey* life in the Azores.

Markus pulled them into LAX long-term parking. "The last thing we want is to forget where we parked after all of this."

Now, that sounded likely.

"What's this ramp called?"

Gabby was focused on collecting her things: ChapStick, phone, bag. About to embark on a mission, about to get fake married. She had the same feeling as she did before she had to give a presentation, not that she'd had to do that recently. Her mind retreated to some dark corner and left her body to go through the motions on its own. She had started to unbuckle when Markus placed his hand over hers. "Hold up, Gabs. You didn't answer my question."

"What did you ask? Oh, parking. Ramp D, fourth floor," she started to say, but when she looked up, she didn't see a man with a parking garage question in his eyes. Markus was deep into her soul, looking at her, trying to connect with her.

Gabby's mind and spirit were otherwise occupied, but she tried to focus on him as best she could in her state of excitement.

"Are you taking my name?" he asked.

"Oh, yeah, I forgot. Yes. I'll take Alexander."

"Nice," he nodded with satisfaction. "I'm really not down with a hyphen situation."

She laughed and took her last sip of coffee before TSA.

"And if we have kids, I'd rather we all have the same name."

Gabby started choking on the last sip of coffee.

CHAPTER 7

Early, day one of the mission, LAX

Gabby tightened her Hermès scarf, pushed her Gucci shades up her nose, and stepped out of Markus's car as Gia Glanville. One second in, and life as Gia was different. She could feel it, the designer leggings soft against her skin, a heavy polished jade pendant nestled between her breasts, and Louis Vuitton luggage rolling along. It wasn't just that the wheels worked better—she was starting to work better.

At the baggage check, Markus lifted her Louis onto the scale. When she started filling out a luggage tag, Markus pointed out an engraved gold tag on her bag's handle.

Markus was beaming at her like she was his entire reason for living. Like he was sharing a secret, he told the checker, "We're getting married this week."

The baggage checker reacted like it was scripted from a sitcom. He clutched his heart and sighed. "I'm upgrading you." With an over-the-shoulder glance, he said, "Don't tell my boss." Without a second thought, he tapped at the keyboard and printed them new tickets. "Enjoy."

Was this how it felt being rich and famous?

The TSA line was their first official appearance as a couple, if you didn't count the baggage counter. Even with priority, they had to weave through a curlicue line, pretending not to notice the people around them. Really, it was just a reality show with no plot—staring at the other passengers and guessing at relationships and destinations.

She could feel eyes on her and Markus. They were *that* couple, fancy luggage, dressed like A-listers, smelling of tropical vacation and designer perfume. A grandma winked at her in a way that Gabby interpreted as "Way to go!"

She snuck a glance at Markus. If she wanted, she could make this real. The ball was in her court.

The entire airport was a dreamscape of Markus holding Gabby's purse, gesturing to let her go through the body scanner first, gently guiding her through lines with his hand on the small of her back in a possessive way, and then there were the endearments. "Babe, do you want a sweater?" "Hey, Beautiful."

Half an hour later, they were boarding the plane. Was it her, or was the flight attendant nicer than usual? With a sparkling smile and a flash of white teeth, the attendant said, "Welcome. What takes you to Boston, business or pleasure?"

"Pleasure," Markus answered without a second thought. It didn't seem like a lie. He pulled her into his side like he cherished her. "We're continuing on to the Azores. To get married."

Gabby was starting to think that Gia probably didn't even know what anxiety was. Gia might not even miss Gabby's old life. Pretty soon Gabby might not miss her old life.

The flight attendant brightened. "Congratulations! That is so exciting!" She held up her hand to let them know to wait. After disappearing into the galley for a few seconds, she returned with two miniature bottles of champagne. The passengers in line behind them weren't quite as excited. "What's holding up the line?" someone griped.

"A wedding or something," someone else answered, not sounding the least bit excited.

The flight attendant shook her head and smiled. "Have fun, you two."

Once secured in seats 4a and 4b, Markus held his glass up and said, "To a successful . . . vacation."

They clinked glasses. At the moment, it felt even better than a vacation, a vacation where they wouldn't be pressured into signing up for zip line adventures, where she would end up standing in line with a woman from Chicago with the vague feeling they were all being swindled and possibly going to die. This was a vacation with purpose.

Giddy from champagne and flattery, Gabby's optimism was lifting off faster than the plane. All the concerns of the last week already felt an ocean away, which they soon would be. She had not been fair to Markus this week. Well, she hadn't been bad to him, but the work-wife thing—at the very least, she could have been clearer.

"Are you even sure it's really a cult?" Gabby leaned in close and whispered. She'd listened to a podcast about cults and was leaning toward "It's a cult" in the way Starbucks or Costco was a cult. Not every cult ended in a suicide pact. Some just left you with an overpriced latte and confusion over whether you'd just been had or you belonged to something that mattered.

"A cult?" someone repeated in an overly loud voice. "I used to be in a cult."

Gabby gasped and glanced up to see a large woman who looked

like she'd absolutely been through it. Her clothes were rumpled, her hair a mess. It looked like she'd rolled down a grassy hill fully dressed with her luggage before boarding the plane.

With a glance at her phone, the woman, who definitely projected just-out-of-a-cult said, "I think I'm in the window seat."

Gabby and Markus stepped into the aisle holding their champagne while the woman squeezed more luggage than looked legal into the overhead and under the seat in front of her. When she settled into her chair with a large Ziploc bag of homemade popcorn, she introduced herself. "Hi, I'm Susan."

"Gia," Gabby said. "And this is George."

Susan smiled. "Nice to meet you, Gia and George. Where are you two from? I live in Encino now, but I grew up in Reseda."

Gabby said, "Encino is so pretty!" She didn't add anything or answer the question, subtly hinting that this convo wasn't going anywhere.

The captain came over the speaker and announced, "Flight attendants, prepare for takeoff."

"I know you wouldn't believe it to look at me now, but I was in a yoga cult," Susan said, not taking the hint.

The flight attendant stopped at their row and said, "Ma'am, can you buckle up?"

"Damn it. I was hoping she wouldn't notice. Can you maybe scooch up on a cheek so I can get this thing buckled."

Markus flashed a conspiratorial look at Gabby.

"A yoga cult, you say?"

"I studied with Guru Jagat for a while, before she went off the deep end." Susan proceeded to shut her eyes and inhale deeply. When she exhaled, part of a piece of popcorn flew out.

"Do you still practice?" Markus asked. Nothing about Susan said yoga or centered. Gabby loved that about her.

"On this trip, I'm going to try some yoga without the crazy." Which is when she noticed that Markus had *Power Couple* pulled up on his TV. "Have you seen that?" Susan asked. "I was going to watch it on the plane."

Apparently, Susan was going to check out Inner-G too.

Gabby shook her head. It had been on her list of things to do before leaving for the trip, but she hadn't gotten around to it. She pulled out her phone to read the plot summary on IMDb.

After reaching international success with movies like *G-Force*, Genesis Love made his directorial debut with *Power Couple*, a story that he'd been working on since high school. Despite being largely snubbed by awards shows, it won the Golden Globe for Best Score and was nominated for Best Costume. Notably, Margo Martindale was nominated for Best Supporting Actress for her role as G's psychic advisor. *Power Couple* became an instant cult classic.

POWER COUPLE

G (played by Genesis Love) is a man who doesn't know that he has been a Silicon Valley office drone. He lives in a condo filled with appliances, glued to his phone, checked out of real life. He is a slave to the machines. After a poignant moment in a garden, which has died on his watch, he realizes that the tech giants haven't stolen his power; he has freely given it.

G declares war on the machines, quits his job, and moves into the woods, gathering his strength to wake up the rest of society. After trying to defeat the machines with lasers, he realizes that he can't win alone. He comes to the conclusion that he needs to join with an equally powerful woman to become a true Power Couple.

At their wedding, they ascend to the fourth dimension. He and his bride become so powerful they destroy the Facebook-esque company they used to work for and pave the way for a better world.

Gabby read it twice, and then a third time.

"What do you think?" Susan asked.

Markus said, "You know how sometimes a star gets too big, and then they make a movie and no one tells them 'no,' and it just turns into a big sprawling post-apocalyptic mess with lasers and too many monologues?"

Gabby nodded.

"That's *Power Couple.*" With a smirk, Markus said, "It's probably not true, but I heard that Kim Jong-Un is G's number one fan."

Kim Jong-Un was going to have to compete with Susan for the top fan prize.

Gabby couldn't handle any more *Power Couple,* so she calmed herself with the flight tracker. At least that made sense. While she stared at an outline of a plane slowly making its way across the United States, Markus picked up his phone and texted someone.

It pinged with a response, and Markus looked at the phone in a way that made her wish it were her. Three more back-and-forths, and Gabby asked, "Who are you texting?"

"G."

"G?" Her voice low and steeped in accusation, she pointed at Susan's screen where Genesis was meditating so hard that a beam of light was coming out of the top of his head. Susan had put on her headphones and hopefully couldn't hear. Gabby leaned in as close as possible and whispered, "You mean the same G we are investigating for abduction and running a freaky cult?"

The corner of his mouth pulled up in unrepentant amusement.

"Markus," she said sharply. She was just a regular spy on a mission with her partner, whom she trusted. She did not sign up for *Mr. and Mrs. Smith.*

"What? He's funny."

"Just don't forget who he is, okay?" she said. *Please don't let me find anything.*

"Gabby, I'm a professional. I've got this."

Was he doing a really good job with undercover work, or was he getting too cozy with a guy they would have to arrest before the weekend was out?

Two minutes later, the fasten seat belt light turned off, and Markus stood to use the bathroom. He left his phone sitting on his seat, just daring her to snoop.

Instead, Gabby stared deliberately forward at the flight tracker.

CHAPTER 8

Morning but feels like midnight, Ponta Delgada Airport, São Miguel

After an unfortunately long layover in Boston and nearly a day of travel, Gabby was both exhausted and wired all at the same time. Her ears were popping, the landing gear was down, and her nerves were set to extra. They were descending toward the Ponta Delgada Airport on the largest island in the Azores, São Miguel. Like Hawaii, it was a volcanic island. Tropical plants, warm weather, beaches—paradise may have been forged in hell, but that was a long time ago. No lava to be seen these days. From the looks of it, it was all waterfalls and flowers.

"We're here!" she said, an explosion of butterflies in her stomach. It was almost go time.

When she turned off airplane mode on her phone, it blew up with a whole day's worth of notifications: The kids had been tardy, the plumber she'd called couldn't get into the house, Granny wanted to know where the plumber was, weather alerts, and the regular news. It was Scorpio season, and things were getting spicy. There were no suspects in the Amanda Duvall murder. Sheridan's disappearance still hadn't made the news.

The plane pulled to a stop on the tarmac, and some people in high-visibility vests wheeled a staircase to the exit. Gabby's first feel of the Azores was a perfect seventy degrees. At the top of the staircase, she took in the tropical island and ocean. Her spirit soared. She was an EOD field operative, landing in paradise to protect the president. Her kids were safe at home, and she was about to save the world, or something like that. Maybe she did have it all. Sometimes. Not last week for sure, but now that she was being paid to go on vacation—maybe.

"Bem-vindo aos Açores!" A flight attendant spoke to them in Portuguese, and Gabby smiled pleasantly like she knew what was going on.

After collecting their luggage, Markus glanced at his phone and reported, "We're supposed to meet a G-Wagon in front of the airport."

Twenty minutes later, a young blonde with yoga vibes and a face that didn't need makeup hung her head out the window of a sporty-looking SUV with surfboards on the roof and honked. "Gia and George?" she called. When they nodded, she said, "My name's Aspen, and I'm your ticket to paradise. Get in."

As Aspen tossed Louis V into the back of the SUV, Gabby said, "Sorry. We probably missed you. We were looking for a G-Wagon."

"Oh, this is the G-Wagon."

Gabby laughed at herself. "I'm always getting stuff like that mixed up." This did not look like the G-Wagon all the LA celebrities and Bentley's mom drove.

"This is the Inner-G wagon," Aspen answered in a profound voice.

Markus whispered in Gabby's ear. "I don't know if Genesis realizes that anyone else uses the letter G."

"Help yourself to refreshments," Aspen said. "There's a mini fridge in the back."

Gabby opened the door to find it stocked with brightly colored juice shots and healthy snacks. "This isn't alcoholic, is it?" If she started drinking, she'd probably forget who she was supposed to be.

"It's kombucha, so not really." As Aspen pulled out of the airport pickup lane onto the highway and accelerated, she explained, "The retreat is on the north side of the island. As you can see, the landscape is mountainous. There are some really amazing hikes if you're into that sort of thing."

That would be a *no*.

After almost an hour in the car, they turned down a long, winding driveway. There was a golf course dotted with palm trees and tropical flowers. Everyone looked rich.

"Big G owns this whole resort." Aspen pulled up to a large structure. "You'll see some of these people in your yoga classes and whatnot, but you are part of the Power Couples Retreat, which is more exclusive and—believe it or not—fancier."

Aspen led them into a luxurious open-air lobby. "Feel free to enjoy any of the resort's features like the tennis or the juice bars, but you two are the real Gs."

Was it just Gabby, or was there some appropriation happening here? Genesis went through culture like a marauding army, taking whatever he wanted. Well, anything that started with the letter G. It was a G-heist.

"You'll have to tell me what the Power Couple life is like because I don't know." Aspen shook her head. "Dating—it's rough out here, people!"

The first view of Inner-G Resort and Spa was impressive—fountains, flowers, stonework. The centerpiece of the lobby was a life-size portrait of Jasmine and the Big G. Or maybe it was bigger than life-size because they looked larger than life.

Aspen noticed Gabby staring and said, "That's their wedding portrait."

"It's, uh, nice," Gabby said. In the portrait, they were standing on a rocky outcropping with the waves crashing at their feet, looking unbothered by anything. They were the model union, the model marriage, not to mention actual models.

"How are we going to find the Power Couples Retreat?" Gabby asked.

If this were a retreat at a Marriott in Cleveland, there would be a banner that read POWER COUPLES with lanyards and agendas printed on colorful paper with stock photos of smiling couples in pant suits.

Aspen just laughed. "You'll figure it out."

Gabby glanced over her shoulder as she walked across the open-air lobby to check if Genesis's eyes were following her.

"I heard that they used vials of their blood to tint the paint red." Aspen smiled and, without missing a beat, went on, "We grow and dry our own sage for burning. It has extra cleansing properties."

A guy in an old T-shirt, shorts, and a dazed look, like he had just emerged from a spiritual journey in a tent, held out a tray of bright green shots of liquid. "Would you like a G-shot?"

"This is Dave." Aspen introduced the guy offering the green juice. "He owns an airplane company, but he's doing his service to G this week."

"Nice to meet you, but no thanks," Gabby said, being of the firm opinion that green was for salads.

Markus flashed a look, reminding her that she wasn't Gabby. She was Gia.

"On second thought," she said, "thank you." As she held it up to her lips, a pungent odor hit her nose. "What did you say this was?"

"I'm going to check in, babe," Markus said, downing his G-shot in one gulp.

"It's a juice shot packed with radical molecules."

Gabby blinked back. She touched her tongue to the liquid. She would describe it as crude oil in texture and taste. "What's it for?"

"It helps you tap into your Inner-G." The man said it like he was speaking the truth.

"Does it boost metabolism?" Because that's the only way she was interested.

"And don't forget to check in your phone," Dave reminded them. "Leave it at the front desk, and it'll be here for you when you leave."

"Of course. I can't wait to get rid of that thing," Gabby said, her phone tucked safely in her purse with the ringer off.

"You'll be a new person without that thing sucking the lifeforce out of you. Clear thoughts, less anxiety, fewer insecurities."

Gabby laughed like she agreed. There was no way she was letting go of her phone. It was bad enough that she had left the kids for a week, but to be out of contact—not acceptable.

Aspen said, "I hope you'll enjoy the honeymoon cottage."

Gabby choked on the last sip of radical molecules. The honeymoon cottage? There was no way she was going to swallow. Instead of coughing/vomiting the juice out, she spit it into a potted bamboo right in front of Markus and the front desk attendant.

Markus rubbed her back. "You okay?"

"I'm sorry. I couldn't swallow, so I decided to just spit it out."

Aspen smiled in amusement. "That's a choice we all have to make."

Jesus, Aspen. Gabby started choking again.

Markus squeezed her hand. "It's okay. Why don't you just catch your breath?"

As Gabby agreed, Aspen handed the key to their door to Markus and an egg-shaped crystal to Gabby.

"Umm..." Gabby turned it over in her hand. All she could think of was Gwyneth putting a crystal in her vajayjay. Sincerely confused, she leaned across the desk and loud-whispered, "Am I supposed to insert this?"

Aspen leaned across the desk conspiratorially. In a hushed tone, she said, "Feel free to do whatever you want in the honeymoon cottage. Spit, swallow, and put anything up there you want."

Gabby blinked back.

"Let us know if you need any assistance. The Loves have left instructions to take particularly good care of you."

Gabby glanced over at their imposing portrait and smiled back numbly. Assistance with what?

Markus placed his hand on the small of her back and steered her toward the room. "Let's get you to the cottage, shall we?"

Gabby nodded. It was time to collect herself before she said something stupid.

The honeymoon cottage wasn't a cottage but a beachfront luxury retreat. Small enough to create a sense of intimacy, but large enough to provide everything a person could want. A bottle of Dom Pérignon sat in an ice bucket on the counter alongside two crystal flutes.

Finally alone, they stupidly stared at each other. Tired from traveling, wired about the mission, and in the midst of a honeymoon fantasy. The silence left space for the awkwardness to bloom.

"Want some champagne?" Gabby asked, shifting the bottle in its bed of ice.

"Not yet, baby," he said. "Let's go for a walk."

What he really meant was "Let's go pick up the spy stuff at the designated location at the designated time." They wouldn't be able to speak freely in the cottage until they swept for listening devices. Markus had arranged a dead drop with their Portuguese liaison at a secluded spot on the beach. All they had to do was casually stroll down the sand until they found a large rattan beach bag filled with countersurveillance equipment, comms, phones, defensive measures, and who knows what else.

"Absolutely. I want to feel the sand in my toes." She didn't, but in case anyone was listening, she wanted to make it sound natural. On her last mission, she'd been pinch-hitting. This was her first mission as a proper field agent who threw around phrases like "dead drop" and "countersurveillance" as casually as "laundry" or "damn it, my kids have a science fair tomorrow."

Gabby wasn't just playing at this anymore. She was a spy.

Besides the dead drop, which she was trying to be very casual about, they had to familiarize themselves with the layout of the resort. They'd studied aerial photos, but things looked different on the ground. They needed to figure out where all the key players were staying, as well as ingress and egress from all important buildings. Not to mention a PACE plan, which was the stop, drop, and roll of communication. Apparently, they required a primary, alternate, contingent, and emergency communication strategy.

Markus slipped on something that she would describe as "James Bond at the beach," black shorts and a casual button-down shirt.

"Are you going to button your shirt?"

He looked down at his chiseled core like it was a roast beef sandwich. No, that's how she was looking at it. "What? This is how you're supposed to dress on vacation."

"Is it?" Maybe it was, but he wasn't supposed to look so good doing it. "It's like I'm about to go on a walk with you and your abs." She pantomimed meeting someone. "Hi, this is my fiancé, George, and these"—she gestured like Vanna White showing off a *Wheel of Fortune* prize package—"are his abs."

He slipped on a smile to go with his bare chest. "Says the woman dressed like Catwoman."

"Stop it. You like this outfit?" She was wearing the black exercise onesie that the Disguises department had packed for her. "I thought it highlighted some of my problem areas."

"Oh, they're problem areas all right," he said, blowing out a breath.

"Really?" She looked down at everything below her bust line.

Markus glanced at the clock. "We'd better get going."

CHAPTER 9

2100 hours, sunset, the beach

The dead drop was a leisurely stroll through paradise. In the Azores, it was the afternoon, and Gabby was on a romantic vacation, but mentally Gabby was in LA, battling to-do lists and traffic. She blinked into the perfect afternoon sun, trying to orient herself.

Markus's shirt billowed like he was on a photo shoot. He had the audacity to take her hand.

"We have to sell the romance," he said, "for our cover."

It was basic spy stuff—a couple draws less attention than a single man, or even a single woman. Especially at a couple's retreat.

"There it is." Markus pointed to a boho beach bag under a designated chair. It looked like someone had forgotten it after sunbathing. Per the plan, the liaison had left it there not ten minutes earlier.

Markus handed it to Gabby. "Look like ours?"

Gabby peeked inside to make sure it wasn't someone's actual beach bag. It wasn't. Underneath a visor and a blanket, she found everything they might need. It looked like the inside of a Verizon store.

"Our cottage should be within range of the listening devices,"

Markus said. "At least, if the liaison was right about room assignments."

Markus slung the bag over his shoulder. "Recon time." Together, they surveyed the length of the beach. At the farthest end, a modern structure hung over the water. The setting sun glinted off its floor-to-ceiling windows, and a waterfall spilled over the cliff, seemingly from underneath the house. "That's the Big G's private residence," Markus said.

"They must be selling some juicy secrets to pay for that," Gabby said.

Markus pointed at one of the luxury "cottages" between their location and the Big G's residence. "According to the liaison, a single woman who meets Sheridan's description has been on the patio every day." Their plan: knock on the door, introduce themselves, and ask if Sheridan needed a ride back to Wyoming.

Gabby took a few strides toward Sheridan's cottage while Markus scanned the area. "Careful."

They could be walking into anything. If Sheridan had been kidnapped, there could be an armed guard. If she hadn't been abducted, she might be colluding with Inner-G.

"Stay alert," Markus advised.

They walked carefully up a sweet, hydrangea-lined path toward the cottage. There was no sign of any security measures. Nothing but tropical paradise, lapping waves, and sand. Just as the liaison had described, a woman who definitely looked like Sheridan was relaxing on the back patio. Seemingly unalarmed, she put her book down and waved at the sight of Gabby and Markus.

"If she's been kidnapped, sign me up," Gabby whispered. The woman had a plate of snacks and an umbrella drink.

When Gabby and Markus made it to the edge of the patio, the woman gave them one look and said, "You're not here for the Power Couples Retreat, are you?"

Was it that obvious? Sheridan might be the real deal.

"Of course we are." Markus forced a laugh. "I'm George, and this is Gia."

"Sheridan." The psychic smiled and held out one perfectly manicured hand. She and Gabby shook hands like they were at a meet and greet at the Cleveland Marriott, not that Gabby had ever been to Cleveland.

Gabby fought to stay present in a reality that didn't quite make sense. She was not the kind of person who functioned off three hours of sleep on an airplane and hit the ground running.

Because they needed to move their conversation out of range of listening devices, Gabby said, "We're so turned around. Would you please show us to the main resort?"

Sheridan glanced at the comfort of her patio but grabbed her flip-flops and led the way.

Anyone else would have said, "Hell no," but Sheridan seemed to know who they were. She was steady and decisive, no indication of any fear.

A safe distance from her patio, Sheridan stopped walking and faced them. "I assume you know who I am."

"Sheridan Lane?" Gabby said.

"And you are?" Sheridan asked.

"I'm Agent Parks, and this is Agent Greene," said Markus. "We're with the CIA. As you can no doubt imagine, there has been a lot of concern over your disappearance."

"I told President Simon I was fine," she said.

"You did?" That's not what they had heard. According to the president, he'd heard nothing from Sheridan.

"Yes."

"You spoke to him yourself?" Markus asked, and Sheridan nodded yes.

They'd given up the subterfuge of needing directions to the main resort and were standing on the beach close to Sheridan's. A couple strolled by with yoga mats under their arms. The man said, "Namaste."

Sheridan returned the "namaste" with a serene smile.

"So you're not being held against your will?" Markus asked. Something smelled fishy about this situation.

"No." Sheridan laughed, as if the suggestion was absurd. "I'm just fine. No one is bothering me. Well, until now." She looked at them pointedly.

"You planned to come down here?" Gabby asked, "Because everyone is pretty worried."

"Hell no, I didn't plan this. I was on my way to Washington to do an aura reading for the president, not of the president but of the Speaker of the House. It was not my idea, nor is it a service I advertise, but he's the president. I was just going to end up telling him to calm down and do his job like a big boy."

Markus's jaw dropped. "What?"

"You heard me. That's the relationship we have. He needs some encouragement. I need a job. That's the way the world works."

Gabby's jaw was on the floor. People always seemed so normal until they opened their mouths.

The couple set up their mats and sat down in lotus pose facing the ocean like they were posing for a brochure about a yoga retreat.

"So how'd you get here?" Markus asked.

"I thought the private jet was an upgrade. When I realized what had happened, I asked them to turn the plane around, and G said no. I was upset for a minute, but then I took a nap. Now here I am in paradise with an umbrella drink."

Markus said, "That's an abduction. He took you somewhere without your consent."

"I don't think consent is a thing G's thought a lot about. No one's probably ever said no to him."

"So he just thought he was going to pick you up and make your day?" Gabby asked.

"Pretty much. And I can't say he was wrong." Sheridan gestured to the surroundings. "I needed a break. He's harmless, so I called and told everyone I was outtie for a week."

Markus gazed into the mid-distance thoughtfully before saying, "What does Genesis want from you? I guarantee it wasn't altruistic."

"I'm a present for Jasmine, his wife. He's under the impression that Jasmine's a huge fan."

Gabby and Markus stared back dumbly for a fraction of a second.

"They've been arguing, and he's trying anything to save his marriage, including kidnapping me from the president, which probably wasn't that smart."

Gabby had no words.

"The funny thing is," Sheridan said, "I don't even think she's a fan. She's aware of me, to be sure, but a fan, I don't think so."

Bringing Sheridan to the resort was Genesis's version of gas station carnations and waxy chocolates. He was Phil as a movie star billionaire.

"Anyway, I need a vacation, and that man needs some advice. It's a mutually beneficial situation."

"Are you sure?" Markus asked, "Because we arrived with the intention of evacuating you to safety."

Gabby looked at the pink sky and the frothy waves crashing onto the shore.

Talk about a bad gift. Genesis had activated national security with his recklessness. On the upside, this mission was going to be short and sweet. All they had to do was clarify the misunderstanding and spend the next couple of days sipping umbrella drinks and writing a glorified Yelp review of Inner-G.

But even if there hadn't been a kidnapping, it wasn't all cool. Markus explained, "Ms. Lane, in your capacity as the president's psychic, you have been read in on a variety of sensitive information. Inner-G is not the kind of place where you or that information is necessarily safe."

Sheridan smiled. "You act like I know something."

"The president thinks you know something."

She arched a brow. "The president is attributing more power to me than I have. I am not a mind reader. I'm a good listener with powerful intuition. There's a difference."

Markus leaned forward. "The point is, if everyone thinks you know something, you aren't safe."

Sheridan stood and pressed the wrinkles out of her caftan. "If we're done here, I'd like to get back to the cottage. I'm binging that new Keira Knightley thriller. Spoiler alert: The prime minister is rotten. You don't need to be psychic to know that, though."

The prime minister is rotten. Was she speaking in code?

"I only have time for TikTok lately," Gabby said. This morning, she'd seen one where a woman had proclaimed that childless, unmarried women live longer and more happily, are less likely to die from suicide or homicide or car accidents, and have better sex.

Looking at Sheridan, Gabby believed it.

Markus said, "Well, consider us your babysitters. We can't leave you down here alone and will be checking in periodically." He handed her a necklace.

Sheridan stopped and gave them a look so pointed that Gabby couldn't help but think she was having a vision. "I can't stop you from being here, but I don't want to go, and I don't want to see you, talk to you, or know you're here."

What? Gabby was surprised. "Don't you want protection?"

"I'm safer without you."

Markus drew his brows together in consternation. "I don't think that's true."

But the thing about a psychic is that you can't argue with their logic because there is none.

At the edge of her patio where they were to part ways, Sheridan stopped and looked back at Gabby and Markus. "You two need a vacation too. Babysit me all you want, but go enjoy a couple's massage and your plunge pool—"

"Oh, we're not a couple," Gabby said.

Sheridan looked between them and smiled like she knew better.

One more question. Gabby asked, "Why do you need a vacation so badly?"

"I'll answer this, and then I'm done," Sheridan said.

Gabby nodded her assent.

"I lost a client recently. It was hard on me."

"I'm so sorry. Who was it?" Gabby asked.

"I said no more questions." She turned and went back into her cottage, done with Gabby and Markus forever.

Back at the honeymoon cottage, they opened the dead drop bag. It was filled with countersurveillance measures, communication devices, cell phones for them to use only for official purposes, and a couple of sidearms. Inner-G looked like the last place you'd need a gun, especially now that she knew the mission was about a grand gesture gone wrong. When you are so bad at gift giving, the EOD gets involved—that was epic.

"That didn't go to plan, did it?" Gabby said, setting her gun back in the bag.

"That was not what I expected," he said. "We can talk it over once I clean up." Clean up: aka sweep for bugs.

"I'll clean up too," she said. Gabby meant a shower.

Washing away travel grime was always refreshing, but Inner-G made it luxurious. The bathroom was filled with products from Jasmine's ironically named brand, Inner Beauty. The shampoo, and conditioner, and body wash, and lotion—everything smelled expensive.

In a robe that felt like a wearable cloud, her hair wrapped in some kind of fancy hair towel, and wearing personalized fuzzy slippers, Gabby lay down on the bed in a state that wasn't quite sleeping but wasn't quite awake. Maybe Sheridan was right. A few days of this might be just what she needed. In her blissed-out haze, she let herself drift off to sleep until she awoke with a start at the feel of the weight of a body on the bed next to her.

"I cleared the room," he said. "We're good."

"Did you find anything?"

He shook his head. "Nada."

"I must have fallen asleep." She propped herself up against some pillows.

With a laugh, he said, "Oh, you did."

"Was I snoring?" She covered her mouth. "Damn it."

"It was cute."

"Really?"

A charged silence filled the air between them. They were sitting on the most romantic bed she'd ever seen in real life. Fluffy, scattered with rose petals, spritzed with perfume, and surrounded by gauzy curtains. It was their own little world. She was naked under her robe. One loose knot from nudity. They were on vacation in the Azores. "So..." she said in a voice that didn't even sound like her own, "we're in the honeymoon suite."

Markus's professional façade cracked and he broke into a big, dopey, lopsided smile.

The nightstand had several bottles of lotions and oils, and something that she was pretty sure was artisanal lube. If she opened a drawer, there was probably more. The honeymoon suite was even sexier than the room Justin had designed, which was saying something.

With Markus this close, she wasn't sure where to look. All her thoughts were turning dirty, and her heartbeat was beginning to tick up. She tried to blink away every nasty thought that was crossing her mind, but it must have been written on her face.

Following her thoughts, Markus's gaze drifted to the nightstand. "They thought of everything, didn't they?"

There was no way to get through this professionally. Work wives was no boundary at all if this was their office. The EOD was pushing them off the cliff into romance.

He slid a little closer and rested his hand on her thigh, just below the hem of the robe. Her whole being focused on the warm press of his hand. She desperately wanted to lean in, to encourage him to hike that robe up. It would be a shame if someone didn't appreciate all that waxing.

Her focus blurred, and she let her head fall back. She was

thirty-eight years old, a grown woman. Screw all her reasons for not wanting to jump into a relationship. What were they even? Her kids? They weren't here. It was time for Gabby to have some fun. It was her turn, damn it.

She inched closer. As she did, the robe hiked up higher, dangerously high.

His voice lower than normal, Markus rasped, "Don't tease me, Gabs." He lifted his hand from her thigh.

Before she had a chance to say anything, he took a deep breath and collected himself. "My bad. I'm respecting the boundaries you set. You were right."

Why in the hell had she set a boundary, again?

When he got up and walked away, she practically groaned in frustration. "Please, come back."

The look Markus gave her was pure inner turmoil.

"Markus," Gabby pointed out logically, "there's only one bed." She said it with conviction, like it was a prophecy. The universe had spoken.

With a chuckle, he said, "Um, yeah. But you were right. I can take the couch."

"That's thoughtful," she said, "But Markus—" Gabby looked up, desperate for another touch. "There's only one bed, and the psychic said—"

"Gabby, did it occur to you that Sheridan might be in on it?"

Gabby didn't think so. If she didn't believe in psychic powers before, she did now.

CHAPTER 10

The ass crack of dawn, the honeymoon cottage

G abby awoke in paradise after almost no sleep. How early did the sun come up in the Azores? Whatever time it was, it was too early. And too bright. She groaned and slipped deeper into the luxury bedding. A lot of relationship confusion and a late night— it was like college all over again, but with a higher thread count and more to lose.

After ten minutes of applying Inner Beauty products with no noticeable effect, Gabby joined Markus on their private patio with a view of the beach. Before she'd met Phil, she'd sold vacations like this but had never taken a trip herself. Here she was, smack-dab in the middle of one of the fantasies she'd marketed: palm trees, turquoise waters, umbrella drinks, and some snorkeling just to say you did it. A couple of people were doing sun salutations on the sand, but far enough away that they weren't a bother. Sort of like if you lived somewhere other than LA and had deer in your yard.

"I think this is too nice to be a cult," she said. Sure, there were weird things: all the nasty green juice and undue amounts of yoga, but so far, the vibes weren't that much different than Whole Foods, which, granted, was a low-key cult.

"We'll have an informed opinion soon, and we have plenty to do. Keep Sheridan safe, even if she doesn't want us to, map out Inner-G's organizational structure, and assess the potential for sensitive information leaks." Markus passed her an itinerary. "Did you see our schedules?"

Her first impression: too much yoga.

Gabby glanced at Markus's. "Why aren't they the same?"

"Something about men going one direction and women another." Markus shrugged.

She frowned at the schedule. "Are the men going to offend our delicate sensibilities by talking about sex and farting too loud?"

"I hope so," said Markus with a grin.

If Gabby could send men to a cult, it would involve patriarchy deprogramming, followed by instruction on how to wash dishes and find things for themselves. *When you walk into a room, look behind and under things. You are more likely to be able to find your things if you put them away. If you see a mess, do you 1) tell your wife, or 2) clean it up yourself?*

That might be the final test. That and refilling the ice cube tray.

On the upside, at least she wouldn't be lounging around with Markus all day, stewing in their mutual sexual frustration. Not to mention, they would cover more ground if they split up.

"We have wedding planning together, at least." Her schedule listed a meeting with Naomi, the wedding planner, at 2:00 p.m.

With a smug grin, he said, "Nope, I'll be fishing."

"For real?" This cult wasn't the least bit revolutionary.

For a second, her ire rose because there was no way she was planning this wedding on her own, but she stopped short. There was no point going bridezilla when the wedding was fake.

"Do your best to keep your emotions out of it," Markus said, "Pick a dress and a cake, stay focused on the primary objectives."

The primary objective was going in and out of focus.

With a sigh that might or might not have indicated understanding, Markus locked eyes with her. For a second, it seemed like he was going to say something, to acknowledge the discomfort of pretending to get married when they were struggling with their own issues. Just as he was about to say something, a device dinged.

"What's that?" Gabby glared at the offending alarm. If only they could be as device-free as the rest of the guests. To spend a day without a phone constantly begging for attention would be bliss.

"I planted a listening device on Sheridan's patio."

"Is that legal?" They weren't supposed to be listening to American citizens.

"It's a FISA order, on the authority of the White House."

Of course it was. It was about the president, technically, but even to Gabby, it seemed like a reach.

Markus set the phone on the table between them and cranked up the volume. The sound quality was good. The unmistakable whoosh-whoosh-whoosh of a ceiling fan on Sheridan's lanai provided the background.

"Do you want some tea?" a female voice asked. That was Sheridan.

"I need something stronger than that," a woman with an Australian accent responded.

"That's gotta be Jasmine," Markus said.

Why did an Australian accent always make a person sound fun?

Well, the accent and the gajillion photos of Jasmine frolicking on the beach. It was so ironic that one of the most famously beautiful women in the world was selling a product line called Inner Beauty.

"Do you want a reading?" Sheridan asked, her rural accent contrasting with Jasmine's down under. "I mean, I came all the way here."

"I'd prefer a divorce lawyer," Jasmine said, "but why not?"

"Well, in that case, I predict a divorce." It was nice the way Sheridan just let things be what they were—sad, happy, tragic—no judgment or attempted fixes or coddling. She was a "just the facts, ma'am" psychic.

Markus guffawed, and Gabby took a sip of coffee and leaned back. This was better than TV.

"Well, I'm going to shut my eyes and tell you if I see anything else." There was a moment of silence, probably while Sheridan shut her eyes and invited a vision. "Well," Sheridan said, "I have a very clear vision of your future with Genesis. I'm not sure what it means."

"What's that?" Jasmine asked, her voice edged with curiosity.

"I feel hot, and I see flames."

"Well, they're not flames of passion," Jasmine said, her voice 100-proof sarcasm. "You sure you're not having a hot flash?"

"Maybe you're not feeling passion, but he did just fly me halfway across the world to impress you." There she was with those facts again. If she quit being a psychic, she could be a lawyer.

"Well, I'll watch out for flames."

"You better," Sheridan said. "You've been warned."

"All joking aside, I know you're the real deal, Sheridan. We had a mutual friend who convinced me."

"Had?" Sheridan asked, sounding less sure of herself.

Before the conversation could go any further, the sliding door opened, and a male voice boomed, "Jasmine! I was looking for you." It was the voice of a confident man, the kind of voice you'd pick to narrate a documentary about the disappearance of the glaciers.

"Genesis," Markus said, but Gabby already knew. He delivered all his dialogue in the same authoritative tone. Half of his lines, even the boring ones, had been memed. "If you can't handle the G's, get out of the kitchen." "Is that karate, or are you swatting flies?" His voice was all over TikTok.

"Sheridan, dearest Sheridan," Genesis said, "you look vital and vibrant."

"Would you like some tea?" Sheridan asked, ignoring the comment. He sounded more like the psychic than her.

"What are you two ladies talking about?" Genesis asked.

"Oh, nothing," Jasmine answered.

"We brought you here for a reason, Sheridan," Genesis said. "Our energy needs your energy."

"No offense," Jasmine's impatient voice cut into the conversation, "but she can't fix us, G."

"This woman," Genesis paused dramatically, "has elevated men to greatness over and over. She might not know it, but she is a synergizer."

"Synergizer?" Gabby mouthed the word to Markus, who shrugged in response.

"I'm not even sure what a synergizer is, G," Sheridan said. In a softer voice, she said, "Are you okay, Jasmine?"

There was a heavy breath. "I'm . . . okay."

Okay physically, but clearly not okay emotionally. Gabby hadn't even met Jasmine yet, but she felt that answer down deep.

"Can you help us, Sheridan?" G's voice was earnest.

"She can't, G. You can't just kidnap a celebrity and hope that fixes our marriage."

Sheridan said, "No worries, though. I'm enjoying the vacation."

Ignoring Sheridan, Jasmine said, "This man"—her voice was filled with pent-up emotion, and Gabby could imagine Jasmine pointing at her husband with accusation—"is cheating on me."

"Oh." Sheridan sounded like this was a surprise to her.

"Jasmine, no," Genesis implored. "Don't say that out loud."

"If she's a psychic, she already knows."

Genesis must have bought that because, in a gentler voice, he said, "Only with my body, not with my spirit."

Gabby choked on her coffee.

Then came the sound of hard shoes on the patio, followed by a sliding door and a "Jasmine, wait."

Gabby and Markus listened for a moment longer, but the conversation seemed to be over for now.

"Well, that was—" Gabby didn't even know what to say. It was tawdry. And confusing.

The Power Couple rhetoric was nothing but a lie. Genesis was cheating on Jasmine, and he'd brought in a psychic to put the marriage back together. No wonder Jasmine was unhappy.

"Good morning," a man's voice called, making Gabby practically jump out of her chair.

She spun around to see a man in a tuxedo shirt with the sleeves ripped off like he was halfway through a striptease.

"Did you ring?" the man asked.

"Ring?" Gabby asked.

"I'm your butler, Geeves. You must have pressed the call button by accident."

"Oh, yeah, I was looking for the light switch. Oops." At home, she'd turned on the garbage disposal when she hit the wrong switch. Here she called the help. Inner-G was weird in ways she just hadn't expected.

"Are you ready for breakfast?" he asked. "I assumed that's what you were calling about."

"Of course, thank you," Gabby said.

After setting the table with cut fruit, G-shots, and some fresh coffee, Geeves presented them each with a conch shell.

Gabby turned it over in her hands. "This is . . . pretty."

"Yes, but at Inner-G, we start each morning with a purge of secrets. I'll walk you through it the first time."

Gabby's ears pricked at the words "purge" and "secrets."

"First of all, hold the conch to your ear," Geeves said.

Gabby did as instructed and listened to the rushing noise of the sea.

Markus was playing along next to her.

"Close your eyes, let the sea whisper its secrets to you. When you have heard your fill, return the favor. Tell the shell your deepest thoughts, fears, and, most of all, the things you can't tell anyone else."

"It's kind of like journaling, huh?" Gabby said, as if talking to a seashell was normal.

"Yes. Start each morning with meditation and a purge. If you want to grow as an individual and a couple, you must do this."

After purging a few innocuous "secrets," Markus scanned the conch with a countersurveillance wand, and it lit up like the Fourth of July. He disappeared into the cottage to secure the conches somewhere where they wouldn't pick up voices. When he returned, he said, "Does anyone fall for that?"

"Hopefully, Sheridan hasn't," Gabby said.

"Well, we have a gold mine for our report already, and we haven't even finished our coffee," Markus said.

"They can just bring all their tricks right to us," Gabby said. She glanced at the itinerary again. "We have a busy day ahead, Markus. I'm going to get ready."

Gabby flipped through the outfits the EOD beauty brigade had packed for her. The attire was a mix of athleisure and cottage-core dresses made from natural fibers and dyes that wouldn't hurt the bees, just her bank balance.

Because of the yoga, she went with athleisure. The EOD agreed with influencers. This week, a bra was a shirt.

When she emerged, she wore her sports bra that had her girls spilling over the top and a pair of yoga pants that outlined her ass with an intentional wedgie and ruching over each butt cheek. These were her "v is for vagina" pants that were all over Instagram, pants she would never be caught dead in normally.

For God and country, she could do it, but she didn't look like a mom.

When she stepped out of the bedroom, Markus's eyes focused on her even as he continued walking across the open-plan living room. The man tripped over a chair.

"I know." She shook her head. "I feel naked and..."

Markus took in her appearance and drew in a breath. "You're not going out in those pants, are you?"

She stared back. Was he into them? It looked like he was into them.

"You heard me."

"You don't want me to wear these pants?" She laughed.

He made some sort of grumbling noise. "Just remind everyone that you're pretending to marry me." He pointed to his chest, and Gabby laughed.

"I'll make sure to let them know."

CHAPTER 11

A little late to Ladies-Only Power Couple Orientation, the wave pool

While Geeves cleared their breakfast dishes, Gabby walked down a rock-lined path that she wasn't entirely familiar with and dialed Granny. No one had noticed that she hadn't turned over her cell phone, and she intended to keep it that way. A week of no communication with her family was a non-starter.

"Hey, Granny, how is everything?"

"It's—" The line fuzzed out.

"What was that?"

"It's…uh…card…Kyle."

Damn it. The signal was almost nonexistent.

"Let me call you back in a second." Gabby faced a crossroads in the path. One direction went up. Maybe if she climbed higher, she'd get a signal, like in one of those lost-in-the-wilderness shows.

She climbed higher and higher, keeping half an eye on the time. All she had to do was check in with Granny, and then she'd run the phone back to their cottage for safe keeping. After reaching the top of a rise, she emerged at a scenic overlook where the view of the beach, the cottages, and the ocean spread below her like a postcard. If she wasn't undercover using a false name, she'd take a selfie.

This was a fantasy that she could not bring home. Not the marriage, the man, or even a selfie. It's not like she could wear a São Miguel T-shirt home from "Cleveland." What happened in the Azores truly had to stay in the Azores. But that begged the question: If she couldn't tell Justin everything in excruciating detail, did it even happen? Or maybe it would be a special secret for Markus and her to share.

Staring at the Atlantic, she hit "Granny" in her recent calls list.

"Gab—" Granny's voice turned to fuzz after one syllable. The signal was still shit. She tried again. Still nothing. She sent a text:

Is everything OK?

The message couldn't be delivered. Damn it.

She shoved the phone in the pocket of her leggings and let her mind wander to its favorite topic: Markus. Her skin flushed as she recalled the way he'd undressed her with his eyes, not that he'd had to do much work in these pants.

"Hello?" A voice called around the bend.

"Um...hello." Gabby took a few steps and peered around a bend in the path.

There he was. Genesis, because the man needed no introduction, reclined in a moderately-sized wave pool overlooking the ocean. His legs were kicked out, and his arms spread wide over the rocky ledge into which the pool had been carved. Or maybe it was just good concrete work. Either way, *Architectural Digest* should do a thing.

Men's Health should probably do a thing too. Big G's muscles were a sight to behold. Gabby couldn't remember all the names—traps, lats, biceps, deltoids—but he had all of them, plus some to spare. His hair was piled on top of his head in a messy man bun. The braided beard gave her pause, but if anyone could pull it off, it was this guy. The Big G was primal sex appeal written in easy-to-understand caveman scrawl.

"I like your pool," Gabby said. She said it in the same voice she would use to compliment Janice at parent pickup about her new Kia Sportswagon.

"The waves are attuned to my natural energy. My heartbeat powers the water."

Well, that sounded like some cult leader BS.

"Would you like to get in?" he asked.

"Umm…" Was this a come-on? He had admitted to cheating on Jasmine, but "only with his body."

Unsure of herself, Gabby shifted her weight from one foot to the other. A second ago, she had felt like a goddess. Now she was out of her element, a mere mortal in the presence of a Greek God. No wonder the Big G ran a cult. What else could someone like him do? He probably couldn't walk through a grocery store without causing a stir.

"You're welcome to join me," he said

She was about to say "No!" when the righteous indignation caught in her throat. Her entire job at this resort was to gather information on this man and his organization. Naked hot tubbing with the cult leader was exactly what she should be doing.

Damn it. She took a breath and steeled herself. If Jamie Lee Curtis could rip all the bows off her dress, slick back her hair, and dance for Arnold, Gabby could peel off her sportswear and skinny dip with this fool.

Do it doucement. Do it very slowly. Phil would sometimes say Arnie's line to her while she was getting ready for bed, usually while she was tripping out of sweatpants and into an old T-shirt. It was a joke.

Primly, even to her own ears, she said, "I have to be at Ladies Orientation, but maybe I could squeeze in some..." How was she going to get these pants off? She might as well try to striptease out of a scuba suit.

Her mind flashed to Markus. He had slept on the couch last night. She shouldn't even feel guilty about getting naked for G, but she did.

Did he want her to dance?

Maybe just some light swaying in her underwear and bra top. Standing on one foot, she tried to get one shoe off. She hopped on one foot until she lost her balance and had to try again while one of the world's biggest action stars watched.

"If only I had a shoehorn," he said, taking in her troubles.

A shoehorn—Gabby didn't know whether to laugh or cry. Good thing she hadn't gone into stripping. Because she wasn't pulling a Jamie Lee, she made a joke. "Loss of balance is one of the first signs of aging. I'm middle-aged, you know," she corrected.

Why had she said that? "Well, thirty-five isn't quite middle-aged."

He suppressed a grin. "I'm older than you."

That's when it hit her. The Big G was sweet, maybe not all the time, but at least today. And he was sad. It looked like it took heavy machinery to hold the corners of his mouth up for a simple smile.

Recognition dawned on his face, a little late, considering she was already getting naked. "You're Lil' G's girl, aren't you?"

"Huh?"

"George's my dude." With a sly smile, G said, "That man cannot stop talking about you."

"Really?" She looked up from putting her socks in her shoes to keep them clean. There's a reason strippers don't wear athletic socks.

And she remembered that she was person first, spy second. Really, the entire reason that she'd been successful on her last mission was because she got to know people.

"Are you okay?" she asked. Her compression leggings were just below her belly button and squishing her muffin top out in a way that she'd prefer they didn't. Luckily, G wasn't even looking.

At her inquiry into his welfare, he blew out a breath. "I feel like I'm losing on every front. Jasmine is mad, and *Power Couple 2* isn't going anywhere. Money is tight." He sank farther into his personal pool. "Sorry. I'm supposed to be supporting you."

"Everyone needs support." Gabby looked down at her shaping underwear with a supportive stomach panel. "I'm not sure if I wore the right underwear for skinny dipping."

"Are you taking your pants off?" he asked, his gaze deepening into a confused squint.

"No, of course not!" She laughed uncomfortably and pulled her pants back up with a snap. "I thought you asked...never mind. I must have heard you wrong."

Just then, footsteps approached. A bigger audience—this was not going well for Gabby.

"Gia?"

At the sight of Markus, Gabby's soul departed her body (in order to survive the intense and overwhelming shame).

He didn't say "What in the hell are you doing?" but from the look on his face, that's what he was thinking. He had definitely seen her pulling her pants back up.

"George, my man!" Genesis called. "You wanna join me?"

She was such an idiot. Apparently, Genesis invited everyone to hop in the pool with him. It hadn't been a sexual thing. It had just been a thing.

"Rain check," Markus said, "You're supposed to be leading orientation right now. I came to get you."

"Really?" G glanced at his dive watch. "I'm not ready. Can you give everyone a welcome? Tell them I'll be there in a minute."

"Sure thing, bro."

While G got himself together, Gabby and Markus made their way down the path. Markus raised an eyebrow, "So...what'd I walk in on? You have something to tell me?"

Gabby's face burned. "He asked me to come into the pool. I was going to say no, but then I figured hot tubbing with the cult leader was exactly what I should be doing. He was obviously naked, and I'm wearing athleisure." Gabby covered her face with her hands. "What was I thinking?"

"Good instincts. You did the right thing."

"Really?" Gabby glanced up with disbelief.

"Really."

"Did you see me trying to get out of those pants, though?"

"To be fair, who could get out of those pants?"

She laughed. "I know, right? You're probably going to have to cut me out of them later."

He glanced her way, and his lips parted as if to offer just that, but she quickly looked toward the trail, too overwhelmed to look him in the face. For a woman who wasn't comfortable in a two-piece, she was getting in over her head.

"You just came out the gates a little hot. Tone it down and blend. Ladies Orientation should be easy."

Gabby took a breath. "I've got this. No one will even know that I'm there."

"Just remember to keep your clothes on."

She deserved that.

CHAPTER 12

Midmorning, the G-hut

Everyone, shut your eyes. Open your hearts," said the woman standing in front of a circle of women at the Ladies-Only Power Couple Orientation. The group was gathered in the G-hut, a circular building made from beautiful stone and gleaming wood that practically dangled out over the ocean. A small circular hole in the floor at the center of the room revealed the rocky cliffs and crashing waves far below them.

Gabby was in the doorway, sweaty and out of breath and running late after the incident that would hereinafter be referred to as, umm, My Bad.

She surreptitiously put the phone she hadn't had time to drop back at the cottage to silent. As quietly as she could, she tiptoed between the women to a free spot.

"Welcome, Gia," the leader said, breaking the spell of the class, if Gabby hadn't already. "I'm Jasmine."

Tall, broad shouldered, boobs spilling out of her top, red hair down to there. In photos, Jasmine was beautiful, an object to be admired. In person, Jasmine was overwhelming. Like the Big G, her presence also screamed "cult leader." Gabby couldn't tear her eyes away.

Jasmine repeated, "Take a seat. Shut your eyes and open your heart."

"Oh, sorry!" Gabby must've been staring.

The gong sounded. As it faded to a distant shimmer, Jasmine said, "It is my mission to share the practice and wisdom of Genesis with as many people as I can. It would be criminal to keep this happiness to myself."

Funny choice of words.

"You will spend the next week finding your Inner-G."

Gabby wanted to ask what that meant, but it seemed like something she was already supposed to know. Like that time she'd zoned out at Best Buy while the salesman was talking to her, and she ended up walking out with an air fryer instead of admitting she hadn't heard a word he said.

A woman in a flowy dress passed out G-shots. Standard ingredient list: seaweed and radical molecules.

Gabby peered into the opaque green liquid. By the end of the week, she'd be speaking fluent G. The more she got into it, the easier it seemed. Sort of like the G version of pig latin. Instead of "ig-pay atin-lay," just add a "G."

G-love.
G-hut.
Inner-G.
G-force.
G-ranch.
G-wagon.
G-spot?

Jasmine said, "Genesis and I are so grateful that you've joined us. This retreat is designed to wake you up."

Gabby looked around. Had she been asleep? Also, how closely was this going to follow the plot of *Power Couple*?

"We are all so stressed, busy, bombarded by information. Very few people are actually awake to the world. Waking up is the first step."

Step to what? Where were they going? This felt like the closest Gabby had been to cult membership since her last visit to Trader Joe's.

"Outside the constant noise of society, you will be able to see the lies that we believe, the lies that we tell ourselves. If you give yourself over to practice, you will be able to see the truth and access your Inner-G."

The women in the circle were eating it up, nodding in agreement and breathing like they'd never gotten a lungful of air before.

"Someone with strong Inner-G walks through a room with confidence, finds romance with ease, makes money hand over fist."

Okay, she was starting to feel it. Maybe all she needed was some more G. It couldn't hurt.

Jasmine was in the flow, the room was humming with energy when...

Briiiing.

Gabby's leg vibrated, and the phone rang. Damn it. She must have turned the ringer on instead of off. Why did she always do that? It was a blaring ringtone against a background of soft music and ylang-ylang scented air. All eyes in the room moved to her.

"I'm so sorry!" Gabby hurried to turn the sound off. "I forgot that was there."

Jasmine glared at her like she'd murdered someone. "You have a phone?"

Gabby stuttered. "Um, it's my family. I really have to be available."

"It's rule number one. No phones."

"It's my Granny, though. I really have to take it." She'd been trying to call all morning.

Gabby looked between her phone and Jasmine and back again. What if Lucas was having an allergic reaction? What if there had been a car accident? It could be anything.

"Just one second." Gabby ran outside and answered the call. "Granny, what's going on?"

The connection was fuzzy. After a few "Can you hear me?"s, she said, "Gabby, you know those shoes you ordered Kyle?"

Gabby deflated completely. "You called about shoes?"

"WHAT?" Her voice was fuzzy, but Gabby could tell she was probably yelling into the phone.

Gabby yelled, "You called about shoes?!"

"They didn't...and Kyle..."

This was not an emergency. Gabby's heart rate skyrocketed. From inside the G-hut, Jasmine was laser-eyeing her. She looked furious.

Granny fuzzed out again, and Gabby ended the call with no more information than before. She pasted a smile on her face and walked back into the hut. "I'm so sorry. It was my grandmother, and I just had to take it."

Jasmine shook her head. "Do you think you're the only one with a family?"

"No."

Gabby looked around the room at all the other women. They

probably had responsibilities and people to worry about back home. Was she being arrogant, thinking that everything would fall apart without her?

"You cannot be a Power Couple or a Power anything if you don't learn balance."

"But I need to learn balance with my family. What am I going to do, not worry about them?"

Jasmine raised an eyebrow. "You answered your own question. Good job."

Ouch.

Jasmine put a hand on her hip and said, "Gia, you can't have a phone. You are going to throw off the energy of the whole retreat. Did you feel how we lost the flow when that phone rang?"

Partially because Jasmine freaked out, but Gabby wasn't going to mention that.

"Not to mention, this is a private space. We need to feel safe sharing. No phones."

Hmm. That was ironic for a group that had been selling its members' secrets to the tabloids.

"You simply can't have it." Jasmine shut her eyes like she was doing her best to stay composed. "The G-hut is a sacred space."

Gabby's eyes widened. "But—"

"There's no exception. If you want to be here, you have to shut off the noise."

Gabby felt it coming. Jasmine was going to confiscate her phone like she was a teenager who just violated a house rule. But this was Gabby's personal phone. Her actual phone number with a gazillion pictures of her kids and Mr. Bubbles. Her cover would be blown. The whole mission would be blown because she wanted her phone.

"I can't believe you didn't hand over your phone when you arrived."

"I, uh, didn't know," Gabby stammered.

"I'm going to have to talk to whoever checked you and George in."

Gabby had to think fast. She needed to get rid of this phone before Jasmine took it. The hole in the center of the room called to her, the sound of the waves giving her the answer to her problems. In the most high-stakes game of cornhole ever, Gabby pretended to trip on the completely flat floor (not a problem because she did that sort of thing all the time) and fumbled her phone but with just enough momentum to send it toward the death drop. She shut her eyes and willed the phone toward its destination. It skittered across the gleaming wood floor and went straight into the hole, disappearing.

Instead of doing a victory dance, Gabby gasped. With a muttered string of "shit, shit, shit," she ran toward the hole. Sure enough, the phone was face down on wet gray rock far below, the bright pink phone case just barely visible.

"Damn it!" she said, with feeling. Inside, it was nothing but sweet relief. A twenty-foot drop onto a rock that was sure to be submerged any minute—her phone was toast. That had been too close for comfort. Jasmine had been seconds away from uncovering Gabby Greene's entire digital footprint. She shouldn't have even had the phone with her on the mission, but really, how else was she supposed to contact her kids?

Jasmine took a centering breath, one of those in-through-the-nose, out-through-the-mouth yoga breaths.

Gabby needed to learn how to do that.

Once again composed, Jasmine said, "That was nothing but karma. The universe righting itself after the interruption."

If it hadn't been clear before, it was now. Inner-G was a cult. The cell phone wasn't just a disruption, it was contact with the outside.

"I'm so sorry," Gabby said, kowtowing to Jasmine like she meant it. "I had no clue about the phone rule. We got in late last night, and this is my first activity. This is orientation, right?" She looked around with wide eyes and an innocent look.

Gabby knew how to play dumb.

"Now you know." With a glance toward the abyss, she said, "I guess you don't have to worry about that rule anymore. Let me tell you, the Big G would not be happy about this." Jasmine shivered. "No phones. Ever. Do you hear me?"

For a moment, Gabby wasn't sure if Jasmine truly cared about the rule or was just scared of G's reaction. How bad was the man's temper?

Then the weird moment was over. Jasmine's red curls bounced, and she scanned the room with nothing but serenity. "Clearly, I need to start from the beginning." She laughed lightly.

Gabby turned bright red and mouthed "sorry" again.

"To develop your Inner-G, you need to do a couple of things. First of all, you have to shut down the noise. No one can think in the constant dinging and ringing of society. Social media, scrolling, sound bites, phones, traffic. We are a society of interruptions and disruptions. ADHD is an epidemic in society, not because more people have focus and attention problems, but because we are not built for the world we have created. That is a core principle of Inner-G: Change the world, not yourself." With a look at Gabby, she said, "That is why we need to get rid of phones."

Did she have ADHD? Instagram kept sending her quizzes with blurry pictures, captioned If you see a dog when you look at this, you have ADHD. Gabby always saw the dog.

"Develop a mind-body connection."

At least she didn't have to be an athlete.

"Develop your connection to nature. Root your person to the earth itself like a tree and disconnect from the noise. Breathe with intention."

Breathing and sitting—that sounded fine.

"The last and most important step of Inner-G is releasing secrets. If you keep secrets locked inside, they will chip away at your power, block the flow of energy. You cannot grow or transform while harboring secrets. You cannot become your best self, and you definitely cannot become a power couple if you are keeping secrets. Stop holding in toxic energy. Stop telling lies."

Well, so much for that one. At this point, Gabby's entire life was a tangled web of lies; the only thing holding it together was the secrets. But she could vouch for the secrets-being-bad-for-relationships thing. Valentina asking her to spy on Markus tied her stomach in knots.

"The first step to a better relationship with your partner and with yourself is purging secrets. You must develop a confessional practice."

A confessional practice—it wasn't very hard to figure out how Inner-G was collecting information to sell.

"The G-hut is a safe space. We're going to go around the circle. I want each of you to share your greatest fear."

What was this, *Harry Potter*? Professor Lupin was going to have them each cast a Patronus against their greatest fear? Kyle and Lucas both loved the Harry Potter movies.

She went to a quiet place in her mind, hoping the bell would ring before her turn. The women to her left piped up with, "Aging," and, "My kids won't need me anymore," and, "Irrelevance," and "Never making anything of myself."

Then it was her turn. Gabby didn't have an answer prepared. She was going to say, *That I'll never find the G-spot*, but when Jasmine looked at her and the gong sounded, her fear spilled out like water from a pitcher.

"That I can't do it all."

Jasmine nodded. "Because you can't."

CHAPTER 13

Before yoga but after chanting, outside the G-hut

Gabby found Markus waiting outside the G-hut, a fanny pack dangling from an extended hand. "You forgot your bag," he said with a smile.

The bag he was holding was empty. He was up to spy business. Thank God, because she needed a break from introspection. Spying was easier.

Jasmine smiled. "Be honest, George. You missed her."

Gabby was sure there was a secret note in the bag.

Markus played along. "Can't blame me for missing my baby on our honeymoon." He wrapped his arm around Gabby and steered her away from the group. "Are you all on break or..."

"Yoga is in a few hours," Jasmine said, then turned to Gabby. "But I'm meeting some of the other women in my office for a matcha before the class. Gia's invited."

Markus grabbed Gabby's hand. "Matcha? I'd never get between Gia and a matcha. I'll have her back before class."

Markus knew she thought matcha tasted like dirt.

As soon as they were out of range, Markus became all business. "Val wants to talk."

"What is it?"

He shrugged. "Something important."

"How was your thing?" Gabby asked Markus as they hustled down the path.

"Genesis was half naked and talking about living in his mind cave."

"I thought you were supposed to go fishing."

"I don't think Genesis can be bound by schedules. How about yours? Did you make any friends yet?"

She snorted. "Not yet."

"Everyone here will be telling you their darkest secrets in no time," Markus said. "I have faith."

"They do seem to be pretty busy unburdening themselves to Jasmine."

Because they didn't want Geeves surprising them, they took the call on Markus's bed, aka, the couch. He moved his pillow out of the way, dialed, and set the phone between them. Gabby tapped her foot at a crazy pace until Markus set his hand on her knee.

Valentina answered, "Special Supervisory Agent Monroe."

"This is Agents Greene and Parks."

"Are you in a secure location?"

"Yes." Markus had swept once more for bugs before calling.

"Strap in, Agents. I just got off the phone with the president moments ago, and he is at a level ten over this operation."

Gabby and Markus exchanged a worried look.

"He skipped the proper channels. Called me directly on my office line. That's how serious this is."

"What's happened?" asked Markus.

"This morning, an incriminating picture of the president was leaked to the media. It's a photo of him and Amanda Duvall."

"The journalist?" Gabby asked. "She was on the political beat, right?"

Markus pulled up the photo in question on his laptop. In it, she and President Simon were relaxing in the White House's Oval Office. She had her head tilted back in laughter, perfect white teeth on display. Now, here was someone who wore her retainer.

The president appeared to be telling a joke. The intimacy between the two was palpable. It was the kind of picture where the internet would unanimously conclude that they were into each other based on the angle of their knees and the sincerity of the smiles.

"There are a couple of issues with this photo. The most obvious being that Amanda was murdered last week and the president would like to distance himself from any fallout or speculation."

Made sense. "Can't he just put out a statement saying that he's met Amanda and mourns the loss of a bright mind in journalism or something?" Gabby suggested.

"I'm sure he will, but there is already a lot of chatter about the photo."

"Yeah," Markus said, "but it's just one photo."

"Is the president funny?" Gabby asked. "He doesn't seem like it." Amanda appeared to be laughing way too hard at that joke.

"I'm sure he's very fun," Valentina said. "He claims Amanda interviewed him for a piece on White House inner workings that never came out."

Hmm. That seemed a little thin.

Markus leaned toward the phone. "Why does this concern us? Did the leak come from Inner-G?"

"We haven't fully traced the photo's source yet, but no one is comfortable with Sheridan hanging out at Inner-G right now."

"She doesn't want to leave," Gabby said. "Also, when we interviewed her yesterday, she said that she'd informed President Simon that she was going to miss their appointment."

"That can't be right," Valentina said.

"I'm just repeating what she told us. It kind of feels like we're chasing down a woman on vacation."

The line was dead for a second until Valentina said, "Even if that was true, her presence at Inner-G is a problem."

"Yes," Markus and Gabby both agreed.

"Someone is lying about that phone call, which we need to look into, but first things first: Inner-G is still in a position to bilk Sheridan for sensitive info and leak it." Sounding more sure of herself, she said, "That's our number one concern."

"Should we just take Sheridan and leave?" Gabby said, feeling like she was stating the obvious. "That would solve the problem."

"We can't. She's an American citizen," Markus said. "She didn't steal classified information. The president just dumped it on her while she was reading tea leaves or whatever she does. If she asks for help, we can. If she's joined Inner-G and wants to get a hot stone massage, we can't stop her."

"Well, put the afterburners on finding that leak." Valentina paused before saying, "The stakes of this mission just escalated. You two have your work cut out for you."

Markus leaned back, and Gabby exhaled in frustration. "So what do we do?"

"Do what you were doing," Valentina said, "but more of it. And faster."

"Ten-four," Markus said.

"Oh, and don't get distracted. I know they put you two in the honeymoon cottage, and I'm here to remind you—this is not a honeymoon."

Be More. Do More. No fun.

When they hung up with Valentina, Markus must have sensed Gabby's waning spirits. He didn't smile or cajole her. Deadpan, he said, "Don't worry. We got this."

"Do we?" She didn't want to remind him about the morning—an unwanted striptease followed by a contraband discovery.

"Gabby, we are Elite Operatives for the CIA. Jasmine invited you to matcha—"

"I'm not sure that was an invitation."

"Close enough. Mingle with her girls—you need to be there. Listen in, make friends, ask questions. Wedding planning might provide you access we can use."

Save democracy. Plan a wedding. Rock a shirt-bra. All in a day's work.

"What are you going to do?" Gabby asked.

"Whatever bullshit Genesis makes up next. Every day with him is like a spirit quest."

He handed her the fanny pack, and she buckled it on like she was strapping in for the mission. "Got it."

"I put a protein bar and some sunscreen for you," he said.

"Really?"

"You can't be saving the world sunburned and hungry," he said.

Gabby blinked back, flabbergasted. It was just a little thing, but still.

Markus walked her back to matcha hour with Jasmine. Within sight of the matcha crowd, he brought her in for a kiss, the kind of kiss shared by two people who have been intimate. The way her cheek pressed against the soft skin of his neck when she tilted her face up just so—it was familiar, but fraught with so much uncertainty. Her blood heated with feverish desperation.

"Don't save the world without me this time," he whispered. Gabby's vision blurred from the scent of his aftershave blooming in the tropical air, and her breasts pressed suggestively into his chest.

Too abruptly for the intimacy of the moment, Markus released her and stepped back. "Go get 'em, tiger!"

CHAPTER 14

Morning tea, Jasmine's "office"

With the smell of Markus's aftershave still tickling her senses, Gabby tripped her way toward Jasmine's beach "office." It was another small building, tucked along the edges of the Japanese gardens. At the door, she stopped to take a breath and collect herself. Her mission: Find out who in the inner circle had motive and means to drag the president's reputation or just seemed like they might have been selling stories to the press.

Jasmine's voice sounded clearly through the door. "Lana, what are you thinking?"

In the interest of spying, Gabby listened longer than was strictly necessary. When Lana didn't give a fascinating answer, Gabby gave a little "yoo-hoo."

"Gia, I didn't think you were coming. I thought George was going to keep you for the whole hour." Jasmine's voice dripped with suggestion. "I wouldn't have blamed you."

"Oh, I wouldn't miss this." A little sassy, she said, "George can wait."

Jasmine's "office" was a luxury beach cabana—a wooden frame with walls made of gauze. Persian rugs, antique furniture, and

China tea service within feet of the surf. It was about ten times more luxurious and sensual than Gabby's redesigned bedroom. Deep pink touchable fabrics and couches you wanted to sink into, open to a salty ocean breeze and frothy ocean waves. Justin would die.

"This is sort of my she-shed. You remember that trend?"

Gabby almost laughed at Jasmine's description of this as a Pinterest-worthy converted garden shed. Gabby had started clearing out a shed in the yard with dreams of painting it mint green and installing flower boxes. By the time she'd moved three rakes, Kyle and Lucas figured out where she was. The she-shed was only an achievable fantasy if the kids weren't already looking for you.

"It's my secret hiding place." Jasmine winked, although who was Jasmine hiding from? The woman had a mansion overlooking the ocean and no kids.

The butler carried in a tray of matcha drinks and cut fruit.

"There's so much good food here," Gabby said, thinking of the swimsuit in her luggage. "I don't know how you all stay so slim."

"When you eat clean, it shows." Jasmine smiled in a way that made Gabby feel judged.

"Are you calling me out on the frozen pizza and wine?" Gabby joked.

Jasmine's expression was one of pure horror. "Definitely."

At least Granny had added some real food to her diet recently, but pierogies weren't low calorie. Gabby was on the babushka diet.

Jasmine gestured to the other women at teatime. "Gabby, this is Naomi Schwartz and Lana Hunt."

Gabby had definitely found the inner circle.

Gabby reached out to shake Naomi's hand. From the dossier EOD had provided, Gabby knew Naomi was fifty, but she could pass for thirty-five. She was built like an athlete, and her brown skin glistened with what Gabby guessed was Jasmine's inner glow serum. Naomi was apparently Jasmine's right-hand woman. She'd been a member of Inner-G for several years and oversaw various aspects of the group.

If Gabby ignored her athleticism, Naomi seemed more relatable than some of the other people at Inner-G.

Lana Hunt was a famous designer. Huntress was the current It Brand. Half of Kyle's friends had Huntress T-shirts. They couldn't afford the clothes, but they could get a T-shirt with the logo. It was a pagan Ralph Lauren, the silhouette of a naked woman on horseback holding a drawn bow. All of Lana's looks were ethereal, lots of gauzy fabric and one-shouldered designs, but with a goth edge. Wood nymphs and fairies, but deadly. Kyle had bought a knockoff Huntress dress to wear to the eighth-grade dance last month. It hadn't been a particularly good look for an eighth grader, but Gabby had just smiled and taken a picture. Looking dumb in eighth grade was a rite of passage.

Lana gave Gabby a quick once-over and must have found her wanting because she picked up her conversation with Naomi like Gabby wasn't even there, which reminded her of Lana's nickname, the Cuntress. Kind of cunty, kind of fancy.

"George and Gia are our newest members," Jasmine said, handing Gabby a bowl of clear liquid.

"Is this broth?" Gabby asked.

"Bone broth."

Gabby stared at the bowl of broth in confusion. It's not like she had the flu. That's the only time she'd ever had just broth.

"Bone broth is deeply healing."

When you have the flu.

"It's very comforting."

Macaroni and cheese was more Gabby's speed when it came to comfort food, but whatever. Bottoms up. Maybe she'd lose some weight before she had to put on a swimsuit.

"On the topic of jobs, what do you do, Gia?" Lana asked. "Are you famous, and I've just missed it?"

With a laugh, she said, "No, I'm pretty boring. My husband is more interesting. He's an inventor."

"An inventor?" Naomi narrowed her eyes. "What does that mean? Does he just come up with ideas and patent them?"

"George invented—" Her mind went blank. Had they said what he invented? What kind of things did people even invent these days? Then an image came to mind. "He invented the fidget spinner."

"The *what*?"

"You must not have kids." Gabby smiled and looked down her nose, mimicking their superior tone.

"I have one, but he's grown," Naomi said. A smile flitted across Naomi's face as she must have been imagining her grown-up son off doing grown-up things.

"Oh, George only came up with this idea a few years ago, but it's huge," Gabby said. "It's like a little propeller you hold between your thumb and forefinger and then spin. It's weighted so it keeps spinning."

"So it doesn't do anything?"

"It spins." Lucas had a box of them she was always reminding him to pick up, his focus toys scattered all over the house.

"The Japanese would call that a chindogu," Lana said.

Lana was clearly hoping Gabby'd ask what that meant. When she didn't take the bait, Naomi said, "A useless invention, something that seems to solve a problem but causes more trouble in the process. Is that what George specializes in?"

Shots fired. Gabby leaned back and assessed Lana. Who did this woman think she was?

"For your information, the fidget spinner is extremely useful. It helps people with ADHD focus," Gabby said, making it sound like a medical device. Lucas had about a hundred of them, all made of plastic and cheap. They were the kinds of things that would forever pollute the ocean. All the kids in his class were using exercise balls as chairs, spinning fidgets, and . . . how that was supposed to help them learn was beyond her, but whatever.

"Okay, so anyway," Jasmine said, "Does anyone need more matcha?"

Gabby said *yes* just to talk about something other than fidget spinners.

While she poured, Jasmine asked, "Did you ever find out if Freddie is sleeping with his assistant, Lana?"

Gabby almost spit out her bone broth. She was out of her league in this group.

Naomi answered for her. "Men are such neanderthals, except for Mr. Fidget Spinner apparently," and smiled in Gabby's direction.

Jasmine passed Naomi her tea and said, "Not that you have to worry about it, Naomi."

"I might be a lesbian, but I have plenty of men to deal with at work." With amusement, she said, "Your husband, for one."

Jasmine laughed. "He counts for at least a couple."

"Did any of you see that story this morning?" Gabby said, doing her best to steer the conversation toward a topic that she was interested in.

"Gia, you're the only one who had a phone," Jasmine chided her.

"Oh, that's right. My bad." Gabby apologized.

"Now you have to share, though," Lana said.

"It's about the Amanda Duvall case," Gabby said, keeping a close eye on Jasmine's reaction. As soon as she said Amanda's name, it was like she'd sucked the air out of the room. All three faces fell.

"What, did you know her?"

"Yeah, we did."

"All of you?"

That was too weird to be a coincidence. "Was Amanda a member of Inner-G?"

Jasmine smiled, the kind of smile meant to paper over something dark. "Let's not talk about sad things right now." She lit some sort of incense and wafted it toward her face.

Wow, this was a hard shutdown of her interview topic. What this told Gabby: Jasmine was hiding something.

"Now that we've cleaned the vibes, let's talk about your wedding. Gia and George are tying the knot this week. Big G has taken them on as his pet project."

Lana set her drink down. "Gia, do you have a dress yet?"

"Um, yes. Nothing special, though."

"Well, I would be happy to have a Huntress gown brought in. There are some shops in Lisbon. Unfortunately, they're only sample size." Her gaze seemed to linger on Gabby's tummy control panel. "I'm not sure if we'd have time to do the alterations."

"Um...thank you." Did Lana just call her fat or offer her a free designer gown, or both?

"You're welcome."

Before Lana could arrange the details, Jasmine brought out a mallet and tapped a small ceremonial gong with a dramatic flourish. When the sound faded, everyone prepared to leave. Gabby had learned two things at matcha hour: 1) No one wanted to talk about Amanda Duvall, and 2) Jasmine didn't have any sense of perspective. Ending a conversation with friends with a gong was bonkers but also a great idea. Maybe Gabby should get one for home.

As she stood to leave, Naomi looked directly at Gabby and said, "Go grab some lunch, and I'll see you in an hour."

Gabby tried to recall her schedule. "Wedding planning?"

"Yep, I'm on duty."

"Really?" Gabby had never expected someone so high up in the organization to help with wedding details.

"Naomi insisted, right, Naomi?" Jasmine said.

"Actually, G insisted." Naomi laughed. "But I'm happy to do it."

"Can't wait!" Gabby was mostly excited to ask some questions without Jasmine shutting her down.

CHAPTER 15

Early afternoon, Naomi's office at the Resort

After a too-long lunch with too few Diet Cokes, it was time for wedding planning. Naomi had an office in the center of the resort. The vibe was boho glam with flowing curtains and soft fabrics with gold fixtures. The walls were decorated with pictures of Jasmine and Genesis.

The TV was on. Naomi wasn't just watching; she was glued to it.

"And I didn't think we got screen time at this resort."

Naomi startled at Gabby's voice. She placed a finger over her lips. "Shhh. We don't. But I'm a recovering CNN junkie."

Gabby squinted. Seeing Naomi in front of a TV reminded her. Naomi wasn't just a news junkie; she had been on the news. "You were a reporter, weren't you?"

"Yep. I got my ass outta that rat race when I got the chance, but I still like to see what my peeps are up to."

Naomi seemed like an obvious candidate to be selling stories to the media. She had the connections.

Gabby filed away that information as she pulled up a chair. "What are we watching?"

"The only thing anyone on TV can talk about," Naomi said. "A photo of Amanda with President Simon has surfaced. But it's not like they have anything to say about it." Naomi picked up the remote to click it off, but Gabby held up her hand.

"No, I want to see it too," Gabby said. Trying to modulate her overeager tone, she added, "I've been going into screen withdrawals, and I've only been here for a day."

"Fair enough. Want a coffee while you rot your brain?"

"Yes, please!" Naomi was rapidly becoming Gabby's favorite person.

Gabby relaxed into the chair with a cup of black coffee and the TV on. "Catch me up," Gabby said.

Naomi went into newscaster mode. "There have been two developments. Number one, the president not only knew her, but there is some speculation that there was a romantic connection between the two."

"Based on what?"

"It's pretty loosey-goosey, but allegedly there are some questionable texts, and it seems President Simon has been to her private residence, which isn't the norm for a president. Why the hell go to her house with his security detail? Doesn't make any sense."

This was juicy.

"The White House Press Secretary is giving a statement and taking questions tomorrow, supposedly."

"Is the president a suspect?"

"There are theories flying all over. A lot of people think someone was trying to keep her quiet before she published some big story."

"A story bigger than having an affair with the president?"

"Don't ask me," Naomi said.

Gabby chewed on that for a second. If Sheridan knew something about Amanda Duvall, no wonder the president was eager to get her off gossip island.

"So how did you all know Amanda? Was she part of Inner-G?"

"She's been here before," said Naomi, nonchalantly.

"What? Like at this resort?"

Was she visiting or doing a story? Alarm bells were going off in Gabby's head. If Amanda was doing some sort of takedown on Inner-G, there were so many more suspects. She was tired just thinking about it. One way or another, it wasn't a coincidence.

With finality, Naomi shut off the TV and turned to Gabby. "But enough of that. We have a wedding to plan."

"What was Amanda like?" Gabby asked.

"Amanda was an icon," Naomi said. "She quit the *Post* when Jeff Bezos bought it to start *ThinkPiece*. Amanda was doing big things, taking down people with money and power without having to please the billionaires running the media." Naomi dabbed at her eyes. "Sorry."

"It's okay. We need more people like her." Gabby didn't want to turn her attention away from the Amanda story, but she had a cover to maintain.

"These are photos from other weddings we've hosted." Naomi pushed some lookbooks her way, and Gabby selected the first one.

"Anything you see in here, we can do without any trouble. Well, except for the zip line one. The bride's dress got caught on some branches on the way down. Ripped the train right off."

Gabby laughed. "No zip lining to the altar, got it."

"Great."

"How long have you been part of Inner-G?" Gabby asked as she flipped through pictures.

"Since the beginning."

Gabby nodded. As far as she knew, that was about five years ago.

"As the Big G says, I'm an Inner-G OG."

Gabby laughed. "Does he know that other people use the letter G?" The letter stood for so many things: Gangsta, homie, grand, "it's all cool." He acted like he owned the letter G.

"Probably not. He's in his own world." Naomi gestured to the surroundings. "That's what this is."

Men were ridiculous, running around the world naming stuff after themselves: kids, mountains, roads, schools. You just didn't see women acting like that. Her name, Gabby, started with the letter G. She had a necklace with a golden "G" charm, but that was it. This man, though, had basically started a religion based on the first letter of his name.

Gabby frowned at the gorgeous wedding pictures. They all looked like fantasy weddings, but they also looked like a thousand choices when she should probably be doing something else, like chasing down the leak. "Can I just pick a wedding package? I'm not much of a planner."

Gabby must have looked overwhelmed because Naomi shook her head and said, "I got you. Let's just start with the basics: a place to say the vows, a menu, a dress—all the standard stuff."

"That's still a lot."

"It's going to be beautiful," Naomi assured her. "Let's just pick a few things." She passed Gabby some cake samples. "We can start with a fun part."

Gabby took a bite of the cupcake. "Ohmygod, is this buttercream?"

Naomi laughed. "Yes."

"Never mind. Let's plan weddings all day." Gabby took another bite and practically melted into the chair while she admitted to herself that she was addicted to sugar. And to screens. It's not like she was eating candy bars at home, but cutting out sugar cold turkey was not good for a person's mental health.

What had Jasmine said earlier? *Sugars and trans fats don't just block arteries and nerve conduction; they block your energy.*

Gabby moaned. "You're my favorite person here." Before she could overthink it, she picked a chocolate strawberry cake. One decision made!

Naomi smiled. "Let's go check out a few spots for the ceremony. We'll see which one has the right energy. You'll know it when you feel it.

"There's the G-hut. It's built for ceremonies, and the view is to-die-for."

Gabby shuddered. The G-hut was too *DaVinci Code*. What else had been tossed down that hole besides her phone?

Naomi laughed. "The G-hut is intensely spiritual."

That was one word for it.

She gestured for Gabby to follow. "Let's take a walk."

The first stop was a large room in the Inner-G lodge. "Here's the sanctuary. This is where we gather for GTs."

Gabby perked up. "Gin and tonics?" Finally, someone was speaking her language.

Naomi laughed her off with a wave. "You wish."

"There really aren't any drugs here? What about ayahuasca?" It's not like she wanted to try it, but if she didn't try it here, when would she?"

Naomi asked, "What do you think?"

It was a beautiful indoor/outdoor space with seating for a small army. "Is there anything more intimate?" She would prefer not to invite everyone who'd ever been involved in Inner-G.

"Outdoor?"

"Definitely," said Gabby. "We're in paradise. No sense being inside."

"You're right. Sometimes I forget." After grabbing some G-shots "to make up for the cupcakes," Naomi led them down to the beach.

"What is a radical molecule anyway?"

Naomi stood up straighter and recited, "An energy-clearing ingredient derived from native plants. When you first get here, G recommends at least five shots a day to clear the toxins." She walked down a beautiful path. "Your toxic load is going to reduce drastically after you're here for a few days. Did they hook you up to a tox-o-meter when you arrived?"

"Um, no."

"It's amazing," Naomi rhapsodized. "Three days of G-shots, clean living, yoga, and a balanced life, and your toxic load just drops. You'll be lighter and think clearer. Better sleep and better—" Naomi cleared her throat. In a loud whisper, she said, "And better sex." She fanned her face. "I didn't know what I was missing until I tapped into my inner-G and detoxed from the noise."

It's not like she didn't want all those things, but it sounded like a MUD\WTR ad, or anything with mushrooms. Her social media was fat with the promise of mushrooms to change her life. "Is there a mushroom component to Inner-G?"

Naomi's eyebrows drew together, her expression confused. "Why do you ask?"

"It's just that I keep seeing ads for mushroom this and mushroom that. They all say better sex, better sleep, better brain."

"Oh." Naomi shook her head. "That sounds like a bunch of

mumbo-jumbo marketing. Inner-G is different than that because it's not a product; it's a practice."

Hmmm. Maybe.

They emerged from a feng shui'd path to a beautiful horseshoe-shaped beach. The G-hut marked one end of the horseshoe, and the other end was a rocky isthmus of volcanic rock. In the way of tropical beaches, the water in the bay was graduated shades of turquoise, ranging from white sand to the color of a romance heroine's eyes, in other words, a shade of blue that no eye had ever been.

"We could put up an arch over there." Naomi gestured down the sand toward the isthmus. "With the lava rock and the water, this place has a lot of elemental energy."

"It's perfect," Gabby said. She couldn't imagine a prettier spot for her pretend wedding.

Beyond the G-hut and the docks, a luxury yacht was in a slip close enough for Gabby to have a good view of the deck. While she took in every detail of the fanciest boat she'd ever seen, Jasmine emerged in a bikini and oversized sunglasses. Her sheer cover-up blew in the breeze like a cape.

Naomi followed Gabby's gaze. With her eyes locked on the boat, she gasped. "Ohmygod. That would be so cool if G let you get married on the yacht." Naomi frowned as she considered G's reaction, which Gabby figured was unlikely.

"G only invites the luckiest inner circle members to the *G-Spot*. It's almost brand-new. He bought it, like, a month ago."

"Did you say the G-spot?"

Naomi smiled. "That's the yacht's name."

Gabby had been looking for the G-spot.

"Sunrise on the yacht. That would be beautiful!" Naomi walked toward the boat as she planned the wedding. "Fairy lights, flowers, a violin player on deck—it would be gorgeous."

"Sunrise sounds too early for me!" Especially for a fake wedding. Gabby stumbled after Naomi.

"Don't worry, Gia. After a week of G-shots and balanced living, you're barely going to need foundation. The initial glow-up is so incredible. I almost want to quit and start over just so I can experience the change again.

"I'm going to see what Jazz thinks," Naomi said, heading even closer to the boat. Just as Naomi started to call out, Jasmine yelled.

"YOU DID WHAT? How are we going to pay for that?"

"...For you, baby," G answered.

"No. Absolutely not! We don't have the money."

"Money's not a problem. Look at us—" He gestured to the surroundings.

She stomped down a staircase in a huff, but he followed. "We have each other. What more could we need?"

Gabby strained to hear more, but they were now behind closed doors.

"I'm sorry you heard that. Sometimes helping everyone else can wear on our leaders."

Gabby smiled, but that sounded like more than a healthy airing of grievances. She'd been there with Phil. He'd tried to buy their way to happiness with things too, as if a bigger TV and a Weber grill could save their marriage. The only ones who really came out ahead in that situation were their creditors.

You can't buy happiness if you're putting it on a credit card. If you're going to buy happiness, you probably need cash.

Before afternoon yoga, Gabby snuck back to the cottage for some internet sleuthing.

She found *ThinkPiece* on Substack, a platform Gabby wasn't quite hip enough to be familiar with. It seemed like Etsy for journalists.

There was nothing specifically about the president in Amanda's list of recent posts, and no article about Inner-G. Believe it or not, there was something about Sheridan. Amanda, apparently, had broken the news that the president had a psychic and had proceeded to dig into the implications for democracy. Gabby hadn't realized there were any.

The President's Psychic

President Simon staunchly defends his choice to consult a psychic on any matter he so chooses, personal or policy. "Sheridan has more common sense than my entire cabinet put together. She's logical, and she doesn't get bogged down with emotion. She's my most clear-headed advisor. Sheridan might be a woman, but she's the best man I know."

Which is the crux of the problem. Our president is leaning on a psychic to make decisions that carry national and international consequences. She

wasn't elected. She wasn't appointed and cleared
by Congress. She doesn't even have an appropriate
security clearance. President Simon found her on
the internet, and she's weighing in on national
policy.

No one cares except a few *NPR* listeners, who, for
the most part, seem to like her. She does seem
to be smarter than the people in charge. But still,
maybe she should run for office herself, instead of
influencing politics through tarot.

Well, this was a hot take Gabby hadn't known was there. Amanda was low-key saying that Sheridan was puppeteering the president, like she was Dick Cheney or something.

Gabby rolled that over in her mind. The way Amanda was calling her out, Sheridan might have motive to: 1) kill Amanda and 2) drag her reputation.

Sheridan, the woman who wanted them out of her face, could be the problem.

CHAPTER 16

Longest day in history at yet another activity, the yoga tent. What is this, summer camp?

Gabby had never liked yoga. Holding an uncomfortable pose until you were bored or about to fall over—it was more like sex with Phil than exercise. And really, it was a waste of time when she had a national security leak to investigate. Gabby needed to Be More. Do More, not contort herself into an awkward position to reach enlightenment.

Skip yoga and snoop around the main offices—that's what she should be doing. Or working on an organizational map of the cult, which probably wasn't the posterboard family tree–style project she was imagining.

Yoga was the last thing she needed. Getting centered and finding balance was a waste of time in the real world, and it was a myth here.

Just as she was flipping around to head anywhere but yoga, she spotted Sheridan outfitted in yoga pants and a Jackson Hole T-shirt.

Damn it. Now Gabby had to make a choice. Follow the woman

she was supposed to be babysitting who didn't want anything to do with her or...

There was no choice. If she had to do yoga to learn something, then so be it.

Gabby fell into step with the psychic and headed toward class.

Sheridan's gray-streaked hair stood out at the resort where everyone else was Botoxed and filled to perfection and slathered in Inner Beauty cream. Sheridan didn't need anyone's approval. Her confidence had a gravitational pull.

"How's the psychological decluttering coming?"

"I told you we weren't talking," Sheridan said sharply, not even glancing Gabby's way.

"Are you going to skip yoga now?"

"No, but I'd like you to."

The yoga tent wasn't really a tent. It had a gleaming wooden floor, a live harpist, pillar candles, and an ocean breeze. It was *The Great British Bake Off* tent on a beach. Gabby defiantly picked up a yoga block. If Sheridan didn't want to talk to her, she'd eavesdrop. After the room filled with women, Gabby placed her mat closer to Sheridan, close enough that she could speak to her if she wanted.

Lana sashayed in and plopped her mat right in front of the two of them. After some hellos, she looked at Sheridan and asked, "What's it like having a vision?"

"Like a bowel movement for your brain," Sheridan answered matter-of-factly.

Gabby felt like her brain took a shit all the time, and she'd never predicted anything.

"I read that piece Amanda Duvall wrote about you," Gabby

blurted out because she wasn't sure how else to work it into the conversation. Interrogation wasn't conversation, unless you were good at it.

Sheridan flashed an annoyed look. "Ma'am, are you trying to rile me up? Because it's not going to work."

The way she answered the question made her seem a little riled up.

Sheridan, hands on hips, answered the question. "Amanda had some fair points. I see how I am problematic, but democracy has worse problems than me: politicians who are owned by rich donors, lobbies that determine votes, an invisible administrative state, the electoral college, and an uneducated and misinformed population of voters. If she was truly worried about democracy, she has plenty of bigger fish to fry." Sheridan gave her impassioned speech calmly, but there was a quiet energy behind her words. Gabby never expected a psychic to be so worked up about government.

Jasmine dimmed the lights and cued the harpist. "Welcome, everyone!" she said in a soothing tone. "I normally don't teach yoga, but Saphire is feeling a little under the weather."

Probably too many G-shots. Blindly drinking anything a cult leader handed out seemed like a bad idea after Jonestown. The Kool-Aid might sound good, but...

Gabby's thoughts drifted to Rasputin. It wasn't like she was a historian, but she had watched the cartoon version of *Anastasia* with Meg Ryan, and she remembered Rasputin trying to take over Russia. Sheridan could be pulling a Rasputin, but it was hard to say. If Sheridan did want to take over, maybe she'd do a better job. Gabby was inclined to cheer her on.

After some light stretching, Jasmine moved into a downward

dog. "Gia, this is an active pose. Push into your heels and engage your core."

For Gabby, the core of her body was something to cover with rouching or drapey fabric that hopefully didn't pooch out and make her look pregnant, even though that's what it usually did.

Jasmine shifted into a plank and then back again, lifting one leg up into the air. She made it look easy.

The rest of the class followed Jasmine's lead like they'd done it a thousand times, a good reminder that Inner-G recruited through yoga studios. This wasn't paradise; it was Gabby's nightmare.

Lana, thankfully, was still blabbing. "How well did you know Amanda? Everyone down here just loved her."

The question seemed to take the life out of Sheridan. Jasmine called out, "Sheridan, stop hunching. I want your spine long from your tailbone to the crown of your head."

Poor Sheridan dropped out of her pose and plopped on her mat.

Gabby asked, "Are you okay?"

A tear rolled down Sheridan's cheek and dripped on the yoga mat.

"Now root your heels toward the earth," Jasmine called. "Become connected."

Why was everything so dramatic with yoga?

When Jasmine pushed down on Gabby's heels, her hamstrings almost broke. At least she was giving Sheridan a break.

Lana, who also must have noticed the tear, said, "Oh, Sheridan, what's the matter?"

A lightning bolt of inspiration hit Gabby. Last night, Sheridan had said she was broken up over losing a client. Now she was crying at the mention of Amanda. It was foreseeable that she and Amanda met through the president. Did a guy introduce his mistress and his psychic? It seemed odd, but that must be how the two met, and how Amanda broke the story.

"Were you working with Amanda?" Gabby asked quietly.

Sheridan didn't say no.

"Even though she wrote that article about you?"

"That wasn't about me. That was about the president for hiring me without clearance," Sheridan said.

That was half true.

"She's dead, and I didn't save her." Sheridan sniffled.

Jasmine walked back. "Ladies! Stop talking or I'm going to kick you out."

Sheridan took a yoga breath like she was trying to keep it together, but her face fell again. "I'm too emotional for yoga. Sorry, Jasmine."

Jasmine nodded her head. "Get centered. Come back tomorrow."

On her way past Gabby, Sheridan stopped and whispered, "Someone is going to die this week."

"What?"

"You heard me."

Was that a threat? Gabby wobbled in her warrior pose while Sheridan walked out of the tent with her yoga mat under her arm and her head held high. Gabby stared after her with her jaw on the floor. Hopefully, Sheridan's brain was still broken because that was not news anyone needed.

Oblivious, Jasmine said, "Root your feet to the earth and reach your head to the sky. Use your core. Many of us have forgotten to do something as simple as stand correctly.

"Gia!" Jasmine said sharply, "I'm talking to you."

Had Gabby forgotten how to stand? Probably.

"Now hold your right leg out perpendicular to your body and grab your toe. You will never stand taller than after this."

Taylor Swift's posture bra sounded like a better option. But it was two hundred dollars, and some of the reviews said it was really hard to get off. You probably needed to do yoga to wear it.

Gabby teetered as she moved to one leg and put her foot back down.

If you can balance your body, you can balance your mind, you can balance your life.

Who could balance after hearing, "By the end of the week, one of you will be dead!" Was Sheridan just messing with her? Probably. She had been really pissed at Gabby for following her and then bringing up Amanda.

At the front of the class, Jasmine was doing the move Ralph Macchio had done at the end of *The Karate Kid*, the one that had finally taken down the blond guy who was really adorable on *Cobra Kai*. She needed to watch the latest season of that with the kids.

As Gabby stood on one leg and tried to hold the other out, her balance started to go. Come on—Be More! Do More! She could muscle her way through this. Just stiffen and clench. Left leg on the ground. Right leg in the air. Compartmentalize. Control. Standard operating procedures. Dead drops. Parent pickup. Conferences. Dinner. Elder care. Her mind clouded with everything she needed to balance. She tried it again.

Was Markus really doing this stuff?

"Squeeze your inner thighs," Jasmine said. "All of these exercises are working your pelvic floor. A strong pelvic floor is the basis of a strong relationship."

"Really?" There was something else she was missing.

"Do you want to find your G-spot, Gia?"

"I was just joking about that. I know it's a myth."

"It does exist. And so does balance."

For a second, Jasmine held Gabby's hand, just barely. She clung to that support for dear life. She could do with a helping hand.

Jasmine let go of Gabby's hand and stepped away. "Trust yourself, Gia. You need to trust yourself before you ask someone else to place trust in you."

Which just made her think of the report she was writing on Markus. No one should trust her.

"Gia, you can—"

Gabby wobbled, and panic shot through her like electricity. Her left leg started to go. She had no balance without support. She let go of her foot and started helicoptering her arms, but she was too off-kilter by the time she got her other foot on the ground.

On her way down, she reached for something, anything to hold herself up. She got a handful of tent flap. Instead of holding her up, she felt the tent give way.

"NOOOO!" Her scream cut through the relaxing harp music.

With the heaving and the creaking of metal and the chiming of sound bowls skittering across the wooden floor, the tent began going sideways. It was coming down on top of them like that parachute in her elementary school gym class, except this could hurt. Gabby froze for a moment.

Luckily, they all were able to make it out before the tent came down. It sort of slow-collapsed.

Outside, Gabby stood on the sand and viewed the disaster with the rest of the class. In the end, the tent looked like a hat that someone had sat on.

Once Jasmine verified that everyone was safe, she shuttled them all to the spa to recover from the drama.

Gabby hung back with Jasmine. "I'm so sorry about that."

"You haven't done much yoga, have you?" Jasmine didn't sound angry.

Gabby flashed a guilty look.

"It's just an observation, not an accusation."

Gabby didn't have the energy to pretend, so she went with her only other option: honesty. "I don't know if you know, but I have a couple of kids. I bought a gym membership, but that's about as far as I've gotten on my fitness journey. I was hoping I could just stay in the back of the class and stay under the radar."

Surprise flashed across Jasmine's face. "I didn't know George had kids."

Gabby blanched. Damn it. Trying to recover from her slip, she said, "Well, they aren't his. Yet. Not until we get married. Then he's going to be a stepdad."

Stepdad—saying it out loud made it real. Releasing it into the air let some of the pressure off. Blended families could work. She saw them on TikTok all the time.

"I haven't seen the kids on Instagram." Jasmine seemed to be thinking aloud.

"Oh, I don't post the kids. Too many low-vibrational people on the internet," Gabby said in an attempt to relate.

Gabby never posted much of anything, actually. Like everyone else, she was addicted, but it was all voyeurism, scrolling through other people's material. It was a blessing now that she was a spy. She had less of a digital footprint to hide.

"Genesis and I tried to have children." Jasmine's voice lilted slightly.

"I'm sorry," Gabby said, legitimately surprised.

"You are lucky, Gia. I have to be satisfied being a mother to everyone at Inner-G."

Gabby smiled back. "That sounds even harder than teenagers."

Jasmine laughed. "Not to mention G. I'm pretty much his mother too."

"I know that one," Gabby said with feeling.

"I think I know what happened today," Jasmine said.

"I can't do yoga."

"It's more than that," she said. "When I watched you going through the poses, I saw a woman struggling to control her body, her environment. Am I right?"

"Yes, but that's what you have to do, right?"

"Control doesn't come through micromanaging. Sure, there is some of that. You have to have intent and drive, but you also have to surrender."

Gabby looked up. Surrender described her pre-divorce life, surrender to the status quo, surrender to the inevitable. Surrender had felt like defeat.

"If you can't control something, don't fight it. You can't be present in the moment or mindful. In that tent, I saw a woman at war with her own body."

That was true.

"And I see the tension in the way you hold your shoulders."

Okay, that Taylor Swift bra might be worth the money.

"As far as the yoga, we'll just scale back the difficulty. Practice presence and surrender in the easier poses before moving on. If you master that in yoga, you will be able to carry it into your daily life."

"Really?" Gabby released a held breath, relieved that Jasmine wasn't kicking her off the island.

"I'm so glad to meet George's fiancée finally," Jasmine said. "Are you upset that your kids aren't here?"

Gabby thought for a second. "It's complicated."

Jasmine accepted that. "Surrender to what you can't control."

Gabby laughed nervously because that described nearly everything and everyone.

CHAPTER 17

1700 hours, recovering from her first and last (God help her) yoga class, the honeymoon cottage

Gabby's mind was swimming with all the information she'd learned today. Even if she wasn't undercover, this was one of the least relaxing places she'd ever been. Had these people ever heard of downtime?

After she got back to the cottage, she sent a quick email to Valentina. She figured that if she sent the preemptive update early, then she wouldn't get a call while she was in the bathtub.

SUSPECTS:

Genesis: Abducted Sheridan, supposedly as a gift for Jasmine. Overheard argument with Jasmine about the resort's money problems (motive for sales).

Naomi: Former news correspondent with connections in media. Not sure about motive, but she had opportunity.

Sheridan: Openly stated that she wished to influence political decision-making as a psychic. Doesn't seem to trust the president or any government, including EOD agents.

Jasmine: Very worried about money problems. Wants a divorce.

Inner-G: Collects secrets through ritualized "purges" into a conch shell outfitted with a recording device. Doesn't allow contact with outside world while on the island except through a landline that I haven't seen. No alcohol (suspicious). Everyone is too nice, and there is too much yoga. Why is everything so vague? Very culty.

Wildcard: Amanda Duvall has been to this resort. Everyone knew her. If the president was involved in her death, someone might want justice and or revenge.

She hit send.

Now, bath time! There was a luxury bathtub and a buffet of free products to enjoy. Gabby had never turned down a Costco sample or a free hotel shampoo, and she wasn't about to let anything at Inner-G go to waste. She dumped about a gallon of Inner Beauty products into the bath and turned the water to hot.

A tiny refrigerator on the counter was filled with fresh produce for facials, which seemed like overkill. Gabby barely ever sliced produce to put on the dinner table, let alone put on her face. There were cucumbers and avocados, a jar of manuka honey, coconut oil, and the ever-present G-shots.

The hair guacamole directions were in a gilded frame on the counter. *Hello beautiful. Mix the avocado and honey, work through hair, and let sit for 10–20 minutes for soft, shiny mermaid tresses.*

Achieving inner beauty was going to be a mess. But if there was ever a time to invest in her appearance, it was her pretend wedding week. Would Markus run his fingers through her hair if she conditioned it? The look on his face when he saw her in yoga pants— she wanted to see that look all the time. She cut the avocado in half and squeezed it into a bowl with the honey and mashed it. Funny considering she never even made guacamole at home. It was always an extra step that she just didn't have the energy for.

Add cayenne pepper to boost the shine and activate other products. Capsaicin is an aphrodisiac.

Maybe Jasmine was just messing with her, but maybe not.

While she was fighting one hard chunk of avocado that kept sliding up the sides of the bowl instead of submitting to its fate, an avocado pit rolled onto the floor and did its lopsided roll to the other side of the room. Green slime and peels all over the counter reminded her why she never made this stuff on a weeknight.

Markus knocked on the door.

"Umm." Gabby assessed the situation. "I've made a mess in here."

Concern in his voice. "Are you telling me you blew up the toilet?"

"No!" She laughed. "I was trying to use Jasmine's products and...Do you have any chips?"

"Chips?" Markus opened the door hesitantly to find Gabby crisscross applesauce on the floor of the bathroom, wearing a fluffy bathrobe and slathered in green tea face mask.

Like she'd just invited him to a party, she held the bowl out and said, "I made guacamole."

"Great, but..." She could hear the question in his voice.

"It's supposed to be a hair masque, but I haven't had anything but vegetables and juice today, and matcha, oh, and one bite of our wedding cake." Matter-of-factly, she reported, "We're having chocolate strawberry."

"Sounds delicious." He rubbed his stomach. "I'm hungry too."

It was hard going straight from the babushka diet to mostly raw food.

"Wait here," he said. Less than a minute later, Markus returned with four bags of airplane pretzels.

"Markus," Gabby said. "I have never been so turned on in my life."

He dangled them from an extended arm. "You want?"

"Oh yes. Truce?" she asked.

"Are we fighting?" he asked.

That was the most male thing she'd ever heard. "We're not fighting, but we're not entirely cool either, are we? I mean..."

He sat down next to her and leaned against the wall. "Yeah, I know what you mean."

She nodded. "It's been—"

"Weird," he finished.

She pushed the bowl of guacamole between them. "It's technically a hair masque, but it's just avocados and there is a little honey in it."

"I'm game, if you are."

"Did you ever play truth or dare as a kid?" She dipped a pretzel in the hair guacamole and closed her eyes.

"Of course."

"I bet you always picked dare."

"Guilty."

Why did this hair guacamole and pretzel taste better than anything she'd ever made?

"I went camping once with Kyle's Girl Scout troop," she paused to look up. "Never again, but anyway, the oatmeal tasted so good that I didn't even really need to put sugar on it. When I got home, I was like, 'Everyone, you need to try oatmeal. It's amazing,' but when I made it, it was just oatmeal."

"That's happened to me before too. I was on this survival expedition, and I ate a squirrel. It might as well have been Kobe beef."

Gabby held up her pretzel. "This is my oatmeal. It's the most delicious food I've ever had. And we've only been here for a day."

"Sometimes everything's more delicious because of the company. If you're sharing it with a special person, everything is special." The way he was looking at her made her believe it.

Gabby glowed with warmth from the compliment. "Is that a truth?"

"Yes." He chuckled softly. "I guess I'm evolving. Not just dares anymore."

"I'm the opposite. My entire life has gone from truth to lies to one big dare."

A surge of boldness overcame her. She was that woman, a woman who dared to go after what she wanted, who took risks. Her thirty-eight-year-old body, which had only recently been exercised, had borne two children. Everything society told her about beauty, everything that she had believed about her own body and its desirability—had it been wrong?

Markus wanted her, and for the first time in her life, she was drunk on her own sexual power. The world wasn't like she'd always assumed it was, a place where sex and pleasure were for the pretty girls at the mall. Middle-aged moms could have their share too.

She and Markus leaned into each other over the bowl of hair guac. It was like the scene in *Sixteen Candles* but with guacamole instead of cake. And Molly Ringwald and the hot guy were slightly over the hill, like if they made the movie today. Molly Ringwald was a national treasure.

Fuck it. Gabby was in paradise.

After years of dormancy, the need had returned. Her breasts ached to be touched. The mission—so what. She loosened her robe and pushed it open.

Markus went bedroom-eyed and laser-focused on her like she was the only woman in the world. He whispered huskily, "Do you know what you're doing to me?"

"Tell me," she breathed.

He traced the line of her leg from her thigh down to her ankle. She dropped her head back and shut her eyes, savoring his touch, aching for more.

He pushed the guacamole and pretzels out of the way. They clattered across the tile floor, and the bowl almost tipped but righted itself. Markus firmly gripped her thighs and pulled her in close. In the quiet of the bathroom, the noise of her scooting across the carpet was amplified. Their breath and the water dripping into the tub she wasn't going to make it into—every noise was a yes, a deeper slide into this moment. Heat pooled between her legs as she straddled him. Markus's eyes were dark with desire.

She was on his lap, her décolletage exposed. Markus gripped her firmly by the ass and kissed the top part of her chest, where she'd just started putting lotion because TikTok reminded her it was about to wrinkle. He didn't seem to notice, exhaling into the tender skin of her neck.

Gabby shut her eyes and leaned into the pleasure.

He started to slip the robe off her shoulders when—

Briiing.

Not now, Valentina.

Briing.

The phone was ringing. His hand stopped moving, and her breath hitched while they silently agreed not to answer.

When the ringing stopped, Markus said, "Where were we?" He nibbled at her collarbone. Gabby gave in to the sensation, the tingles running through her body, the feeling of his skin on hers sending her into the stratosphere. How had she lived without this?

The phone rang again.

This time, the mood was broken. She couldn't sink into the pleasure anymore. "We have to answer. She's not going to give up."

Markus groaned in frustration and threw on a fluffy white hotel robe monogrammed with the letter G. "Give me a minute. I'll be back."

Gabby started to say something, and he shook his head. "Don't talk. I'm trying to focus on not sexy thoughts." When he had won the war against his erection, he picked up and put Valentina on speakerphone.

"I was about to send in backup."

Markus sighed. "I was in the shower."

"There are two of you. Were you both in the shower?" After Valentina said it out loud, she seemed to realize that was probably what happened and admonished, "Jesus, you two. This is a *work* trip, not a honeymoon!"

Markus didn't answer. "Okay, what's going on?"

"The president is freaking out. He wants Sheridan evacuated from the resort immediately."

"I think you should give us a day," Markus said. "We haven't pinpointed the leak. If someone is trying to get information from Sheridan, they'll likely do it again. Let's leave the bait out and find them."

That sounded smart. Also, Gabby wasn't ready to leave yet. She glanced at Markus, replaying the scene in the bathroom, a scene she'd like to finish.

"Gabby, I haven't had a chance to tell you, but we were invited to an exclusive dinner for the Inner-G higher-ups. It's in forty-five minutes. It's a good opportunity to get closer to anyone who might be selling intel."

"Where is it?" Valentina asked.

"Genesis and Jasmine's house."

"Depending on security, we could break into his office," Gabby said.

Last time she'd broken into an office, the security had been intense. A whole team of agents had spent all night preparing.

"Can we plan an op on such short notice?" Gabby asked.

Markus nodded. "Let's do it. His private computer is in his office. We can look for any financial trails."

Before she hung up, Valentina said, "And don't forget what we talked about, Agent Greene." Gabby froze at Valentina's last line, which was clearly a reminder to keep an eye on Markus, stated right in front of Markus. The audacity.

"Your ex-wife sure has some timing," said Gabby.

"You mean your boss?" Markus countered.

She gave a half-hearted laugh, but the truth was, Valentina belonged to both of them at this point.

"Truth or dare?" said Markus, suddenly.

For once, she was going with dare. For a spy, she was not a good liar. "Dare."

He raised a brow. "Okay, I guess you're breaking into his office while I cause a distraction."

"Deal." Adrenaline shot through her veins and lit her body up like the Vegas Strip.

While they were getting ready, Markus asked, "What was that cryptic 'what we talked about' stuff?"

Gabby improvised, "Just that she wants me to stay on task and not get distracted by romance."

"Oh." He snorted in derision. "Tell her to politely fuck off. With all due respect."

To hammer home the point, he leaned in for a kiss. "We'll just have to save this for later. Duty calls."

CHAPTER 18

Activated mocktail hour, the Big G's mansion

Gabby put on some pants that looked really good but were also really tight. Hopefully, this mission didn't require any bending or stretching. She could sit carefully, but that was about it. Still, pants seemed more practical than the sexy dress the Disguises department had packed.

Gabby applied some of Jasmine's makeup samples. With Inner Beauty, she looked basically the same as before, although she had to say that her hair looked pretty good...even if she ate the hair masque instead of using it.

From the other room, Markus said, "Do you have a purse?"

"The fancy beaded one," Gabby said.

"I'm going to tuck a USB drive in it. Is a taser good enough, or do you want a gun?"

"A taser, please." She did not want to shoot anyone at dinner tonight.

With a snort, he said, "As I recall, you're pretty handy with those."

She laughed. "I know. I really got the hang of it." She'd tased

Markus before tying him up last time. "I promise not to use it on you."

Stomach in, fanny out, she stepped out of the bathroom like it was no big deal, like she always looked like this. She rolled her shoulders back and tried to look casually gorgeous. No big deal. Discreetly, she glanced at Markus, ready to catch his reaction.

But damn him, Markus looked even more like James Bond than usual.

"Markus," she said, annoyance edging into her voice, "can't you let me be prettier than you sometimes? I mean, really. It's not very thoughtful at all."

A smile spread across his face at her compliment. He knew he looked good. But he gave her an up-and-down, lingering on her hips in a way that sent a spark right through her core.

"It's not funny. I'm not sure we can go on a real date unless you tone it down a little. This"—she gestured to his whole person—"is too much."

"Stop being dramatic. You look good enough to eat." The way he said it, she almost believed him.

"Our first party as a couple," he said.

"I'm actually a little more worried about the break-in."

"You're going to be great." He offered his arm. "Gia," he said, leaning into her new name, "you ready?"

"Yes, George. Let's do this."

Jasmine and Genesis's house was an avant-garde structure made of curved glass and steel that overlooked the ocean. The building wrapped around a courtyard with a Japanese garden and a stream that ran right under the house, through the courtyard, and spilled over the cliff toward the ocean in a fantastic waterfall. The design was very villain's lair.

Around ten or fifteen people were mingling in black-tie attire, holding cocktails. Well, not cocktails exactly. They were drinking mocktails with "activated compounds," whatever that meant. The beverages looked like regular fancy cocktails, and no one looked like they'd just done bath salts, so Gabby took one and hoped for the best.

While finding her shoes, Markus had explained the layout of the house to her. The office was down the hall, close to the bathroom. The plan was simple: pretend she needed the bathroom and slip into the office. Markus would play lookout.

While she scanned the guests, the crowd parted, and Jasmine and Genesis appeared. He was a full head taller than any of the other men and glowing with charisma. Jasmine was on his arm, looking all va-va-voom with long, slim legs, wrapped in an evening gown that was both elegant and daring.

As individuals, they were charismatic; as a couple, they had a gravitational force. The Loves were selling that Power Couple branding without even trying. Jasmine tilted her head back, exposing an elegant neck, and threw back some activated radical molecule drink. Gabby went from suspicion to "I'll have what she's having." Inner-G looked good.

Gabby took a sip.

"Is it hot in here?" she asked Markus, fanning her face.

He shook his head. "Your face looks a little rosy, though."

She exhaled in frustration. "I might be allergic to Inner Beauty."

He laughed. "No, you've got plenty."

"The product, I mean."

Markus wrapped his arm around Gabby's waist protectively as they approached.

Genesis locked eyes with her. "Gia, it's so good to see you again," he said, taking one of her hands. He held it an uncomfortably long time. "I can see why George fell for you. You have a glow that comes from deep within." He said "deep" in an actual deeper voice. And gestured to her lower belly.

She laughed uncomfortably. Was he trying to point out her uterus? Because she knew for sure that's not where the glow came from. Just cramps. And a small fibroid, according to her gyno.

"Any glow I have tonight, I owe to your wife," Gabby said. She turned to Jasmine. "Thank you so much. I was wondering, though, is this redness normal?"

"I'm sure you're fi—" Jasmine started to say before doing a double-take. "Don't use whatever you used tonight again."

That would have been everything.

Genesis said, "Maybe you should start testing that stuff on animals. Speaking of animals"—Genesis pointed to some tuna poke canapes—"Jasmine let me have some meat tonight."

Jasmine patted his arm. "Genesis is such a typical man."

…If reclining in his personal wave pool with his extra-large D out for the world to see was typical.

"How did the wedding planning go today? Naomi mentioned that you looked at places for the ceremony." He looked at them intensely. This man was as invested in her love for Markus as much as her mother was in her relationship with Phil.

"Yes, I'm thinking the beach," Gabby said because she was a good girl, "I want to be connected to nature when we say our vows."

Markus squeezed her hand, either because she was doing such a good job schmoozing the cult leader or because he was having feelings.

"Jasmine and I got married on this property before we bought the resort," Genesis said with a faraway look like he was reliving the moment. "A fox appeared to me that morning."

Was that good or bad?

"We'll take any tips you have," Markus said. "About marriage."

Not about wildlife. Gabby got the impression Genesis didn't know much.

"I got you, Lil' G." Genesis clapped Markus on the back.

Gabby almost choked on her molecules at "Lil' G." Maybe Valentina was right. Was Markus his sidekick?

G put an arm around each of them. And with more intensity than felt manageable to Gabby, he said, "Having you say your vows at the retreat, marrying into Inner-G—I am grateful for the trust you have placed in Jasmine and me. Especially you, Gia. This is a leap of faith for you."

Gabby smiled, an actress playing the part of a peaceful bride, but G left her feeling anything but peaceful. His presence was unsettling on a molecular level.

Like inspiration just struck, G said, "You know, how would you like to get married on the yacht?"

Gabby gasped. "Really?"

"Surrounded by the ocean on all sides. You can tap into your Inner-G as a couple and begin your journey into oneness in connection with the life-giving force of our planet." He was not using an inside voice. G was always preaching, it seemed. "It would promote abundance and fertility."

Gabby choked. Fertility?

Markus did an *aww yeah* head nod, totally fine with the concept of knocking someone up. Gabby tried to remember his stance on children. If he wanted more than an eight-year-old and a fourteen-year-old, they might have issues.

"We'd love to get married on the yacht, but only if you perform the ceremony," Gabby improvised. "It would mean so much to George and me."

Genesis swelled with importance. "I would be honored."

"Would you like to meet some of our inner circle?" Genesis asked, taking Gabby's arm and steering her toward a group of old white guys who looked like they could be congressmen, even if they weren't.

Gabby nodded. "I would love to meet the Inner-Gs, but first, could you point me toward the restroom?"

After G pointed down the hall, Markus gave her a head nod and squeezed her hand. He turned to G and said, "Give me all your marriage advice. I'm all ears."

G started ominously, "In the beginning—"

Gabby took a deep breath like she was jumping off the boat for a scuba dive, not that she'd ever done that. She was a sunhat, SPF 50, and a book-on-the-beach kind of girl, not that she had the attention span to read a book these days.

Her whole being was vibrating with fear and excitement. Her brain was useless and panicking, leaving her body to walk down the hall of its own accord. Normally, she wouldn't even go to a dinner party without a hostess gift, and here she was breaking into G's office.

Like Markus had said, the office was just past the bathroom. Noise from the party dimmed as she went farther down the corridor. Just the high notes of clinking glasses and a peal of laughter that carried above the conversation like a flute solo.

At the office, obvious from its furniture, she slipped in and pulled the door shut behind her. It was dark, only lit by the screensaver and moonlight filtering in from the windows. In the center of the room, there was a huge desk that looked like it was made from a reclaimed redwood tree, chunks of bark still attached and root structure still visible along the base. A fancy monitor sat atop the tree desk. When Gabby wiggled the mouse, the light from the monitor spotlit her face and the wall behind her like a high beam police light.

She paused before continuing, but there was no sign she was caught. The sounds of the party carried on uninterrupted, no one the wiser to her snooping. No steps in the hall or jiggling doorknob. So far, so good.

She typed in the password using a password decoder from the gadget department. It took a couple of minutes. While she waited, she couldn't help but think about Sheridan's prediction. She felt like the most likely candidate to die at the moment. Not likely, just most likely.

She didn't have time to sort through and analyze the data in the office, so she was copying the entire hard drive. With the USB inserted, the download bar popped up on the screen. Estimated time: ten minutes.

What was she going to do for ten minutes? Wordle? A quick nap?

She spoke into her watch. "Ten minutes to download." Just to let Markus know how long she needed. "If I'm not back in ten minutes, come looking."

Maybe she should go to the bathroom. After tapping her foot, she decided, why not. Might as well pee. It would be weird if, after spending fifteen minutes "in the bathroom," she had to leave to pee again. Jasmine would probably prescribe her some herbs for a UTI.

After peeing, washing her hands, and inspecting the skin on her nose, she walked back to the computer. Inner Beauty hadn't shrunk her pores yet, and there were still eight minutes remaining.

Before she started yoga, the doorknob jiggled. Gabby made for the closet and threw herself in. Her fingernails dug into her palms. If they were coming in to do something with the computer, they'd know what she was up to. She'd have to use that taser in her purse.

Please, please, please.

A couple spilled into the room, all giggles and rustling of fabric and frantic hands. Someone plopped on the desk, and a woman said, "You are driving me wild in that dress."

Gabby couldn't place the voice.

"The way it's riding up."

There were more giggling-kissing noises.

"We need to talk, though. I moan—"

"Stop talking."

I moan? Gabby couldn't follow this. Were they using "moan" like a verb? I moan. You grunt. He gasps. It was probably some kind of cult-speak.

They moved closer to the closet. "What do you think of Gia and George? Who gets an invite to dinner this fast?"

"G loooves him some George."

"Hmm. I don't get it. Seems suspicious."

"Agreed."

Hmmm. Guess they weren't totally in the clear. Gabby couldn't get a glimpse of whoever was talking. She'd only heard one voice and giggling and nonverbal sounds from the other, but both sounded feminine. Was there a lesbian couple? Gabby couldn't recall.

"Gia!" Someone called her name from down the hall.

"Oh shit." Gabby heard the couple scrambling to put themselves together.

Someone else opened the door and said, "We're looking for Gia. Genesis won't start dinner without her."

"Oh, she's not in here," the woman said, cheekily.

With their stolen moment interrupted, the couple left the room, and Gabby snuck out of the closet. She breathed a sigh of relief. The download was complete. She grabbed the USB drive, tucked in the desk chair, and made for the door.

Halfway there, footsteps padded down the hall. "Gia!" someone called.

Oh fuck. She was found out. She moved toward the closet, but the person was just outside the door. They would see her getting into the closet, which would be even weirder than lurking in the office.

"It's dinner!" Jasmine called, her Australian accent giving her away. Gabby froze in fear for a moment. Fuck, fuck, fuck. What was she going to do? Markus wasn't here—no kissing in a closet excuse. No…

In a flash of brilliance, it came to her. She did a deep squat in the too-tight pants, and the sound of splitting seams and rending fabric met her ears. She had done it.

She owed this excuse to frozen pizza, boxed wine, Starbucks, and the Taco Bell drive-thru. Taco Bell had officially just saved her life.

A second after Gabby's pants completely split, Jasmine opened the door. "Gia, what are you doing in here?" She scanned the room as if to see what was stolen, clearly sure that Gabby was up to something.

Gabby felt herself blush and said, "I was seeing if there was anything I could do with these." She turned to show Jasmine the split ass of her pants.

Jasmine blurted out a laugh. "Ohmygod. Really?" She shook her head. "Come with me."

Gabby relaxed. Bumbling ineptitude was on her side once again, and the USB was tucked safely in her pocket.

When they sat down to dinner, Markus squeezed Gabby's leg and whispered in her ear, his breath tickling the nape of her neck, "Nice work, Agent."

His hot breath and the whisper of a kiss momentarily transported Gabby. She glowed with happiness at the praise from Markus and the anticipation. She wouldn't mind sharing that bed tonight, as long as he never found out that she was spying on him. Or maybe that was just the business? It was only her second mission.

With a questioning look, he asked, "Is that outfit—?"

Jasmine saw the look on his face and said, "Do you like? I was dying to have Gia try out my refined loungewear collection."

Sweatpants. She was wearing sweatpants, and they felt so good. "I love them so much, Jasmine. I've never felt more at home in a pair of elegant pants." This might be the one souvenir she would bring back.

"You don't find them too casual?"

"Not at all." Gabby smiled. For the first time since she'd been on the island, she felt like herself.

After dinner and dessert, Naomi called across the table, "Sheridan, when are you going to do readings for everyone here?"

G said, "Naomi's a genius. You know it was her idea to bring Sheridan to the resort?"

That was news to Gabby. She glanced at Naomi, who was taking a sip of her mocktail.

"I'm such a big fan of *Uncommon Sense*. How about a reading, Sheridan?" Naomi asked again.

Sheridan politely declined, but G stepped in. "I can do you one better. I have something special for you all."

Gabby's heart sank. Couldn't they all just go to bed?

She and Markus exchanged an annoyed look. But if the guy you're spying on invites you to stay "for something special," you can't say *no*.

CHAPTER 19

2100 hours, past bedtime, Jasmine and Genesis's screening room

Genesis was a movie star first, cult leader second, at least based on his screening room. It wasn't just a theater; it was a small planetarium. The seats reclined to almost horizontal, and the screen extended onto the ceiling. The walls were draped in velvet, and the air clouded with incense. It might have been a floral incense, but a cloud of smoke never reads as floral. It reads as opium den.

"Are we going to watch a movie?" Gabby whispered to Markus. He shrugged. "Don't know."

Something was off about the vibes, like they were sliding fast into real cult territory. Gabby imagined a sacrifice, ritual sex, partner swapping—every yoga cult on HBO did that stuff. Gabby glanced at Markus for reassurance.

After everyone had settled into their chairs, G stood in the front of the theater and said, "It's time for the purge."

Gabby's eyes went wide, and she mouthed "The purge?" to Markus. Did they need to run? She gripped her purse with her taser tightly. She'd seen *The Purge* with Ethan Hawke. As she recalled, he was cute, but there was a lot of murder.

"He doesn't realize how other people use that word."

"Recline your chairs and open your eyes," Genesis said, like he was about to take them on a magical journey.

Gabby began to relax. Markus wouldn't let them get murdered.

Like an actual planetarium, the screen displayed the stars. The Milky Way and the Big Dipper twinkled overhead. When Gabby was in college, she'd gone to a "The Dark Side of the Moon" Full-Dome show, Pink Floyd's songs and futuristic images on the planetarium's screen. She'd forgotten about that until this very moment.

Instead of Pink Floyd, meditation music filled the room, and a yawn replaced Gabby's nerves. She was going to have trouble staying awake. If Genesis kept this up, she would probably sleep through the ritual sex.

Before she drifted off for real, recorded voices played over the shimmery sounds of reflection and gentle rainwater. A woman confessed, "I don't love myself. I try, but I don't think I'm lovable. Did my mother love me?"

She reached for Markus's hand and glanced into his eyes. What was going on? "Who was that?"

A man's voice said, "I hate my job."

They kept coming. Different voices, but many similar complaints.

"I hate my wife."

"I cheated on my taxes."

"I cheated on my husband."

"I cheated—"

"I cheated—"

They were listening to confessions. Were they from the conches? It was confirmed when Gabby's own voice filled the room. "I'm so stressed all the time. I want to have it all, whatever that means, but I feel like I'm killing myself to get it. What's the point?"

Okay, that hadn't been too bad. It was her conch confession from the first day. Sheridan's podcast had been running through her mind. Concerns that she was just "doing it all" instead of "having it all." Like most women.

Genesis called out over the recording. "Sister Gia, you *can* have it all. Tap into your G and set sail."

She couldn't. Beneath the whole universe, or at least a picture of it, Gabby knew she was just a conglomeration of dust that had once been a star, but now owned a van and could barely handle her daily life. The rat race she was engaged in seemed not only impossible but inconsequential, at least in the moment.

The recording sped up, a frenzy of confessions: broken trusts, infidelity, insecurity. More voices were layered on top of each other, so many people echoing the same inadequacies and insecurities. All the people in this room self-flagellating together. Had they known this would happen? Probably. They'd all been here before.

Markus's voice cut through the din of voices. "I'm not happy."

She could barely see his eyes, but she looked in his direction and squeezed his hand.

Gabby's voice filled the room again, hers isolated. "I have cold feet."

Someone snickered, and she gathered they were going to have to talk about that one.

Genesis yelled out, "That's normal. Everyone has cold feet."

Markus's voice came through again. "I'm scared I'm not enough."

Something about the weird experience had her turning toward

Markus and him to her. It was strangely intimate. They were inflicting this embarrassment and shame on themselves and this weird moment of forced vulnerability with a group of supposedly important people, some of whom she'd only read about in magazines until today.

After the secrets were done, a gong sounded. They all lay completely still until the sound shimmered and trailed into nothingness.

Genesis had been right. It had been a purge. A toxic purge of everything they were holding inside. Weirdly, Gabby felt lighter.

And they'd learned something. Genesis wasn't necessarily selling secrets. Tricking people into telling secrets and playing them for group consumption was kind of creepy, but it wasn't the same as selling them to the media. Theoretically, he could still sell the really juicy ones and save most for ceremonies, but it seemed like he was collecting them for this.

Like after a yoga class, Genesis said, "Wiggle your fingers, wiggle your toes. Open your eyes." It didn't sound right coming from his booming voice.

"Your secrets are no longer yours. You've released the burden. That is the first step to intimacy. You cannot be a power couple if you aren't honest with one another."

He had a point, but also, you probably had to confide in your partner more than once a year when you whispered secrets into a conch shell in the Azores. But she agreed with the honesty thing. She and Phil hadn't been, and look where they'd ended up.

"Now it is time for me to share the deepest part of myself with you. To share my truth and secrets."

Gabby waited with bated breath for Genesis to share a truth, maybe something that would matter to the investigation, but no. *Power Couple* came up on the screen.

For fuck's sake.

Big G shut his eyes and bowed his head. "Before this movie, I thought I could do it alone. I thought I was enough. I didn't realize that I needed my better half to accomplish big things. That's really what this movie is about.

"When you are doing big things, making big moves, your partner has your back, and you have theirs. It's not just you against the world, it's you and your other half against the world."

Why was the world against them?

"When you become a power couple, you can do anything."

It was 9:00 p.m. and Gabby was trying to fight sleep. This job might have provided her an opportunity for a satisfying love life for the first time in forever, but it was really just a big tease.

Markus pushed up the armrest on the chair between them, put his arm around her, and pulled her in tight.

Maybe they were undercover being indoctrinated by a megalomaniac cult leader, but they were also out for their first movie. She snuggled into the crook of his arm and rested her head on his chest. The position was a little awkward, but she wasn't going to move. The heat they were generating between them was enough to power a small appliance, a toaster maybe. They were a power couple, at least for tonight.

CHAPTER 20

2300 hours, the beach, on the way back to the honeymoon cottage

After the movie at Genesis and Jasmine's, Markus and Gabby walked down the beach in silence. Gabby wrapped the refined loungewear sweater tighter around herself to block the chill in the air. The breaking and entering part of the evening had been simple in comparison to the rest of the night. It was more like leaving a couples' therapy session than a dinner party.

"Good job with the mission," he said.

"Thanks." She still had the USB drive tucked in her pocket. The plan was to upload it and send it back to EOD headquarters for review.

"While I was downloading, a couple came into the office." She tried to recall their conversation, but it was fuzzy. "It was kind of hard to hear from the closet. Besides making out, they talked about us. More like they mentioned us," she amended.

"Oh?" he said, his voice pitching up in curiosity.

"They were suspicious. And then one of them said, 'I moan' something something. I don't know what she was talking about, but it struck me because it was odd."

"Could you tell who was talking?"

"No, two women. As far as I know, there wasn't a lesbian couple at the party tonight. They might have been staff or..." She had no clue who they were. "Mostly, I was glad that they didn't find me hiding in the closet."

For a few paces, they didn't say anything. In the theater, things had felt cozy, but on the beach, talking about the mission, the uncertainty was back. Gabby was walking separately from Markus, her arms across her chest.

"So you have cold feet?" he asked.

"Oh, that." She laughed off her conch confession. When he didn't seem to buy her dismissal, she said, "How could I have cold feet for a pretend wedding? It was just something I said."

It wasn't. Their cult wedding might be fake, but it was a dress rehearsal for real life. They passed by the still partially collapsed yoga tent, gleaming white in the moonlight, evidence of her complete lack of balance. Gabby had seen a team of people trying to put it back up earlier and had overheard something about ordering new tent poles. If she wasn't careful, her whole life would become that yoga tent, collapsed around her.

Markus stopped in the path, unfortunately right in front of the metaphor for her life, which he didn't seem to notice. It's like he couldn't see her flaws when they were as big as a collapsed British Bake Off tent.

The moon was full and shining over the water. His expression was earnest. "Gabby, there is no one on this earth I would rather pretend to marry."

That was sweet, but sweet only counted for so much. "I've got a lot of baggage," she said. "You know that, right?"

"Kids aren't baggage. They're part of the package."

Kyle's face when she saw Markus pick her up for the airport

was seared into her brain, a stop sign that appeared every time she began to lose herself in the fantasy. "That's why I have cold feet. I'm not twenty and freewheeling. Every time I make a choice, it's like trying to steer a ship, slow and arduous, sometimes impossible. I'm a tanker. You're a sports car."

Markus accepted that. "Okay. That's fair enough."

They took another few steps in silence down the beach. It had been a long day. Instead of circling everything that had happened, romantic and career-wise, Gabby took a breath in through her nose and released it through her mouth. She surrendered to the moment she was in, to the experience. There was too much control. She couldn't guarantee anything to anyone, really.

Before they got back to the cottage, Markus said, "Earlier, we started—" A smile spread across his face.

"I remember."

"We're adults, and I want to talk about where we're at before we do anything more."

Her stomach about dropped to the ground.

"Last week, when you asked me to be your work wife—"

"Ohmygod, don't bring that up again."

"No, here we go," he said with a half laugh. "I had my feelings hurt at first, but I had some time to think, and I get it."

"Really?" That caught her off guard. Then the surprise turned into something mellower and sweeter all at the same time. Hope fluttered in her chest. A romance with Markus—she wanted it so badly she ached. So bad that she might risk too much.

But if they were honest with each other, or at least as honest as two spies could be... He knew her fears and desires. She knew his.

"But is it a dumb idea? Who keeps their romance at the office?" At the moment, her office was a moonlit beach. Ohmygod—was he? He was. Markus was dropping to one knee in the sand. The moon hung low over the water, and a breeze ruffled her hair.

With mischief sparkling in his eyes, he said, "Gabby Greene, would you be my work wife?" He searched in his pockets. "I don't have a ring, but would you take this flashlight taser combo as a token of my affection?"

"Markus!" she rebuked. "A taser?"

"What? It's a sign of trust after you tased the shit out of me on the last mission."

Gabby took the taser like it was actually a ring. "Thank you."

"Just make sure not to hit that button," he pointed at a feature of the taser, "unless you want to tase someone, hopefully not me."

She was living her dream. It was just backwards and inside out, but the feelings were the same. If they were work wives like she'd originally wanted, she'd be a secret agent with a romance by day. She'd hang up her trench coat and drive home to her kids and spaghetti at night. With the right workarounds, she could have it all.

As if they were on top of the Eiffel Tower and he'd just pulled out a diamond ring for her, Marcus said, "What do you say? For better or worse? At least while we're on the job."

She shook her head but couldn't stop a smile. "You just wanna—"

He smiled, no hint of apology.

Why spend their week arguing? She'd never been to the Azores. Didn't she deserve to enjoy herself?

"I kind of figured we would have dinner first. One Starbucks date hardly seems like the foundation for a solid fake marriage."

Markus shook his head. "We're having dinner together every night this week. And"—he cocked his head toward the cottage—"I plan on laying plenty of foundation."

Her cheeks flamed, and her stomach went weightless like she'd just gone over the top of a roller coaster.

Gabby desperately wanted this man in front of her. Handsome, self-assured, out of her league—her stomach flip-flopped at the idea. He still wanted her, even after she'd confessed all her insecurities and reservations. They were walking into this together with their eyes open. If it was dumb, at least they'd chosen it together.

He gripped her hand and said, "Do you want to go back to the cottage?"

"As long as you're not sleeping on the couch."

"Hell no. We can save that for California. Sleeping on the couch has been the hardest mission of my entire life."

"Oh, really?" Gabby's face was starting to hurt from smiling. "Tell me more."

"It's harder than that time I went undercover in the drug cartel. It's more torture than the time I was actually tortured."

"Oh no!"

Markus didn't pause to explain the whole torture thing. "Gabby, I can't stand knowing you are in that big bed all alone just on the other side of the wall when I have been dying for this moment since we met."

At the cottage, butterflies erupted in her stomach. Operation One Bed was about to commence. The anticipation had risen to a fever pitch. She looked to Markus. "Are we—?"

He smiled and gave her a nod. "You ready?"

Her heart racing, she nodded.

"Let's do this." And he unceremoniously rolled his travel bag into the main bedroom. For some reason, it felt like they were really moving in together. That intimate moment when you've chosen to share your space with someone, to split a closet, to brush your teeth at the sink together. To be in your pajamas in front of him without makeup. At the very beginning, before it becomes old hat.

It was after midnight, but Gabby was wired.

"Which side of the bed do you want?" she asked. "I put my stuff on this nightstand, but I don't care. It's not like I have a phone to plug in." Not since she threw it into the ocean. It felt like that had happened a lifetime ago. "Did I tell you I accidentally dropped my phone into the ocean?"

While unbuttoning his shirt, Markus began walking slowly toward her. "By the time I'm done with you, I don't think you're going to know which end is up, Gabby."

"Oh—" Her jaw dropped, leaving her staring, gape-mouthed.

He dropped his pants, leaving him standing in a pair of boxer briefs that left nothing to the imagination. She'd seen him without his shirt before. Now he was giving his body to her. For a flash, her own stupid body spiked with anxiety. What was she going to do with it? Did she remember what to do?

With heavy-lidded eyes and full lips, he angled his gaze down at her. "How did I get so lucky?" he said.

"Um, actually, I'm the lucky one. You're—"

He slipped his hands around her waist and slid them up under her shirt.

"Markus, I'm not very good at this." She was so round and imperfect compared to this man. Cellulite on her thighs, a stomach pooch, stretch marks. She knew she was strong, but she mostly looked lumpy. "Do you want to turn out the lights?"

"I want to see you." Huskily, he breathed out the words, "All of you." With hypnotizing slowness, he was rubbing the pads of his thumbs over the sensitive skin of her waist, her ribs, that soft secret part of her tucked under her breasts, slipping under the rubber band of her bra, teasing. He tugged at her shirt, a suggestion, and when she nodded, he helped lift it up over her head.

"Um…"

"Do you know what you do to me?" he whispered while trailing kisses from the sensitive skin of her neck down to her collarbone.

"You haven't seen me without my clothes, Markus."

"Gabby." The way he said her name almost broke her. "Feel what you do to me." He pressed his hardness against her, and she gasped. If anything could convince her that he wanted her, it was that steel rod in his pants.

"That's for you."

"For my big, lumpy butt?"

"*Definitely* for your absolutely perfect butt." He let his hands skim her bottom.

She exhaled her insecurities. If he could love her big mom butt, maybe she could too. "Those pants are soft, aren't they?" Jasmine's refined loungewear pants felt like a cloud.

"Shhhh," he whispered.

"Are you sure you're not just really horny?"

With a laugh, he said, "I'm sure. I know what I like, and it's you."

"I like that you think you're going to like my thighs, but I'd rather turn the lights off."

"Fine, but I'm lighting a candle."

The waves lapping against the shore outside, the candle flickering against the walls, the scent of ylang-ylang, and the distinctly male scent of Markus.

Markus groaned. "There's my girl." He picked up where he left off, trailing kisses down the soft skin of her collarbone, down,

down, down to where his mouth set her on fire. She sat up for him so that he could unhook her bra.

"They go where they want, Markus," she warned him, just in case he expected them to stand upright.

Markus shut her up with a kiss. "I'm familiar with how they work, Gabby. Yours are perfect." He cupped one.

"It's not quite as perk—"

She couldn't get out the rest of the word when he dropped his mouth to her pink crest. Lightning rods of pleasure shooting from his mouth to her—

"I love this breast. I love this stomach." He trailed his tongue down her stomach past every one of her stretch marks to...

"Hmm. I wasn't expecting this," he said as he slipped her panties to the side. "Are you stripping on the side?"

She managed an almost-laugh, except that she could barely talk. "The EOD made me get a wax."

"What'd they think you'd be doing down here?" he asked, running his finger along a smooth lip.

Before she could explain double standards, he tugged the panties down.

"Markus, don't."

He slid back up her body. "Don't what?"

"You don't have to feel like you have to—"

He drew his brows together. "Don't have to? What if I want to?"

"You don't have to pretend that you want to taste me down there. There's no way you want..." She trailed off. Phil had never gone down on her. A college boyfriend had a couple of times, but she hadn't come, and it had just seemed like—there was no way anyone wanted to be down there. She hadn't accepted her thighs, let alone her... she wasn't even sure what to call it. Women threw around the word *pussy* so cavalierly. Her vagina was Voldemort, the part that shall not be named.

"I know what I want. I want to taste you."

"Oh," she said.

Markus slid her to the edge of the bed, pushed her legs back, and...

"You really don't...Oh."

He was going so slow, so, so slow, driving her insane with wanting more, taking his time. Before, it had always been a mad rush.

"I hope I don't taste like bong water."

He slid a finger inside of her while he moved his lips upward.

"I don't—" Her eyes almost rolled back in her head as he moved his fingers in and out of her canal while teasing, sucking, and licking.

"Markus," she said his name. "Ohmygod."

"Mm-hmm," he murmured.

"Mark-us." She breathed his name out, no longer a call for attention, but a cry.

"Markus!"

She arched her back and gripped the covers, all the while making noises that had never come out of her. When her body clenched around his fingers, he said. "Good job."

In her wanton haze, she giggled. "Do I get a gold star?"

"Yes."

"Markus," she released his name in a soft exhalation. "Thank you." She didn't even know that she could enjoy intimacy like this. It had never happened for her. She was Sleeping Beauty, awoken with a kiss, not a chaste kiss on her perfect, pink, pouty lips, but down there. Her Prince Charming had gone to work.

Finally, he entered her, sliding in and out, skin to skin, moving with one another in an erotic dance that had never felt like this. When he came, he cried out in pleasure, a guttural throaty exhalation. She had done that.

Twenty minutes later, they were lying on the bed. She was tucked into his chest, feeling treasured in a way she never felt before. This was going to be hard to give up at the end of the week.

CHAPTER 21

Morning sex, the honeymoon cottage, who cares what time

Gabby knew she was dreaming. She kept her eyes shut so as not to burst the bubble.

Markus rolled over and draped an arm over her rib cage, a comforting, solid weight. A dependable weight. Last night, she'd broken into a cult leader's office and copied his hard drive and slept with her hot handler. Gabby Greene had unlocked the secret to happiness and success, and the rest of her life was going to be nothing but sliding down rainbows into pots of gold.

Markus murmured and kissed the back of her neck. "Good morning."

"Morning." The sound of her own voice brought her to full consciousness. She wasn't lucid dreaming. She was in bed with Markus, his arm draped over her, and an erection pressed firmly into her backside. Reality was damn good.

He kissed behind her ear and whispered, "Good morning, *Mrs. Alexander.*"

"Who?" she said before recalling that was his fake last name. "Did I agree to take your fake name?"

"I thought so," he said. "Didn't we discuss this?"

"Gia might want to stay Glanville," she teased.

"Glanville. Don't joke. We both know you don't like that name."

The alarm went off and interrupted their flirtation. Markus turned it off with zero hesitation. "Let's not get up."

"Oh, really?" she said, not the least bit opposed.

"Yes. I have some important undercover work to do," he said, rolling her onto her back and straddling her in a fluid motion. He pulled a sheet over them. They were in their own private tent.

Gabby didn't even laugh at his joke. She was too turned on. "Your undercover work is quite good, Agent Parks. I think we can make time for that."

"What did you like about it?"

"Hmm. Strong observational skills and adaptability. Your mission last night was a success. Your between-the-sheets work is A plu—"

He pressed his lips to hers, cutting off her sentence.

"Maybe I could demonstrate some of my against-the-wall work."

"What is this, *Magic Mike*?"

For some reason, that made him laugh. "It might be."

He got out of the bed, all the while she was telling him, "Markus, let's just stay lying down. Or I could scoot down to the edge." What if he threw out his back lifting her up? No thank you. "I just don't want you—"

Before she could finish her sentence, he had her in the air.

"Markus!"

With her legs wrapped around his waist, he started walking to the shower with no sign of strain.

"What is all that working out for, if not this?"

"So *this* is what you've been training for?" she teased.

"Definitely."

Then the phone rang.

"Damn it," he said. "Every time."

Maybe, as his ex-wife, Valentina had some kind of psychic connection. She could feel it when he was about to get laid.

Reluctantly, Markus took a few steps and picked up the phone. Gabby was still wrapped around him, her breasts pressed against his chest.

"Just set me down, Markus," Gabby said.

Instead, he pressed her against the wall and set the phone right on top of her boobs like they were a table. Looking pretty satisfied with himself, he managed to answer the phone.

"Agent Parks here," he answered in a serious tone while securing his grip.

Gabby suppressed a "Put me down, Markus!" but she silently gestured with her head to the floor.

Markus smiled like he thought the whole thing was funny.

"Morning, Agent Parks." In an all-business tone, Valentina said, "Is Agent Greene available? I'd like to talk to both of you."

"Agent Greene!" Markus called, as if she wasn't wrapped around his waist.

Gabby waited a second to pretend like she had to walk across the room. "Yes, I'm here."

"Oh, that was quick."

Markus gave up on sexy times and set Gabby down gently. Before letting go, he squeezed her cheeks in a way that said, "This is mine."

"Any updates?" Valentina asked.

"I have a report," Markus said. While talking, he made eye

contact with Gabby. "Agent Greene, this will be news to you too. I didn't get a chance to debrief you fully."

Maybe not this morning.

"Last night, Agent Greene overheard someone use the phrase 'I moan.' I knew I'd heard it before somewhere, and now I remember where. IMoan is an online disruptor. They've taken credit for several leaked stories. I spent a few hours last night trying to chase down anyone associated with IMoan."

All while she'd been sleeping.

"I traced the group to Kalkofnsvegur two in Reykjavik."

"Nice work, Agent Parks," Valentina said emphatically. "Do you have any idea who's behind it?"

Gabby tied a robe on. It's not like Valentina could see her naked, but still, it felt wrong.

"Unfortunately, the address is a dead end. A shell named Privacy Withheld is sheltering hundreds of illicit companies using this address." A smile quirked his lips. "Get this, though. It's the same address that houses the Icelandic Phallological Museum, the home of 320 mammalian penises, and an H&M. They're thumbing their nose at us."

"Fucking Iceland."

"The penis museum is Switzerland for anyone being a dick on the internet," Markus reported.

"That's not funny," Valentina said.

"It's a little funny."

It was funny. Gabby was now imagining a trip to Iceland. The penis museum sounded fascinating.

"The person using IMoan to generate temporary scandal could very well be the same person looking to escalate things with the leaked photo of the president and Amanda Duvall. It's at least worth looking into."

"Who's our ambassador to Iceland?" Valentina asked. "Probably some small fry. We'll have to see if they can do anything."

"You can track that down on your end," Markus said.

"We will. Is that all you have for me?" She didn't sound too impressed.

"Yes," Markus said. "But Agent Greene is getting in close with the inner circle. As usual, she's making friends with everyone, and no one suspects a thing."

Valentina said, "Good job with the hard drive last night. We're not finished sorting through everything, but a fifty-thousand-dollar payment hit one of G's accounts from what appears to be a dummy account shortly after the picture with Amanda Duvall and the president was leaked."

"That's suspicious."

"I agree. And it confirms my decision to evacuate Sheridan. She's coming home today."

Gabby tightened the belt on her robe. "If we let her stay for another day, we might figure out who she's communicating with. It's an opportunity that won't re-create itself."

"This is not a conversation. President Simon wants Sheridan's cosmic advice on how to deal with the scandal, so she's coming home."

"But—"

"What aren't you understanding, Agent Greene? I've given you a direct order. The president of the United States wants his psychic back. Do your job and nothing more.

"Sheridan's evac is a go for this morning," Valentina said. "You two stay and chase the money trail for the rest of the week. See where it leads."

When they hung up with Val, Markus slipped on some running shorts and a pair of tennis shoes. The sun was just coming up over the ocean. It looked like another perfect day in paradise.

"I'm going to run down and talk to Sheridan, explain the situation. Why don't you go to yoga so you don't raise suspicion." When she gave a nod of confirmation, he said, "Let's meet back here in an hour."

In his best impersonation of David Hasselhoff, Markus *Baywatch*ed himself down the beach in a pair of shorts, no shirt.

Gabby, with a glass of water, sat down on a chair on their private patio for a moment. Just one moment to collect herself before she dove back into the insanity. Before she even managed a second sip, she noticed Markus's phone sitting on the chair opposite from her. Gabby grabbed it and hurried in the direction he'd gone.

"George!" she called. He might need the phone for evidence gathering or, god forbid, to call for help.

No response. He was already out of hearing range, trotting down the sand in...where was he going? Sheridan's cottage was in the opposite direction from where he was headed.

Damn it. If he was up to something, she was going to have to actually spy on him. And after last night! But her doubt blossomed into a suspicion she couldn't ignore as he cut up the path toward the wave pool.

Gabby knew what she had to do. She grabbed the Crocs that Kyle had slipped in with her things. When she tried to slide her foot in, her toes bumped up against something jammed in the toebox. A quick inspection revealed the offending object to be a silicone sunflower keychain. It was attached, so Gabby squeezed it through a hole in the Croc, leaving it to dangle on the outside of the shoe. Her heart squeezed at the sight of the flower from Kyle, but she tightened her monogrammed G robe and took the short-cut to the G's personal wave pool. It was probably nothing, but she had a job to do. Just walk up there and make sure everything was cool.

The wooded path was so pretty with lush tropical plants and smooth gray stones that would go for twenty dollars apiece at the garden store by her house. The scenery did nothing to help with her feelings. With each step, her stomach sank further. Now that they'd slept together, this little tattling on Markus's side quest was even worse.

Before she got to the wave pool, she heard Genesis's voice. "Lil' G!" he called out in greeting. Gabby tucked herself behind a bush on the side of the path.

"Big G," Markus responded.

They were so dumb. If she didn't know better, she'd think they were just a couple of bros. Markus was covering something up.

The Big G said, "I've got an idea of how to make this really special."

"What do you mean?"

"You want it to be natural, but also a little extra. A surprise."

They were planning something, probably no big deal, but…

"When are you thinking?" Markus asked.

"Either the night before or during."

Gabby leaned in, and her hair caught in some branches. She couldn't make heads or tails of this conversation.

Suddenly, the Big G turned on the music. Boyz II Men's "End of the Road" came on, and she heard him call out over the music, "This is a classic."

What the what? This was so confusing. It didn't make any sense. Last night, he'd gone down on one knee and given her a taser. Admittedly, a little weird, but also a gesture of trust. And then later. Her toes curled in her Crocs as images from last night flashed across her mind—Markus had been so gentle and sweet, and so-o-o-o much more.

She wanted to stay and suss out what was going on, but footsteps started down the path her direction. Markus could not find out she had followed him! Gabby disentangled herself from the bush and hurried back down the path as fast as she could, catching just a line of the Big G belting out, "Still I can't let go." And then in a goofy voice, "Don't leave me, Markus."

"See you in a bit, man. Gotta get back to my lady."

Was G into Markus? This was so confusing.

Not a minute too soon, Gabby crashed out of the wooded path onto their patio and flopped into one of the patio chairs like she'd been doing nothing but chilling. She reached for her coffee only to realize it was green tea. Not enough caffeine and no Starbucks carbs. She was not built for this.

When Markus wandered onto the patio, she looked up from her cup like she had been staring into space, relaxing for the last twenty minutes. "Hi, how was your run?"

The EOD was worse than *Grey's Anatomy*. She'd been recruited into a den of hotness where everyone had dated everyone else, but despite being up in each other's business, they were all still harboring secrets. Spying was nothing but a soap opera.

"Good." Markus started stretching in nothing but a pair of low-slung shorts and shades. No shirt, no shoes—but this man would get service. The sun was glinting off his warm brown skin. He was glowing, probably from all the lying.

"Did you find out anything at Sheridan's?" she asked, all innocence.

"She wasn't home," he said, no mention of G. "I'll have some green tea and try again in a minute."

Fuck. Her spirits sank. Changing plans was one thing, lying about it was another.

Then he said, "I've got something special planned."

"Oh yeah? Tell me about it."

He smiled. "You'll find out."

"Markus," she said, "this is not the week for surprises."

He just smiled. "I have one surprise you'll like," he said. "I ran into Geeves and ordered some pancakes on the sly."

Her mouth started watering. Maybe she didn't care if he was double-crossing her.

As promised, Geeves brought out a stack of vibrant pinkish purple pancakes with a butter pat, dripping in syrup. He set a plate in front of each of them, explaining, "Ube is a purple potato rich in antioxidants. It's a staple in Okinawa, which is one of the Blue Zones."

"Is that why you were allowed to serve this?"

He nodded. "Just don't tell anyone I gave you syrup." He shook his head. "They wouldn't understand."

After Geeves left, Markus said, "I know Val dumped a lot of pressure on us this morning."

"We got it, as long as we're working together," she said with intentionally direct eye contact.

Markus parried. "No leaving me tranquilized and tied up this time." As if she was the problem.

She smiled without meaning it. "Don't worry. I would need Justin's help to pull that off again. I think you're even bigger than the last time I had to haul your unconscious butt into a storage room."

"Thwarted by the laws of physics, I guess."

She trailed her bite of pancake through as much syrup as possible without meeting his eyes, because she would definitely haul his butt into a storage room if he kept sneaking around behind her back.

Halfway through her stack of pancakes, Gabby knew that she was addicted to sugar, and not in a casual way, but in the I-will-sell-my-firstborn-for-my-next-hit way. Before finishing, she felt the energy hit her system, and she was ready to tackle the day, running through a field of daisies picking flowers and singing. She might even be able to write music. It was the kind of high she normally associated with hard drugs.

"I know not everything's perfect between us..." He looked into her eyes like he really meant what he was about to say. "I'm just so glad that I can trust you."

Could he, and should she trust him?

Before they left for the morning activities, he picked up the pale pink conch, football-sized with its weirdly feminine slit, or maybe she was the only one with a dirty mind.

Markus feigned licking the conch, and she laughed. Nope. She wasn't the only one.

"I am the luckiest man in the world," he said to the conch, "I have no secrets from my beautiful fiancée."

But then, what was Markus talking to Genesis about, and why was he lying about it? Gabby might be sleeping with the enemy.

CHAPTER 22

0800 hours, after breakfast but still hungry, the main lobby, just passing through on the way to yoga

Dressed in yet another pair of high-waisted, butt-enhancing yoga pants and a bra that was masquerading as a shirt, Gabby set off to yoga. After a night of life-altering sex, she should be floating through the resort, confident for the first time ever in a bra-shirt, but her mistrust of Markus had dimmed her glow-up. She tugged the shirt down and walked into the lobby.

Because the yoga tent was still crumpled on the beach after Gabby had single-handedly taken it down with the worst crane pose ever, yoga was being held in the main resort.

To avoid a guy pushing G-shots and a woman checking in, she skirted the edge of the room. A familiar voice stopped her in her tracks.

"I already *told* you, it's booked under Elena Greene. Check it again. I have a reservation! Y'know what, can you just let me speak to your manager?" the woman said.

Gabby's heart plummeted as the voice ramped up in intensity. It couldn't be. She must be hearing things.

Bracing herself, she turned around, sure she was hallucinating. Nope. There was her mother. In a polo, khakis, and a golf visor, her mom was killing the meditative vibe of the entire resort. Gabby stood frozen as she watched her worlds collide in the worst way possible.

How had her mother ended up on her spy mission? Just the thought made her brain explode with the absurdity. She was an undercover spy, Top Gun of the spy world. She was the best agent available to protect the president's reputation, and her mother had just followed her to work.

She fought back tunneling vision and a feeling of faintness like a pilot trying to hang on to consciousness before the g-force took him. G-force—the word jogged a memory of Jasmine's advice yesterday. *Avoid distraction. Focus.* She had to get her mother out before anyone noticed.

All her mission goals were irrelevant, except to protect her cover and try not to kill her mom.

As the yoga class started their deep breathing, Gabby did one yoga breath with them. In through the nose, out through the mouth.

Isolate the problem and contain it. She'd offer the woman her mother was talking to an explanation, shuttle her to the cottage, and form an evac plan. As far as the resort was concerned, she would just be an annoying guest who went to the wrong resort. That was essentially the truth. Her mom was definitely at the wrong resort.

"The credit card should have gone through..." Her mom continued talking about payment.

As she took a step in their direction, Genesis, looking like a mountain of man flesh, wearing what could only be described as a loincloth, entered the lobby.

Shit. Shit. Shiiiiiiit.

Gabby slipped behind a display of tropical plants to stay out of view. Worst-case scenario, at the moment, was that one or both would spot her and they'd all end up chatting in front of the reception desk, everyone she was keeping secrets from in one casual conversation from hell.

"Cult leader, whom I'm undercover investigating, meet my mom, who thinks I'm a secretary. Nothing suspicious is going on at all. I repeat, nothing suspicious!"

Behind the plant, she crouched and took some deep breaths. *Get it together, Gabby. Get it together. Think. There has to be a way out of this.*

Her hiding place failed her. As Genesis walked past, he grabbed a G-shot off a tray and handed it to her. "Looks like you could use some help there."

She stood up with a nothing-to-see-here smile. "I'm just a little off-kilter this morning."

"Uncovering the truth will do that for you. You'll get there. Sometimes I feel naked walking around the world."

Gabby laughed, "G, you kind of are naked."

"Good point," he said, but corrected her in a sensitive voice, "I mean naked in the emotional sense."

With a quick goodbye, he was off. Gabby breathed a sigh of relief just as her mom yelled, "Gabby!"

"Mom, what are you doing here?"

"Gabriella, I am so tired from traveling, and I just can't seem to get through to this woman. Can you please help me clear this up?"

What the hell was happening? She was supposed to be doing important national security work, protecting the reputation of the president, and here was her mother throwing a fit on her mission. She hadn't even wanted her mom to chaperone field trips when she was a kid. This was next level.

Gabby marched forward. It was time to isolate and contain the problem.

When children yelled all the time, it was usually because they thought they had to yell to be heard. Gabby walked up to her mom and spoke very softly like she used to do with the kids, "Mom, I hear you. Why are you here?"

"Granny said she called you. Didn't you know we were coming?"

"What, no? She said something about shoes, and then the call dropped."

"I'm sure she called back. Didn't you answer?"

Gabby's phone was in the Pacific Ocean, but how was this even something she should have been worried about. She had been concerned that Kyle wouldn't make it to horseback riding or that they'd run out of groceries. This—this had never crossed her mind. Really, it just validated all the over-worrying she'd ever done. Apparently, she could have worried even more because her family was more ridiculous than she ever could have imagined.

"How did you even pay for this?" A last-minute trip to the Azores and a stay at Inner-G? Could regular people even stay here? Markus had spent a year working his way into the group, and her mom had just shown up.

And then it got worse because there was her ex-husband walking over to join her mother at the front desk.

"Phil? What in the actual—" She couldn't even finish the sentence.

He was scowling.

Gabby's mind exploded. Maybe her mom and Phil hadn't followed her. Maybe they had come here of their own accord.

Had Phil and her mom joined a cult? Were they fu—? She couldn't even finish the thought in her own mind. It couldn't be, but what else was going on? Her mother might have been the woman with whom Phil was cheating. And she'd thought it was bad he'd replaced her with a younger woman. This was SO MUCH WORSE.

Gabby was paralyzed completely, standing in the lobby, blinking like a plastic baby doll. When he started to answer, she put up a hand. "Save it. I'll talk to you in a minute."

Rebuffed, Phil sulked while she turned to the woman behind the counter. She needed to remove this potential collateral damage, because that's who they were to her now. And she needed to do it before they compromised her mission even more than they already had.

Like all the workers at the resort, the receptionist was a member of Inner-G, who was paying for her membership with labor. It was essentially like an organic food co-op. The woman took a deep breath and said, "It's fine. It'll take more than a credit card problem to rock my inner-G."

Gabby said a prayer of thanks. "I need to take lessons from you."

"You can."

Gabby laughed. "I'll look into that. For now, I'll just bring them back to my rooms. I'll sort this out later."

Gabby escorted her mom and Phil to the cottage. With every step through the luxury resort, Elena's wordless judgment grew louder. It was all head shaking and back-of-the-throat noises. When they stepped into the honeymoon cottage, it got even worse. Ten minutes ago, it had looked like her fantasy, now—a full-on nightmare. She'd rather be grocery shopping with two toddlers.

Hands on hips, Elena did a slow sweep of the room with her eyes. Seething with repressed anger, she said, "Gabriella Greene, what is going on?" Elena gestured to the luxury beach resort. "This is not Cleveland."

Instead of shouting, "It's none of your business!" like she wanted to, Gabby took a yoga breath (thanks, Jasmine) and tried to collect herself.

Elena did a slow sweep of the honeymoon cottage. In a syrupy voice that made Gabby's skin crawl, she said, "You're being awfully good to yourself, Gabby." The subtext was clear. Gabby didn't deserve this.

Phil excused himself and went out to the patio to ride out the argument that was clearly coming.

Gabby spun on Elena. "My question is, what are *you* doing here?" Gabby violently gestured to the patio. "With my ex-husband, your ex-son-in-law."

"You are the one who needs to be answering questions, Gabriella." Her mom wasn't the least bit apologetic, like she had a right to do whatever it was she was doing. Even though there was no rational explanation for her presence.

"Did you join a cult together?" Gabby asked. "Are you cheating on Dad with my ex-husband?" Gabby could barely get that sentence out. They could have kept the Jerry Springer show on the air for a few more seasons with that one line.

And even if she and Phil were having some sort of freaking cult-fueled fling, what were the chances that they would go to the same cult that Gabby and Markus were investigating?

Maybe it was like that Elizabeth Gilbert book *Big Magic* that Gabby had read three chapters of. Elizabeth Gilbert had said something about ideas floating around in the air, and sometimes the same people reach for the same very specific idea because it's ready to be picked or something. She'd been talking about creative ideas, but it probably applied to this sort of thing, except this wasn't good magic. It was Big, Shitty Magic.

"Why are you here?" Gabby asked.

"When Kyle showed me where the AirTag had finally stopped moving, I went straight to the airline and ordered tickets for Phil and myself. I was going to bring Granny and the kids, but she didn't want them to miss school."

"AirTag?"

"The one Kyle put on your shoe, Gabby." She stared down her nose. "You didn't see it."

Gabby's mind exploded. The silicone flower jammed in her Croc wasn't a cute charm. It was a tracking device. She and Kyle were going to have to have a conversation.

While Gabby was still processing the "gift" from Kyle, Elena went on. "Oh, and I used your credit card. It was stored on your computer. Because this trip is a rescue. You're welcome."

Gabby rubbed her temples. That was her government card. Her mother had charged last-minute tickets to the Azores to the US government. How was she going to explain that to Valentina?

"How the hell is this a rescue?" Gabby said, her voice pitching up. "I'm on a freaking work trip."

"Work?"

Okay, she wasn't going to convince anyone that this was work, not unless she started from the beginning and explained that she was an undercover agent, which she wasn't going to do. If anyone should not be trusted with a secret, it was her mother.

But she had to tell her *something*. So she was going to have to let her mom believe some version of Gabby ran away to paradise and was being irresponsible. That didn't go down easy. For once, she wanted to get a "Good job, sweetie!"

The fact that she was even in this position...If she were in a Bugs Bunny cartoon, steam would be coming out of her ears, and her top would be rattling like she was a screaming teapot.

"This is not work, Gabby." Her mom was struggling to catch her breath. "You left your eighty-three-year-old grandmother with the kids to go on a luxury vacation with some guy. You are a mother, Gabby!"

Gabby rubbed her temples. All Gabby had done for fifteen years was do her best at mothering, to the point she had lost herself. Admittedly, she might be out of balance now, but Elena was out of line. Gabby practically hissed, "You are telling *me* to be a good mother? That is rich."

"If chasing your daughter across the globe to rescue her from a bad decision isn't committed mothering, I don't know what is."

Her mom was delusional.

In a quiet but deadly voice, Gabby said, "Sometimes there are good reasons to lie. I have my reasons. You should not be here." Gabby paced the room. "Don't unpack a thing because you can't stay."

Her mom laughed. "I will do whatever I want."

Gabby considered tasing her mother. She wanted to. Before she could act on her current deepest desire, her mom said, "I'm going to splash some water on my face and cool off."

Good.

Gabby turned to the patio.

Phil. The man was sitting outside in a light drizzle, just letting it rain on his face. Maybe it was as good as crying for him.

"Phil, do you want to come inside? It's raining." Why was she being pleasant to him?

"Gabby," he said, his voice filled with defeat, "I came out because I was so pissed. You know you're supposed to inform me if you get married. It's a violation of the custody agreement."

She wasn't even getting married. This was the dumbest day on the planet. Plus, she'd missed yoga, and she needed to be worried about Sheridan, who needed to get off the island ASAP per the president of the freakin' United States' direct order.

"*You* built that in because you were worried about me introducing 'some ho to the kids behind your back.' Do you remember that?" He glanced in her direction.

She laughed softly and nodded. She did remember that, but she didn't think it was necessary to inform Phil about a fake marriage for undercover work.

"And I thought there was a good chance you were in trouble. Pretending to go to Cleveland but instead running off to some cult-y island with *that guy*." He choked out "that guy." He'd met Markus once, and they'd had a pissing contest over a small home repair. Markus's presence had inspired Phil to change a lightbulb that Gabby had been asking for help with for about five years.

"Now I'm here, and I…" He shook his head. "Look at this." He gestured to paradise. "Look at you." He gestured to her.

Phil looked beaten. He dropped his head to his hands. It must be hard to see your ex do better than they did with you. Maybe the divorce was finally sinking in. Hopefully. Seeing her get fake married to Markus might be just what the doctor ordered.

Then Markus strode onto the patio, tall and handsome with a freshly exercised glow. He looked right at Phil, clearly confused as hell and rightfully so. He blinked as if to clear Gabby's ex-husband from his vision. She'd already tried that.

"Phil?" he said. "What the hell?"

At which point, the patio door opened, and Elena poked her head out. "Is this George?" she asked. When Gabby ignored her, she looked directly at Markus and asked, "Are you George?"

Without answering or saying anything to the family, he made eye contact with Gabby. "We need to talk. Now."

CHAPTER 23

Only 0900, but it feels like a full day has passed, the honeymoon cottage

While her family sat on their private breakfast patio, where she and Markus had enjoyed ube pancakes and macadamia nut lattes only an hour ago, they walked to the beach, far enough away so that they couldn't be overheard but close enough so that they could keep an eye on the Worst Family Ever. It was official.

And Markus—she couldn't forget that he'd lied to her this morning. Fooling around in the woods with Genesis when he said he'd be working on Sheridan's evacuation.

The wind kicked up and blew her hair across her face. Gabby sputtered to get her windblown strands out of her mouth. Markus's shirt clung to his abs.

"Did you talk to Sheridan?" Gabby asked, pulling the hair from her mouth.

Markus raised his eyebrows. "Really? I think we have bigger problems at the moment. What the fuck is your ex-husband doing here? And your mother?" He looked absolutely flabbergasted. He shook his head and blew out a breath like he was trying to get a hold of his emotions.

But she was mad too. Hands on hips, Gabby stared him down. It was questionable what their biggest problem was: her mother or Markus's lying.

"Why are they here?"

"I sure didn't invite them," she said, seething with rage. Had a family ever followed an undercover agent on assignment before? It sounded crazy, but she was two-for-two.

"If you didn't invite them, then why are they here?" Markus looked frustrated beyond belief. "Our jobs are on the line. The mission could be jeopardized, and Phil is here acting jealous about a fake relationship."

The way he emphasized "fake" hurt.

"They're here to stop the wedding." Gabby couldn't believe she'd just said that out loud. But that's what had happened. Her nosy mom and her jealous ex had crashed her undercover wedding.

Markus looked like he was going to melt the sand into glass with his glare.

"How the fuck do they even know there is a wedding? I heard you tell everyone we were going to Cleveland. And here they are—" He gestured to the beach. "How?"

A crab skittered by on the sand, unaware of the human drama unfolding above.

"Kyle put an AirTag in my stuff and informed everyone in the house that we were not in Cleveland. Granny apparently called to warn me, but the call dropped, and then I lost the phone."

Markus started laughing. But not a joyous laugh. More like a we're-so-fucked-there's-nothing-to-do-but-laugh laugh.

The crab found another shell. Gabby wished she could hide under something and skitter away.

"At least the kids aren't here. I think there's a good chance we can get rid of my mom and Phil without causing a fuss. I'm sorry. I'll tell Valentina everything. You shouldn't take the fall for this. I should have known something was up when Kyle gave me a pair of Crocs." Hindsight.

But she knew that, if this mission failed, they'd both go down, especially *this* mission. You couldn't use a fourteen-year-old as an excuse. Agents were supposed to plan for all contingencies. Although she would have needed a psychic to predict today.

"What happens if we report this?"

"We'll be fired." With a grim look, he said, "We have to report this and request an evacuation. Your family can't be here. Our covers are most likely blown or will be any minute."

They hadn't even gotten around to talking about Sheridan. They were supposed to be evacuating her from the resort. Instead, they were dealing with Gabby's drama.

Before they could dial Valentina, Gabby caught movement in the corner of her eye and turned to see Sheridan running full speed toward them. Sheridan was wrapped in nothing but a towel that she was doing her best to hold up. Her knee was bleeding, and her legs were scratched.

Sheridan, the woman they were supposed to be babysitting, was in obvious distress while she and Markus were arguing about her family. This wasn't good.

When she reached them, she stopped and tried to catch her breath.

"What happened?" Gabby asked. No one appeared to be chasing her, but Sheridan had been running for dear life. Her hair was soaking wet. Some of the suds from a recent shampoo were popping in the breeze.

When she'd almost caught her breath, she said, "Someone broke into my cottage while I was in the shower."

Unlike Gabby and Markus's place, Sheridan's cottage had an outdoor shower with a little garden. She must have just grabbed a towel and run.

"Are you okay?" Gabby gestured to Sheridan's knee.

"Yes. I had to climb up the retaining wall to get out the back. They're just scrapes."

"Let's get you to shelter," Markus said, standing between her and the direction from which she had run. "You're safe with us."

"Thanks," she said shakily.

In a calm voice, Markus asked, "Are you sure it wasn't a butler or someone dropping by?"

Sheridan stopped walking forward and gave him a scathing look. "Would I have climbed up a retaining wall naked if I thought they were friendly?"

"Why were you sure they weren't?"

"I heard someone cock a gun. There was no way I was going to hop out of the shower and ask them polite questions."

"Are you sure it was a gun?"

"I'm from Wyoming," she said. "I know what a gun sounds like. Whoever it was, they weren't dropping by for tea."

Also, she was a psychic.

Gabby and Markus exchanged a look. They didn't have much choice. It was either take Sheridan back to her place with a possible bad guy or to the family reunion going on at the honeymoon cottage. No one wanted to introduce her to Phil and Elena, but ex-husband and mom beat bad guys.

In action mode, Markus said, "You take Sheridan back to our cottage. I'm going to check her place out."

"Markus," Gabby paused and reached out to him. The wind whipped her hair around as words caught in her throat. She didn't know what she wanted to say, but even if he was lying his ass off, she wanted him safe. "Please be careful."

Markus didn't reach back. Apparently, her mom and ex's arrival was too fresh for forgiveness. "Get her back to the cottage safe. I'll be back." And with that, he was trotting down the beach toward the bad guy. She was pretty sure he didn't even have a weapon.

Gabby escorted Sheridan to their cottage, scanning the area for danger and hurrying as best she could. Because they weren't living in a movie, the only place where towels actually stayed up, Sheridan was struggling to keep the towel on. Luckily, it was an extra-large, fluffy one.

"Just to warn you, I have unexpected guests at my place." She was about to tell Sheridan more, but what was the point?

When she slid the patio door open to the honeymoon cottage, her mom said, "Gab—" before catching sight of Sheridan. Elena's jaw dropped, and her hand flew to her mouth in genuine shock. "Sheridan?"

"Yes, Mom, this is Sheridan. You know her?"

Gabby mouthed, "I'm sorry," to Sheridan. To her mother, she said, "Sheridan needs to get changed. Sit tight out here."

She took Sheridan back to her room and found a comfy one-size-fits-all outfit. "I'm going to check the perimeter while you get changed."

Gabby could barely believe she'd just said "check the perimeter" in a serious voice. She tucked a sidearm in her yoga pants and pulled on a hoodie to conceal it from prying eyes.

While she was clearing the rooms, Phil found her and started following her around. "Gabby, we need to talk."

"In a minute," Gabby said.

"Why is Sheridan Lane here?" her mom asked. "And why was she naked?"

"She's wearing a towel," Gabby said, as if that was normal. "I'll explain in a minute. I left something outside." To give her mom something to do, she said, "Will you make some coffee or tea? I will explain after I—" She didn't say check the perimeter.

Phil said, "I'm coming with Gabby."

"No, wait here, Phil. I'll be right back."

Phil followed anyway, breathing heavily before he'd even walked a foot. "Gabby, are you really marrying this guy?"

Gabby scanned the wooded area behind the cottage and the beach. Some of the trees bent in the wind, and the leaves rustled, but she didn't see anyone. Markus had scanned for surveillance devices earlier.

"It seems really fast. Has he even met the kids?"

The terrain behind the cottage wasn't meant for walking. Gabby scrambled up an embankment and walked through some underbrush that could provide cover for an intruder.

"Are you sure this is what you want?" He gestured to her. "You're not really acting like yourself."

"I dropped something out here earlier."

"What?" he asked, scanning the ground.

"Umm, a necklace," she improvised.

After circling the entire cottage and finding nothing, Gabby was satisfied. She headed back inside while Phil trailed behind, still talking about her abrupt choice to alter her life and that of the kids.

"What about the necklace?" Phil asked.

"I give up," she said.

Markus returned from Sheridan's place about two minutes after they'd gone back inside. Gabby gave him the "all clear" nod.

"Mom, Phil—" Gabby said, "Markus and I are going to take a moment with Sheridan. Then we can talk."

"Do you have a session?" her mom asked, clearly trying to make sense of it.

"Yes." Gabby nodded.

"That's good. At least you're listening to someone." Under her breath, she said, "Although I don't know why she was wearing nothing but a towel." Her mom cleared her throat. "Do you even remember you have children?"

Gabby escaped to her room before her mom could sling any more barbs. Instead of sagging against the door like she wanted, she said, "Hey, Sheridan. Are you doing better?"

Gabby picked up a pile of her clothes on the floor and tucked them away. Nothing like having your bra and undies out for an important work meeting.

Because they were in a bedroom, there wasn't anywhere to sit. This was an unwelcome escalation of the one-bed situation. One bed was supposed to force you into sex, not whatever this was, but here they were—sitting awkwardly on the bed interviewing Sheridan Lane.

Markus balanced on the edge of the mattress like it was a chair. "Let's cut to the chase," he said. "You were right. Your door was tampered with, and it was also wide open when I got there, like someone took off when they heard me. It wasn't obvious whether they took anything."

Sheridan nodded. "Glad I wasn't hearing things at least."

Markus said, "President Simon already ordered your evacuation." He stopped to perform some calculations in his head. "We can get you out on a plane by this afternoon."

"Nope." Sheridan shook her head adamantly. "I'm ninety percent sure President Simon or someone in the White House wants me dead."

"What?" Gabby's jaw dropped. Why was no one cooperating today? "Why do you think that? Did you have a vision?"

"I've had a premonition building since the morning Genesis took me here. I wasn't sure what it was about, but over the past week, it has been getting stronger. When that person broke into my room, I had a flash of clarity." She made direct eye contact and in a serious voice announced, "The president killed Amanda Duvall. He knows I know."

Markus rubbed his temples and groaned. "And your evidence is a vision?"

"I thought you were psychically blocked..." Gabby said.

Sheridan was adamant. "Now that I've sensed the truth, I can't unsee it. It makes too much sense. Who else would want me dead?"

Markus stood up and started pacing the room. "We can talk this over with the EOD. They can provide you with a security detail."

"Please," Sheridan pleaded, "don't send me to DC. I won't be safe."

Gabby was turning all of this over in her head. "I thought you trusted the president."

"Did I say that?"

"I guess not." Sheridan had been flying to Washington before being unexpectedly diverted to Inner-G. Why would she go to Washington if she hadn't felt safe?

"I didn't know what was wrong before. Fate intervened on my behalf with Genesis."

Gabby didn't know what to say. Just a few hours ago, she'd woken up in this bed, wrapped in Markus's arms. She thought she'd had everything figured out.

"Do you have any evidence?"

"I keep notes and records of my sessions on my phone. When I think back, he asked a lot of questions about Amanda." She wrung her hands. "He kept asking if he could trust Amanda."

"What'd you say?"

"I told him to stop thinking with his dick, do his job, and end it. He accepted my wisdom and said, 'I know what I have to do.'"

Gabby was on the edge of her seat.

"I thought he meant divorce his wife or break up with Amanda. He meant end it permanently."

Markus dropped his head to his hands. Quietly, he said, "Where are your recordings?"

"Just on my phone. I use Voice Memos. It's nothing fancy, but it backs up to the cloud." She reiterated, "No one knows."

"Jesus F. Christ. Where's your phone?"

"In the bathroom. I didn't grab it."

"We need to get the phone, and we need to tuck Sheridan away somewhere, even if it's to keep her safe before the evacuation." Gabby tried to talk slowly and calmly to de-escalate things.

Markus looked up. "I'm all ears."

"I have an idea," she said. "You're not going to like it, but I think it'll be perfect."

CHAPTER 24

1000 hours, main resort

Jasmine was only too happy to book two extra rooms at the resort, one for Gabby's mother and one for her ex-husband. If anything, Jasmine looked a little too delighted, like she'd tuned in to an episode of Jerry Springer and was waiting for the brawl to break out.

"Your mother?" Jasmine had asked. *"And* your ex?"

Gabby had nodded beatifically. "They just couldn't let me get married without being here to support me."

Jasmine had clasped her hand to her heart. "That's beautiful." With a confused look, she had asked, "How does George feel about it?"

"George is delighted," Gabby lied through her teeth and smiled like she was running for office.

After securing a safe place to stay, Gabby stormed through the door of the cottage. "Pack up, people. I got you all rooms." They didn't have time for talking through their feelings, so she said, "Mom, Phil—Markus and I joined a cult, changed our names, and we're getting married. Down here, we are Gia and George. Gabby and Markus are dead. I don't want to hear those names. I don't want to hear any more questions about our decisions. You are here through our good graces, and the minute you lose them, you will be uninvited."

Phil loudly cleared his throat again and said, "What's with the G thing?"

"Markus and I joined Inner-G's Ultimate G package. That means that they assigned us new names. I think they're both great names. I'd appreciate it if you all respected them."

"Your name already started with G," Phil pointed out.

She inhaled sharply but answered in a calm tone, "No more questions. I'm Gia. This is George." All she'd wanted was a couple of dates without mixing the family in—was that too much to ask?

"Sheridan." Gabby looked at the psychic. "You are going to stay with my mom. It's our best option at the moment."

"Was George able to find my phone?" Sheridan asked.

"He's working on that now."

She and Markus were officially putting their careers on the line based on a psychic prediction and some weak circumstantial evidence. Why Markus was going along with it so easily was beyond Gabby. She should add it into the suspicious behavior column. For her part, Gabby was doing it because she saw real fear in Sheridan's eyes. There was no way she was putting the woman on a plane in this state. What if she got off in Washington and something happened to her? Gabby could never forgive herself.

Elena squinted and looked between Gabby and Sheridan Lane. She looked torn between complaining and celebrating the chance to cozy up to a minor celebrity.

"Mom, Sheridan needs your help because she's trying to stay out of the way of the paparazzi. She doesn't even want the butler to know she's with you."

"There's a butler?" Elena's eyes went big.

"Yes, it's very nice here. Basically, you're Sheridan's bodyguard. She needs peace and quiet while she works on her . . . podcast. The paps found her in her private cottage this morning. She asked for our help."

Her mom didn't think to ask why Gabby felt responsible, or maybe she was just excited to be involved. Elena just gasped. "Poor dear! We'll have a nice, private vacation."

Sheridan listened to all of this without comment, clearly resigned to her fate.

There wasn't even a standard operating procedure to cover what was happening here. They were too far off the books, but Gabby knew what she was doing. Her mom was the worst because she was relentless, but that same doggedness would make her a great protector. If she committed to a task, she committed a thousand percent. After this, she would probably be offered a Secret Service gig.

Phil couldn't stop clearing his throat. Was he going to hawk a loogie? "So if Elena's the bodyguard, what am I?"

"Just relax in your luxury suite. Don't come out unless necessary." She made it sound like a time-out, but maybe that's what he needed. Gabby couldn't have them wandering around the resort, blowing her cover.

"Mom, Phil, grab your things. Let's get you checked in." Gabby walked them over to their rooms in the main resort and they took the elevator up to the third floor from the lobby. Gabby waved at Lana as she walked by. Apparently, the news had spread because she ogled Phil and Gabby's mom with a satisfied smirk. Rule number one of working undercover was lying low and not becoming the biggest source of gossip. Oops.

The rooms were on par with the rest of the resort. They had ocean-view balconies, soaker tubs, and small kitchens. Gabby wouldn't be able to get her mom out of here without a pry bar.

A moment after Gabby arrived with Phil and her mom, Markus arrived with Sheridan. He'd ferreted her in through a back staircase.

"Sheridan," he said, "stay off the balcony and keep the blinds drawn."

Sheridan nodded. "I'm ready to settle in."

"But the view is so nice," Elena said.

For a second, Gabby worried about putting her mom in danger. "He's serious, Mom."

"The paparazzi aren't too good for open windows," Markus said. "It's the price of fame. And they try to get the ugliest pictures. They always publish the ones where you're chewing."

Nice touch, Markus. That might actually get her mom to keep the shades drawn.

"And Mom, you should stay in the room too. Keep away from classes or spaces where you might end up interacting with other guests. I need you to take care of Sheridan."

"But—"

"No. I'll come get you if you need to be anywhere."

Elena's expression hardened, but Gabby could not risk her mom blowing her cover. Having them here was bad enough, being here and causing trouble would make this mission unsalvageable.

After they'd settled everyone in, she and Markus took a collective sigh of relief in the halls outside the rooms. Markus destroyed the peace immediately when he said, "We should call Val."

"She'll fire us." If she lost this job, she'd be back to square one.

It's not like she could put "former undercover spy" on her LinkedIn page. She was not letting her ex-husband show up, wreck the mission, or anything else.

"We can get this done. I believe in us." She meant as a spy team.

He chortled. "I'm not there yet."

"You were this morning."

"There's been some backsliding on that front."

"What now?" Gabby asked. She didn't mean the mission, but he said, "Seems like our mission is clear: find Sheridan's phone and the person who broke into her cottage. They will likely be together."

So they weren't going to talk about their relationship. Fine.

"What do you think about Sheridan's theory about President Simon trying to kill her?"

"It sounds paranoid. It's not like he can ask the military to assassinate an American citizen, and I find it highly unlikely that he's hired some kind of off-books assassin to do her in."

"But if she has dirt on him—" It seemed like the president of the United States would be able to figure out a way to make that problem go away.

"It's more likely that whoever wanted her phone was willing to scare her to get it."

"I believe her." Gabby just wanted to disagree with Markus. With the way she was feeling at the moment, she had half a mind to head back to the room and write a report to Valentina about his secret meetings with Genesis. Not that she had room to criticize anyone with Phil and her mom showing up on their mission.

Back in their cottage, she and Markus called Valentina. They were both relieved when she didn't answer the phone. Instead, they sent her an email: "We will not be evacuating Sheridan at this time. The risk to her safety is greater in Washington than here. Will explain later."

Valentina must have been in a meeting, but she had enough bandwidth to respond with a quick "WTF?"

"If there's even a hint that things are getting out of hand, I'll call for an evac," Markus said.

"Fine."

This morning had been so perfect, a fantasy, well, almost. A couple of hours later, and there was nowhere to turn. Markus was standing at a deliberate distance from her, cold and unflinching. They had skipped over all the usual arguments: the dishes, him leaving his laundry on the floor, or her stealing the covers. Nope, straight to whether the president had taken out a hit on a psychic.

"How do we find this person who was after Sheridan?"

Markus shook his head. "No clue. Search everyone's rooms for her phone."

"Use Sheridan as bait?" Gabby suggested. "Or me in a brown wig."

"I'll figure something out. In the meantime, show yourself at one of the classes. It probably looks like three people have disappeared right now. We need to get out there and act like nothing unusual is happening."

He was right. The next step in this mission: act normal.

CHAPTER 25

1400 hours, main resort

After a quick stop at the cottage to splash water on her face and scan the schedule, Gabby decided on meditation with Jasmine. She'd show her face, act normal, and then go search someone's room. Feeling determined, she marched to class.

"Gia!" a voice called. She looked up to see her mother.

"Mom, what didn't you understand about 'stay in your room'?" Gabby glanced around to see if they'd been spotted.

"It's fine. I didn't fly all the way here to sit in a room." Her mom tightened her fanny pack and said, "Have you talked to Phil yet?"

Gabby shut her eyes. What was this, *The Parent Trap*? That show was only cute from a kid's perspective.

"It's not because George is Black, is it?" Gabby side-eyed her mom. Her mom might be annoying, but Gabby never thought she was racist. Fingers crossed she was right on that one.

"No!" Elena sounded annoyed at the question. "It's because you were married to Phil. You have children with Phil. He's a good man."

Not racist—phew, but still, Gabby fought the urge to hip-check her mom off the path.

"Phil came all this way—" Her mother gave her a critical look. Gabby's blood pressure was skyrocketing.

"Do you want a Xanax? You're sweating a lot, honey."

Gabby scoffed and in a superior voice said, "I'm not going to pop a Xanax on the way to meditation. How bad off do you think I am?" She was pretending now. A Xanax would probably be a good idea.

With a look of distaste, like when Gabby wore an outfit she didn't like, Elena said, "Gabriella, I'm not sure if this marriage is the right choice for you, not if you're this stressed already." Managing to look sad and judgmental at the same time, Elena said, "And if you weren't even comfortable introducing George to your mother, there must be something wrong."

Dear god.

Elena narrowed her eyes and scanned her daughter's expression. "You're hiding something."

In a quiet voice, only because she was trying to shove her rage in a box before it burst out and made a mess, Gabby said, "I changed my mind."

"About the marriage?" her mom said, suddenly all ears.

"No," Gabby said. "About the Xanax."

Her mom unzipped her fanny pack and made a production out of dispensing a pill from a typical prescription bottle. This was something she'd expect from someone Granny's age, not a woman a few years older than JLo.

Meditation was in the G-hut again. Gabby tripped on one of the carefully placed rocks. The path was too narrow for her and her mother. The entire resort wasn't big enough for the two of them.

Elena oohed and ahhed all the way out there. "Is George paying for all of this?"

"Geez. It's not why I'm with him, Mom."

"What does he do for a living again?"

"He invented the fidget spinner," Gabby said flatly, using the same dumb line she'd used with Lana and Naomi. What did her mom care anyway?

Her mom scrunched up her face in confusion over that one. "Those obnoxious toys?"

Gabby kept her eyes ahead. This Xanax had too much anger to push through to really make a difference today.

"Is inventing even a job?"

"Yup."

"I just don't understand young people these days."

"That's obvious."

"Gabby, you're not being very welcoming. "

Gabby stopped and looked at her dead in the eye. "I didn't invite you."

"Hmmph." Elena loudly swallowed her judgment.

In the G-hut, Jasmine was setting the mood with incense. A beautiful woman with silky black hair that flowed over her shoulders and touched the floor was creating a sound bath. Until Gabby entered the room, it had probably been very relaxing.

Her mom leaned back and at an ear-splitting volume, said, "Ohmygawd. Isn't this a treat?"

Gabby braced herself. She looked at Jasmine and then back to her mom. She had two choices: Pretend like nothing was going on or bite the bullet. Pretending required patience, so she walked up to Jasmine and said hello.

"Gia," Jasmine trilled, "we missed you at yoga this morning. I hope it was for honeymoon reasons."

If only it had been for honeymoon reasons. Mind-blowing sex already felt like it had been a lifetime ago.

Gabby laughed like it wasn't physically painful and said, "Nope, it's door number three." She gestured to Elena. "Jasmine, this is my mom, Elena. Mom, this is Jasmine."

Elena's jaw dropped. "My goodness. You are even more beautiful in person."

Gabby should have known her mom would know everyone here. Elena was the queen of the gossip rags. TMZ was the only news she watched.

"It's so nice that you're here to support your daughter," Jasmine said diplomatically. Truthfully, she looked skeptical about Elena.

Elena smiled. "She's my only daughter."

After meditation, Jasmine pulled Gabby aside. With a meaningful glance at Elena, who was across the room, she said, "Are you okay?"

Gabby shook her head. "Sort of. No, not really. It's a lot."

"My mom is a lot, too," Jasmine said.

"To tell you the truth, I could have done without this particular surprise visit, even though it was sweet of them."

"Sit down, Gia. Lotus pose, palms up."

Gabby copied Jasmine, sitting cross-legged, albeit with her knees sticking a lot higher up in the air. Jasmine had clearly discovered stretching before the age of thirty-eight.

"Gia, I want you to repeat after me."

Gabby shut her eyes and embraced the experience. She trust-falled into the Xanax, into Jasmine's mantra. Jasmine seemed okay so far. Her only crime was marrying an absolute dick. A charming one. Gabby had also married a dick, one who wasn't charming, handsome, or nearly as rich as G, so she had no room to judge.

For a while, they hummed. It seemed silly, but Jasmine made her do it so long that she forgot herself.

"Now repeat after me: I am not alone."

Okay, Mulder.

"Repeat after me, Gia."

"Oh, oops. I am not alone."

"Even though sometimes I might wish I was."

Gabby giggled.

Together they repeated the saying, "I am not alone, even though sometimes I might wish I was."

It didn't offer any wisdom or fix, but there was solidarity in the mantra. Maybe she wasn't alone. There were other people out there being tortured by their families too.

"Misery is best shared," Jasmine said.

"Misery is best shared," Gabby repeated with feeling.

"That's not part of the mantra," Jasmine said.

"It should be. That's the truest thing you said," another voice piped up, and Gabby opened her eyes to see Naomi.

The way Naomi and Jasmine smiled at each other made Gabby believe that they'd been through it together, or at least they thought they had. Could anything be that bad with millions of dollars?

"Where were you, skipping meditation?" Jasmine gave Naomi a look that communicated some subtext that Gabby didn't understand.

"Sometimes I find weed to be more helpful than mantras," Naomi said with a smile.

"Stop it, Moni!" Jasmine exclaimed.

"What if I want to wallow?"

Gabby took a deeper glance at Naomi. What did she have to be so miserable about? The woman was in paradise, living her best life.

On the way out of the hut, Jasmine sidled up to Gabby. "Moni's up in her feelings about Amanda Duvall today. Naomi wanted her to join."

"Weren't you worried that she'd do a story about you or something?"

"Oh, we would have loved that! I tried to convince her to do a story on us, but she told me that, if we were ever in one of her stories, it would be a bad sign."

Amanda didn't do puff pieces. Gabby had noticed that.

"You don't have anything to hide?" Gabby asked, watching Jasmine's face carefully.

"Oh no! We have no secrets here." Ominously, she said, "Inner-G is not a place for someone with things to hide."

CHAPTER 26

1900 hours, getting ready for the soiree, honeymoon cottage

Jasmine and Genesis were having a thing, a soiree of some type. "You are invited to Together." Jasmine and Genesis were so big that they didn't need to make sense, and you knew it was important because it only had one vague name. It was the Madonna of parties, or a café circa 2010, when everything had a name like "Toast" or "Bread." Tonight, it was "Together."

From an event planning perspective, the concept made sense. For most of the retreat, the couples had been separated. The women had been doing yoga and learning... Gabby had been trying to get laid without commitment and spy on all the other members, so she couldn't say what they'd been learning. It hadn't stuck. The men had mostly been shirtless and spear fishing or something. It looked a little *Lord of the Flies*, or maybe just CrossFit—same difference.

Gabby slid into a cocktail dress that must have cost the same as her monthly mortgage and struggled to zip it halfway up. Markus appeared in a button-down shirt, only half buttoned with the sleeves rolled up, highlighting his chest and forearms, his best features. He had on pants, but it was hard to tear her eyes away from his chest.

Enjoying a fantasy date was a big ask after the amount of drama they'd suffered today, but they were professionals. Gabby smiled softly at Markus, testing the waters.

Markus didn't smile back.

"Markus..." she said.

They needed to talk.

"In a couple of years, we're going to laugh at this," she said.

"I don't know, Gabby. I'm—" He took a breath. "Let's just finish this mission and get everyone out safe."

She turned the flashlight taser over in her hand. It sent her heart pitter-pattering, and then her head jumped in with thoughts.

"How did it go today?" he asked, softening his tone a touch.

"Eh. It went. I think I'm getting closer to Jasmine." She groaned. "I wish they weren't so supportive of Phil and my mom. It's exhausting." Genesis had been inspired by the concept of support from family and friends.

"Genesis must not have a family, the way he's romanticizing it," Markus joked. "I mean, I love my family, but—"

Well, there was something they had in common. Gabby snorted at the cynicism. It was a relief to be able to let down and shit-talk her family. "I guess that's why it's important to have friends." She would give anything to talk through all this with Justin. He could make sense of anything.

Maybe she was imagining it, but it seemed a flash of sadness crossed Markus's expression.

"So, uh, you and G seem pretty close." Now was as good a time as any to make things worse. Might as well ask about his weird behavior.

Markus shrugged off the statement. "It's kind of depressing. Here we are fishing and talking about women, and it's pretty likely to end in an arrest."

That did sound like the worst bromance ever. "You think he's guilty?"

"No, but I can't not consider the possibility, right?"

"There's not anything you haven't told me?" She searched his face for signs he was lying. "You're not planning anything on the sly with G?"

"Nope, nothing." He looked her dead in the eye. God, that man could lie.

Genesis's version of black-tie was slightly less naked than normal. He was wearing a loose shirt with not a single button buttoned. For the occasion, he had some of those white shells braided into his beard, the kind high school boys used to wear in the nineties. The man was barely civilized, and she had to admit that she saw the appeal.

Jasmine, who was dressed like a redheaded Aphrodite, clinked her glass with a fork. "Welcome to Together, everyone."

Genesis took the fork from his wife, leaving her standing with a glass, about to make a speech. Jasmine smiled tightly, like she was having difficulty stretching her lips around all that rage.

I see you, girl. Gabby had been there.

Maybe this is just how a Hollywood marriage to an action star worked. Gabby understood having your head turned around, feeling mad one minute and forgiving the next. Marriage was complicated, and so were the individuals in it. And Genesis was a lot: cult leader, action star, claimed to generate waves with his heartbeat. That was too much ego to fit into one marriage.

"Tonight, we are celebrating Togetherness," he said. "We will no longer do everything separately. From this point on, we will be together."

Why did that sound like a threat?

"Instead of unburdening yourself to this shell, you will tell your partner your secrets, your fears, your hopes. You can't forge a true connection with someone without honesty."

Jasmine was no longer attempting to smile. She looked like she might kill him. He looked like he wouldn't see it coming.

Genesis held the shell high and then smashed it to the ground. It cracked in two as it hit a lava rock below. Gabby jumped back as a jagged piece skipped across the hard, packed sand.

"You are one step closer to becoming a Power Couple," Genesis said. "Tonight, we're celebrating that achievement with Together."

"Four fists, two hearts, one unstoppable force!" Phil chanted the tagline to *Power Couple*.

G's energy was off, a little too high, in danger of spinning in the wrong direction. He almost shouted "Never not together!" in answer to Phil's chant, confirming Gabby's opinion that the movie probably wasn't for her.

Phil sidled up next to her. "You look nice...Gia."

What circle of hell was this?

"Gia and George have brought togetherness to another level," Genesis added. "Gia's mother and even her ex-husband have joined them in support." Genesis looked at Phil. "This toast goes to Phil. Way to put your own feelings and pride aside to support the mother of your children and the greater good."

If only.

"If more men could be like you, we would be a better world."

Gabby started choking on her champagne.

Phil gave a deep nod and held his cocktail in the air.

Gabby took the opportunity to tell him, "Phil, if you were actually here to support me, it would be different."

"How am I not here to support you?" he said, sloshing liquid out of his drink. "I'm supporting our family. You know, we were a power couple before, Gabby."

She looked at him. "Phil, to be a power couple, both members of the couple have to have power. It can't just be one person with all the power while the other one does the laundry." Trad wives made it look good, but real laundry wasn't nearly as satisfying. Plastic baskets with broken handles, unmatched socks, period underwear, and no one ever said thanks.

Phil scowled. "That's not what we were."

It was, though. He knew it as well as she did.

"Enjoy the food and the music." Genesis held his glass up again and said, "Let's eat."

Back in the day, before kids, she and Phil had gone to Red Lobster on Fridays after work. Now Gabby's mouth watered at the sight of the tables piled high with a seafood feast that would put the chain meals to shame.

"Gabby," Markus caught her attention, "let's grab a place by G and Jasmine."

Smart move, Markus.

She and Markus and her ex–Red Lobster date sat down with Jasmine, who couldn't seem to focus on conversation. G didn't sit down at all. He was circulating, clapping people on backs, but obviously distracted, scanning the crowd instead of actively listening to anyone. He was looking for someone.

As Gabby dug into her sushi, Phil said, "The finances on this place just don't make sense. The coastal property, luxury everything. And is it just me, or does this All You Can Eat Seafood spread remind anyone of—"

He didn't even have to say it.

"God, I miss those biscuits," Gabby said, with true feeling.

Phil caught her eye and said, "Me too." For a second, they were both back in 2010 when things hadn't sucked.

The boxed make-at-home version had never turned out as well. Same went for their marriage, it turned out.

Phil gestured to the table of seafood. "All you can eat shrimp— that's how Red Lobster went down."

Markus said, "They declared bankruptcy, but they're still around. They weathered the storm."

Phil nodded meaningfully, like that could be them, and Gabby quickly said, "I'm sure it's not as good as before. Sometimes you have to know when to call it." She was looking right at Phil.

Phil was right back to finances, though. "What does it cost to stay here? Are the guests paying *that* much?"

Phil wouldn't know. The EOD was picking up his tab.

"I don't know the international tax situation. Maybe they've found some loopholes." Phil popped a shrimp in his mouth. Just like the old days.

G stalked toward them, nothing casual about him. "Have you seen Sheridan today?"

Gabby shook her head. "No. Is something wrong?"

"She hasn't shown up for anything." He glanced around. "Where is she?"

"I'm sure she's at her cottage," Jasmine said.

"Her stuff is all there. She's gone."

"You need to drop it, G," Jasmine said. She walked off as if to get another cocktail, but it was really just because she couldn't deal with her husband. Gabby could read the signs.

She and Markus exchanged a glance. Two things: 1) G seemed legitimately upset, which was a point in his favor regarding the attempted murder-slash-break-in that had happened earlier. 2) Gabby lost her train of thought. It'd come back to her.

A few minutes later, Genesis sat down. He dropped his head between his knees and rubbed his hands through his hair until it was super messed up. "Fuuuuuuuck."

Phil was seated next to him and looked over while eating a shrimp. "You know, I loved you in that movie."

"*Power Couple*?"

"No."

"*G-Force*, that was so fucking cool."

"Wasn't that the one about guinea pigs?" Gabby asked. She was sure she'd watched a *G-Force* movie with the kids.

Phil shook his head with disdain. "No. It's the one with Genesis where he's jumping out of planes from extra-high altitude into danger zones."

Gabby held up a hand before they went on a plot deep-dive that was even weirder than the one she was experiencing. "I'm sure she's okay, G."

"Where the fuck is she? It's not like she went to the mall."

"I heard she went into San Juan de Miguel to meet a friend," Gabby said.

"Really?" He scanned the group again. "People were already upset that I brought her down here. Jasmine accused me of kidnapping her. She loves it though. I thought so, at least."

As she suspected, Genesis wasn't the best with consent, but his intent was good.

A man of action, he stood up. "I'm going to call the police."

Gabby's throat constricted. "Don't just yet. She's visiting a friend, and it'll be a lot of fuss for nothing." Gabby didn't want to explain to the local authorities that she'd hidden Sheridan with her mother, especially given that Valentina hadn't approved that particular move.

"Jasmine's worried about the resort's reputation. She's worried someone will bring up—" He ran his hands through his hair again and groaned.

"What is she worried about?" Markus asked. He and Gabby waited with bated breath.

Phil talked over any answer that might have come. "These shrimp are great. What's in this sauce?"

Gabby stroked the taser in her pocket.

"I'm calling." Genesis stood up definitively and headed toward Jasmine, where they began exchanging words and angry looks.

Uh-oh.

The angry looks escalated to violent gesturing. Gabby couldn't hear everything they were saying, but it was getting louder by the minute. The music paused at just the right time. A "NO!" from Jasmine punctuated a jazzy number with a flamenco beat.

Things were coming to a head, and the guests couldn't ignore it anymore. Almost everyone was watching like it was a reality TV show. Some people were pretending not to listen, but conversation had stopped.

"Together" had been the wrong name for this party.

Markus reached for Gabby's knee under the table, not in a

sexy way but more to get her attention. He gestured with his head toward the buildings away from the party, and Gabby followed his thinking.

This was the perfect moment to sneak out and snoop around the rooms.

Gabby tracked down her mom. "Mom, Markus isn't feeling well, and we're going back to the room. Please let me know if I miss anything exciting."

No one was better suited to catching the hot goss than her mother.

CHAPTER 27

It's been a long day, the Togetherness Soiree, 2300 hours

Markus and Gabby left "Together" as quietly as they could and made a beeline for G and Jasmine's place. The mansion-iest mansion presided over the party from atop a cliff a short way down the beach.

Gabby's dress and pumps were the wrong choice for anything but a cocktail party. She slipped the shoes off and scurried along the hydrangea-lined path, trying to avoid rocks. Why had she worn heels?

"Maybe we should check someone else's room first," Markus said, "You already searched G's office."

"I overheard Jasmine talking at the tea party. She does all of her actual work from her walk-in closet. There's probably a computer or an iPad or something in there."

When they arrived at G and Jasmine's door, everything was quiet. That was good, but the house was locked.

"How are we going to get in?" Gabby peered through the window into the empty house.

With a self-satisfied smile, Markus punched the code in and swung the door open for her like it was no big deal. "Madame."

"How'd you do that?" Gabby glanced at him with a hefty appreciation. Nothing was sexier than a competent man in a tux.

"I watched G enter the code last time," he said, like it was no big deal.

In the interest of being efficient, they bypassed the kitchen and great room and headed up the stairs to the main bedroom, which occupied the entire second floor of the mansion. It was everything you'd expect it to be. Floor-to-ceiling windows overlooking the ocean. A private deck with sliding doors that let in the noise of the waterfall spilling onto the rocks below.

Gabby put her hands on her hips and looked around. "Do you like it?" she asked. To her mind, it was beautiful but not very cozy or welcoming.

Markus stopped to appreciate the room. "It's big, nice lighting, but where's the TV?"

"I know, right?" It wasn't a space designed for regular people, which made sense, given that Jasmine and Genesis weren't very regular. "I like mine better. Justin really did a great job."

"Oh, you like your bedroom better than this?" He angled a look at her.

"You should see—" she started to say before cutting herself short.

"Should I?" He raised a brow.

Gabby made a show of looking out the window and testing the sliding doors. "I like the deck, though." She was not thinking about the deck, and Markus was boring a hole through her back with his gaze. She didn't need to be a psychic to feel that.

More gruffly, he said, "There," and made toward what must be Jasmine's closet.

The term "closet" didn't really reflect the room. Her closet was the size of a Blockbuster Video. After the party earlier, Gabby was going down an early aughts rabbit hole.

The back wall was nothing but designer clothes, racks of shoes that looked like they'd never been worn, and more bikinis than a person could wear in a year. There were framed photos of Jasmine's modeling days, including one of her kneeling on the beach and making bedroom eyes into the camera with her arms crossed over her breasts. The frothy surf crashed over her shoulders.

Gabby said, "I feel like the ocean is cumming on her back in that one. Am I wrong?"

"No, I believe that was the artistic intent," Markus said dryly.

"And if it's a swimsuit ad, where's the swimsuit?" Gabby asked.

"That one is for Inner Beauty's new fragrance line."

Gabby found Jasmine's office in the form of a small desk tucked against the wall, between a display of purses and jewelry. At first glance, it looked like a makeup desk, but there were no brushes or powders to be seen. Tucked in a drawer, Gabby found some snapshots and a sleek Apple laptop.

She thumbed through the photos, mostly pictures of Genesis and Jasmine dressed up for various occasions. Then there were pics of her and some of the girls. Selfies of her and Naomi with smiles plastered across their faces. Then she found one of Naomi, Jasmine, and Amanda Duvall with the same big smiles. Amanda looked like Inner-G material.

"How about a USB?" she asked. "Do we have one?"

Markus searched his pockets. She saw him come up with a condom but no USB drive.

He saw that she'd seen. They locked eyes for a moment, neither saying anything. If it had been yesterday, they definitely would have made a joke or maybe made use of it.

Markus shoved it back in his pocket. "Let's just take the whole laptop. We'll return it later."

After a cursory search of the premises for Sheridan's phone, they were ready to skedaddle. Just as they were shutting the front door behind them, Genesis appeared, looking downtrodden.

"Hey," he said, barely glancing up.

Gabby started stammering. "Oh, hi ... We were just looking for you." Which didn't make any sense after she said it because they knew damn well that Genesis was at Together, the worst party that Inner-G had ever hosted.

He gave a nod, seemingly unconcerned that they were leaving his house. "Well, you found me."

Gabby tucked the computer under her arm more tightly.

"Want a drink?" Genesis asked. With a heavy sigh, he said, "I know we're a dry resort, but I need a drink." Genesis looked ten years older than he had earlier that night.

Gabby and Markus exchanged a glance. She thought they came to a nonverbal agreement—definitely not staying.

Just as she said, "No," he said, "Yes," which about summarized their communication. With a shrug, she said, "Just one."

Genesis opened the door for them and ushered them over to his bar. He poured two fingers of whiskey into highball glasses for each of them. "Together was a bust. Jasmine is off with the girls, not talking to me." Genesis looked at Gabby. "I thought you might be with them."

"Sorry, man," Markus said, clapping him on the back. "Some nights are like that."

"It feels like everything is falling apart." He threw back the whiskey. "Did I tell you I was set to make *Power Couple 2*?"

"Really? That's awesome." Markus sounded truly happy for him.

G shook his head. "The finances are falling apart."

"Can't you fund it?" Gabby asked.

G shook his head. "No, we just look rich. The outside investors aren't coming through."

Phil's comment about the All You Can Eat shrimp buffet crossed her mind.

After one more drink than they agreed to, Markus said, "I'm going to walk Gia back to the cottage. If you want, I'll meet you for another drink after."

G waved him off. "I'll see you in the morning." He gave Markus a hug. "Thanks for being here for me, man."

"Same," Markus answered.

Back at the honeymoon cottage, they made quick work of duplicating the hard drive.

Just as they were finishing, the phone rang. It was Valentina. Gabby grimaced because this wasn't going to be good.

"At least we have the hard drive," Markus said, sounding unconvinced.

"Agents?" Valentina said. "Are you both there?"

"Yes."

"Good, because I want both of you to hear how fucking disappointed I am. What the hell happened today? I was expecting a psychic to get off a plane no later than twenty-three hundred hours EST, and we have no psychic and no communication from you."

Markus rubbed the back of his neck like he was trying to get a knot out.

"She refused to leave, Agent Monroe," Gabby said. "She believes she's being targeted by President Simon."

Valentina was silent for a beat. "Where the hell is this coming from?"

Gabby started to explain, and Valentina cut her off. "That's absurd. You need to get her off that resort and on a plane to Washington."

"We did duplicate Jasmine Love's computer tonight."

"That's fine, but you disobeyed a direct order to evacuate. This is about chain of command. When your senior officer says go, you GO. When the president of the United States says to move, you fucking hustle. What did you do?"

Gabby was silent.

"You went to a party and copied a hard drive. You continued with the mission against direct orders. Sheridan Lane is supposed to be in Washington, DC, and she is still on the fucking resort in the Azores."

Uh . . . that was all true.

"This is the simplest, most luxurious mission that anyone at the EOD has ever been assigned, and you two are screwing it up. I could have asked an intern to do this job." With finality, she said, "You're done."

"But—"

"No 'buts.' You're off the case. I'm placing you on administrative leave, effective immediately, and expediting your paperwork. Do not leave that cottage and wait for evacuation."

"Val—"

"Sit tight and don't do a damn thing until we get there."

"We found—"

"I don't want to hear it. You are civilians now, and if you do anything, you will be arrested. So stay put or say hello to the Portuguese government for me."

The call went dead.

CHAPTER 28

0000, late at night, honeymoon cottage

Were we just fired?" Gabby was shell-shocked. She hadn't
been fired since she worked at Chili's in the early aughts.

"Not yet," Markus said, "but expect to be when we get back."

Gabby blinked back tears. This mission had taken a hard turn.

"I'm going to have that drink with G," Markus said. Shoulders
slumped and looking generally defeated, he took his leave.

Damn it. Damn it. Damn it. They had lost their jobs, and it
was her fault. And now she was supposed to sit in the room and
wait to be evacuated. It was humiliating. Poor her. Poor Markus.

Gabby had done fucked up good this time.

She sat there for a few minutes before coming to the conclusion
that she wasn't going to give up that easily. Gabby slipped on her
new favorite pair of sweats (thank you, Jasmine), her Crocs (eh,
Kyle), grabbed the laptop, and hoofed it to Phil's room. Markus
had gone back to have another drink with Genesis, so she didn't
even need to explain that she was going to her ex's room for a work
question and not because she was in a dark place having regrets.
Sure, she'd just been fired, but was she low enough to relive Red
Lobster? No biscuits were that good.

Gabby was ready to fight the good fight for justice and for her sweet, sweet government bennies. Lucas still needed braces. She padded through the night, her route barely lit. The paths were intended for daytime use, not for spies darting about at midnight. She clutched her engagement taser tightly. Palm trees swaying in the breeze and ocean waves met her ears.

The main building was empty, the front desk unmanned. When Aspen, etc., went to bed, the main building shut down hard. The cheerful "ding" of the elevator's arrival sounded like an alarm in the night.

Upstairs, Phil answered the door in much the same shape as Genesis, reeking of whiskey and regret. He was wearing an old T-shirt from his college days, a shirt Gabby herself had worn to bed many a night. It was threadbare and a little stained, kind of like Gabby and Phil.

"Gabs?" he said, as much a question as a greeting.

"Hey, Phil, I was wondering if you could help me out?"

"With what?" He drew his eyebrows together in concern. "Is Markus, er George, or..." Phil gave up on the name. "Something happen to him?"

"He's fine," Gabby answered brusquely. "I have a finance question."

He glanced out the window at the darkness outside. "At this time of night?"

Gabby could see the wheels spinning in his head, so she said, "I can't sleep unless I figure it out, and I saw your light on."

When he looked unconvinced, she reiterated. "Just finances, Phil."

"Oh-kay." He wandered back to the couch and put his feet up. "Hit me."

She sat down next to him and pulled up the laptop. How to phrase it . . . "Jasmine was trying to figure out the finances of Inner-G. She offered me a discount if I could sort through some of it."

"She asked *you* for financial help."

Gabby flashed a self-deprecating smile. "She knows I'm an executive assistant at an investment firm and seems to think I know more than I do. I could really use the discount. These rooms are expensive."

With a shrug, Phil took the computer. "Sure, I'm not doing anything else." Clearly, Phil's eyes on this were illegal, but if Valentina hadn't fired her, she would have used internal help. Now Phil was her only option.

Gabby got him to the page of resort financials. "Do you see anything suspicious here?"

"Um, apart from insane deposits." He started laughing at something. "What the fuck are these people up to?"

"I thought maybe that was normal. They're operating on a different level."

He nodded and looked a little deeper. He pointed to a line. "Look here, you have a twenty-million-dollar deposit into this account a couple of months ago. A five-million-dollar deposit another month back."

Those numbers sounded big, but everything here was so outsized.

He spent a little more time scanning documents. "The numbers don't add up. I don't see how they're bringing in enough to pay for this place."

"So where's the mystery money coming from?"

"Some holding corp, PowCup Financial."

"What's that?" Phil might as well be speaking Klingon when he started talking finance.

Phil slipped into his business voice. "A holding corporation owns a controlling interest in other companies, usually, but without offering goods or services themselves."

Aka, rich people stuff.

"Who owns PowCup?" Gabby asked.

"How should I know?" He slumped back onto the couch, done with his analysis. "Ask Jasmine or G." Phil narrowed his eyes. "What's really going on? Is Jasmine leaving G? She's trying to secure her assets before divorce, isn't she?" Phil threw back the rest of his whiskey and swirled the remaining ice cubes. "I guess I'm not surprised after tonight."

"Probably," Gabby said, letting Phil supply whatever answers kept him figuring out what was actually going on. "Don't say anything. It's on the down-down-low."

"It always is."

Not ready to give up, Gabby pulled up Jasmine's email and scrolled through, looking for financial or legal entries, anything besides back-and-forth with Naomi and Lana. Maybe there'd be a quick-and-dirty answer about where that money came from.

One with the subject line "Red dye number six" caught her eye. The message suggested a number of more expensive but natural red dyes for the Inner Glow blusher, to which Jasmine responded, "Stick with number six." Gabby was pretty sure that ingredient wasn't on the packaging.

After another twenty uninteresting emails about resort business, she came across one with the subject line: Power Couple 2. The author of the email, supremeleader@koreanre.co.kp, wanted to know when he was going to get to see *Power Couple 2*. Gabby hadn't realized that one was in the works.

Genesis had responded, "Soon. It's going great."

She kept scrolling and showed Phil an address that sounded business-y.

"Linkman and Schmidt," he said. "I've worked with that firm before."

"Really?"

"Down in the Caymans. Brad and I play golf sometimes." He made a thinking face and amended, "Well, like three times."

How many golf games were required for what she needed? "Can you ask him? Would he know?"

"Yeah, but he's not gonna tell me."

"Can you give it a shot?"

With a shrug, he said, "Fine, I'll try." Phil was trying. He was trying really hard to time travel back to 2010 when Red Lobster had been financially solvent and things had been "good." Gabby felt guilty for leading him on for a second, not that she had promised a damn thing, but let it pass when she remembered how often Phil had done the dishes: never.

After some general "Bro" texts regarding golf and some chick named Jenny, Phil got to it:

> **Phil:** Yo Brad. Know anything about PowCup?
> **Brad:** PupCup duuuuuude.
> **Phil:** ...
> **Brad:** I'm not here to say anything bro but daaaayyyum.

"It was worth a try," Gabby said. "Thanks for the help."

Instead of heading back to the cottage, she padded through the dark to G's. As she'd hoped, he and Markus were still there, and Jasmine wasn't back yet.

"Hey, boys," Gabby said casually. "I've come to collect my fiancé. I need him."

"Lucky man, George. Go get her!" G hooted with drunken enthusiasm.

"You boys finish up," Gabby said, "I'm gonna run to the bathroom."

While Markus wrapped up with G, she tucked Jasmine's computer back where she'd found it. Maybe she was going to be fired upon arrival, but at least she was giving it her best shot.

Markus was a little drunk. "I'm not mad at you, Gabs."

She took his arm. "I'm not mad at you either. I mean, depending. Have you done anything I don't know about?"

With a laugh, he said, "Noooo!"

"Markus," she said, "I know you're drunk, but in all seriousness, I'm going to finish this mission and get us our jobs back."

"Gabby—" He let her name hang in the air, not jumping up and down with enthusiasm about her proposal, but also not saying no.

"Are you in?"

"Do I have to be?"

"Actually, yes. Our cover is all about the wedding. You can't give up before me."

"You could switch me out for Phil."

"Markus." She stopped walking.

Halfway back to the cottage, he relented. "Might as well. What else am I going to do, fly home and meal prep?"

She laughed a little too hard. "Your lunches are so dumb. All those little containers."

"You know you're jealous," he teased.

"Of course I'm jealous."

At the door to the honeymoon cottage, her stomach flip-flopped with nerves. After their day from hell—attempted murder, her mom and Phil arriving, all the spying, and now getting thrown off the case—she couldn't handle awkwardness with him too. But it was inevitable.

The porch light cut across his face, leaving him partially illuminated. "Markus, don't sleep on the couch tonight. I don't know what we're doing, but I don't want to be alone in bed. I hate this awkwardness." When he didn't jump in with a response, she said, "We don't have to do anything. I just..."

"Me too, Gabs. It's been a lot. Let's just—"

"I just want to lie down, shut my eyes, and forget our troubles for a few hours."

He reached out. "I've got you. I want that too."

Five minutes later, she lay with her head on Markus's chest as he pulled her in close. With his warm, solid body pressed against hers, she was overcome by a sense of peace, especially after their hot mess of a day. Lying to her family, lying to the people at the resort, lying to Markus.

Remembering how she'd started the day following him around, ready to report him to Valentina, filled her with shame. She squeezed him harder, overcome by tenderness. If they made it through today, what couldn't they do?

CHAPTER 29

0600 hours, waking up with regret, the honeymoon cottage

Gabby woke up before Markus. In the light of a new day, her uncertainty was gone. She'd had a decent amount of sleep, a satisfying cuddle, and was ready to Be More, Do More her way out of this mess. No one was going to save Gabby's ass but Gabby, so she might as well get to it.

The Top Gun action hero always went rogue and got fired until they saved the day, and the boss saw how great they were and begged them to come back. When she thought about it, she was just following the script. Lose big. Win big. Get hired back.

She buzzed Geeves for coffee and breakfast because, if you have a butler, you should use him.

"Markus." She walked back into the bedroom with a cup of coffee for him. "Are you ready to save the day?"

He rolled in her direction without sitting up. In a tired voice, he said, "Gabby, we're government employees."

"Not anymore," she reminded him cheerfully. "It's time to get up and action hero our way back into your ex-wife's good graces and catch us some bad guys." Her voice crackled with a little too much energy, like she'd finally accessed her Inner-G and added caffeine.

Markus gave a muffled laugh but sat up enough to accept the coffee.

After she'd chugged three G-shots and wolfed down some sort of high-protein, raw, vegan something or other, she gave Markus a salute because that's how keyed up she was. Risking prison to save their jobs and the mission was hitting her harder than a couple of lines of coke, energy-wise.

"I'm off to plan our wedding," Gabby announced. Talking too fast, she said, "See you in . . . When will I see you next?"

"I haven't checked the schedule, but uh, Gabby, we're supposed to stay in the room and keep a low profile."

"I thought we were going to finish the mission—" She let the sentence hang.

He took a sip of coffee. "We can keep our ear to the ground, but I don't want to do anything that could be interpreted as espionage and get ourselves arrested. We are civilians and do not have the authorization or backing of the United States government to do anything that might be interpreted as espionage. Do you want to be charged with violating the Espionage Act?"

Gabby frowned.

"Do you want to end up in a Portuguese prison, Gabs?"

"No, but . . ."

He exhaled a frustrated breath. "Can we keep it light at least?"

She nodded. "I'll be careful."

Markus was right, but in some ways, the mess she was in today was easier than a regular day. No one had to go to the dentist, the kids didn't have a day off from school on a day she still had work, there wasn't a science fair, and she didn't have to cook or clean anything. The toilet wasn't clogged. Even if it was, she could call Geeves. This is probably what it felt like to have a wife. Gabby had this mission in the bag, even if she was trying to do it on the down-low.

Partway to Naomi's office, a male voice (Phil?) yelled her name. Her real name. Damn it. She was going to strangle that man.

"Gabby!" he yelled again.

Gabby looked frantically around to make sure no one else had heard and saw . . . "Justin!"

He was running across the sand like she was water in the desert or like she was his long-lost lover returned from war.

She ran toward him with her arms open. "Justin!"

He wrapped her in a huge hug and then leaned back and said, "Bitch, what is this I hear about you getting married?"

Gabby gave him a you-know-better-than-to-ask look. "Justin, I didn't think I had to tell you this is an EOD thing."

"Okay, great." He swiped his hand across his forehead in relief. "I figured, but you never know."

"If you knew, then why are you part of this weird family drama to rescue me from my own bad decisions?"

With a sly smile, he said, "How else was I going to get Hugh to go to the Azores with me?" Hugh was standing on the sensible part of the beach where your feet didn't sink, and you could still walk around without filling your shoes with sand.

Gabby sighed. She saw his point.

"And there was no stopping this family intervention. Phil—" He shook his head in despair. "That man was throwing such a bitch fit when he found out you were in the Azores getting married to Mr. Hottie. I could hear him from my patio."

Phil. Maybe she should feed him to the sharks.

"Justin, this is serious. Someone tried to kill"—she looked around for potential eavesdroppers before whispering—"Sheridan Lane."

Justin gasped dramatically and held his hand to his heart. "Not *the* Sheridan Lane."

"That's her."

He squared his shoulders and adjusted his beach bag. "Consider me on the case. I love that woman with my whole being. She is the reason that I married Hugh."

"What?"

"A column she wrote in *InStyle* ten years ago about trying new things. I was reading it at this nerdy book café when Hugh walked in. I'd never seen anyone who was less my type, and I was like— 'You know, Sheridan, maybe I will try new things.' And here we are today, nine years happily married."

Hugh looked like he was starting to burn. He didn't have an easy complexion for the outdoors.

"Have you checked into a room yet?" Gabby asked.

"Yes, it's gorgeous. I'm going to have to send the CIA a thank-you note."

"It's the EOD. We're an elite division."

"Whatever. Send them my regards. The room is very nice. Where are we going now?"

"I have to work on wedding planning," Gabby said. "My wedding is supposed to be in two days."

"Well, that isn't much time, even for a fake wedding. Or is it real?" he asked as they walked toward Hugh. "If it's real, I'm also into it. I mean—" He fanned his face.

"It's fake. Markus and I are...I don't know what we are.

We—you know." Gabby gave Justin a look that explained everything. "But now, you know?" She shrugged and sighed.

"Girl." He shook his head.

Hugh squinted at them. "What happened?"

Justin waved off the question. "I'll fill you in later, baby."

"Well, let's go plan this thing." Justin scanned the area, probably trying to gather his bearings.

"The people here are already planning it."

"*Were* planning it, you mean. There is no way I'm going to not plan your wedding. How many times is my best friend getting married?"

"This makes the second time, and it's only pretend, so three times easy."

Justin poo-pooed her statement with a wave of his hand. "Wild horses couldn't drag me away from planning this party. Where are we at with flowers, food—" Crescendo-ing with drama, he said, "the dress."

"Well, Lana Hunt is here, so she is flying out one of her Huntress dresses from Lisbon."

"Really?" He grimaced. "Are you sure about that choice?"

"What? I thought you'd be excited." How could a man who name-dropped his picnic table on the regular care about Alphonse de Picnic Table but not Lana Hunt, designer to the stars?

With his nose in the air like he was smelling something bad, he said, "She's going to have to sell me on it."

As they approached the resort's main building, Gabby whispered, "Call me Gia while we're down here. I'm Gia Glanville, an executive assistant with a couple of kids."

"They really aren't challenging you with these covers," he said.

"For once, I'd like to see them give you something like truck driver or burlesque dancer."

"Justin, stop."

"No, really. They need to challenge you."

"I'm not trying to win an Oscar!" Gabby said. "And what is this about Lana Hunt being over? I thought everyone was wearing Cuntress. Huntress, I mean. I keep forgetting the real name."

"Gabby," he said, "Cuntress is so last season. She is going to need to step it up for me to agree to it. I'd rather have you get married in a simple cover-up and a bikini."

"Why is everyone putting me in a bikini?"

"Oh, stop. You're going to look great. Now, what about venue?"

"Genesis's yacht, I guess. I haven't been, but we're supposed to be all excited that we're allowed on it."

Justin leaned back and gave her a firm look. "Okay, that, I'm down with."

"What is it with everyone and Genesis?"

Jasmine breezed into the room. "Well said, Gia. I'm glad not everyone is swooning over my husband."

"Don't worry, I'm swooning over you and your husband." With a long look, Justin said, "Forgive my honesty, but you are so hot." He held out his hand. "I'm Justin, by the way."

"Justin," Gabby said in a cautionary tone. He needed to take it from a ten to a five.

Ignoring Gabby, he asked, "What's your secret?"

"Inner Beauty, obviously."

"The product line or actual inner beauty?"

Gabby waited for Jasmine to kick him out of Inner-G for mouthing off. She hadn't seen anyone do anything but suck up to

Jasmine so far, but Jasmine only raised an eyebrow and answered, "Both."

She linked arms with Justin and said, "Let's discuss the ceremony, shall we?" And she walked ahead with Justin, leaving Gabby in their wake. Apparently, Jasmine and Justin were going to plan her wedding.

"What kind of flowers does George like?" Jasmine asked over her shoulder.

"George has never once mentioned flowers."

"Of course he hasn't. He is Lil' G."

"Gia," Justin announced, "I am so excited. This is going to be a wedding no one will ever forget."

Justin had wedding planning in hand, so Gabby decided to check on her prisoners, aka, her mom and Sheridan. Gabby found Elena in the lobby talking loudly on her phone.

"Mom! You're not supposed to have a phone here!" Gabby glanced around the room frantically. Her mom was going to be the death of her.

Her mom waved that off, "They're not serious about that one. Come on, everyone at this place kept their phone."

Come to think of it, her mom might be right about that, but still. "Try to hide it though."

Elena said, "Do you mind if I call you back? I want to hear the rest of that story, but I can't focus right now."

"No problem," the woman said loudly. "I'm on the couch all day. This ingrown toenail is killing me."

"Have you soaked it?" Elena asked, suddenly nothing but helpful.

"I think I need it cut out."

Elena cringed.

"I'll give you the name of my podiatrist. It's worth a visit even if you don't have foot problems. That man is a looker!"

OMG, Mom. Gabby face-palmed.

When Elena hung up, she asked, "What did you need to talk about? Did you call me earlier?"

"What? Of course I didn't call you. We're not even supposed to have phones!"

"Oh, I guess it didn't really sound like you. I've never heard you talk about 'counting your chickens before they hatch.'"

"What?" Was her mom talking in riddles?

"Whoever it was said something like, 'Saddle up.' Then the call broke up. I meant to ask you."

Saddle up—that sounded like Sheridan.

"Does Sheridan have your number?" Gabby asked, on a hunch.

"Oh, you're right. That does sound like something she would say."

"Have you been calling each other?"

"Just if I'm out and she needs something."

Something fishy was going on. Sheridan had told Gabby and Markus her phone was missing. Why lie about that if she wasn't hiding something? The woman could play innocent with the best of them. At this very moment, she was probably cozying up in her mom's room, arranging sales to God knows who to besmirch the reputation of President Simon, after pretending to be scared of him.

Gabby had been played. She could feel it.

"Mom, I have to run." Now that she knew she'd screwed up, all she wanted to do was rewind time, or at least fix it as fast as possible.

Did she and Markus lose their jobs protecting this con artist? Ire rose in her like mercury on a hot day.

"But what did you want to talk about?" her mom asked.

"Just stop using your phone in shared spaces!" Gabby called over her shoulder on the way to have a serious discussion with Sheridan.

Gabby was too keyed up to wait for the elevator, so she hoofed up the stairs, taking them two at a time. When no one answered, she keyed into Sheridan's room. "Hello!"

The room looked the same as earlier, except with some belongings strewn around and the scent of her mom's perfume, Opium by Yves Saint Laurent, which had always seemed to be a bold choice for a cul-de-sac mom.

No one responded to Gabby's call, so she scanned the room more thoroughly. Right there on the kitchen counter sat Sheridan's phone. Unbelievable. At least she hadn't searched every room at the resort looking for it.

She picked it up. The numeric passkey Sheridan had given her earlier worked just fine. The messages were pretty innocuous and sparse, so she went to recently dialed numbers. Her mom's number was on there. She had called one number over and over again most recently, not her mom. Gabby didn't recognize the number, so she hit redial.

With each ring, Gabby tensed. Would it be a newspaper or a reporter? What would she do when she got them on the phone? A journalist wouldn't share any information unless they thought she was Sheridan—protecting sources and all that. She had found the smoking gun, and she couldn't flub it. Her strategy: pretend to be Sheridan.

When a woman answered with a "Howdy," Gabby said, "Morning!" in a slightly rural twang. She cringed at her own bad accent, but the woman didn't seem to notice.

"I bet you're calling to check on Leonard." Before Gabby could say anything, the woman launched into an explanation of Leonard. "Oh, I had to pick up another bag of food. They were out of the kind he normally eats, but he seems to be doing okay on this other brand. It's some sort of primal kitty brand. Has he tried that before?"

"Um…"

Before Gabby could get a word in edgewise, the woman on the phone started in again. "And that darn cat won't let me cut the poop out of his fur. He's being a real pickle about that."

Gabby dropped her face into her hand. Nothing could be further from national security than Leonard's poopy tail.

To make it sound like the line had gone bad, Gabby pressed "speaker" and held it next to a running faucet. From a distance, she said, "Thanks. That sounds great."

"I can barely hear you, Sher," the cat sitter yelled through the line.

"How about now?" Gabby moved farther from the speaker.

"I'm losing you."

"I'll try back later," Gabby said and hung up.

Gabby collapsed on the couch, a little dejected. So much for an easy answer, but at least she hadn't been duped by Sheridan.

While she caught her breath and tried to figure out her next move, Sheridan came out of the bathroom.

"Agent Greene! I didn't even hear you come in!"

Gabby looked up.

"How's everything?" Gabby said. "I dropped by to check on you."

"I found my phone," she said.

"Where was it?"

"Agent Parks dropped it by."

"What?" Gabby had had about enough with Markus and his lying. "Did he say where he found it?"

Sheridan shook her head.

Markus was in hot water.

CHAPTER 30

1000 hours, midmorning, just outside Phil's room

Gabby marched over to Phil's room. Maybe he'd made some progress on the finances. Probably not, but she might as well check while she was right there.

Before she knocked, Genesis burst through the stairwell door, looking absolutely frazzled. His eyes were wild, and his man bun in disarray.

"G, are you okay?" Gabby asked.

He stopped short and ran his hands over his hair. Gabby had never seen G anxious, not even when he was arguing with Jasmine, but right now he looked freaked-the-F out.

"I need to find Sheridan." He peered down the hallway over Gabby. "Who are you visiting?" he asked, sounding suspicious.

"Phil, my ex."

"Really?"

Genesis squeezed in next to her and knocked on the door before she could.

Phil opened the door in swim trunks and no shirt, like he was about to hit the beach. She had to admit that he'd been working out.

"Hey, Phil," she said, "how're you this morning?"

He opened the door wide. "Hey, Gia, and...hey, Genesis." Phil dropped Genesis's name from his mouth with all the grace of someone delivering a ten-pound baby. "I'm surprised to see you."

"Mind if I come in?" Genesis asked, but not really.

Phil opened the door wide looking slightly more excited than confused.

After a cursory glance around the apartment, G said, "My apologies. I'm desperate to find Sheridan."

"I'll let you know if I see her," Gabby said.

And with a quick apology, Genesis was off again. "Sorry again. I'll see you both later."

"Well, that was weird," Phil said. "Also, he's going to find Sheridan if he searches your mom's room."

"Let's hope not," Gabby said, feeling good about her choice to hide Sheridan. G was way too worried.

"Sit down," Phil said. "Take a load off."

"I didn't come to stay. I was just wondering if you'd made any progress with Brad. Did you find out who's behind that holding corp?"

"Want some coffee at least?"

She glanced over his shoulder to see if he was already making some.

"I'll take that as a yes," he said with a smile that would be cute if she wasn't trying to get in and out. Phil looked like he was about to take advantage of the fact that she needed him. What she needed was to get hired back ASAP.

"Are you really getting married in two days?" he asked.

"Yes," she answered with zero hesitation.

"That means no more spousal support," he said.

Jesus. Phil was probably going to cut her off because she was getting fake married for her job that she was about to be fired from. At this point, she really needed him to kick it up a notch with the data analysis.

"Phil, do we have to talk about money right now?"

He slumped on a stool. "Is Markus a decent person? I think you should introduce me to someone who is going to live with my kids. I can't believe you ran off to marry someone without even talking to me."

"Phil, really?"

"Yeah, I'm worried. I still care about you...a lot. And the kids."

Gabby couldn't with this. She'd been trying to have a conversation with the man for fifteen years, and this was the time he chose to show up. She needed him so many other times, when she had post-partum and was trying to figure out how to breastfeed, but Kyle wouldn't latch, when the kids were little and she was trying to get back to work. She could forgive him, but she couldn't forget.

"Markus is a great guy. Very upstanding and reliable. And I don't think you want to start this game. I've seen some of the women you've been with since we divorced. They don't look like PTA members."

Phil ignored her. "What does he do for a living?"

Here they went again. "He's an inventor. Of children's toys."

Phil made a noise of discontent in the back of his throat. "Is that even a job?"

She stared down her nose at him like he had farted. It was easier than answering a question about Markus's job. "Phil, it's not like you get a vote in who I marry. This was a spontaneous decision. You weren't the first person I thought to call. But you're informed now."

"I don't think that's proper notice."

Gabby hadn't read her divorce decree recently, no, make that ever—that's what she overpaid a lawyer for. She certainly wasn't aware of the legal requirements, but she didn't think they were as serious as Phil was making them out to be.

"Phil. You left me. You moved out. Did you think I was going to stay single?"

"I didn't think you'd get married this fast." The railroad tracks formed between his eyes. "It's too fast, Gabby, and it's not like you. It took you a year to pick a paint color for the kitchen."

Damn it. All she'd wanted was a little office romance.

"And if you're signing up the kids for a weird religion, or whatever Inner-G is, then I think I get a vote in that."

"Phil—" She bit her tongue. She wanted to tell him to take a long walk off a short pier, but not until after he helped her with the financial analysis. "I need you to take a step back."

"A step back?" He raised his voice just enough to make her pulse jump. "Gabby, we were married. We have kids together. I still..."

Was he going to say he still loved her? If she asked, Geeves would probably drive Phil to the airport right now.

Gabby boxed up her emotions to refrain from screaming. This fool had endangered her whole mission with his meddling, not to mention her relationship with Markus. Actually, he might have wrecked that, or at least significantly contributed to its likely downfall.

"Gabby, I just want to say that I lo—"

"It's Gia." Gabby didn't let him finish that sentence. "And I really need to know what you found out from your Cayman Island buddy."

Like she'd flipped a switch, he changed his expression. "I think Brad might be fucking with me."

"What do you mean?"

"It's too weird. I can't even say it out loud."

"Say it."

"No. I need to double-check it. It's too dumb."

Too dumb meant it was the right answer.

"Let me talk to Brad, and I'll get back to you."

"Fine. I'll be back in an hour."

CHAPTER 31

1100 hours, Inner-G pool

Gabby left Phil's room with her head spinning. She was officially too overstimulated to solve any national security crises or get her job back. Every time she thought the answers were coming into focus, the whole board would reset.

It had seemed like Sheridan might be the prime suspect, sending pictures to the press to smear President Simon's reputation. She had the access to stories. She had opportunity. It would have tied up the case with a bow. But no, her only contact with the outside was her damn cat sitter. Leonard and his poopy tail.

Back five squares.

Genesis—his computer was clean. There was nothing of interest on there, except a lot of bad ideas for more dumb movies. The script for *Power Couple 2* had circulated around the EOD office, apparently.

Forward two squares and back another five.

Jasmine—all those huge payments were certainly suspicious. Apparently, the answer was dumb and all hinged on Brad, a guy Phil had golfed with three times. Gabby wasn't holding her breath.

The men in her life were not making this easier. Phil and his jealousy, Markus and his double-crossing. Her mom.

Just thinking of everything, Gabby stalled out so hard that she couldn't go one step farther. It's not like she wanted to sit down in the poolside chair. It was more like she wasn't able to stand any longer. Gabby succumbed to inertia and collapsed by the side of the pool in a chaise lounge. She would just live here now. It was over.

"Would you like a mocktail, ma'am?" a waiter asked.

She gave up. "Can you make it a cocktail? Charge it to my room." Valentina could buy her a drink at least.

The waiter laughed. "I'll see what I can do."

A minute later, he dropped by with an umbrella drink and handed it over with a wink.

"I might as well order the next one now," she joked. "Keep 'em coming."

He laughed. "One of those days, huh?"

"Yes."

Fuck the game. What was the point in playing? She was going to live her best life unconscious by the pool. She pulled her sunhat low over her face and sucked down a pineapple-guava-whatever.

Only halfway into her drink, she heard voices. It was her mom, Phil, and Markus. Gabby pulled the hat lower and sucked harder. What the hell was Markus doing with her mom and Phil? What fresh hell was this?

"When is the wedding?" she heard her mom ask. Gabby's mercury rose so fast that she tried to get out of the chair, but between standing up too fast, uncontrolled rage, and too much pineapple-guava-whatever, she fell out of her chair.

Markus gave her a shocked look.

"I'm working," she said from the pool deck. Even to her own ears, it sounded ridiculous. She was day drinking by the pool.

Her mom inhaled sharply. "What time is it? Are you drunk in the morning?" Looking around, Elena said, "Where did you even get the alcohol?"

Gabby wasn't sure if that was judgment or sincere inquiry.

"What are you doing?" Gabby asked, still hanging on to her glass.

"Just talking," Phil said.

Gabby narrowed her gaze.

Looking at her mom and Phil, she said, "I need you two to stay out of the way. You both showed up uninvited to interfere in my life and..." Gabby couldn't say anything else out loud because, even if she was about to be let go, she was still a spy, at least for today.

Instead, she said, "I'm so mad at you two!" She sounded like a child with a limited vocabulary, but it felt good to get it out.

Her mom looked shocked. Phil shrugged.

"I'm done," Gabby yelled. "Don't talk to me for the rest of the trip." She was gesturing too wildly with her second drink, and some of it sloshed over the rim. Whatever the waiter had put in this cocktail was serious. Or maybe it was hitting her harder after two days of healthy living. Her body no longer recognized alcohol.

Markus gave Gabby a hand and helped her to stand. He brought her in for a hug. "It's okay. We're gonna get through this."

"Are you sure?" she asked, tears pricking the back of her eyes. It didn't feel like they were going to get through any of it intact.

The voice of reason, Markus said, "I think this has been stressful for all of us. Weddings are difficult. If we could all just relax and support each other."

Gabby snorted. They weren't even getting married.

Her mom didn't look sold on anything. "Wait till I tell Mason about how unwelcoming you've been to me when I only came down to help."

To help—now that was funny. "Who's Mason?" Gabby asked. "Do you mean the dog sitter?"

"I tell Mason everything. I have a better relationship with him than I do with you."

That wouldn't be hard.

Gabby tried to recall a Mason. He'd been a neighbor for a long time, one of those older men with a lot of weird opinions on everything, the kind of guy you couldn't get to stop talking once he'd started.

"Mason brought Prince to the vet last week after a chocolate scare. He didn't have to do that, but he did. You didn't even invite me to your wedding."

An idea smacked Gabby right between the eyes. If her mom was buddy-buddy with Mason, then maybe, just maybe . . .

"Ohmygod. I have to go." She just needed to quickly call Sheridan's cat sitter and see if Sheridan had a Mason in her life too.

Her mom looked extremely disgruntled.

"Thank you, Mom!"

"Gabby, are you hormonal? What is going on with you? Where are you going now?" Her mom called after her, but Gabby was already headed back to the second floor.

Markus trotted after her.

Gabby kept her head down, focused on the mission. She wanted to take the stairs, but the pineapple-guava-whatever had been stronger than she'd thought, so she hit the button on the elevator.

Once inside, Markus pulled the emergency stop button. "What are you doing?"

"I have a hunch. You'll see." She made angry eyes at him. "Sheridan told me you returned her phone. Why didn't you tell me that? Why didn't you tell me where you found it?"

"Sorry," he said, "it slipped my mind. After getting fired, it didn't seem like it mattered anymore."

"Oh, it mattered," she said.

"Gabby," he said sharply, "what about 'sit in your hotel room and wait to be evacuated,' didn't you hear?"

"All of it," Gabby retorted. "What part of *Die Hard* did you miss? The part where Bruce Willis is abandoned by the department and then does the right thing on his own? Or *Beverly Hills Cop*, *Lethal Weapon*. There is nothing more American than a rogue cop. It's who we are."

Gabby was a little drunk, but she was also right.

"This isn't a movie," Markus said.

"If Glen Powell got fired, he wouldn't quit. End of story." She'd seen most of the Glen Powell movies on Netflix.

"Who's Glen Powell?"

"He's in everything the last couple of years. I don't totally get it. I mean, he's cute and all." She took a breath to stop the rambling. "But anyway, you can thank me when you get your job back." She depressed the Stop Elevator. They rose to the second floor, and the doors opened, everything normal but them.

She marched down the hall to her mom and Sheridan's place.

Sheridan answered the door right away in one of her mom's shirts, with her hair piled in a messy bun. "Agent Greene, what are you doing here again?"

"I'm here for security reasons," Gabby said. "I need to see your phone."

"Fine," Sheridan said, "I don't know what you want with it, though." Sheridan didn't look worried at all.

When Sheridan handed it over and unlocked it upon Gabby's request, Gabby hit redial on the cat sitter.

"What is Lainey going to tell me?" Gabby asked Sheridan, doing her best impersonation of a hard-boiled detective.

Sheridan groaned. "Ugh, I shared too much."

"What do you mean?"

"I've been a little bored. Lainey asked me to tell her about everyone here, and I blabbed my theory about Naomi and Jasmine." She cocked her head. "Well, it's not really a theory. They just don't talk about it openly."

The pieces in Gabby's mind reshuffled to see the picture: the way Naomi and Jasmine looked at each other, the snapshots in Jasmine's closet, and that time Naomi had finished Jasmine's sentence (just once, but still).

They must have been the women Gabby had overheard the night she was hiding in the closet. Two women making out. One of them had mentioned iMoan...

"I was chatting about Jasmine's affair," Sheridan said. "Lainey has a big mouth, but I certainly didn't sell anything."

"Did you tell your cat sitter anything else?"

Sheridan shook her head.

"Has that story gone public?"

Gabby wasn't sure, but it seemed like there was a good chance that Lainey had been doing a lot more than cleaning Leonard's poopy tail.

"I'm taking your phone," Gabby said.

Sheridan handed it over.

"If we clear you, you can have it back. At the moment, it's evidence."

After they shut the door on Sheridan, Gabby said, "What do you think? Did Lainey cause all the trouble?"

Markus chewed his lip. "I would have HQ look into Lainey, but that's not an option. If Valentina finds out we're doing EOD work, she will have the Portuguese authorities arrest us. You are not lying low, Gabby."

"If you hadn't been talking to Genesis behind my back for this whole mission, I'd be more inclined to trust you."

Markus stopped in place. "What did you say?"

"You heard me."

CHAPTER 32

1300 hours, Naomi's office

If Markus didn't want to help, Gabby could handle this investigation on her own. She could Be More, Do More without a man. After fifteen years of marriage, she was used to that.

Maybe Markus was scared of rotting in a European jail, but Gabby was more scared of returning home without a job or benefits. What was she going to do if this didn't work out? Work at Bloomingdale's or as a Walmart greeter? She might have to go back to school and finish her degree and...do what? Gabby wanted to be a spy.

Her mission: Find Jasmine and get to the bottom of this affair. Sheridan's cat sitter might be leaking some information, but Gabby had difficulty believing that was the whole story.

Gabby headed toward where she'd last seen Jasmine: Naomi's office.

Before she could see them, she could hear them. Justin was still there with Naomi. "Absolutely no pastels!" he was saying.

"It's a wedding. It's supposed to be soft and romantic. Pastels are soft and romantic."

"Gia's a Scorpio," Justin shot back.

Gabby poked her head in. "I'm looking for Jasmine."

"Gia, do you like pink? Be honest."

Once Justin brought up signs, there was no talking to him. It was like arguing about religion. For him, it was a question of faith, and if you didn't have it, you were probably going to hell, and most likely a Sagittarius. (His most significant ex was a Sag, which apparently had nothing to do with why he didn't trust Sagittariuses. Yeah right, Justin.)

A sudden moment of perspective struck Gabby. Everyone was just looking for answers, for comfort. That's what all of this was. The people at Inner-G trying to tap into their G. The president talking to a psychic. So many people talking to a psychic. Religion. Astrology. Even marriage. Phil running home to her like she would save him. Gabby would like some answers too, but where was she going to put her faith?

Her mouth still hanging open, her opinion on pink not yet voiced, Justin said, "Well, Gia doesn't like pink. At least that shade of pink."

Dear god, maybe they could compromise.

"You guys are doing great," she said. "Thanks, Justin."

"You are going to be such a beautiful bride," he said. "I would never miss one of your weddings."

"Do either of you know where Jasmine is?"

"She went home."

A plan emerged, and by plan, she meant that she was going to walk up to Jasmine and ask her if the rumor was true. She almost wished it wasn't. What did Naomi have to do with anything? This one was coming out of nowhere.

Ten minutes later, Gabby stood at the door to Jasmine and Genesis's place. She was poised to knock when a raised voice stopped her in her tracks.

"You can't call the cops," Jasmine said. "Gia said Sheridan went to town to see a friend."

"She left her purse!" G retorted. "Where's she going without money?"

Jasmine huffed. Gabby heard someone violently reorganizing some objects in the living room.

"She's a psychic. Psychics are not dependable."

"I don't know," G said. "Her whole thing is common sense."

"Just go surfing or something. I need space."

"Why is everything a problem lately?" G said with a frustrated exhalation. Angry footsteps approached before the door swung open. The Big G almost walked right into her.

"Oh, hi!" Gabby said, taking a step back to avoid a collision. "I was just stopping by to ask Jasmine a question."

When he saw her, G took a breath. Ignoring that she might have heard the argument, he said, "She's inside."

"Thanks."

"Did you say Sheridan went into town?" he asked.

"Yep." Gabby smiled. "She was excited to meet some friend or other."

And then he was off, probably to soak in the wave pool.

"See you later," she called after his retreating form.

She pushed into the house. "Jasmine," she called.

The living room was a mix of magical tropical garden and luxury accommodations, but here was Jasmine slumped in the chair at the edge of the water feature that ran through the center of the house, looking devastated, and with good hair to boot. You weren't supposed to be devastated in a multi-million-dollar mansion. You were supposed to be able to work through the small problems.

"Is everything okay?" Gabby sat down in a chair next to her. The creek burbled around gray river stones.

"Eh." Jasmine shrugged. "It's a little rough at the moment. I'm struggling."

Gabby smiled softly. "I'm sorry. It's probably hard. You two have to be perfect all the time to be the Power Couple."

"Tell me about it." Jasmine huffed out a laugh. "I'm not even sure whom I'm married to anymore, who we are."

Gabby let her have the space to let it out. Like a real friend. She was a pretend friend, but apparently, she was pretty good at it. Jasmine was letting her in.

A tear rolled down Jasmine's cheek. Gabby walked to the bathroom to get her a tissue. Gabby was no longer the honest, trustworthy person she was in her own mind. She could see how Markus had ended up lying, almost no one ever told the truth in this job. Everything was so gray. There were so many permutations of the truth that the capital T truth slipped into the fog with all the other secrets, a shifting cloud of facts.

"Markus and I are having trouble too," Gabby confessed. "He's been lying, hiding a relationship from me." Gabby looked down at her knees while she twisted the truth of his relationship with G into something else.

"Is he cheating?" Jasmine looked up in shock.

"I don't know." Gabby really didn't know. "I'm not even sure if I'm mad at him. I just want him to be honest. I want to know where I stand."

Jasmine took a deep breath and released it, as if ready to release her own truth. It had to be weighing her down. Gabby was betting on it. "How are you and G?"

"Same as you and Markus, except messier. We've been married longer."

"Is G cheating too?" Gabby asked.

"Yeah, he has, but I'm worse. I'm in love with someone else."

Jasmine looked up through wet lashes. She paused for a second and then admitted it. "Naomi. It's been going on for a while. You probably already knew."

"No, I didn't."

"Well, you do now." Jasmine laughed.

"Are you going to leave G?"

Jasmine dipped her toe into the water running through the center of the house. "I don't think I can."

"Why not?"

"I'm in too deep. And I've turned my whole life into supporting him. I'm not independent anymore."

That rang true. Gabby had been financially powerless in a world Phil created, supporting his career, living in a house he bought.

"I don't even know everything I'm involved in. He has a lot of money coming in, and I don't think it's for anything good. It's messy, and I'm up to my eyeballs in the muck."

"What's the money for?" Gabby asked.

Jasmine shook her head. "All I know is that it's from bad people. The finances are a disaster. The taxes—I don't know. Inner Beauty would be a success, but because it's tied to the rest..." She trailed off.

"It was kind of sweet that he brought Sheridan here for you."

"Gia—" Jasmine gave her a sharp look. "You know that's a lie, right? He's never been good at gift giving, but he's not that bad."

Gabby had completely bought the gift-giving line.

"What would you do to leave him?" Gabby asked.

"Anything."

"What if I could get you and Naomi out?"

"You?" Jasmine looked up and gave Gabby a deeper look. "What are you going to do?"

Gabby shut her eyes and centered herself. There was no great reward without great risk, so she decided to gamble. "I'm an agent with the CIA, well, actually, the EOD, which is a division, but no matter. I can secure you immunity in exchange for testimony regarding Genesis's criminal financial activity."

Jasmine shot out of her chair. "What? What are you talking about?" Gabby started to say something, and Jasmine interjected, "What about George? Ohmygod. Are you undercover?"

Gabby didn't answer.

"Of course you are. You've never even done yoga." She laughed manically. "You took the whole tent down."

Jasmine stood up and walked to the kitchen, and then abruptly sat back down.

"I'm here for you," Gabby said, gambling that Valentina would help her deliver on any promises.

"What do you have on him?" Jasmine asked.

"Abducting Sheridan for one. We're digging into the financials now and about to put together enough evidence to arrest him." Gabby bluffed. It wasn't true yet, but they'd get there faster if Jasmine's testimony backed them up.

Jasmine's eyes went big. "What?" With fear in her voice, she asked, "What's he been doing?"

Gabby needed to show just enough of her hand to get Jasmine to talk. "Do you know about iMoan?"

Jasmine wrung her hands. "What's that?"

"We think your husband is financing this resort in a variety of illegal ways. You don't want to go down with him."

Jasmine looked directly at Gabby. "What do you need from me? I'll do it, but only if you can get Naomi the same deal."

Gabby did a silent touchdown dance. She had him!

Jasmine shut her eyes and exhaled a troubled breath. "It's more than finances, Gia."

"What's he really up to?" Gabby leaned forward eagerly.

"It's not like he tells me his nefarious plans," Jasmine said. "G is up to some shit, and he's using this psychic as leverage."

"What do you mean?"

"He didn't bring Sheridan down here as 'a gift.' I think he's using her to blackmail the president. He knows she knows things."

"What does she know?" Gabby asked, desperate for any crumb of an answer.

"Something about Amanda, I assume. I think the president did it. I don't know what G is asking for, cash or political favor, but he's getting something out of this." Jasmine struggled to maintain her composure. "I've been waiting for the other shoe to drop."

That would explain why the president wanted Sheridan dead, assuming he did actually want her dead. Sheridan's psychic intuition was the main evidence of that so far.

No matter what, Gabby was in the middle of a lot bigger mess than she realized. God, she hoped the president wasn't the killer, but so far that was the one thing everyone agreed on. Sheridan and Jasmine were consistent on that.

And how was she going to get her job back if the bad guy she was offering up was President Simon? That posed a problem.

Thirty minutes later, Gabby walked out of Jasmine's place filled with terror and anxious energy. She had just offered a deal to Jasmine without being able to back it up. If she didn't make this look good and convince Valentina there was a chance she'd spend the next few months, or maybe even years, of her life in a Portuguese prison. What would happen to Kyle and Lucas?

On her way to Naomi's, someone called her name, and she turned to see her mom. She seemed upset, but Gabby couldn't deal with her anymore.

"Not right now, Mom."

She'd had enough manufactured drama for one day, especially when she was busy creating plenty all on her own.

CHAPTER 33

1500 hours, the beach

Now it was coming together for real. Sheridan's cat sitter might be a little loose-lipped, but she was not selling stories to the press, and she certainly had nothing to do with all that money Phil couldn't figure out. Genesis, for all his good-natured charm and movie star looks, was behind all of it. Of course he was.

Gabby was so close to wrapping this up, she could taste it.

Now she just had to ensure Naomi would give testimony so that Jasmine would. It reminded her of when Kyle would only go to camp if Sierra went, and she had to call the camp and make sure they were in the same group, which, in retrospect, had been a lot of effort to accommodate some whining. But at any rate, she had managed to get Kyle and Sierra to camp, and she could get both Jasmine and Naomi immunity. Then take down the cult, get Markus's and her jobs back, and everything would go back to normal, which wasn't perfect but was better than not normal.

Gabby wanted to talk to Naomi before Jasmine had a chance to warn her, so she went directly to Naomi's cottage. Naomi was on her way out, striding purposefully toward the beach in a bikini and wielding a paddle. Naomi might be older than Gabby, but she had the look of a lifelong athlete, someone who was so confident in her own body that she was just as comfortable naked as in a fancy dress. Gabby still hadn't worn any of the swimsuits the EOD had forced her to pack.

"Naomi, can we talk?"

"I'm getting on my paddleboard. You're welcome to join me, but it's probably not the best place to talk wedding details." It was a polite way of saying, "Bye bitch. I'm busy."

Gabby groaned. On a normal day, Gabby would say, "See you later. Have fun." Today, she was on a deadline. She had gambled big, offering immunity to Jasmine, and she needed to lock down the deal before her fake wedding to Markus.

"Sure." How hard could paddleboarding be?

"Do you have a suit on under that outfit?"

"No, I don't mind."

Naomi was just looking for excuses to leave her behind. Gabby would go swimming in full athleisure if she had to.

"Gia, put on a swimsuit," Naomi commanded. "You're being weird."

"Maybe I am weird," Gabby responded.

"Suit yourself."

Gabby just wouldn't fall in. They weren't going swimming. A paddleboard was essentially a boat. She'd seen Kyle's friends on them at a birthday party once. Naomi waded out into the water with her paddleboard. Gabby grabbed another one of the boards. There were plenty to pick from.

Gabby scrambled to get her board in the water to catch Naomi, but when she climbed on and gave a strong push, it wouldn't budge.

"Your fins are stuck in the sand," Naomi yelled. "You're still on the beach." Hands on hips, she said, "Gia, if you want to talk to me about the wedding, I'll meet you in my office in an hour."

"I've always wanted to go paddleboarding," Gabby said with a smile that probably came off as maniacal. After she dislodged the fins from the ocean bottom and pushed the board to deeper water, she tried to climb up the back, but its nose popped up. The whole thing slipped out from under her like she had just tried to catch a greased hog at the county fair.

"Get on in the middle." Naomi frowned. "Have you ever done this?"

"Just a little rusty," Gabby lied.

"The middle, Gia. That's where it's most stable." Naomi frowned and reoriented the board for Gabby.

Once again, the board slid out from under her, and she flopped in the water. As if she were having so much fun, Gabby laughed. Really, she couldn't think of a worse way to spend time. Why did people torture themselves like this? With another fake peal of laughter, she said, "I can't believe I forgot how to do this."

"Don't lie. This is your first time."

"It is not!" Gabby smiled big.

"Were you airlifted onto the paddleboard last time?"

Gabby laughed again. After about ten more tries and a lot of direction from Naomi (put your left foot here; no, I mean here; grab the board in the middle; yada, yada), she was on her knees in the middle and trying not to breathe lest she tip the thing again.

"When you get a little momentum, rise to chair position."

"What is that, yoga?"

Naomi glared at her. "Gia, this is a yoga cult. Chair pose is second only to corpse pose in simplicity."

"So it is a cult?"

Naomi flashed a cagey smile. "I call it a cult with affection. It's no more a cult than Peloton."

"What makes something a cult?" Gabby was asking for personal reasons at this point. Naomi seemed pretty smart.

"A lot of things are cults," Naomi said, "but I don't think they're dangerous unless they take your money, harm you, and won't let you out." Naomi gestured to the surroundings. "This is just a fancy spa in the tropics."

"Jasmine wants out of Inner-G," Gabby said. It was now or never. "I know you're together. She wants to be with you." Gabby was trying to paddle to keep up with Naomi.

Naomi's poker face was solid.

"And I know Inner-G isn't harmless. I think it's more of a cult than you think it is, or that you're letting on."

The waves lapped over the front of her board.

"Genesis kidnapped Sheridan and brought her here. There are some real problems with his finances." Gabby hedged her bets there because she wasn't sure what "dumb" thing was going on. "If I'm right, you helped Jasmine sell stories through an illegal media group."

Naomi shrugged defiantly.

"This place is going down. If you talk, you will be protected. So will Jasmine."

If she got testimony from Jasmine and a member of the inner circle, plus the financial records, Genesis would be toast. Job back. Ka-ching!

Naomi shook her head. She didn't look surprised. With a half shrug, she said, "Men," in a very matter-of-fact, what-did-you-expect tone. "I'm a lesbian for a reason."

"There are some good guys out there still, right?" Gabby implored. "My guy...George."

"Lil' G?" Naomi raised an eyebrow in judgment. "You mean Big G's sidekick?"

Gabby's ire spiked. Instead of jumping to Markus's defense, she schooled her expression.

"So how are you going to help me?" Naomi said. "Are you CIA or something?"

Gabby stiffened her spine, but it threw off her balance, and a wave sloshed over her legs. "Yes."

She stopped paddling and said, "You know what pisses me off?"

"What?"

"You're here, ready to save the day, but you've missed everything." Naomi looked sincerely upset.

"What'd I miss?"

"Are you listening?" Naomi's expression was intense, even though she appeared to be having zero trouble balancing.

"I'm listening." Gabby listened as carefully as she could over the lapping waves and raucous water birds. "How'd you know her?"

"I was a political correspondent, and she worked for the *Post*. We met, got to be friends." A big duck landed right next to Naomi, and she swatted at it with a paddle. "I brought Amanda down here a couple of times."

Gabby nodded. "How does that tie into Sheridan? Does Sheridan know something about Amanda's death?"

Without answering the question, Naomi smiled sadly and said, "She was better at paddleboarding than you."

"Wouldn't be hard, huh?" It was time to give up the lie that she knew what she was doing.

Gabby held her breath and braced her knees, trying to keep her balance on the damn board. Just as Naomi was about to speak, someone from the shore yelled, "Gia!" and Gabby looked while trying not to jerk her head too rapidly and tip the whole thing over.

"Is that your fiancé?"

It was. Markus was standing on the beach, interrupting just when she was starting to get answers.

She waved like she was excited to see him. She wasn't. This is what happened when partners weren't communicating.

Gabby yelled to shore, "I'm busy! I'll see you later."

Markus frowned back, clearly wondering what was going on. She was solving everything on her own—that's what. And Markus was not giving Glen Powell vibes at the moment. Gabby might not be able to kneel on a paddleboard or have washboard abs, but she was about to take down the president of the United States, if Naomi's story agreed with Jasmine's that is. This is what happened when you gave a woman a week to do her job without kids. Or maybe she'd end up in prison. Gabby was rapid-cycling between visions of triumph and despair at this point.

Naomi, apparently done with the distractions, was gliding away looking like some sort of Athleta cover model. Gabby tried her best to keep up, but she was putting a ton of energy into going nowhere, a move she was familiar with in and out of the water.

"Naomi, wait up!" she called. "Geez, how are you going so fast?"

Naomi glanced over her shoulder. Even without seeing her expression, Gabby could tell she was annoyed.

"You know I'm not some vapid girl who will spill everything for love. Love—" She let the word hang in the air, not sounding convinced. Had she been burned? Or maybe she was too practical to be guided by softer emotions.

"Isn't love worth it?" Gabby said. "Sure, it's not perfect, but don't you want someone you can weather the storm with? We all need a safe harbor."

Gabby glanced at Markus onshore. A day ago, she would have fantasized about Markus as hers.

"I might love Jasmine, but I'm not silly enough to think this is our ticket to happiness. The timing isn't great, Gia. She's still married, and I don't understand fully what's going on, but if I need an immunity deal to be with her, that's not a good sign."

Gabby didn't want to hear it. "Maybe it's right person, wrong time currently, but I'm fixing all that. It's going to be the right time as soon as you testify."

Naomi laughed. "What are you, a matchmaker?"

Gabby wanted Naomi to have it all. "Naomi, just testify. Get immunity and run away with Jasmine. You don't even have kids to worry about."

"George is waiting. You can go have it all with him." Naomi smirked. "Or try to, anyway."

"Maybe I will," Gabby said.

Gabby's dream was slipping away. It's not like she expected an all-you-can-eat buffet-size portion of having it all, just a small slice of everything. A career to be proud of and someone to watch Netflix with after the kids went to bed. Also, how had Naomi twisted this conversation to make it about her? Gabby was supposed to be working Naomi. Instead, Gabby was questioning her love life and choking on salt water, barely staying on a paddleboard. She had lost the upper hand, if she'd ever had it.

Was this what happened when you tried to have it all? You ended up drowning under your own expectations while the men in your life watched from the sidelines?

"Jasmine needs help. If you offer testimony against Genesis, Jasmine could leave without worrying about him."

Gabby, who had been on all fours, rose to her knees and tried to balance. She wasn't doing chair pose, but at least she was on her knees. Maybe if she were in a pool instead of the ocean, she could stand up.

"What do you say? Will you talk? Get off this ship before it sinks, Naomi."

Naomi looked back. Her expression wasn't hard or defiant anymore. She looked lost and unsure.

"Naomi, if you know what's going on, tell me. Make sure I get it right," Gabby called.

Naomi began paddling. Gabby tried to stand to follow her. "I'll take care of you!" Gabby tried one last plea.

"I'll be fine, Gia. Have fun with your choices." And she was off. Conversation over.

Gabby dug into the water with her paddle, but the board went right out from under her, leaving her dog-paddling.

Markus came up behind her. "You're supposed to use a leash." He pointed to a curlicue phone cord that was attached to his ankle and clipped to his board. "And a life jacket."

"I'm never getting on one of these again," she sputtered.

Markus narrowed his eyes. "We need to talk, Gia."

He needed to talk? That was rich. "Great, because I need to talk to you too."

CHAPTER 34

1500 hours, the beach

Gabby stood on the shore, dripping wet, her yoga clothes sealed to her skin. Getting out of an already too-tight bra top that was soaked—she might need to cut the thing off.

Gabby braced herself for what was coming.

"What the fuck are you doing?" Markus said. "I said *no espionage*." He gestured to the paddleboard. "I'm guessing you weren't doing that for fun."

Gabby filled him in in a rush of words. "Naomi and Jasmine agreed to provide testimony against Genesis. Well, Jasmine did, and Naomi is going to agree. I can tell."

He held up his hand for her to stop.

"Gabby, this is your second mission. You can't just blow off direct orders and pretend there are no consequences."

"I'm doing my job!" she shot back.

"News flash," he said, "we don't have jobs anymore."

A seagull walked up toward them, looking for a handout. The waterfowl were reflecting her internal chaos today.

Markus rubbed his neck like the tension was killing him.

"Gabby, remember how I was trying to get my career back on track with this mission, how I asked you to have my back?"

"I do." Of course she did. "That was right before you started sneaking off to meet with Genesis, I believe." She put her hand on her hip. She was facing into the wind, and her hair whipped behind her dramatically.

Over the bay, a bird was catching air and floating like a hang glider.

He huffed. "Oh, you think I'm up to something?"

"I do. Texting G surreptitiously, hanging out when you're supposedly going to Sheridan's. G's our number one suspect! What did you expect me to think?"

"I expected trust."

"You know, Valentina asked me for a report on your behavior." Gabby leaned forward. "She doesn't trust you either. This isn't all my fault."

"What?" He reared back. He shut his eyes and took a breath, clearly trying to control his emotions. "I can't believe that. I've been a field operative for six years. Six years!"

"I didn't want to," Gabby said, her heart filling with regret now that she'd said it out loud.

"After six years, I haven't earned the benefit of a doubt from my ex-wife or you. Whoever you are to me. Work wife, my ass."

Gabby let him get it out. He was rightfully mad.

"I needed this one, Gabs, and you're a fucking double agent, spying on me and playing my girlfriend." He looked so hurt.

Gabby was silenced by guilt. He was calling her on everything.

He nodded. "I see how it is."

"I'm sorry about that, Markus, but I've been in a bad position too. I didn't know what to do, and you didn't let me in! If you had just told me what you were doing and why…I asked questions, and you just brushed me off." It was Gabby's turn to be mad. "Do you see the position you put me in?"

He gave a nod. "Fair point. My communication could be better."

"Thank you," she said emphatically, like she'd just won.

But he didn't elaborate, just stood there silently when there were too many times that he'd snuck off to talk to Genesis.

"You returned Sheridan's phone without even mentioning that to me," she reminded him, again.

"I had too much to drink. Sorry." He looked out to sea. She could see the angry words gathering like a storm cloud. "You're one to talk, Gabby. You're conducting an illegal mission without my approval."

She was in the most beautiful place she'd ever been. They should have been working together, enjoying everything about this place—the turquoise waters, the waves, the honeymoon cottage with a butler so she'd never have to lift a finger. Here they were arguing. It was hopeless.

Cold and emotionless, Marcus said, "I should have known from the beginning. I saw you hesitating to agree to dinner." He let out a hollow laugh. "Work wives. How did I not see through that?"

"I was just trying to find a workable compromise."

They'd compromised until there was nothing left. A vision of Naomi laughing at her on a paddleboard came to her. Why did she think she could handle more than anyone she knew when she couldn't even operate a paddleboard?

"I want you, Markus, but I also want a career, and I already have a family I need to take care of." Overwhelmed, she added, "I just don't know how to have it all."

"Did you think you could have it all?" he asked, his question more of an accusation.

For a hot second, she did think she could have it all. All she needed was better planning. That color-coded schedule she had worked so hard on. Ten minutes for kids in the morning. Phone calls in the car. Romance at lunch hour. A tight schedule, clear boundaries, and labels—that's how women did it. Not to mention, strategic compromises: a work wife instead of a boyfriend. Working out for fifteen minutes before she left work.

She couldn't even have it all playing pretend in the Azores in a honeymoon cottage.

Gabby had always thought she wasn't good enough for Markus— not in his league with too much baggage—but tonight she knew that had been her insecurity talking. She was enough. There just wasn't enough of her to go around.

Coldly, he said, "Valentina's coming."

"Why?" Her voice came out in a squeak.

"Her ass is on the line for trusting us."

Suddenly, Gabby was just tired. All her anger was spent, all her suspicions from the last week out in the air. And there was still more mess to mop up.

As they walked back to the cottage, Gabby said, "There's still the matter of Naomi and Jasmine. They are willing to provide testimony against G in exchange for immunity."

Markus groaned and walked a few more steps. "Fine," he said. "We might as well throw that Hail Mary."

She nodded. "It's our only chance to come out of this employed."

"New plan," he said. "Get their testimony, save our jobs, and get the fuck out."

"Even though they're taking G down?"

He nodded. "If he's guilty, he's guilty. I can't save him."

Gabby had almost had it all for about two minutes. Now she had no romance, but at least she had her partner back.

Steely eyed, she said, "Let's do this. What's next?"

"We need to go get ready," Markus said.

"For what?" Gabby didn't have energy for anything anymore.

"You have to be at a bachelorette party in an hour."

At that, Gabby started laughing. "Fuck me."

CHAPTER 35

1600 hours, Inner-G resort, the bachelorette party

Gabby's bachelorette party had started two minutes ago. Markus had just broken up with her. What fresh hell was this? She wanted to turn on Sarah McLachlan, cry, and lie in bed. That was not a luxury she could afford at the moment.

Work and romance—she should have known better. She'd jumped headfirst into the deep end when she'd known damn well she should have kept it at a coffee date. She squeezed her eyes shut to keep from crying. That fucking Inner Beauty mascara probably wasn't even waterproof.

Gabby needed to pull it together. It was time for a bachelorette party.

But she couldn't bring herself to get dressed up. She could show her face, but it wasn't going to be pretty. Any inner beauty she had was going to be natural, and she was wearing Jasmine's "refined loungewear." She hadn't double-checked while getting broken up with, but if she remembered right, the party was at Jasmine's.

Storm clouds loomed on the horizon as she made her way down the beach. The breeze was transitioning from perfect to "why did I bother brushing my hair anyway?" It didn't matter. Who cared about her hair? Her relationship was over before it even started. You would think this would make it easier, but what Gabby was feeling wasn't a superficial hurt.

What did they say? Love was chemistry and timing. She and Markus had the chemistry, but the timing… She exhaled. Markus didn't fit into her current life. If they'd met before she'd gotten married and had a family, it would have worked. But it's not like she could undo the last fifteen years of her life, and she wouldn't if she could.

"Wait up," Phil called.

Yep. Someone was torturing her for sport. She did not have the energy for Phil. Not right now. She knew he was a decent person, the father of her children, but the timing… The relationship was over, Phil!

"Can we talk?" he asked.

"I don't have time right now, Phil," she said, picking up her pace. "I came here to get married to someone else. This isn't about you."

He sighed. "I really need to get this out. It's important."

Hands on hips, she turned to face him. "You have two minutes."

"I'm sorry," he said, looking deep into her eyes.

She raised an eyebrow. Where was he going to start?

"In meditation today, I sat in self-reflection and—" He shook his head. "I've been an ass, following you down here, getting in your way. I don't want you to get married. I want to give us another shot, but I've been doing it all wrong."

She nodded. That was all true.

"I probably blew it."

Finally, he was getting it.

"But I love you. I love what a good mom you are. I think it's great that you're trying to grow as a person, joining Inner-G, and meditating, and all that."

For fuck's sake.

"I need to do that too."

It would be nice if he did his growing on his own time, not on a work vacation he had invited himself to. "Great. Self-improvement is important."

"I officially signed up to join Inner-G today. I'm going to stop being a hater and try to grow and evolve, to access my inner-G."

Gabby actually sobbed. It was sweet and so misguided. He'd just joined a cult she was about to take down, but he was trying. It was the nicest thing he'd ever done for her.

"If I become a better man for you, would you consider taking me back? I'm ready to grow together."

Why would you bite into a lemon twice? As far as husbands went, Phil was a lemon. And he had been disruptive, disrespectful, and in her way this week.

"I still love you, Ga...I mean, Gia."

"Phil—" She held up her hand in a stop gesture.

But then again, he was fighting for her. Hadn't she always loved that scene where Colin Firth and Hugh Grant fought each other in the street? But now that Phil was pulling his version of Colin Firth, it just didn't work. She wanted to give him a hug, not marry him. If you were going to fight for love, the love had to be worth fighting for in the first place.

All she had been thinking about for the last week was how awful he was, but from a different perspective, maybe it was romantic. He loved her so much he couldn't let her go. And there was Kyle begging her to get back together with her dad. It hadn't been a perfect family before. Phil had never been around. They weren't a team, but...did she owe it to her daughter to try again? Markus had broken up with her before they even got off the ground. It was just her and Phil. A weight settled on her chest at the thought.

"Phil, did you ever figure out where that money was coming from? You were going to follow up with Brad before you got back to me."

"It's *that* important?"

"Yes. It's extremely important."

"I got a little more out of him. Do you want to sit down?"

She didn't want to sit down, but she relented and perched awkwardly on a beach chair meant for lounging. Phil sat across from her and scrolled through his email. Apparently, no one *actually* gave up their phone in this place. That was Inner-G's least effective rule.

"The holding company is called PowCup Financial," he said. "According to Brad, it exists to fund *Power Couple 2*."

"I didn't think anyone liked that movie," Gabby said. She'd tried watching *Power Couple* three times now.

"It has a cult following."

A cult following. Now that was funny.

"Have they even started the movie?" Phil asked.

"I don't think so," Gabby said. The way G talked about making *Power Couple 2* reminded Gabby of the way she talked about finally getting to Lucas's baby book: i.e., it wasn't happening.

"I only ask because the money is gone already." Pointedly, Phil commented, "That yacht is brand-new, right?"

It was. Gabby nodded.

"I'd bet G bought it with the twenty mil." Phil drummed his fingers on the table. "They might want to return it."

"Can you return yachts? Asking for a friend," she joked.

"You might have to sink it and hope insurance pays for it."

"Do you know who's behind the holding company?"

Phil shook his head no.

"If you find out anything else, let me know. Don't worry about waking me up," she said. The web of evidence around G was tightening, but she needed more, preferably something to corroborate any testimony from Jasmine.

Gabby continued to Jasmine's house. First Markus, now Phil. Silver linings: She was out of men to break it off with tonight, not that she'd exactly broken it off with Phil. She just hadn't gotten back together with him. Just as the first rain droplets fell on her, she let out a delirious laugh.

Yep, she was cracking up. The only way she was going to make it through tonight was loud music, dark lights, and Jell-O shots. She needed to hide her feelings in a throbbing mass of people. To lose herself in mindless motion.

When she finally got to Jasmine's, she was informed the party was at the G-hut.

At the G-hut, Gabby found a gathering that was anything but a bachelorette party. There were no cocktails, no strippers, no jalapeño poppers. Justin, Lana, Naomi, and Jasmine—awkward! Her mom was nowhere to be seen. This didn't seem like something she'd miss, but maybe she and Sheridan were watching *The Bachelorette* or running late. Everyone was in cute outfits, except for Jasmine, who had opted for a ceremonial robe, and Gabby, who was in sweats.

Justin caught her attention and made crazy eyes with a discreet nod toward Jasmine, who, to be honest, looked less stable than G tonight. Gabby would feel more comfortable about hinging her entire plan on Jasmine if she looked a little less crazy.

Between the pitter-patter of rain, the sound bowls, and the incense, they were clearly about to meditate.

With the party assembled, Jasmine opened the ceremony. "Tonight, our goal is to prepare you spiritually for your union with George. Our cultural tradition of bachelorette parties leaves women walking into marriage dazed, hungover, groggy, and just going through the motions."

That sounded perfect. How else was she supposed to pretend to marry a man who'd just dumped her?

"Gia, are you listening?"

"Yes," she lied.

"Tonight, we are going to sit with our feelings."

Anything but that.

"Before we get started, has anyone seen my mom?" Gabby asked.

"I don't think she's coming," Jasmine answered.

Hmm. Missing a party wasn't her mom's style.

Jasmine said, "When we are all clear in heart and mind, we will begin."

Begin what? Jasmine's outfit said "about to make a blood sacrifice."

"Let's start with silent meditation. We will meditate for as long as it takes to reach clarity."

Gabby was barely holding it together as it was. Her feelings were so close to the surface. Markus had exposed all her hurt and desire. The sound bowls normally just provided background noise, but today, they struck a chord. All her feelings were spilling out already, and she couldn't help herself. First one tear fell, then another. Pretty soon, tears were quietly streaming down her face. She couldn't stop.

This was a nightmare. She might not have wanted to start a serious relationship with Markus yet, but she didn't want to run through a whole relationship and fast-forward to a breakup. What had even happened? And then Phil. All while she was supposed to be solving a murder and figuring out who was selling secrets. She didn't have time for feelings.

And why was she crying? She was an adult woman with children and important things to worry about. Somehow, she'd been going through life, making the choices that were expected of her. Getting married when it was time, to a man who was a good provider, having kids when she was supposed to, autopiloting her way through.

Now there wasn't any room for the choices she wanted to make, something she felt deep in her bones. There was no room for Gabby in her own life, and it was her own damn fault. All of it was her own fault. A million choices she had made without thinking, and here she was. She had no room left to choose Markus.

And how long was this godforsaken sound bath going to last?

She tried to discreetly wipe her eyes with her dress. When she glanced up to see if anyone had noticed, Jasmine was watching.

"Look up when you're ready," Jasmine intoned in the voice she reserved for yoga classes and meditation. Jasmine must have realized presence wasn't an achievable goal for this group. She said, "Now that we have clear minds and open hearts, I would like to go around the circle. Each member, please share a piece of wisdom. Let's start with Lana."

With a disinterested expression, Lana said, "I think you should drink nothing but water and fresh juice before tomorrow. That wedding dress is a little tight."

Jasmine nodded. "Practical advice is always welcome." She

turned to her lover. In a softer voice, she said, "Naomi, your turn. What advice do you have about marriage?"

Looking straight into Jasmine's eyes, Naomi said, "Pass. I'm not in a place to give relationship advice."

Justin had had enough. "Does anyone else want to crash the bachelor party?"

Lana stood up like she'd been ejected from her Japanese floor pillow. "Yes, please. I think they have liquor."

"And music, I hope."

Even Naomi was on board. "I'm starving, Jasmine. Do they have food?"

Like a gang of twenty-somethings club-hopping, Gabby's bachelorette party of middle-aged and better women piled out of the ceremonial hut and went in search of the men to see if they had anything better going on. It wouldn't be hard.

Despite the circumstances, the spirit of the moment was infectious. Just a bunch of girls off to look for some cocktails and hot guys.

"Jasmine, you need better lights," Lana complained about the poorly lit path after stumbling over some uneven terrain.

"We didn't want to impede anyone's view of the stars."

Justin laughed. "Which they'll be able to see great after they land flat on their ass."

"I heard that!" Jasmine giggled and said, "But fair point."

"There they are!" The bachelor party was on the yacht, its reflection glimmering on the water like a Monet. The boat was anchored within sight of shore.

Jasmine pointed to a dinghy for them to take to the yacht. "Shall I call for a driver?"

"Jasmine, no!" Naomi said. "We can drive ourselves."

The entire bachelorette party piled into a smaller boat. Naomi started the motor, and it roared to life and burbled. "Everyone ready?"

"One second." Justin finished securing himself in a life jacket and passed one to Gabby. He mouthed, "These women are unhinged."

Naomi took no offense. While the rest of the women found seats, she expertly untied the small boat and steered their course through the inky black waters. Like an actual pirate, she hooked the smaller boat to the yacht. Naomi had definitely driven a boat before. Paddleboarding, boating—the woman was competent.

"Prepare to be boarded!" Justin yelled. "Did you hear that, Gia?" He whispered. "I might use that again later."

Gabby laughed. She didn't really want to be crashing a bachelor party. If she were on good terms with Valentina, she would have already evacuated Naomi and Jasmine for their statements to be taken. Instead, she was driving around the bay in the dark looking for liquor.

To be a good spy, you had to go along for the ride, though. *You don't control the action, you are just there to observe*, Gabby reminded herself. This was the job. Going along for the ride was her specialty. She'd been going along for the ride, wondering what the hell she'd agreed to, for most of her life.

Genesis leaned over the edge of the yacht. "Ahoy there. Be thou friend or foe?"

That was a good question. Most likely the latter.

"Oh, we're friendly," Justin said in a heavily flirtatious voice.

Genesis lowered a ladder. "Welcome, friends. It's good to be Together."

Gabby had never felt more like a spy than climbing a twenty-foot rope ladder to board a luxury yacht in the middle of the night, even though the main suspect was helping her up. All her senses were on high alert.

After she huffed and puffed her way up the side of the boat, Markus gave her a hand onto the deck, where she found the guys hanging out. Most of them had fishing poles. As soon as her feet hit the deck, Markus took her elbow and steered her to the far edge of the boat for a quick catch-up.

Someone hooted when they noticed Gabby and Markus walking off for a private moment and started chanting, "Kiss, Kiss, Kiss."

Markus gave a good-natured laugh. "That's for the reception."

They were met with a "Kiss, Kiss, Kiss."

The last time they'd seen each other, they'd argued on the shore and broken up officially, but they had to play the part. Gabby attempted to disassociate as he leaned in. His lips brushed hers lightly, and he whispered, "Sorry."

Sorry for breaking up, or sorry for kissing her after, or sorry for breaking her trust? Spy work was not easy on a relationship.

After the kiss that wasn't sexy enough to satisfy the partygoers, they stayed in the embrace. Gabby leaned her head on his chest for comfort. Everyone lost interest, and they continued to the other side of the boat.

"So how's the bachelorette party?" Markus asked.

Gabby looked across the glittering bay. "Have you seen the Festivus episode of *Seinfeld*? Instead of Christmas, George's family has an airing of their grievances around a steel pole?"

He laughed. "I take it that's why you're here."

She nodded. "How was the bachelor party?"

"As good as deep-sea fishing with your ex-husband and a megalomaniac cult leader can be. It's a catch-your-own-dinner situation, but no one has caught anything yet. I think Justin's hubby, Hugh, might be taking notes to write an academic paper on the experience."

Despite herself, she smiled. The whole week was unhinged.

"I don't think Inner-G really knows how to throw a wedding."

"No shit. This is a terrible wedding so far."

After their non-updates, Gabby felt better. At least she and Markus were in it together, even if they were not together-together. They walked over to the group. Phil had gone below deck and come back with the liquor.

"Someone had to do it," he said. "Who wants a Jägerbomb?"

There was loud agreement.

Meanwhile, he hooked up his phone to the boat's speaker system. "Fuck the fish, we need some tunes."

He was going to get them kicked off the resort with this dumb idea. It was the most frat-boy thing she'd ever seen. Gabby leaned in and apologized to Jasmine and Genesis. "I'm sorry. I think he's having some feelings about me getting remarried."

Genesis nodded. "Poor guy," and said, "Sure, Phil. I'll take a Jägerbomb."

Just then, the sound came on. Gabby face-palmed when she realized what he was playing. It was Andy Samberg and T-Pain singing, "I'm on a boat, motherfucker."

Gabby started coughing. She had to admit it was a good one, a lot of posturing about owning a boat. How could she not have seen this coming? Phil loved this song, and he was on a boat. She watched through her fingers for everything to fall apart, but it seemed to be a relief for everyone.

Lana was twerking. Jasmine had tossed the ceremonial robes aside to reveal some club wear. Genesis was raising the roof. The song might as well have been written for him. It was a lot of "I'm on a boat! Look at me!"

With the energy whipped up to a frenzy, Lana yelled, "I'm on a boat, bitch!"

Hugh looked a little disconcerted, but Phil threw his arm around the history prof's shoulders and chanted, "I'm on a boat with my boys."

When the song ended, it was like they'd really gone through something together. The group had started as one thing (snobby and buttoned-up) and had moved to another (drunk and disorderly).

The next song came on, which was some grinding on the dance floor number from their college days. Phil went up to Naomi—lol, good luck Phil—and started doing a little middle-aged footwork, an invitation for her to join in. Unfortunately for Naomi, and for everyone, Phil's only dance move was thrusting with a pretend lasso. Gabby had never taken him out before.

As a pickup line, he said, "Her name's Naomi. That's 'I moan' backwards."

Naomi's eyes went big, and she glanced at Jasmine. While some wordless exchange of information passed between the two women, Phil started explaining the quote. "It's from *Van Wilder*. You know, the movie?"

"No, I haven't seen that." Naomi collected herself and schooled her expression into a benign smile.

Phil raised his glass with one hand and started the lasso with the other. "Sorry, but consider it a compliment."

Gabby and Markus exchanged a look, clearly both having a lightbulb moment: Naomi was iMoan backwards. That couldn't be a coincidence. Had they just found the person behind iMoan? Gabby recalled details: an illicit business sheltered by Icelandic privacy laws, housed out of a building with a penis museum and an H&M.

Naomi had worked as a TV reporter. It wasn't inconceivable that she would start an illicit business to sell secret stories. The name seemed more like Phil's style, but it's not like she knew Naomi well.

No matter what, Gabby wasn't going to figure it out on the deck of a yacht while Sir Mix-a-lot was playing. It was going to be embarrassing for Gabby if it turned out Naomi was behind it all.

She looked at Markus to ask about leaving right as Sir Mix-a-lot rapped, "I like big butts, and I cannot lie." Markus looked away in a "Who? Not me, nothing to see here" way.

He was lying. From personal experience, she knew he liked big butts. Hopefully, that's all he was lying about right now because they had a mission to finish, and she needed him.

"Markus, it's time to go."

Before Gabby and Markus made it back to the cottage, she was hit by a lightning bolt of worry. When she'd been standing outside G and Jasmine's place, her mom had been there, trying to get her attention. Gabby had dismissed her so quickly, so cavalierly. She'd forgotten to worry about her mother's safety. Elena was a civilian in the middle of an EOD operation. She was at risk and Gabby's responsibility.

Worry chased all the exhaustion away.

"Markus, can we take a quick detour? I want to check on my mom and Sheridan."

"Of course," he said. "Are you worried?"

"My mom was trying to flag me down on the way to paddle-boarding with Naomi, but I blew her off. I assumed she was just going to say something shitty, but what if she wasn't?"

Gabby picked up her pace.

"I'm sure it's fine."

Gabby wasn't so sure. Like Markus had pointed out, Gabby'd been running around the resort in a frenzy of last-ditch espionage work. Jasmine had told her that G could be dangerous, and Sheridan had already survived one break-in/attempt on her life.

On the way through the main lobby, Aspen called out, "Gia, your mom left a note for you at the front desk."

Okay, this was weird. Gabby hurried over to the desk and tore into the envelope that Aspen handed her.

"Are you two excited? It's almost the big day!"

Gabby smiled. "We can't wait!"

The note read: "Don't worry. Changed rooms. Sheridan had a premonition. If you really need me, Jasmine can help."

Gabby smiled at Aspen. "Thanks!" She turned to Markus and said, "On second thought, let's let my mom rest. We should get some sleep."

CHAPTER 36

All hope is lost o'clock, the honeymoon cottage

When Gabby and Markus pushed the door open to the honeymoon cottage, it was dark. At first glance, it looked like their place had been ransacked, but it was just their mess. Clothes were strewn around from getting dressed for their parties in a hurry. There was the blue dress she had almost worn slung across the bed.

"Do you think it's weird that my mom and Sheridan changed rooms?"

"It's probably fine," he said. "And we have bigger problems than that at the moment." He caught her eye. "What are we going to do about all of these deals you offered? We can't back them up without Valentina."

Gabby started tidying up just to give her something to do with her hands. "Before we call her, what about iMoan? Naomi is clearly involved and I offered her a deal too." Gabby groaned. "Jasmine won't talk without her."

Really, she had nothing solid. Not even Markus. It's not like he'd explained himself when she'd confronted him about meeting behind her back with G.

Why had she been worried about professional boundaries? The only person she had an effective boundary with was the one she had been trying to let in. Just going through the motions, same as she did at the end of every night, she started tidying up.

"Pull it together, Gabby," Markus said. "You got this. We got this."

She wanted to believe that, but could she trust him? Texting G, meeting with G, dropping Sheridan's phone off when he knew damn well it was providing her with a means of delivering classified news to the outside world. Gabby hung an unworn dress in the closet and lined shoes up neatly against the wall. The room might be clean, but her mind was still cluttered and dark, and she was dead on her feet.

"Do we got this, Markus? Are you working with me or . . ." She let the words trail off.

"I got this" had been the refrain in her head since she took this job, which kept pushing her into "Be More, Do More" territory because she wasn't enough. God, it was almost like she was repeating all the mistakes she'd made as a stay-at-home mom. Taking on too much, over-promising and underdelivering. Different job, same problems.

Markus sat down next to her. "We need backup. This rogue-cop thing only works on TV."

"I really thought I had it for a minute," Gabby said.

"And at this point, we need to tell Valentina so she can save her own ass. If there's a disaster down here, she's going to take the fall right along with us."

Oof. Gabby hadn't been thinking about that. A rogue agent's supervisor probably didn't get a promotion when things went sideways. Not to mention, Markus. He wasn't just admitting failure to his boss but to his ex-wife. The EOD was such a mess. It was like a reality show with spying. She had made it even messier.

It was time to admit defeat. She hadn't gotten the job done. If anything, she'd made it worse.

Valentina answered the phone on the first ring. After Markus and Gabby explained, Valentina took a deep breath and said, "You're fucking kidding me. What am I supposed to do with you two assholes?"

Gabby and Markus remained silent. They both knew when to shut up.

"Neither of you can offer anyone immunity. You're supposed to be locked in your rooms awaiting evac."

"It's my fault," Gabby said.

"This is a group project, Agent Greene. You share a grade. Agent Parks knows that."

Gabby flashed a look of apology Markus's way.

"I'll be there tomorrow. I'm not sure what time, but as soon as I can possibly get there."

Gabby gasped.

"What should we do?" Markus asked.

"Don't fucking offer anyone any more deals. No espionage."

Gabby said, "Tomorrow is our wedding. Should we call that off?"

"No, don't change anything. At least you'll be too busy to get into trouble."

The engaged-to-Markus assignment had officially changed from a fantasy to a punishment.

"When I get there, you better be married and acting like newlyweds. If either of you does anything that could be construed as espionage, I will personally arrest you myself."

CHAPTER 37

The wedding day, the honeymoon cottage

The next day, Gabby woke alone in her large honeymoon bed and walked out to the patio to enjoy a special wedding day breakfast. She had slept for approximately an hour. Markus was seated, already dressed and clutching a half-empty coffee.

She glared at him for leaving her alone and sad all night. Rationally, she knew it wasn't his responsibility to comfort her after breaking up with her, but normal rules didn't apply when you were in the middle of a mission going sideways. She wanted a hug, and she wanted this whole nightmare to be over.

They ate in an unhappy silence.

When Justin finally showed up on the patio, she dissolved into a pile of raw emotion. Here was the person she could lean on through thick and thin, and especially when she had man trouble.

"Hello!" he trilled. "I'm here to make you beautiful."

Gabby'd never been so happy to see her best friend, except for maybe the last mission when he helped her haul mobsters into a supply room, no questions asked.

"Gabby's already..." Markus cut himself off. "It's just that I don't think any woman needs makeup to be beautiful."

Gabby guffawed. If he thought she was that beautiful, he wouldn't have broken up with her.

Markus looked up in surprise. "Why are you laughing?"

"Why do you think?" she asked.

Okay. Apparently, she'd gone from sadness to anger about the breakup in the space of a minute. Anger fit like a glove. A boxing glove. Sadness, no thank you. Also, she was mad at herself for even thinking about her breakup when she had more important things to consider, like keeping her job and health insurance.

"You're misinterpreting what I said," Markus shot back.

She raised an eyebrow. She wasn't.

"Don't question me at work."

"Grow a pair, Markus," Gabby snapped back. "And check your ego."

Justin looked between them. "What is going on here? Is this how you two are together because…" He looked down his nose in judgment. "I can't tell if I like it. I mean, is this your kink or are you just like old married people who should have gotten a divorce thirty years ago but didn't 'for the kids' and now everyone has to suffer through you?"

They turned to shoot identical laser eyes at Justin.

"Fine, be strong and silent with me. I can be into that. Just take me to your fancy honeymoon bathroom."

Markus said, "I'll see you later. I'm going over to get ready with G."

Good riddance. Gabby couldn't handle the breakup. A relationship should provide a solid foundation to stand on, a base. All week, their relationship had been like the ground during an active earthquake, shifting and cracking beneath her feet. It was making everything else harder. How could she do her job when she was always bracing for the next seismic shift?

Justin oohed and aahed over the splendor of the bathroom. "Ohmygod. Look at all these full-size products." He held up a bottle of something like he was from *Indiana Jones and the Temple of Doom*.

"This is probably a thousand dollars of makeup and skincare products," he said.

"It makes me turn red and rashy. I don't think Inner Beauty is for me." Now that she had read Jasmine's emails, she realized it was probably the red dye number six. Gabby wasn't a dermatologist, but she knew that if it was an ingredient in Flaming Hot Cheetos, it probably wasn't also an ingredient in inner beauty or outer beauty. It might actually be an ingredient in cancer.

He sounded disappointed and squirted a bunch onto his palm and started rubbing it into his own face. "This is too expensive not to use."

Despite everything, she couldn't help but relax as Justin started to do her makeup.

"What's with you and Mr. Sad-Sack Spy out there?"

Gabby shook her head. "He broke up with me."

Justin gasped. "Shut. Up. On your wedding day?"

"Technically, last night, right before the bachelorette party."

"Do you want me to fight him? Because I will. I might be good with makeup, but I have a right hook like Tyson, and I will bite his ear off."

"Not yet. Keep that move in the queue, though. We might need it later."

"I hope so."

"Don't you think those eyebrows are a little strong?" Gabby asked.

"No, you want people to be able to see them from the audience."

"I don't think there's going to be an audience. We're all going to be on the deck of the boat. It's supposed to be intimate."

Justin leaned back to get a look at his handiwork. "Well, the person in the back of the boat. Maybe the captain. You want them all to see how great you look."

This was the danger in Justin doing makeup. She was going to look like a drag queen. And Markus would just be Markus.

Next, Lana Hunt arrived with the dress. When she unzipped the garment bag, she revealed Gabby's dream gown. The timing of this was cruel.

After one look at the makeup, Lana said, "Pretty, but let's tone it down. This is an outdoor ceremony, not Broadway."

Thank you, Lana.

Justin huffed. "What about pictures?"

"Take it down a couple of notches. She's wearing one of my gowns."

When Gabby was ready, she looked like her dream as a little girl. Her hair was curled so prettily that it almost looked natural. Justin had pinned it up in a chignon that would go viral on Tik-Tok if he'd recorded it.

Justin was pissed. "Look at this!" He pointed at her. "She's magnificent, and I can't even take a picture. What is it with the no phones policy? Did anyone really feel more centered and connected in 1988? Connected to what?"

Lana answered seriously. "Yourself, the world around you, your creativity."

"Do you see this updo?" Justin said. If he'd had a mic, he would have dropped it.

The dress had a full skirt with a train that was supposed to be pinned up, making it even fuller. At the moment, it was unfurled. The plan was for two people to walk Gabby to the boat. It was the kind of gown they shut the red carpet down for at the Met Gala, not a tactical outfit for a mission, but there was no getting in the way of Lana. She explained how to pin it up after the ceremony.

As long as no fighting broke out on the boat, it'd be fine. And that was the plan. No espionage until Valentina arrived. Gabby wasn't causing any problems.

Justin asked, "I don't know, is it too much?"

"That's what I wanted. Do you not see the belting details in the corset?"

"It's giving Dom at Prom—is that what you were going for?"

Lana ignored him.

"Has anyone thought about a sailor hat?" Justin said. "I know it's on the nose, but..."

Lana inhaled sharply like she'd been slapped.

Well, there wouldn't be any fighting about national security issues, at least.

Ignoring her shock and horror, Justin said, "Because I brought one."

Before he could answer, Jasmine herself arrived, poised and polished. She was dressed in another flowing robe, or maybe it was a cover-up? It was hard to say. Either way, you could see her bikini. Or maybe it was her underwear.

Justin waved hello and called to Gabby. "Come try on this sailor hat."

Lana shot back. "It's going to ruin my dress. Justin, why don't you wear it?"

He said, "I have one too. I'm the maid of honor."

Jesus.

Jasmine put it on. "I'm in charge. I'll wear the hat."

She looked calm, happy, and focused on the matter at hand. She gave Gabby a wink, like she was excited to leave it all behind shortly.

"Why don't you all head to the boat?" Jasmine said. "I want to meditate with the bride for a moment before she takes the plunge."

Still bickering about accessories, Lana and Justin left the honeymoon cottage and headed to the yacht. "I'll see you there," Justin said.

As soon as they left, Jasmine collapsed in a chair. She reached for a bottle of lotion and screwed and unscrewed the cap, like it was a fidget toy.

Gabby filled with warmth, flattered that Jasmine trusted her enough to let her guard down.

After she was sure everyone had left, Jasmine asked, "Did you secure an immunity deal for Naomi and me?"

"I'm working on it," Gabby said.

"Working on it?" Jasmine set the lotion down and came to attention in a way that made Gabby want to excuse herself.

Gabby nodded. "If everything goes to plan—"

"If what goes to plan?" Jasmine cut her off.

"I'm sorry. I misspoke. I'm waiting on approval from higher-ups, which should come through any minute." Gabby smiled serenely and tried to project calmness.

"This is not a comfortable position for me or Naomi. What are we supposed to do in the meantime?"

"Act normal."

She let loose with a peal of laughter. "Normal, huh?" She gestured to Gabby's princess dress. "This is a fake wedding, I assume?"

Gabby nodded.

"That's good because there's nothing worse than being in an unhappy marriage."

Gabby's heart went out to Jasmine. If your life was built on a partnership with a person who didn't respect or love you, the rest of it was bound to crumble. "You're going to feel so much better once we get you out from under Genesis's thumb."

Jasmine seemed to relax. "Thank you, Gia."

CHAPTER 38

A sunny afternoon, time to get fake married, the G-Spot

Gabby walked out to the dock in her Huntress Couture wedding dress, her train wadded up in her arms, and a pair of Crocs on her feet. The two attendants to help with the train had never arrived. It was so bulky that corners kept escaping and hitting the ground, dragging in the dirt in a way that would definitely bother Lana. It was like carrying a full load of laundry with no basket, trailing socks through the house.

If anyone had a career in espionage ahead of her, it was Kyle. Here she was about to get married with her AirTag still stuck to her shoe. She'd added a few other non-Lana-approved items to the outfit during her thirty seconds alone. Instead of the traditional garter belt, Gabby had strapped her engagement taser to one thigh and a knife to the other.

Naomi, who was making a simple sheath dress look like a million bucks, fell into step beside her. It was the first time Gabby had seen her alone since the paddleboarding disaster.

With a smirk, Naomi said, "Nice Crocs. You know Lana is going to absolutely lose her shit. I don't think that's how she normally styles her gowns."

"I've got bigger problems than Lana," Gabby said.

"You say that now." Naomi slowed her pace. "I know it's not a good time, but I have something for you."

Gabby's skin prickled with anticipation. After yesterday's paddleboard fail, she hadn't been sure that Naomi would take her deal, let alone spill secrets. Not to mention, iMoan was clearly Naomi's thing. "I moan is Naomi spelled backwards" couldn't be a coincidence. Yet another thing she'd put a pin in to deal with later. Gabby had A LOT of things to come back to later.

"I have time," Gabby said. "The wedding can't start without me, right?"

"Guess not."

"But just so you know, I don't have the immunity agreement settled yet." If Naomi gave her evidence and got locked up anyway because Gabby hadn't done the proper groundwork, she would feel even more like trash than she already did.

Naomi waved her off. "I'm gonna do the right thing, and I trust you to do the same."

"You realize I'm the government," Gabby said.

Naomi gave her an up-and-down. "You're not selling that right now. But I made up my mind. I'm going to email you a file."

Which email address should she give Lana? She couldn't remember the password for the Gia Glanville one. She wasn't supposed to be working, so she shouldn't use her EOD address. Valentina would see evidence coming in from Inner-G if she looked. Luckily, she still maintained the bake sale account for Queen Palm Elementary and Middle School. "C-O-O-K-I-E M-O-M at gmail.com," she said.

Naomi raised an eyebrow. "See, you're barely the government."

"That's what my boss said too. It's a problem." They turned a corner, and the yacht came into view. The *G-Spot* was scrawled in fancy lettering across the side. And to think that she'd never thought it was a real place.

"Open the email as soon as you can," Naomi said. "It'll explain everything."

"Everything?" This had to be one hell of an email.

"Don't tell anyone you got it from me."

Gabby nodded solemnly. "Deal.

"One more thing. I have a question for you." Gabby stopped walking with the boat in sight, but far enough for privacy. She gave Naomi her best Mom look, the kind of look that would force Lucas into an immediate confession that he was the one who had spilled a gallon of paint on the driveway and then tried to clean it up with all the new monogrammed bathroom towels. Kids.

Naomi squared off. "What now?"

"IMoan, please explain."

Naomi shrugged. "Oh, that. I've been selling stories here and there. Nothing that really hurts anyone. It's a side hustle."

"That's it? Is Jasmine in on it?"

"Yeah, but it's nothing compared to what I just sent you. If you don't look past my little side hustle, you'd be crazy."

Gabby smiled. "If you want to be TMZ, just start a TikTok or something. People get paid for that, right?"

"Who says I'm not on TikTok?"

Gabby accepted Naomi's statement. It had the ring of truth, which she couldn't say for everything she'd heard this week.

They started toward the boat again, and a corner of the train drooped into the path. "Let me help you onto the boat with that dress." Naomi picked up the sagging fabric. "I'm not interested in having to rescue you after you trip off the dock in that thing. It might as well be a concrete block as a couture gown if you fall in the water."

The water sparkled, and the boat gleamed in the afternoon sun. The yacht was decked out in its wedding finery. The railings were strung with flower garlands and fairy lights. A violin was playing...

"Is that the theme from *Power Couple*?"

Naomi nodded. "It's classic John Williams. Kinda sounds like the *Jurassic Park* soundtrack, doesn't it?"

It did.

Naomi followed her up the gangplank while the quartet played from the part of the movie where G had moved into the redwood forest to start training for the coming apocalypse. It wasn't exactly Pachelbel's Canon in D.

Inside, most of the guests were congregated in the luxury dining room with a carved antique bar and chandeliers. Gabby's breath caught in her throat at the sight of Markus dressed for their wedding. It was really hard to remember they had been fighting just a few hours earlier. But really, what wedding couple hadn't been fighting just a few hours before the ceremony?

Markus must have felt her eyes on him and turned. The look on his face when he saw her in the dress sent her spirit twirling, while her feet were planted to the floor in complete paralysis. She tripped, and Naomi scolded her. "You remember how to walk, right?"

From the way Markus was looking at her, it was obvious that he thought she was beautiful. It wasn't an expression of casual admiration. His eyes were shining, and his smile was so big that it took over his whole face. He was smiling like he forgot they were on a mission.

In this moment, in a wedding dress and tux, nothing felt like pretend. She forgot he'd broken up with her yesterday and that they were spies currently trying to salvage their careers. This was better than any wedding she'd ever seen on TV.

Genesis broke the spell. He appeared dressed in a flowing open robe over a golden Speedo. On his head, a turban. If anything could distract from the splendor of the yacht and wedding decorations, it was him.

She and Markus exchanged a glance of shared amusement. They might be broken up, but there was no one she'd rather enjoy this moment with.

All the players were present. Phil was downing a cocktail and wearing an expression of resignation. The OG members of Inner-G were looking snobby and strangely not hungover—all those G-shots maybe. Gabby preferred them after a Jägerbomb.

Phil gestured to the string quartet. "A string quartet on a boat—it's a little *Titanic*, huh? Remember when we saw that together? 'I love you, Jack.'" His eyes shone with tears as if he were the one sinking into the ocean.

"Phil." Gabby shook her head. How many times did she have to remind him that he had left her? It was too late to pretend he was Jack.

Before any official wedding stuff started, she had to sneak away with Markus for long enough to check Cookiemom@gmail.com. She grabbed his hand and led him toward a room with a door. "We have to talk."

"Gabby, I'm sorry," he started to say.

"Ooh, hold that thought. We have some EOD business to attend to."

She dragged Markus into what turned out to be a utility closet. Her giant train barely fit. It took up more space than the two of them. As soon as he managed to shut the door without the train jamming it up, Gabby asked, "Do you have a phone?"

He pushed the train out of the way to get to his pockets.

"Can I see it? I need to check my email. Naomi said she sent something that will explain everything."

Before Gabby pulled up her email, someone knocked. "Hey, guys, it's your wedding."

"One sec!" Gabby called.

She typed in her password three times before she pulled up the account. Sure enough, there was an email from Naomi. No subject line. No writing. Just an attachment. It was an article. Chills raced up Gabby's spine at the author's name: Amanda Duvall.

It really was all circling back to Amanda.

The headline: Could a Hollywood Cult Spark an International Incident?

> A few years ago, Genesis Love was the top-billed action star in the world. After one epic box office flop, he disappeared. The flop, though, wasn't a regular flop. *Power Couple* became an instant cult classic. The movie's biggest fan: Genesis himself.

Strains of the *Power Couple* overture filtered into the closet, an ominous soundtrack to the moment.

> Like he does with everything, he took it to another level. Genesis turned his cult classic movie into a literal cult, Inner-G.

> After ten years of mismanagement and bad decisions, Inner-G's financial decisions are set to ricochet across the globe. Among the weirdest

of Genesis's problems, he's taken millions upon
millions of dollars from *Power Couple*'s second
biggest fan, North Korean dictator Kim Jong-Un.

According to a source from Inner-G, Jasmine Love
has been spending all the money on luxury goods
instead of its designated purpose: filming a sequel
to *Power Couple*.

This isn't a joke. North Korea might not have a lot
of power on the world stage, but it will not take
this lying down. If Genesis doesn't make good on
his promise to deliver a movie that Kim Jong-Un
has paid for, he risks assassination. North Korea will
undoubtedly take ownership of the luxury goods
that its money paid for or, perhaps, even the resort
itself. There will be fallout.

Someone pounded on the door again. Gabby blinked at the
article. She knew most of it, but the North Korea bit was—maybe
she should have guessed, but it was just so weird. The president's
psychic was the most down-to-earth person at this resort, and
North Korea was footing Inner-G's bill. Gabby was living in the
upside-down.

It doesn't end here. Inner-G's line of luxury skincare,
Inner Beauty, makes all the usual claims: vegan,
cruelty-free, no parabens. In actuality, the line is
using cheap, non-medical grade products and
selling them at a luxury price point.

> The cherry on top: visitors to Inner-G should not
> expect privacy. The Loves will sell your secrets to the
> tabloids, as more than one pop star has found out.

> Genesis has done everything short of murder to
> pay for his luxury resort, private jet, and most
> recently, a world-class yacht.

Markus whistled. "Amanda was about to take Inner-G down. This would have led to a federal investigation, charges, the whole works. They would have lost the resort and maybe ended up in prison if the charges stuck."

Gabby said, "And the unnamed source—that's gotta be Naomi." When Gabby thought about it, Jasmine was the only one mentioning running away together.

Someone pounded on the door again. "Hey, it's your wedding, not spin the bottle."

Markus said, "We can't do anything till Valentina gets here."

Gabby nodded in confirmation. "Guess we're getting married."

In a loud voice, Genesis said, "Enjoy the appetizers and music. Keep your eyes out for whales. The ceremony will start when we get out to sea."

CHAPTER 39

Almost time to get fake married, the G-Spot

Gabby clung to the railing and watched the land fade into nothingness. They were going farther and farther into the ocean on a boat about to be repossessed by North Korea with people who had no scruples at the helm. Genesis, it seemed, would do anything for money. Amanda had, unfortunately, been right in her article: Inner-G had done everything but murder.

At the moment, there was nothing to do but float out to sea in a really over-the-top, couture wedding dress, hoping for the best. Except for the couture part, it wasn't an inaccurate description of her first marriage. She hadn't planned for anything after the dress with Phil.

Justin put his arm around her. "This is the most beautiful wedding I've ever been to."

Gabby choked on a laugh. *Oh, Justin.*

About thirty minutes out, the boat came to a stop, and Gabby's heart dropped to her stomach. This was it. The fake wedding to the former man of her dreams.

"Before you say your vows," Genesis announced, "the men have a surprise for the ladies."

Gabby's breath hitched at the word "surprise." No thanks to any more of those.

"Gia, this is for you, but it's also for Jasmine, for Lana, for Hugh. George and I have been working on this all week," he said. "Gia, this goes out to you."

Markus caught her eye from across the boat and confirmed with a curt head nod. This was indeed for her. She braced herself for what must be the comedy section of the night he had warned her about.

"Jasmine wouldn't let me have a live band," G added.

Gabby scanned the deck. Before she could think about it too much, the music came on. A cheesy nineties synthesizer filled the night air. The opening chords of "I'll Make Love to You" by Boyz II Men came on and struck a chord in Gabby's heart. Markus, Genesis, Geeves, and Hugh started walking calmly to the front of the boat. They were wearing hats and walking in step.

Boyz II Men started singing, "I'll make love to you, like you want me to." All of them lip-synced while making uncomfortably direct eye contact. Gabby didn't know if she should laugh or... what should she do?

"Relax, let's go slow," they lip-synced. Genesis was slipping his robe off.

Markus looked at her. So much information passed between them in that one glance. The first layer of information was practical. Markus wasn't doing any illicit spy work with Genesis. The man was rehearsing for a groomsman's dance. Of all the dumb things. Gabby started laughing and couldn't stop. He hadn't been double-crossing her; he'd been working on choreo.

Markus looked good. He was selling this groomsman's dance like it was his job, because it was.

After the first few verses, the track changed to "Pony" by Ginuwine, and they broke out their *Magic Mike* moves. Markus dropped to the ground and did one of those athletic humping-the-floor numbers, the kind that made everyone wish they were the ground.

He was just showing off now. Gabby didn't even have words for the moves he was doing. She'd been doing yoga and cleansing while he was in the woods rehearsing dances like he was a thirteen-year-old girl at a sleepover. Life was a joke. This week, the joke was on her.

Her eyeballs were wider open than they'd ever been. Her jaw was on the floor. Markus was... Dear lord. She fanned her face.

Justin whispered in her ear, "G flew out a choreographer, that guy who never took his Beats headphones off. Did you get a load of his abs?"

Her emotions were all over, crying because they'd worked so hard on this dance for her, scared that she and Markus were about to lose their jobs and maybe spark off an international incident. Then anger flashed hot—but why didn't Markus tell her what he was doing? They were on a mission. He should have said, "Yo, Gabs, just so you know..."

Did Markus want this to be an actual surprise?

The men did some sort of move where they were in a line so that you could see all their arms but only one body. Hugh was in front doing his thing. He looked a little too stiff and had some of the movements only partly down, but Justin was dissolving into tears and clutching his chest like his heart was about to burst. Gabby had never even seen Hugh walk quickly before, and here he was swinging his hips and hitting marks in the most epic groomsman's dance ever.

For the finale, Big G hefted Lil' G onto a perch on his shoulders like Markus was one of those tiny cheerleaders. There was no flipping or throwing, but lifting him was impressive enough. And then G turned in a circle while holding Markus up as high as he could. Hugh and the others did some sort of jazz hands move while Geeves twerked. Gabby didn't understand it, but she truly loved it. Cones of sparklers went off at the front of the boat. It was . . . a triumph. It was ridiculous and over-the-top. And it absolutely sent her over the edge.

Now Gabby was crying happy tears instead of angry, sad, mad ones. The emotional roller coaster was real. That's why adults don't need to get their adrenaline rush at Space Mountain. Gabby dabbed at her eyes. She was overcome.

Next to her, Phil looked like they had invented a new level of sour candy and were forcing him to suck on it at gunpoint.

Gabby didn't care about anyone but the man who had just tangoed to "Señorita" with a three-hundred-pound cult leader. He was for her.

As the smoke cleared, Big G called out, "Gia, I think George's ready to share some of these moves with you."

This was going to make arresting Genesis later so much more awkward.

After accepting the wild applause from two to three people, Markus caught her eye. Without breaking focus, he strode toward her like she was the only one who mattered.

"Did you like it?" he asked earnestly, out of breath, his shirt plastered to his back.

"I loved it." She leaned in and whispered, "Markus, ohmygod. You—" She fanned her face again. "You should have told me—"

"That I'm so good at dancing," he finished smugly.

She slapped him playfully. "No, you should have told me

something. You know Valentina was asking for reports on you."
She whispered that last part just in case someone was listening.

"Hindsight. I'm sorry," he apologized. "I'm sorry about everything. This week has been a lot. I thought it would be fun to be
on vacation together, but—" He laughed. So much had happened.
He didn't need to say it.

"I'm sorry too." Gabby glanced down at the Crocs she hadn't
changed out of. "I'm sorry for not trusting you. You're the one person I should have trusted," she said with true feeling. She wiped a
tear away and then another. "I'm so sorry. I thought you were...
and you know..."

He nodded. "I know. You were in a bad position, and I was
being secretive. It was my fault." He moved closer, so close she
could feel his heat, so close that Lana called out a warning about
staying away from "her dress" until he toweled off. Ignoring Lana's
wardrobe anxiety, Markus said, "I love you... Gia."

"I love you too, George." She leaned into his name.

Maybe they'd used fake names, but this wasn't a performance.
She didn't think.

It was real. She thought.

Markus pulled her into his arms and leaned in for a kiss. Gabby
shut her eyes and surrendered to the experience, to her feelings for
Markus, and all the chaos, to all of it.

Wearing nothing but his Speedo and turban, Genesis wedged
himself between Gabby and Markus. He put his arms around
them and inhaled. "This is it, you two."

Gabby laughed nervously. It was awkward being embraced by a

nearly naked man. Maybe he was comfortable with his nudity, but it's not like she grew up in the ballet or anything.

"This moment, this is what the Power Couples is all about. Bringing two people together, amplifying their energy, until they are unstoppable." He said "unstoppable" like the word had clawed its way out of his belly.

Geeves began circulating with flutes of champagne.

"As a power couple, there will be a lot of attention on you. You will have admirers, and you will have haters." He was still talking like he was narrating a trailer for an action movie. Gabby could see why Jasmine had a problem connecting with him. It was hard to get past all the performing.

"You never know where the attack is going to come from. But when you have power and charisma, there will be attacks."

Genesis was such a big dummy. The man seemed to have no clue. They couldn't have done a worse job on this undercover mission, and he was eating it up.

He narrowed his gaze and explained, "A power couple always has each other's backs. No matter what. You don't ask questions."

Jasmine testifying against him was going to come as a big surprise.

"A power couple is a battle couple. When the going gets tough, when you're outnumbered and outgunned, you stand back-to-back and karate kick the hell out of anyone who is attacking. It's called radial ass-kicking, and it's what you need to do."

Gabby remembered this scene in *Power Couple*. Genesis and the heroine had linked arms back-to-back. He'd lifted her into the air on his back and spun in a circle so she could kick the shit out of the bad guys.

Phil wandered over with an appetizer. Why was this man always snacking? He said, "We were a power couple once, Gabby."

"No, we weren't, Phil."

Jasmine stood and clinked her glass and said, "Does everyone have their champagne?"

"Raise your glass to love and togetherness on this beautiful day."

The final rays of the sun caught the raised glasses, turning the deck into a golden hour painting. It was a Renoir masterpiece of paradise. She might be stressed, but Gabby took in the beauty. The delicate noise of clinking glasses tickled her senses. A migratory bird flew overhead and cawed.

Except for Phil, this was a beautiful wedding.

Markus was smiling like it was the happiest day of his life. Maybe they'd have to arrest his new best friend. Maybe they wouldn't. It was always something.

For the first time this week, Gabby was truly relaxed.

So relaxed.

Almost sleepy.

No, woozy.

"I need to sit down," she said, turning to lean on Markus. But Markus did too.

Together, they slumped against the railing and down to the deck in a slow, mutual deflation as the world went black.

CHAPTER 40

2000 hours, upper deck of the G-Spot

Gabby blinked herself into consciousness a while later. There was no dancing or music, no chatter of partygoers or clinking of glasses. The sun was fully down, and a cool wind raised gooseflesh on her bare arms. When she tried to swipe a hair out of her face, she found her hands were bound behind her back. So much for staying out of trouble before Valentina arrived.

Markus was next to her, his solid weight pressed into hers, but not in the sweet way she craved. He was dead weight.

"Markus," she whispered. When he mumbled something unintelligible, relief shot through her veins. At least he was alive.

Phil, reeking of one of Jasmine's colognes, was on the other side, his face dropped to his chest. Everything was foggy.

The three of them were sitting ducks. She could feel the knife and taser still strapped to her legs, but she had no way to get to them. A moment later, Markus snapped awake. "Damn it," he muttered. "You've got to be kidding me. Again?"

"It wasn't me this time," Gabby said.

He gave her a withering look. "I wish it were."

From across the deck, someone said in a marked Australian

accent, "I didn't think you two would be so kinky. It's always the ones you don't suspect."

Damn it. Gabby had offered the immunity deal to the wrong person.

She turned her head to see the captain's chair slowly spin around to reveal Jasmine. The flowy cover-up was gone, and she'd changed into a jumpsuit. As the chair spun, she recrossed her long legs like it was a choreographed move and casually rested her arms at her side. She had on the sailor's hat that Justin had brought for Gabby.

Fuck. Gabby felt like smacking herself in the forehead, like after you walk out of a test and realize you picked the wrong answer. But so much worse.

"I like your ponytail," Gabby said. "I've never seen your hair up." It really did look good.

"Thank you," Jasmine said. "I don't like to risk breakage unless the situation warrants."

Murder warranted an updo. Now that was a fashion tip.

"I'm guessing your husband wasn't funding Inner-G selling gossip." This woman was not along for the ride. She'd bought the boat with misappropriated funds from North Korea, and she'd packed a jumpsuit for hostage-taking. Right now, Gabby's only hope was that Jasmine had to pee soon. Jumpsuits were cute until you had to get fully naked to take a leak.

"Took you long enough to figure it out, super spy." Jasmine flipped her murder pony. "Gabby Greene, I know who you are. You're not exactly a genius at this."

"Where's everyone else?"

"Don't worry, they're all enjoying an absolutely delicious dinner, none the wiser about this situation. They think you canceled the ceremony and are having a couple's spat on the upper deck."

Phew. That was a relief.

"I don't think they'll even notice they're locked in until well after dessert. No one is going to come looking for you two." She looked at Markus and said, "Pro tip: Try not to pick such a dumb cover next time, Mr. Fidget Spinner."

Gabby whispered. "Sorry. My bad."

Jasmine cocked her head to the side. "What's with Phil, though? Who does he work for? Because his cover is working."

Gabby rolled her eyes.

"Just kidding. I know he's your ex. And he's not getting up anytime soon. He drank all the champagne."

This was her life. You have kids with someone, and they're coming along for the ride, no matter what. They'll show up at work, on vacation, and eventually be taken hostage with you. You can't just cut someone out of the photos and be done with them. If she and Markus made it out of this and stayed together, they were always going to have an entourage. Valentina, though—Gabby couldn't complain. She only hoped Valentina hurried up.

Markus said, "A team of agents is on the way. You still have a chance to de-escalate this."

Jasmine *tsk-tsk*ed him. "Stop bluffing. It doesn't suit you." She turned to Gabby and said, "Guess what? Today, we're going to play Sophie's Choice. You get to pick one man."

That was easy. Markus. "I already did. The divorce is final."

Jasmine laughed. "I was kidding, I'll have to tell Phil how quickly you were ready to throw him to the sharks, though."

"Is this about the article Amanda wrote?"

Surprise flashed across Jasmine's face. "How'd you know about that?" She narrowed her eyes. "Naomi?"

"No."

"You can tell the truth. Naomi chose her sides when she didn't snap up your stupid immunity deal. She's dead to me."

Yikes. "Cut her some slack, Jasmine. It kind of makes sense that she'd want to think about it before she abandoned everything." Why was Gabby arguing for them to stay together?

"Doesn't matter now. But yeah, Amanda came out here a couple times. I thought she was joining, and then last month, I got that trash in my inbox. She was giving me the chance to comment before she published. The woman was a snake in the grass." Before Gabby said anything, Jasmine said, "I commented all right."

"Did you kill her?" Markus asked.

Jasmine cocked her head. "Amanda wrote that 'Inner-G has done everything but murder.' It was practically a dare." She stood up from the captain's chair, walked to the railing, and gazed out over the water. It was a starless night. Fog was rolling in and undoubtedly frizzing Gabby's hair.

"What did she expect me to do, go to prison?" Jasmine said, still looking out to sea. "It isn't hard to hire a hitman if you have enough money."

This was the problem with starting a Substack instead of working for a bigger newspaper. No one probably even knew she'd sent the article to Inner-G for comment. No one else knew the article existed.

"How does Sheridan come into it?"

Jasmine laughed, and the wind whipped her hair. It whipped Gabby's hair too, right into her face, but her hands were tied, so she couldn't fix it. Jasmine kept giving her evil villain speech, while Gabby could barely see through a curtain of red.

"I really need to get going, but someone needs to appreciate this with me, and now that I've met your ex, I think you're just the woman."

"Was she really a gift?" Gabby asked.

"Yes, which was bonkers because I wasn't even a fan. That dummy just doesn't pay attention. I mean, I was freaking out about her when G brought her down here, but only because I'd murdered Amanda and thought she might know something."

Gabby laughed. "I don't think she knows."

"Well, now I know that." With a flippant smile, she said, "Hindsight."

Gabby scanned the horizon for any sign of Valentina. Now would be a great time for a rescue.

"So basically, if my man hadn't given me the most epically stupid gift of all time, we wouldn't be in this situation." Jasmine shook her head.

There was an art to gift-giving. Besides having good taste, you had to know the person, you had to have history with them. You had to pay attention. Sometimes, no gift was better than a bad one.

The taser on her leg—now that had been a great gift, if only she could get to it.

"I didn't want a reading," Jasmine said. "Especially from her. Sheridan's really not much of a psychic. I got all worked up for nothing about her."

"She's just stressed. It's hard to make a prediction when you're stressed." Plus, could you really make predictions about yourself? Gabby still believed in Sheridan and her uncommon sense.

"And the president?"

"What about him?" Jasmine said as if she'd never given the man a second thought.

Gabby would have face-palmed if her hands weren't tied behind her back. After all that, the president had nothing to do with it. Amanda's murder and attacking Sheridan—it was all about protecting Inner-G's reputation. One spot-on Substack piece had caused all the trouble. How many followers had Amanda even had?

"You know, Jasmine, you can't blame G completely. If you'd talked to him, he would have known—"

"Would have known that I had spent all the money he wanted for that stupid movie, and I'd killed a reporter to protect myself?" She shook her head.

"What are you going to do, kill us all? There are a lot of people on this boat, Jasmine." Markus looked at her seriously.

She didn't respond.

"And how are you going to explain this?" Markus asked. "Have you thought of that?"

"Yep. I think it's plausible that you two undercover idiots and Genesis get in a big fight after he realizes who you are. There's a struggle, the boat catches on fire, somehow, and...I'm the only survivor."

"It seems like there could be a simpler solution than lighting a brand-new yacht on fire and burning us all alive." As Gabby said this, she recalled her conversation with Phil. If Jasmine sank the ship, she could collect the insurance and get out from under her North Korean debt. It sounded crazy, but that hadn't stopped anyone yet this week.

And thanks to Gabby, Jasmine might just get away with it. Last time Gabby had talked to Valentina, she'd told her that Naomi and Jasmine needed immunity and that Genesis was behind everything.

"Jasmine!" A yell came from the other side of the boat. It was Genesis.

She muttered a swear word and growled before composing herself. "Yes, baby," Jasmine said. "I'm coming."

For a split second, it seemed like G was in on it, until Jasmine muttered, "I should have given his three-hundred-pound ass more drugs."

She pointed a finger at them like a mom telling them to behave themselves. "Don't get into trouble. I'll be right back."

As her footsteps faded, Markus whispered, "We're about to do that wedding game where the groom gets up under the bride's dress and rips off the garter with his teeth."

"I've always hated that one," Gabby said.

"Can you help me? Move in this direction. I don't have free hands here."

From the other side of the boat, Jasmine's voice was rising in pitch.

Gabby spread her legs and tented her dress as best she could. Markus wormed his way under the full white skirt until he got to the thigh holster.

"This would have been nice yesterday," Gabby joked. She shivered at the touch of his lips along the tender skin of her thigh. He planted a kiss in response. "Later, baby," he said.

"Promise?"

"Mm-hmm. Let's just take care of the bad guys first." Apparently, there was nothing like the threat of death to show two people what matters more in life.

From across the boat, they heard Jasmine and Genesis still talking.

"Hurry," Gabby gasped.

"You can't hurry me when I'm between your legs." His voice was muffled because he was so busy doing other things, but she understood him well enough.

"Ohmygod, Markus. The knife is on the outside of my thigh!"

"Oops, yeah. Just going on muscle memory down here."

Gabby maneuvered one leg over his head, and he gripped the handle between his teeth and managed to get it out of the holster. He backed out from under her skirt with a knife between his teeth.

"Here. Come over here, and I'll try to saw through those cords."

Before Markus had finished, Jasmine yelled, "I want a divorce, G!"

A scream tore through the night, followed by the unmistakable sound of a gunshot.

CHAPTER 41

Final showdown in the rain, upper deck of the G-Spot

Jasmine was about to make a break for it. Like she didn't have a care in the world, she was carefully lowering a ladder over the side of the boat.

Gabby ran through their options. Her feet were untied, and her wrists, almost. None of Markus's ropes were undone, but his ankle ties were loose enough to shuffle. Conceivably, Gabby could charge Jasmine and tackle her, but she only had one chance.

Phil still hadn't revived. He was going to sleep through the entire high-stakes escape. Maybe he was drugged, but it reminded Gabby of how he'd slept through the kids' holiday program last year. Not even the sixth-grade trumpet section had woken him up. At the end, he'd said, "Great job, kids," not having heard a thing. If he survived this, it would be the same.

"You know that radial ass-kicking move that Genesis loves?" Markus whispered. "The one from *Power Couple*?"

He couldn't be serious. "I took down a yoga tent when I tried to stand on one leg and kick."

"I'm here too." Markus locked eyes with her. "We've got this, Gabs."

And it hit her. She had a partner. "I got this" had never been doable, not with the amount of work that she had on her plate. She was a mom and a spy. But a love life didn't have to be another thing that she needed to squeeze into her schedule. True romance brought a partner, someone who she could kick butt with together. Someone who could lift her up when she was down, even if it was to strike Jasmine in the face.

Just because Phil slept through holiday programs didn't mean every guy would. She had forgotten that. A real romance wasn't about flowers and chocolate; it was building a life and taking care of each other. It was *we* got this.

Without a partner, Gabby didn't have it all; she'd just been doing it all. While her brain was exploding with this epiphany, Markus tried explaining, "It's like that yoga move, but we're going to do it together. I'll do the balancing, and you do the kicking. It's the one from the end of *Power Couple*."

Gabby was overcome, overheating, and melting at the same time. Tears pricked at the back of her eyes. They might be at the beginning of a physical battle, but she'd just come out victorious in a mental battle she'd been fighting for years. Gabby'd rather fight a bitch any day than be trapped in her own self-imposed, over-scheduled hell again. She took a steadying breath and pulled it together.

"We've got this," she said, echoing a tagline she really believed in now. "You can count on me. Next time your ex tells me that you've joined a cult and are colluding with a megalomaniac, I'll ask you first. I'm sorry I didn't trust you."

He laughed. "Deal. Same." With a nod toward Jasmine, he said, "Let's do this."

Gabby and Markus hustled across the deck as quickly as possible. G was sprawled on the deck, bleeding.

Jasmine saw their concern and said, "If he's not dead now, he will be soon." Then, evil villain-style, Jasmine pointed a flare gun at the boat itself and fired. The flare lodged in the deck, glowing hot and red in the wooden floorboards and spewing smoke. It looked bad, but easy enough to put out, if they got to it quickly. If they didn't…

"Is that flare gun enough to set the boat on fire?" Gabby asked, already knowing the answer.

Markus nodded.

Those were the flames Sheridan had seen in her vision. The *G-Spot* was about to burn up with everyone on it.

With a look of annoyance, Jasmine said, "And now I'm going to have to do something about you two pains in the asses."

Instead of shooting them, Jasmine squared off *Mortal Kombat* style. "I always enjoy a fair fight."

Gabby didn't point out that Jasmine was the only one with a gun, and Markus was bound. Hardly fair, Jasmine.

Before Markus had a chance to prepare, Jasmine kicked him in the chest. But even tied up, he hopped back and avoided the full impact of the kick. That was it. Gabby wasn't going to take any more. It was time for radial ass-kicking. It seemed like a move that only worked in the movies, but with their wrists bound, it was their only real option. Even if it wasn't, it's not like they had time to make another plan.

Markus turned so that he and Gabby were back-to-back. They locked arms, and he hefted her into the air.

Jasmine started to laugh. "Are you two really? This is great."

Gabby gripped Markus with all she had and bicycle-kicked with her legs, smacking into Jasmine and cutting her evil laugh off mid-chortle. Gabby's feet connected squarely with Jasmine's center mass with enough force to send her sprawling backwards. Jasmine's flare gun clattered to the ground.

In a weird flourish, the immense train of her stupid dress swooshed over Jasmine's prone form. In the background, the deck was starting to smoke.

Gabby and Markus might not have attended all the classes or paid that much attention at the Power Couple Retreat, but they were *the* power couple, fighting back-to-back against their enemies.

Gabby kicked the flare gun farther away from Jasmine, unholstered her engagement taser, and depressed the button. The electrodes launched with a loud snap, and Jasmine's muscles seized up as the taser hissed.

"That was better than a ring," Gabby said, holding the taser up.

"I knew you'd like it." He smiled. "And I'm glad you didn't use it on me this time."

With danger averted and their argument done, Gabby turned to Markus and he to her. He leaned in, about to kiss her, when Phil groaned from the other side of the deck.

"I suppose we better untie Phil and let the hostages out first," Markus said.

"Also, the boat's on fire," Gabby pointed out. It was starting to smell like a gunpowdery bonfire.

After Markus found a fire extinguisher and put out the developing blaze, he checked G's pulse. "He's alive!" Markus said, already putting pressure on the shoulder wound.

Gabby had been sure he was dead. Sheridan said one person was going to die this week, and she'd just heard Jasmine shoot G. Mean girls were the worst. You wanted their approval and love so much that, by the time you realized it wasn't worth it, they'd killed a journalist and tried to pin it on the president of the United

States. Gabby had to hand it to Jasmine. That was ballsy. If only she'd done actual work instead of figuring out loopholes, she would have been a superstar.

"Do we have any gauze?" Markus looked up from the wound.

Gabby looked around and said, "How about tulle?" Before he could answer, she cut a section from under her skirt and handed it over. Then she ripped the cups out of her bra to pack the wound. They always fell out in the wash anyway. Bra pads were becoming the loose socks of the 2020s.

"He's gonna be fine," Markus said.

"That's good because he's your best friend lately. It'd be a shame to lose him."

While Markus tended to his friend, Gabby untied Phil, who had suffered just enough of an injury to feel like he'd done something. And really, he had. Phil had served a valuable role analyzing the finances and using his endless font of movie quotes to unlock the mystery.

Speaking of exes, a cigarette boat appeared on the horizon, going about one hundred miles per hour. Bow up and its engine roaring like a jet, the boat was coming in like *Miami Vice*.

Gabby's thoughts turned to pirates or maybe drug dealers.

Markus glanced at his watch. "Valentina's late."

No, she was right on time. If she'd arrived any earlier, Gabby and Markus wouldn't have had time to clean up their own mess and prove their worth.

Gabby sat back in awe of the woman's style. Even if Jasmine had managed to escape, Valentina probably would have caught her. She was only a few minutes behind.

"I don't know, Markus. Our exes really showed up for us today."

Valentina cruised in, barely losing speed, whipped the boat

around, and docked alongside the *G-Spot* like she was a professional boat racer, if that was a thing.

"I love her," Gabby said.

Markus laughed. "Let's just hope she doesn't fire us."

"She's not going to. We saved the day. Plus, CYA. And that means covering our asses too, so she can claim this win along with us."

Valentina climbed up the ladder that Jasmine had lowered for herself and came aboard looking like one of Charlie's Angels.

"Thought I'd drop by and see how things were going," she said, looking around and nodding at the two subdued suspects. "Looks like you have things handled."

"We do. No casualties, and you're here for the glory part of the mission. It's time to free the hostages."

While Valentina surveyed the scene, Gabby pointed to her train. "Would you help me with this, Markus?" She was going to trip if she had to run around in a damn wedding dress. "Lana showed me how, but I can't do it on my own."

"I'm going to DIY it," Markus said. He wadded up a bunch of fabric and zip-tied it like he was making an arrest. He eyeballed his work skeptically. "Don't tell Lana I did this."

"She's going to see it in two seconds," Gabby reminded him. "But you can remind her that you just saved her life."

"No, we saved her life."

As Jasmine had advertised, the hostages were enjoying a delicious dinner in a *Lifestyles of the Rich and Famous* dining room with chandeliers, and Persian carpets, and tables appropriate for royals. It was all smooth jazz and oysters, zero awareness of danger.

"So what's going on, you're not getting married anymore?" Justin asked. "Jasmine made some sort of announcement about you calling it off before we started dinner."

"Not tonight," Gabby said. "We can talk about it more later."

To Gabby's immense relief, her mom and Sheridan were alive and well, dining with the rest of the guests. Gabby hurried over to them. "Are you both okay? I was worried!" Her mom seemed caught off guard when Gabby wrapped her in a hug.

"Gia, I owe you an apology. Markus seems like a very nice young man."

"Now that he saved you, huh?" Gabby teased.

"What?" Her mom's expression was pure confusion.

"Oh, nothing." Apparently, even her mom missed the danger, which was fine. Gabby would prefer not to explain it. "You were saying?"

"I'm sorry. I never should have come down here to interrupt your wedding. You're a grown woman, and I need to respect your choice." She took a deep breath and said, "I'll stop meddling."

You could have knocked Gabby over with a feather.

"I've been talking to Sheridan, working on my uncommon sense."

Gabby opened her arms and embraced her mom. "Thank you. Apology accepted."

Sheridan sidled up to Gabby a few moments later. "What happened? I know you're hiding something."

Gabby quickly summarized the situation, explaining that Jasmine was the real threat but was now zip-tied and ready to be booked.

Sheridan released a breath. "Damn. I got everything wrong. It's mortifying."

"Don't worry. You'll get your psychic vision machine working again after an actual vacation. If you were stressed to begin with, this must have made it worse."

Sheridan nodded emphatically. "But no more vacations. I need to make dinner and shovel my own walkway, get re-centered."

With everything wrapped up, Gabby hauled herself to the bridge. She stood with Valentina and Markus by the controls. As the resort came into view and they aimed for the Inner-G docks, they debriefed Valentina on everything that had happened.

"In addition to Amanda Duvall's murder, Jasmine's going to be charged with quite a few counts of attempted murder, blackmail, extortion, invasion of privacy...who knows what else."

"What about Genesis and Naomi?" Gabby asked. They appeared to be clear of everything the EOD had originally suspected them of. Gabby hoped so. It was nice for Markus to bro out with a friend.

"They're not going to get away scot-free. At the very least, Genesis violated the executive order that prohibits American citizens from doing business with North Korea, and I'd be shocked if this place filed taxes. Plus, the entire Sheridan abduction." Valentina thought about it for a second. "But they might get that immunity deal now, or at least reduced sentences, for flipping on Jasmine."

Gabby should have known that anyone who was selling inner beauty in a bottle was rotten. Shame on her for falling for it.

As the yacht pulled into the shelter of the bay, Valentina said, "I'll withdraw my request to put you on administrative leave."

Gabby exhaled with relief.

"Good job, Agents."

Gabby stood tall and proud. For the second time, she'd accomplished the nearly impossible and saved the day. And she'd given birth twice and risen from her divorce like a phoenix. At this moment, she was feeling all of it.

"Just never bring your family on a mission again, and for fuck's sake, follow an order if I give it to you." Valentina gave them both a severe warning look and then sighed. "You two get some rest tonight. I'm going to book Jasmine and take Genesis and Naomi in for questioning. We'll be executing a search of the main offices and the Loves' mansion."

Valentina walked down below, leaving Gabby and Markus standing on the upper deck as the rest of the passengers disembarked.

Gabby stood on her tippy-toes in her Crocs, and Markus leaned down and wrapped her in his arms. With the stars sparkling on the ocean waves and a cool ocean breeze whipping through her wedding updo, Gabby's heart set sail. It was just them. No more lies. Well, they would continue lying to everyone else because it was the literal definition of their job, but no more lying to each other.

She shut her eyes and pressed her cheek to his. "We did it."

"Let's go enjoy that honeymoon cottage," he said. "We earned it."

EPILOGUE

Evening, Avocado Avenue, a gathering around Alphonse de Picnic Table at Justin and Hugh's place

"We don't all need to sit around this table, Justin." They'd been back for a week, and Justin was hosting an Azores-inspired dinner for the family. He was treating this party as a bigger emergency than anything that had happened in the Azores.

"There aren't enough matching chairs!" He exhaled dramatically and clutched his pearls. He was wearing his version of a casual afternoon BBQ ensemble with about ten layered necklaces from local estate sales.

"It's fine." Gabby was wearing her refined loungewear from Inner-G.

"What am I supposed to do, bring in a folding plastic table with folding plastic chairs to accommodate overflow?" He shut his eyes at the imagined horror. "I'm a party planner."

"An overflow table sounds reasonable." A kids' table was always a great idea.

"It is the most unreasonable thing I've heard." He held a hand in the air as if he needed a shield from the plastic table acceptance energy Gabby was bringing. "I bought this table to elevate my dining experience, so that's what it's going to do. There are just too many of you."

Gabby laughed. He was preaching to the choir on that topic. "Well, who do you want me to cut?"

He popped a hip out and angled his head. "Do you want to go there? I have suggestions."

It was too late anyway. The kids, and Granny, and Burt filtered into Justin's backyard, all talking at once. Mr. Bubbles ran to Gabby and started jumping like she'd been trying to teach him not to for his entire life. He was just too cute for rules.

"Uncle Justin? Can I play in the pool?" Lucas was already running toward the deep end.

"Just don't splash anything," Justin said.

Gabby raised an eyebrow. Had he met Lucas? "Thank god you didn't have kids," she said with a laugh.

"Actually, Hugh and I haven't decided yet. He brought it up on the plane ride home."

"You're kidding." Justin and Hugh were both well above forty and just now thinking about it? Gabby sighed. Oh, to be a man.

"We had such a nice trip, and we got to thinking." With a glance to Lucas, Justin said, "You know I love the kids. Even though they're so sticky and loud."

"You're serious?" She couldn't believe it.

"Look at what you have, Gabs. You might be drowning, but you're drowning in love."

Cause of death: too much of a good thing. It was better than being taken out by a serial killer, probably.

"Well, they're yours too, you know. You've been with them forever. If you decide to add a family member, I'll be there for them."

Justin grimaced like he was really struggling with the thought of expanding his family. "Maybe just a bunny, I don't know."

"Or you can stick with taxidermy." Gabby gestured to his collection. "I still have Tarragon in my closet if you want him back. He's easier than a kid."

Elena and Phil had walked across the street together. After meddling with Gabby's relationships and making a nuisance of herself at the resort, Elena had toned it down. She was overdoing it in the other direction now.

Phil, who had been too drugged to see much of the showdown, had no clue what had happened and happily went along with the story that he was the smart one.

Inner-G actually hadn't imploded. As far as cults went, it wasn't too dangerous. She'd rank it somewhere between SoulCycle and Disney, maybe a mash-up of the two. It was unclear what the consequences would be. But Gabby didn't see any world in which they could keep the resort and stay out of jail due to the contributions from Kim Jong-Un. As for *Power Couple 2*, investors besides North Korea were showing renewed interest now that Genesis had been in the news so much. But in the meantime, he had signed on to play a detective on *Will Trent*.

Lucas did yet another cannonball into the pool, and an epic splash hosed down Justin, silk shirt and all. Hugh patted Justin on the back and handed him a cocktail.

"Lucas Daniel Taylor!" Gabby yelled and was headed to the pool to remind Lucas to stop acting like he was at an eight-year-old's birthday party when she felt someone come up behind her.

"Boo," Markus whispered, his breath tickling her neck.

She turned to face him, all worries forgotten. "Thank god

you're here," she said, nuzzling his neck and breathing in his scent. He was still wearing the Inner-G cologne. The smell transported Gabby to the Azores, and she suspected it always would. It was their first trip together.

"Thanks for coming."

"I wouldn't have missed it."

She leaned against his chest and shut her eyes for just a moment. The family had bought the story that they'd joined a cult, run away to get married, and changed their names, and then changed their minds and changed their names back to normal. As far as the family was concerned, it was just the worst wedding ever.

Hugh said, "Did you see the news today?"

Gabby nodded. "Yep."

Amanda Duvall's article had finally run. Gabby figured Naomi had had something to do with that. Naomi was a bit of a wildcard. Last Gabby'd heard, she'd actually moved to Iceland.

Everything was quiet for a blessed second.

"When are you and Markus getting married?" Elena piped up, for the third time that day. Now that she'd accepted Markus, she wanted the party.

While Gabby choked on her blueberry matcha lemonade, because Justin could never serve anything normal, Markus answered, "We're just going to take it easy for a while." Really, he should have said, "Are you crazy?" given that they'd just returned from the last disastrous wedding where Elena had literally flown across the world to break them up.

"If you do, give me some notice," Burt said. "I'll break out my dancing shoes. Gotta start getting my stretches in now."

Justin seated them all around his designer table, which really was too small for ten people.

Gabby hadn't explained the details of her work at the EOD to Kyle, Granny, Hugh, or Burt, but they all had at least some idea. Justin, of course, knew she was a spy. Ironically, Elena and Phil, who had done the most spy work in the Azores, had no clue. The mission's success owed more than a little to their meddling.

"So if you're not getting married, what's going on? Are you together?" Burt asked. The whole group stopped talking, waiting for an answer.

Gabby looked to Markus.

Markus looked to Gabby.

"Of course we are," he said. "Nothing changed."

Everyone nodded and kept on doing their thing. Markus was officially old news, not that big of a deal.

He was a big deal to Gabby, though, and potentially to her kids, but...they were also just two people figuring it out. No one was perfect. As long as there were enough seats around the table, or pretty close to enough, and you weren't out of ketchup, life went on.

But sometimes you made a dumb rule, the work-wife thing, for instance, and you had to strike it. It was okay to make mistakes, to surrender to the chaos around you.

When the party was over, Gabby's crowd walked down the block to their home. It was Saturday. Kyle was sleeping over at Sierra's. Lucas was about to pass out.

"Want to spend the night?" Gabby asked Markus. "Like a secret sleepover?"

"Sneak out in the morning like a teenager kind of thing?" Markus asked.

Gabby said, "Let's do it."

Markus nodded like she'd just given him a mission assignment. "You're on, Agent Greene."

"I really liked the idea of going on a work vacation, but the work really got in the way."

He smiled knowingly. "Who would have thunk?"

"Work wives is out," Gabby said. "That was a dumb idea. But what does that make us?"

"Get your butt to the bedroom," he said, "and you can call me whatever you want."

"Coffee date?" she teased while walking down the hall.

"I don't think that's going to cover it," he said in a way that sent shivers down Gabby's spine.

"Boyfriend?" she hazarded.

"If you're ready for it," he said, sounding unconvinced. "I'm not scared."

"How about George?"

"Hell to the no." At the door to her beautiful bedroom, he said, "How about Gabby and Markus?" She stepped into the bedroom, and he followed.

"Deal."

ACKNOWLEDGMENTS

To my agent, Pam Gruber. Thank you for your excellent edits and for always being there. To Alex Logan. Thank you so much for being smart, logical, and patient (especially this time!). You are a dream to work with. And many thanks to everyone else who worked on this book behind the scenes, Kristin Errico, Mari C. Okuda, and Brieana Garcia. Thanks for making me look good! David Purse, thank you for the ideas, the collaboration, and for semi-regular pictures of your bulldog traversing the Scottish Highlands.

Thank you to my family. Terrell, you got the dedication this time, but all of you suffered through this project with me. Lila, Daphne, Silas, and Jr., you made it through a busy year of deadlines with me. I love you and hope you are one day willing to admit to your teachers and friends that your mother writes books that might or might not contain sex. Also, I promise to leave the computer at home on our next vacation.

To Larissa Zageris. With one phone call, you gave me renewed purpose and energy to tackle a daunting revision. You are a master of romance and action. Thank you for sharing your gifts.

To Erica Holland. Thank you so much for your friendship and

honest sensitivity reads. I refuse to publish anything you haven't put your stamp of approval on. Thank you.

To the members of Smut University, who rallied funds to replace my computer after I poured a fresh cup of coffee into the keyboard, especially Jennifer Kirkeby. And Mary, thank you so much for walking me through hedge funds and holding companies. I blame that plot line on you.

To my writing community who always support me and make time to meet me for coffee, even when I've been an inconsistent friend due to my deadlines and four-kids situation. Thanks to my brother for always being willing to discuss absurd hypotheticals. And thank you to Jennifer Smith, who tried to insert logic into my plot. You fought the good fight.

To the members of the United States military and people who I think might be spies who asked not to be thanked or acknowledged in any way (you know who you are), I appreciate you taking the time to answer my questions and, very occasionally, making me sound like I know what I'm doing.

Thank you to the bookstores that carry my books and the booksellers who talk me up. I couldn't do this without you. But as always, mostly, thank you to my readers. I appreciate you more than you know. Thanks for going on every wild book journey with me.

ABOUT THE AUTHOR

When not writing romcom/mystery mashups, author **Sam Tschida** (pronounced cheetah) is probably flipping channels between *Dateline* and the latest reality dating show. She braves the Minnesota winter with her four resigned children, two snuggly dogs, and one sizzling-hot husband. She doesn't drink alcohol, never touches caffeine, and is always on time. Just kidding—did you read how many kids she has?

RAISING READERS
Books Build Bright Futures

Thank you for reading this book and for being a reader of books in general. We are so grateful to share being part of a community of readers with you, and we hope you will join us in passing our love of books on to the next generation of readers.

Did you know that reading for enjoyment is the single biggest predictor of a child's future happiness and success?

More than family circumstances, parents' educational background, or income, reading impacts a child's future academic performance, emotional well-being, communication skills, economic security, ambition, and happiness.

Studies show that kids reading for enjoyment in the US is in rapid decline:

- In 2012, 53% of 9-year-olds read almost every day. Just 10 years later, in 2022, the number had fallen to 39%.
- In 2012, 27% of 13-year-olds read for fun daily. By 2023, that number was just 14%.

Together, we can commit to **Raising Readers** and change this trend. How?

- Read to children in your life daily.
- Model reading as a fun activity.
- Reduce screen time.
- Start a family, school, or community book club.
- Visit bookstores and libraries regularly.
- Listen to audiobooks.
- Read the book before you see the movie.
- Encourage your child to read aloud to a pet or stuffed animal.
- Give books as gifts.
- Donate books to families and communities in need.

BOB1217

Books build bright futures, and **Raising Readers** is our shared responsibility.

For more information, visit **JoinRaisingReaders.com**

Sources: National Endowment for the Arts, National Assessment of Educational Progress, WorldBookDay.com, Nielsen BookData's 2023 "Understanding the Children's Book Consumer"